VIRGINIA BRIDES

*Homespun Love Warms Hearts
in Three Complete Novels*

CATHY MARIE HAKE
VICKIE MCDONOUGH
SUSAN PAGE DAVIS

BARBOUR
PUBLISHING

Spoke of
Love

by Cathy Marie Hake

Dedication

To my Lord and Savior, Jesus Christ.
And to all of the dear women who are my sisters because of Him.

Chapter 1

Virginia, 1750

Frost silvered the grass of Fredrick Town's common, making it sparkle in the first light of morn. Samuel Walsh stood at the door of the inn and glanced out, knowing he needed to be on his way soon. His breath condensed on the crisp morning air. Pulling his thick wool cloak tighter against the biting chill, he scanned the area. A small movement caught his attention, and he sucked in a surprised breath. There, chained to the hitching post, huddled a woman.

Seeing her set him in motion. No one ought to be treated so cruelly—and especially not a woman. Concern quickened his pulse and lengthened his stride.

The woman formed a tiny ball in a futile attempt to conserve what little warmth she created. She'd tucked her legs under the ragged homespun dress and rested her head betwixt her imprisoned arms. The wind blew, and she failed to even shiver. *Is she alive?*

Samuel pressed his fingers to the side of her cold, cold neck and detected a thready pulse. "God bless you, woman! You're nearly frozen." He whipped off his heavy cape and enveloped her in its warmth. A short chain looped over and around the hitching post, manacling her to the center. As a result, the woman didn't even have enough length to permit her to draw in her arms to conserve her own heat. Sam squatted to serve as a windbreak for her as he reached up to chafe her icy hands.

It took a full minute before the woman dully opened her eyes. They matched the pale gray of an early spring morning mist, and her dazed expression told him she couldn't comprehend why such degradation and suffering were visited upon her.

"There, now," he crooned as he cupped her frigid face between his hands. "You'll be warm soon."

A piteous moan curled in her throat.

Sam looked around. No one else stirred on the common. Metal items cost dearly, but a paltry half-dozen links held her fast. Fresh scrape marks on the wood bespoke her attempts to reach the edge so the chain would fall onto the support piece and allow her to draw in her arms. His hands roared with heat in comparison to hers as he chafed them.

She'd not been here last eve when he arrived. 'Twas already gloaming then, and he'd made haste to see his horse stabled ere he wearily signed the inn's register, partaken of a hot meal, and filled space in the bed he'd hired in the upstairs. Frost on her eyelashes, hair, and shoulders told him she'd suffered out here during the time he'd burrowed under thick blankets.

Resolving to put a stop to this travesty, he squeezed her hands to gain her attention. "Where is your master?"

She opened her mouth, but no words came out. Her head sagged between her arms again.

Samuel briskly rubbed her arms, then cupped her pale cheeks. "I mean to help you."

She stared at him. Tears silvered her eyes, formed rivulets down her grimy cheeks, and disappeared between his fingers. Hopelessness radiated from her.

"I'll be back." Sam rose. "Right back." He stalked toward the smithy. Surely he'd find an ax there. He'd chop through the hitching post and free the woman in a trice.

"What's this?" A deep voice growled from a distance.

Samuel wheeled around to see a stocky man snatch the cloak from the girl. "Replace that at once!" Samuel ran back.

The pock-faced man booted the woman in the thigh. Even though the action scooted her a good nine inches to the side and stretched her arms to the point that the chain pulled, she barely winced.

"Cease that! There's no cause—"

"She belongs to me." The stranger spat at her feet. "I hold no particular affinity for her, though."

"That's plain enough to see!" Sam reached them and yanked his cloak from the stranger's hands. As he engulfed the girl within the woolen folds again, Sam felt the awful thinness of her shoulders. "Even a beast shouldn't be mistreated so." Samuel gently slid the woman back into place. His glare dared the owner to object. After he'd repositioned her in such a manner that her arms wouldn't be twisted so painfully, Samuel demanded, "Free her and explain yourself."

The man's jaw jutted forward, and he folded his arms across his chest.

"Free her," Samuel snarled. "Now."

Her owner's beady eyes took on a wary cast, and he produced a key. Samuel knew the woman's shoulder and arm muscles would cramp once the heartless owner freed her from the chain. He wasn't sure she could even comprehend much, but he knelt. "I mean no disrespect," he murmured as his hands delved past the sides of her bosom and turned beneath her arms to support the stick-thin limbs as they fell free from the shackles.

Her scrawny muscles twitched and spasmed, yet she compressed her lips and made no sound. Moisture in her eyes tattled on the pain she felt, but she stayed silent. Could it be she was alert enough to realize he'd championed her? *Aye.* A spark of something in her glistening eyes told him 'twas so.

"You'll ne'er be chained again. I vow it." He pulled the cloak tight around her, then rose. Keeping one hand on her shoulder, Samuel glowered. "Explain yourself."

"A ship's captain sold her to me as she slept." The stranger cast a loathsome look at the pitiful woman. "Only five of the dozen brides survived the voyage."

"Twice in the last five years, the store's imported brides. After six weeks at sea, the women could barely walk, let alone wed and work. Couldn't you show her mercy?"

"She deserves none."

"I know not whence you've come," Sam gritted, "but here, slaves and indentured servants normally sleep in the stable, if not on a pallet in the inn."

The stranger merely shrugged.

"Women deserve to be protected and appreciated. If you cannot care gently for her, turn her over to someone who will."

"She's defiant." A sneer twisted the man's features. "I've had her a full fortnight, and she refuses to speak a word. I cannot wed her without her consent, so I've had to take to punishing her until her tongue loosens."

"Poor woman is likely mute!"

"Nay." The man shook his head. "Silence in a woman can be a good thing and in a slave a very good thing, but her silence is not from birth, for she mutters in her sleep. Best she stop this nonsense and learn who's her master."

"So you would leave her to the elements simply because she's been stubborn? This isn't discipline—'tis cruelty!"

"The widow was sold to pay off her husband's debts. I paid good coin for her and won't be cheated."

Sam went back on his knees beside the woman and tightened his cloak about her. "Have you never read the scriptures about caring for the widows and orphans?"

Hands on his hips, the man glowered. "Do you make me an offer?"

Samuel thought of the leather britches he needed. He also recalled how desperately his son Christopher required a shirt. *My family's needs must come first, and someone else will buy the woman. Whoever does, she'll not be much of a bargain. Small, thin, filthy, and mute, she'd make for a pitiful servant. No man would pay a bride price for her—clearly she is far too frail to bear children.*

He looked at the heap of humanity before him and tried to force himself to refuse to part with what little money he had.

She hung her head in a move of abject misery.

She needs my compassion more than she needs my cloak. I promised her my assistance. "I've not much. What do you ask?"

Sam knew full well the scarcity of women. Though neither pretty nor prizes in any other way, the brides in previous shipments didn't step foot inside the store ere men bought them. Indeed, the community gave grieving widows only two or three months of mourning. After that passage of time, the parson approached them about the natural order of living under a man's domination. A marriage usually followed on the very next Sabbath.

Avarice glinted in the stranger's eyes. "Twenty-eight pounds. With only two women for every three men here in the New World, I can get my price. You know I can."

Samuel let out a disbelieving snort. "This one's almost starved and mute!"

"Twenty, then."

Shaking his head, Sam heaved a sigh.

"Eighteen and not a single pence less."

Lord, You know I haven't anywhere near that much. Watch over her and give her to a man who'll treat her with kindness. Regret swamped Samuel as he turned loose of the cloak. The woman slumped sideways. He caught her ere she landed on her side.

The stranger cleared his throat. "Fifteen."

Father of Light, You know I have just over six. What would You have me do? Samuel couldn't let go of her.

"Fifteen pounds," the man repeated.

"A third of that, and you've done better than you ought. She's so weak, no man will offer you more."

"Now see here! Passage alone cost nearly six pounds."

Sam scoffed. "Do you take me for a fool? Six pounds would fund a private cabin. You said there were a dozen brides. Passage for the whole lot of them barely cost six."

Muttering curses, the man tugged the cloak from the girl and yanked her to her feet.

No woman ought ever be subjected to such base language and rough treatment. Samuel made one last attempt to redeem her. " 'Tis abundantly clear her state isn't merely from a difficult voyage. She can't weigh so much as six stone."

Again her owner spat into the dust at her feet. "She's not worth feeding. She rendered no service to me."

Samuel stepped between them to protect her from the other man's crudity. Anger vibrated in his voice. "If she dies—and from the looks of her, that could well happen—those men you said would pay so dearly for her will convict you of murder."

Sam sensed her collapsing behind him, but he didn't move.

Fear flashed in the stranger's eyes. "Five pounds—in coin only. No paper money."

Elation filled him, but Sam kept his expression chilly. "The only papers will be hers, and you'll yield them to me at once."

"They're inside."

Samuel grabbed his cloak from the ground and shook it. "Go fetch the papers." He knelt in the dirt by the woman and tucked his cloak about her yet again. "Just a little while longer. I'll have you away from him. Just awhile longer." Sure the owner was out of sight, Samuel yanked off a boot. Two toes poked out of a hole in his stocking. Perhaps the woman would be able to darn it, but from the looks of her, not for a moon or longer. Coins spilled into his hand, and Sam counted out five pounds, then hastily dumped the remainder into his boot and tugged it back on.

No more had he gotten to his feet when the man returned. "Her papers. Give me the money."

Samuel inspected the papers. Finding all in order, he yielded the hard-earned money and turned back to the woman. He softly called her by the name on her papers. "Garnet Wheelock?"

Her eyes opened.

Samuel gave her what he hoped was a reassuring smile and brought the woman to her feet. Her legs threatened to buckle, but she caught the hitching post and stayed upright. No doubt, sheer dint of will was all that kept her on her feet. He wound an arm about her waist to lend her support and warmth, then bade, "Come."

Her head wobbled in what he took as nod of agreement, and she put one foot in front of the other. Her gait seemed oddly stilted. Sam quickly deduced she locked her knees with each step so her legs wouldn't give out. He felt the iron resolve beneath the shivering of her reedlike body. "I'll lift you. Your limbs cannot serve to step o'er the doorsill."

It took nothing at all to sweep her into his arms, and Samuel knew a moment's remorse for having given over such valuable coin for her. She would be too small and weak to serve at hard tasks. She must have sensed his hesitance, because the girl slid a hand out of the cloak and clenched his doublet in desperation.

"Rest your fear. I'd not give you back to such a fiend." He strode back to the inn and headed straight for the hearth. Once there, he settled her into a rough-hewn pine chair. "Stay here to gather warmth, and I'll fetch food for you."

"Eh!" The serving wench flapped her arms like a farmwife trying to shoo a pesky murder of crows from her newly sown field. "Get that baggage out!"

Placing a hand on his "baggage's" thin shoulder, Samuel steadied her ere she tumbled over. "The woman will partake of the meal intended for me. Have mercy on her."

"Mercy? Only the Almighty can do that! This is a proper place. We allow none of her ilk."

"The poor woman is near frozen and in need of sustenance. I'll not permit any to gainsay me." He gave the wench a piercing stare. "I've not asked more than my share. Since I've allotted my portion to her, you've no cause to object. Bring the food."

The serving wench's nose assumed a defiant tilt.

Samuel drew up a three-legged stool directly in front of the frail woman, eased his weight onto it, and gently tucked a tangle of hair behind her shoulder. He'd never seen such a filthy woman; but 'twas not her doing, and he couldn't fault her. On the other hand, he did hold the serving wench to blame for her cold manner. He turned and gave her the same stern look he used for his children when they balked at doing a chore.

Lips pursed as though she'd tasted something sour, the wench flounced to a scarred pine sideboard and ladled a modest portion of the barley-and-oat gruel into a chipped pottery bowl. She cast a sly look at him.

Unwilling to let her goad him, he pasted on a smile. "You have my thanks, mistress, for adding both butter and cream to that."

Once he accepted the bowl, Samuel stirred it. He took a small bite to test the temperature. Satisfied, he lifted a generous spoonful of gruel to his charge's mouth and quietly urged her to eat. She obediently swallowed, but she wasn't able to take in much. When it became apparent she'd eat no more, Samuel finished off the bowl and set it aside.

"Do you thirst, little one?" The small flicker of her smile was answer enough. Choosing not to trouble the serving wench again, Samuel rose and paced to the sideboard. Pewter pitchers of milk and ale rested there. He poured a tankard of the former and carried it back to the little scrap of a woman he'd purchased. She remained huddled within the thick folds of his cloak. She needed to warm up, and as he'd deemed her too weak to hold the beverage, Samuel resumed his seat on the stool and tilted the tankard to her cracked lips. Sip after sip she took—small ones, but they added up until she managed to drink half of the milk. She then looked at him, lifted her chin, and seemed to silently urge him to finish the rest.

"You may have it all. There's plenty."

She shook her head. It was more a weak wobble than anything, but since she communicated her refusal clearly, he drained the remainder of the creamy milk, then twisted to the side and set the tankard on a sticky tabletop.

He turned back to her and gently rested his palm on her thigh. She cringed at his touch, and her face twisted in embarrassed dismay. "Calm your heart, woman," Samuel rumbled softly as he gently rubbed his thumb back and forth a discreet inch. "I merely wish to inquire whether his kick did you any damage."

She shook her head.

"Very well." Samuel rose. He had no goods with him, so he simply lifted her into his arms. "Because I've matters to attend, you'll need to pass a bit of time."

Her lips parted slightly as her brows knit.

"Don't be troubled. I vow I'll come back for you." The way she shivered cut him to the core. Was it from fear or from cold? Most likely both, and that vexed him. She deserved every shred of reassurance and comfort he could give. He stepped over the threshold and murmured, "Since the woman here displays neither mercy nor charity, I'll bear you off to the stable. It can shelter you until I return."

The woman blinked.

"I count it a pity that wench showed you no understanding. Forgive her, if you can. 'Tis a small heart she must have, and that will make for a miserable life."

He snuggled the mute closer and injected a bit of merriment in his voice to ease the dread in her eyes. "As for you—I suppose you could ponder upon the fact that sleeping in a stable is a blessed thing to do. Our Lord spent His very first nights in one."

She let out a sigh and rested her temple lightly in the crook of his neck.

The stable lay a stone's throw away from the inn. The stalls boasted generous heaps of fresh straw. Any of the servants or slaves who slept here last night had arisen and started their duties. Satisfied she'd be alone and safe, Samuel easily carried his burden to the farthest stall. Once he reached it, he shook his head. His horse had been watered, well fed, and warm for the night; the woman in his arms hadn't received even a fraction of that basic attention.

He nudged his mare to the side. The stall still held a fair layer of straw, which Sam kicked into a small heap. He knelt before it. For a moment, the position brought to mind all the times he had knelt at the fireside and gathered his sons for a bedtime prayer. Odd that such a thought should flash through his mind, yet he felt the presence of the Lord in that warm, quiet moment.

"Rest here." He laid the woman in the straw. "I must get supplies, and then I'll take you home with me. I fear I left my blanket in the wagon over at the miller's. The straw may itch, but it'll keep you warmer. Pray, forgive me." He tucked his cloak around her more closely before he took an armful of straw from the adjacent stall and piled it over her thin body. He made sure her face stayed clear, but the achingly sad beauty of her eyes took him aback. He gave her a tender smile and whispered roughly, "Rest."

At first, Garnet Wheelock thought this was a tall, broadly built man who possessed an exceedingly kind heart; but now, she knew different. With the morning sun shining through the open stable doors far behind him, a strange, golden nimbus radiated around the edge of his dark brown hair. Golden shards brightened the centers of his deep brown eyes.

He must be an angel—the angel of death. *I never knew death would wrap me in warmth and whisper kind words. Lord, I'm ready. I come not on my own merit, but because the Lamb's blood covered my sins.*

"Rest," the angel bade her.

This moment of security was probably the euphoria of a dying mind, but she sank into that comfort and thanked heaven for the mercy of being given a peaceful dream in her final moments. Heaven was but a breath away.

"I'll soon take you away from here."

Everything rippled as if a pool of blissfully warm water were closing around her. As she started to drift off, her last sight was of the angel's compassionate smile. Soon the terrible memories would be purged from her mind.

Chapter 2

Samuel knelt by the woman and watched as exhaustion claimed her. Plainly, the flame of life within her barely flickered anymore. Filth streaked her face and clothes, and she was gaunt with near starvation. He'd seen the depth of emotion shimmering in her eyes, though—and he knew that deep within, the woman possessed a soul worth fostering.

Deciding he'd done the right thing, Samuel rose, led his horse to the stable yard, and mounted. At the miller's, he reclaimed his cornmeal, rye, and wheat flour. The miller withheld the customary sixth of the grain as his payment, and Samuel helped him load the balance in large barrels onto the wagon.

" 'Twas excellent corn," the miller praised. "Fine flavor. My woman made hasty pudding with it last eve."

" 'Tis a blessing to have a goodwife who cares sweetly for you."

"Aye." The miller curled his flour-dusted hand around a wagon wheel. "Your milling bore a third of one more barrel. I'm willing to trade for more of it. Would you accept maple syrup?"

"I've syrup aplenty."

"I've cider—sweet and smooth. Perchance a basket of apples and three jugs of cider?"

Samuel looked at the barrels of cornmeal, then back at the miller. He didn't want to make an enemy, but the deal seemed less than fair. "A basket of apples?"

A sheepish smile tilted the miller's lips. "Make it three baskets of apples and four jugs of cider."

"Done."

When the miller's apprentice brought out the first basket of apples, Samuel's eyes widened. "I mistook your barter for a bushel! I feel it unfair to take three baskets now. 'Tis not an even barter."

The miller chuckled. "Yonder is my orchard—look at how fruitful it is this year. I'll truthfully not miss the apples at all. Your willingness to reconsider the barter to my advantage pleases me. Take all three in good health as a blessing to your house."

"You have my heartiest thanks." Samuel actually needed help hefting the crate-sized baskets up onto the wagon. The miller's apprentice grunted as they finished the last one.

Samuel cleared his throat. He didn't want to have to pay for the beautiful, large baskets. "I'll return these containers when next I—"

The miller let out a boisterous laugh. "Don't bother. An old man and his lackwit son live in the woods beyond the edge of town. They weave these baskets and barter for flour and meal with them. I've more baskets than sense, and I'd rather have you come back to me for milling than to go elsewhere. I'll consider it an investment in hopes of getting more of your corn next season."

"Be assured, I'll return. I venture God will reward you for this kindness. I and they are blessed by your generosity." He shook the miller's hand and drove off in a well-stocked wagon.

Samuel took the grain to the mercantile. With no wife at home, he'd been forced to barter or pay for simple items. It rankled him to have to rely on his wife's sister to keep his sweet little daughter, Hester. Naomi had been a shrewish wife to him, and her sister, Dorcas, held the same temperament. If the woman he had just bought turned out to be half as stubborn or foul natured, he'd have her gone in a trice.

Lord, 'tis badly done of me to think such dark thoughts about her. I've prayed You'd make a way for me to bring home my beloved Hester. If this woman I've bought is of godly persuasion and sweet spirit, she'll prove to be a blessing. I've no wish to marry again. Since she's been sold off to pay for her husband's debts, she's likely soured on the notion of marriage, too.

"Ho, now," the shopkeeper said as he approached. "What can I sell you today?"

"I've grain to barter," Samuel started out. "I require molasses, an ax head, and powder for my flintlock."

"I presume you'll also want metal for molding bullets."

Sam shook his head. "I've enough at home, but you can show me a shirt length of cloth, a needle, and thread."

"Cloth and metal are expensive," the shopkeeper warned. "Especially since the Crown passed the Iron Act, cost has gone up considerably. What grain did you bring, and how much do you have to trade?"

His harvest rendered a slightly larger yield than Sam expected, but he hesitated to part with much. Adding little Hester and the woman to his family meant more mouths to feed. Bartering away much of the surplus would be foolish. "I'd need to know your prices before I can estimate what I'll spare you."

"They're posted on the counter." The shopkeeper wandered toward a woman who stood by a small shelf before a display of spices. "Cloves. Fragrant, aren't they?"

Sam reviewed the prices and winced. He desperately needed leather britches. Woven ones wore out too fast, and he couldn't afford to buy more cloth—even if the woman he'd bought this morning sewed for him and spared his family the expense of hiring a tailor. A leather pair would last indefinitely, but after spending so much on the waif, Samuel knew he'd have to make do with what he currently owned.

Any misgivings he felt in the store disappeared when he returned to the stable. "Ma'am," he said softly. The woman didn't respond to him, so he gently pushed away the straw. A wayward strand of hair fluttered in the shallow currents of her silent breaths. Though he addressed her again, the woman didn't rouse in the least. Sam slid his arms beneath her and lifted.

Never had he seen an exhaustion so profound, yet surprise rippled through him when the move didn't cause her to stir or make her breathing hitch. Carefully, he placed her in the back of his wagon in the spot he'd left free to accommodate her.

When the sun almost reached its zenith and they had traversed a quarter of the way to his homestead, the wagon hit a rut deep enough to jar it badly. She woke with a gasp and bolted upright.

———

"All is well; all is well," a deep voice murmured.

For a few moments, Garnet felt disoriented. She couldn't recall where she was or whom she was with. Shoving back her snarled hair, she saw her angel of death. It took a moment to realize he wasn't a heavenly being but a mortal man. Memories of his kindness that morning surfaced. *Lord, if 'tisn't my time to be borne to Your bosom, You have my thanks for letting me belong to a compassionate man.*

"How do you fare?"

His inquiry jarred her out of her musings. Though embarrassed, she timidly looked off to the side of the road and hoped he'd guess at her quandary.

"You've slept a good while. I suppose you'd like a moment to yourself. We'll stop yonder. There's a small stream there."

Garnet nodded and folded her hands in her lap. When the wagon stopped, the man wrapped the reins about the brake, jumped down in a single, lithe move, and reached up for her. "Here, now."

I'd rather scramble down unassisted, but that might offend him.

A winsome smile tugged at the corner of his mouth. "I didn't judge well. There's a mud puddle over on the other side."

His admission disarmed her. Garnet half stood, and he cupped her waist. It took every scrap of her self-control not to flinch. Her fingers fleetingly made contact with his broad shoulders as he lifted her down.

Instead of immediately letting go, he braced her waist. Fire streaked from his fingers clear up her back, but she tamped down her urge to twist free.

"I see slumber restored a bit of your strength."

She nodded.

"Do you need me to carry you behind the bushes?"

She emphatically refused by shaking her head.

He finally turned her loose and cleared his throat. "Then go and be assured of your privacy. I vow I'll give you your due. Take your time and fear not."

She twitched what she hoped would pass for a smile and went off behind a bush. A wary glance over her shoulder confirmed the man kept his word. He stood with his back to her, so she gratefully ventured to the edge of the stream. Shoving up dirt-encrusted sleeves, she knelt on the bank.

Her reflection left her gasping. Snarls, oil, and dirt abounded in her tresses. She'd been able to see how grimy her hands had grown, but her face was even worse. Rivulets streaked her cheeks from when she'd wept this morning. Her new master must possess infinite kindness for yielding over so much money for her. She couldn't remedy her hair at the moment, but at least she could wash the worst off her flesh.

Sand from the bank bit into her palm. *Sand, Lord. You've provided sand so I can scour away the filth.* Face, arms, hands, and even the back of her neck—the cool water and abrasive sand scrubbed them clean. Another glance let her know her master continued to face away, so she even furtively lifted her skirt and whisked dampened hands over her legs.

When she returned, the stranger reached out and took her hands. A smile creased his kind face. "Being slovenly clearly isn't your way. The papers give your name as Garnet Wheelock, but that is all. I've no notion what to expect of a woman bearing such a fanciful name."

How can I make this man understand I'll work hard for him? Garnet went down on her knees and placed his hand on her head.

"I'll have none of that. No one ought kneel to another. Such obeisance is reserved only for the good Lord."

Garnet rose.

He nodded his approval. "I am Samuel Walsh, a planter by trade. In the days ahead, we'll come to learn more about one another. For now, I'm eager to be on the way. My sons are staying at the Mortons'." He frowned as she tried to dust off her skirts. "First, we'll go by Goodwife Stamsfield's. Perchance she has a bit of soap we can buy."

Garnet thought for a moment, then wrung her hands.

"You're nervous?"

The pantomime hadn't transmitted her meaning. She tried again, rubbing her palms together, and then holding them side by side and blowing on them. She then formed a circle with her thumb and forefinger to depict a soap bubble rising.

"Soap!"

Her head bobbed, and she tapped her breastbone to transmit that she'd make it for him.

Samuel Walsh grinned. "Ah, so you can make soap. I'll ask you to do that soon. I've little left at home."

She bobbed her head in assent. Mayhap things would turn out passably well.

Chapter 3

Garnet Wheelock wasn't a brazen woman. Indeed, she acted as bashfully as any modest woman might. Samuel kept a mental catalog of her traits. Since he knew nothing about her, he had good cause to wonder about her character. To this point, she had exhibited the virtues of modesty and cleanliness. He'd not yet seen a vice, but those might remain hidden for a short while ere she became comfortable and let down her guard.

After assessing the length of the shadows on the ground, he proclaimed, "We're making good time home. Let's continue." He lifted her into the wagon. Pain flickered across her features. "Are you ailing?"

She averted her eyes and shook her head.

After climbing up, he turned her back to face him. His hand cupped her jaw. "I'm not a man to value deception."

Her slender fingers shook as she haltingly reached up and gingerly wrapped them around his wrist. She hadn't the strength to remove his hand, but it was clear from the way she stiffened and shied away that she was not one to welcome a stranger's touch, however innocent it might be.

"As you wish." He sighed, then turned back, grabbed his cloak, and swirled it about her. "At least keep warm. I'll have Goodwife Morton see to you."

She clutched the cloak around herself and let out a soundless sigh. The wagon set into motion. They continued on in a strange but companionable silence. At one point, Garnet patted his arm and pointed ahead a short distance.

"Grapes, eh?"

She nodded and hopped off the wagon. Heavily laden, the conveyance trundled slowly enough to allow her to scamper ahead. A timid smile creased her face as Samuel drew close. Having identified wild grapes, she gathered a handful and raised them to him. Sweeping her hand back toward the vines, she arched a brow.

"Whoa!" The wagon halted, and he looked behind him in the wagon for something to hold the unexpected bounty. Nodding to himself, he stepped into the bed and rummaged. "I bought cloth. . . . Here it is. By knotting it, I might be able to empty most of the apples from one basket into it. Then we can fill that basket with grapes."

She shook her head and gestured.

"No?"

Garnet pointed at each of the baskets, then held her hands apart.

"There's a fine plan. I'll remove some apples from each basket and knot them into the cloth; then we can pile grapes on the top of the baskets."

Garnet beamed and nodded.

The stop took very little time, but Sam considered the yield more than worth the moments spent. When the baskets were full, Garnet harvested one last bunch. Samuel got the water jug he kept under the wagon seat and rinsed them. They shared the unexpected bounty as their nuncheon.

Samuel lifted Garnet back into the wagon and got underway. Juice stained his fingers, and he noted her hands and lips were tinted, too. She looked a bit better all washed up and rested. "I confess," he stated as he leaned toward her a little, "I'm experiencing the sin of pride. I'm returning home with a woman to help my children, apples, and grapes that were all unexpected."

She folded her stained hands together as if in prayer, then pressed her lips to them and opened them. She lifted her palms heavenward, as if in thanksgiving.

"Aye, we give thanks to God for His generosity."

When the sun hung low in the sky, he pulled to a small bend in the road. "We'll need to stop here to pass the night." She seemed to understand, but he wasn't sure what kind of life she formerly led. A country girl would have full understanding of what an evening stop entailed; a city-born one—either slave or servant—would be completely ignorant of the necessary tasks. This stop would reveal a fair bit about her. "There's a creek just behind that stand of trees. I'll water the horse."

She nodded and let him help her down. As he unhitched, she looked around and gathered up some twigs and a few pieces of wood.

Samuel watered the horse, returned, and nodded approvingly at the well-constructed formation of tinder and small pieces of wood in the center of the stone circle she'd created. He felt a small flare of relief. She might well serve his family in acceptable fashion by at least doing mild tasks about the homestead. "Well done, Mistress Wheelock. I've flint in the wagon under the seat."

She hastened to the wagon for the desired flint and soon had a small fire going. Once it caught, she went off for a necessary moment. On the way back, she gathered more wood.

"You're not a sluggardly woman, I must say." He handed her an apple after she released her hold on the wood and allowed it to tumble to the ground.

She smiled her thanks for both the apple and the praise, bowed her head in thanks, then jerked away when his hand covered hers.

Samuel looked at her somberly. Her eyes were huge, and her lips began to quiver. *I scared her.* He made a note to be more cautious with his contact. Using the low, lazy tone he employed when soothing his children from their nightmares, he said, "You can count me as a friend. I merely wished to voice the blessing, seeing as yours is one I cannot hear to share." He gave a simple, heartfelt prayer, then let go of her. He skewered a sausage on a green stick, and she silently took it from him.

She was such an enigma. Filthy, but cleanhanded. Gentle, yet strangely remote. In spite of her ragged clothing, she showed an odd dignity. She knelt gracefully by the fire, nudged a small log so it would burn more evenly, and cooked the sausage. Instead of holding the stick over the flames, she skillfully propped the end of it between two heavy stones so the sausage arced over the fire and roasted.

Samuel made no pretense about studying her. He needed to take her measure. A city girl might have enough common sense to take care of a fire, but she'd not know to prop a cooking stick in this fashion. She'd have chosen a dry, brittle stick instead of a supple, green one, too. She wouldn't have identified the grapes at such a distance, either. Garnet showed more promise as the day passed. What she lacked in strength, she made up for with knowledge.

Samuel watched as Garnet checked the sausage once more. She seemed satisfied that it was beginning to sizzle its way to perfection. That done, she took a pair of apples from the wagon. After wrapping the fruit in a few large leaves, she carefully put it in the ashes to cook.

"There's a good idea. It'll be a sweet treat, and one to warm you a mite."

She turned the sausage. It put off a savory aroma, and the way it sizzled made his mouth water. A handful of minutes passed ere the sky went dark. The warmth and light of the fire were welcome against the eerie black of the night.

Samuel sliced the sausage in half and handed her one. Garnet tore her portion in half yet again and gave him the other piece. Her smile faltered as she kept only a quarter of the offering.

"Aren't you hungry, little one?"

She lifted her piece of sausage and the apple, as if to say, "This is enough."

He sighed. "I suppose it is sufficient for someone so small and depleted." The leery look on her face spoke volumes. He quickly tacked on, "Garnet, I do not anticipate hunger this winter. God has been gracious, and in time, you will gain enough from His bounty to fill out into a healthy form. I've no plans to cast you off in your frailty."

Tears of gratitude sparkled in her eyes.

"Sit and eat," he bade.

Garnet waited until he scissored his legs and folded down into a comfortable spot; then she sat a good yard away. Samuel said nothing about the distance she put betwixt them. When she finished eating, she got up and rubbed sand, then tall grass between her hands to clean them. Although the stream wasn't far off, it had grown too dark to wander away from the fire.

Using a knot he pried from one of the pieces of firewood, Samuel put it on a thin, flat rock and set it afire. Garnet looked intently at the odd arrangement.

" 'Tis a knot lamp." He tilted his hand so she could see it more easily. "I presume you've never seen one afore, but all about us is a bounty God provided to meet our needs. This will last a fair while and provide enough light to take care of essential trips. I'll step away a moment. When I return, you might well use it for your privacy, too. I'll not want you to rise in the night. There is safety only by a fire."

She acknowledged his words, and he left. When he returned, Garnet accepted the knot lamp and left the immediate area. She attended to her needs and swiftly returned to their tiny camp.

The small knot lamp illuminated her features softly, and Samuel wondered if beneath all of the grime she might actually be pretty. He sternly reminded himself that appearance was a worldly matter, and one that didn't bear much thought. The quality of her character needed to be determined, for that was where a person's true beauty lay. He'd learned that bitter lesson soon after he'd wed.

As he put a few more pieces of wood on the fire and watched them catch, Sam stated in an even voice, "I've but my cloak and a single blanket, Garnet. The night will be bitterly cold. We had frost this morn, and from the look of the moon, we'll have a thicker one again tonight. I vow I'll not abuse you, but I plan for us to share those coverings."

Garnet gave him a wary look and ventured to shake her head tensely. She knelt by the fire and patted the ground there, as if to let him know the fire's warmth would be enough for her.

Ignoring her, Samuel took the blanket over to a shallow indentation in the ground he'd filled with leaves and pine needles. He spread the blanket over them, wishing he could offer her something warmer, more comfortable, and all her own. When he looked up, she glanced over at the wagon and pointed. Then she folded her hands and lay her cheek on them.

"Nay, Garnet. I'll not have you sleep beneath the wagon. Though that would normally be the best way for us to stay warm, you've coughed a bit already today. The flour and cornmeal put off a fine dust, and 'twould sift down on you. I've gathered more wood—that fact should bear witness of my certitude we'll have a cold night."

She stared at the pile of wood he'd supplied. The corners of her mouth drooped.

Sam walked to her and held out his hand. "Come, Garnet. I've given you my word. You've nothing to fear from me. I'm an honorable man. I'll give you my back this night."

Even by firelight, he could see how her face flamed. He felt ungallant for this insistence, knowing full well this turn of events appalled her. Still, the temperature had already begun to drop. She was piteously thin and had barely survived the previous night. If she weren't kept warm, little Garnet wouldn't make it through another cold night without taking ill.

A small whimper trembled deep in her throat, and her eyes stayed huge. Garnet bowed her head.

"Come, then." He stooped, lifted her, and carried her to the blanket. She seemed so frail in his arms. She probably didn't weigh any more than his ten-year-old son. Samuel paused for a moment and gently swayed her from side to side in a small arc, much as he had his children when they were babes and in want of soothing. The way she'd gone so tense in his arms and stopped breathing cut him to the heart. *God, bless this woman. Only You know what she's endured.*

He laid her down to face the fire, then took the knife from his sheath. She jolted upright as a strangled sound of fear curled in her throat. Samuel restrained her with one hand while he flipped up the edge of the blanket and laid the knife beneath. That hand came up to cup her gaunt cheek. "I gave you my knife for the night. I hope having that at hand gives you reassurance."

If anything, her shoulders curled inwardly even more.

Samuel carefully checked his flintlock, and she watched his every move. He observed her out of the corner of his eye. As he set another smallish branch to the fire, the widow lay down. Aye, she did, and he noted how her fingers located the knife beneath the blanket. Not that he blamed her. Sam took his place beside her, then pulled the cloak up to cover them both. The leaves crackled and rustled beneath them. His back pressed against hers, but she immediately shifted a few inches away.

"Sleep, Garnet. Your fears are groundless." He made an effort to breathe slowly and evenly. It might make her believe he was falling asleep. In truth, he didn't feel overly tired. He knew she must be, though. Clearly, the rest she'd gotten today was insufficient. The deep shadows beneath her eyes bore mute testimony to that fact.

Radiating warmth from the fire teamed with the heat he created. Her weakened state and a full belly conspired against her. Samuel knew from the way she shifted and shook her head that Garnet tried to battle the fatigue, but it eventually overcame her defenses. Finally, she went still and slack. At least she'd found refuge in sleep. He whispered a word of thanksgiving for that small favor. Rest would restore her.

———

She wept in her sleep.

Her thin shoulders heaved with the harsh sobs. Samuel rolled over and tucked the cloak around Garnet more closely and studied her. He wasn't sure of her age. According to her papers, she was a widow. Since she'd been sold to cover her husband's debts, he must have died quite recently. Young and fragile as she seemed, he'd addressed her as Mistress Wheelock all day. Standard convention would change that to Widow Wheelock. Samuel determined to give her the choice of which address they'd use. Fresh grief might well be causing her to weep now, and calling her widow would twist the knife of cruelty into her.

Jumbled sounds came from her mouth, mixing with her heartrending sobs. Her mouth was lush, but a scab darkened her lower lip. Clearly, her owner had struck her. He'd kicked her, too. *And she was terrified when I explained how we'd have to spend the night.* Sickened to the depths of his soul at how she must have suffered, Sam watched the firelight flicker across her delicate features. *Lord, You alone know everything this poor little woman's suffered. Even when her body has long since healed, her heart will ache. Be merciful to her. You've placed her in my keeping. Allow her to find safety and peace.*

Sam quelled the almost overwhelming urge to smooth her tangled hair and soothe her. He'd given his word he'd give her his back. If she woke to his touch, she'd panic. Instead, he carefully leaned over Garnet and forcefully shoved another log on the fire. Unable to break his word and hold her, he very gently murmured, "Garnet, come now. Roll over." To his relief, she obligingly turned over.

"Good, good," he whispered as he took her far hand in his. Samuel lay down again and gave Garnet his back once more, but he shifted back and tugged her palm so she half squirmed until her chest and cheek were pressed to his spine. A choppy sigh exited her, and she seemed to calm—at least he hoped she'd calmed. To his relief, she no longer shuddered with those oh-so-quiet, body-wracking sobs that tugged at his heart and soul. He lay there and clasped her small hand in his.

She was nothing more than a hank of tangled hair and a few thin bones—and a gentle smile and possessed of a tender spirit. His feelings took him by surprise. He tamped them down. The woman needed brotherly love. She'd tried to clean up, but in truth, she still stank. He smiled wryly as he let that realization dampen the attraction he felt. A short while later, he drifted off to sleep with her cuddled up behind him.

Samuel woke before she did. He carefully slithered a few inches from her and quietly rose. She lay burrowed in his cloak, her face obscured by its folds and her snarled hair. He tucked the edges of the blanket back over her. She'd shivered the whole night long, and he'd struggled to keep his vow. Had he been able to envelop her in his arms, he'd undoubtedly have warmed the wraithlike woman far better. Her conduct from the start kept him more than aware of her opinion of men, though, and he couldn't very well expect her to hold him in any esteem if he proved to be a liar.

The way she cringed from even the simplest touch and cried in the night troubled him. What harm had come to her in captivity? There was no way for her to tell him, though he couldn't help being curious. Then again, it was none of his business, and to bring those memories up might be too much for her.

His neighbor's wife might be of some help. Ruth Morton had a quiet way about her that made it easy for others to divulge confidences and troubles. Mayhap keeping company with a woman would bring Garnet some peace of heart.

Just before daybreak, he'd added the last bit of wood to the fire and silently prayed she'd at least not suffer any untoward effects from the biting chill. She'd be safe enough now. Samuel stalked off. After visiting the creek and watering the horse, he knelt and reluctantly shook Mistress Wheelock's shoulder.

She bolted up and scrambled back away from him in a reflexive move.

Chapter 4

Good morrow." Master Walsh studied her. After a long moment, he gave her the slightest smile and gestured at a small pot at the edge of the fire. "I've made corn mush. There's but one spoon. Go on to the creek to splash yourself awake and break your fast. We must journey onward."

The pounding of her heart slowed. Garnet nodded. After eating, she took great care to make sure to extinguish all the embers. The task left her feeling warm and sticky.

"Well done." Master Walsh nodded toward the fire ring. "One spark, and the whole area would be aflame. I'm done hitching Butterfly to the wagon, so let's get on the way."

Garnet gave him a quizzical look and mouthed, "Butterfly?"

A pleasant chuckle bubbled out of him. "My daughter named the mare. 'Twas the most beautiful thing she could think of, thus the name. I humored her."

Affection rang in his tone, and Garnet couldn't help smiling. Yesterday, he'd said they'd stop and pick up his sons. He'd not spoken of his daughter. Neither had he mentioned a wife. Her smile faded. *If only he would tell me more of his family.*

"Come, we must move on." He beckoned her. As soon as she reached his side, her master reached for his cloak. "The morning air still holds a chill. Here."

Garnet stepped back and patted the blanket.

"No, no." He shook his head. "I'm plenty warm enough. You're a tiny bird of a woman. Let this warm you." He enveloped her in the folds of his cloak.

She cringed.

His eyes darkened, and the gold centers dimmed. His face went somber, as did his tone. "You need never fear me."

Unable to respond with words, she twitched him an apologetic smile.

" 'Twas an explanation, not a chide," he said softly as he cupped his hands about her waist. "Now up you go."

Garnet scooted to the far side of the bench. Once they set out, she couldn't decide what to do. The cloak made her too hot, but when she shrugged out of it, she started to shiver.

"Put it across your lap, girl." His voice stayed low and gentle. "We've half the day's travel. Soon you'll see an open meadow. Game likes to graze there, and I make it a habit to keep my flintlock loaded."

She nodded. Only a fool left his firearm unloaded. Garnet looked at his flintlock and knew a raw twist of memory. Her husband had owned one. She knew how to clean and load it. In truth, hunger once drove her to fire it. The bruise on her shoulder lasted three weeks and served as a remembrance of that fruitless effort.

Garnet never fired it again—not because she feared the inevitable pain in her shoulder but because Cecil wagered and lost the flintlock. It was yet another vital thing he'd sacrificed due to his gambling. In the seven months of their marriage, they'd work their small farm by day. By night, Cecil had squandered anything their labor achieved—hay, ham, milk, a bushel of peas, the pewter dishes from their table, and even the blankets from their bed. Item after item disappeared from their humble home—each toted away by someone who bested her husband at cards.

She wondered about Samuel Walsh. He hadn't said, "A woman to help my wife" or "A woman to help my family." Was he a widower? He'd mentioned a daughter and sons—how many did he have? How old were they? He provided well for them. Then, too, he was a man who showed generosity and compassion—and restraint. He'd not touched her in an untoward manner. Garnet shuddered.

He shot her a questioning look. She dipped her head and fussed with the cloak, pleating its folds over her lap.

"Your silence gives a man ample room to exercise his patience and control his curiosity."

Garnet peeped out of the corner of her eye. Was he mad? No, his lips were tilted in a grin. She let out a relieved sigh and rested her hands beneath the thick woolen cloth. Quiet descended between them. Birds' songs, the wind soughing through the trees, and the mare's steady *clop-clop-clop* filled the crisp air. Her previous owner spent most of the time berating and punishing her. This man's silence carried no bitterness or anger, and the lines radiating from the corners of his eyes hinted that he laughed often and easily.

Almighty God, have You brought me halfway around the world and now blessed me with safety? Please, Lord, let it be so.

Weariness dragged at her. Garnet wakened, horrified to discover she'd slumped against her new master's side. Her face rested against his sleeve. It smelled of smoke, pine, and lye soap. She gasped and sat upright at once.

"You barely rested at all," he stated mildly. He was kind enough to omit mentioning how she'd made use of his arm for a pillow. "I'd suppose you're in need of much rest yet. Did you have a rough voyage?"

She nodded grimly and stared bleakly off to the side. He seemed to respect her wish to reveal nothing more, and for that she was grateful. The wagon wheels hit a rut and cracked loudly. The sound alarmed an enormous bird that hid in tall grasses not far off.

The flintlock boomed loudly next to her, making her jump.

"Bless us! We'll have fowl this night!" He put down the firearm and jerked back on the reins at the same time. Once the horse halted, her master was off to get the fowl he'd downed. He held the bird by the legs and strode back to the wagon.

Resting the stock of his flintlock on the floor of the wagon, Garnet clamped the long barrel between her knees. It measured four feet long, so she needed to rise up on tiptoe to pour a spoonful of powder into the muzzle. She made a patch with a small bit of buckskin and a ball from the bullet pouch, then tamped it down with the rod. She carefully put her master's firearm back in the exact same location and the very same angle as it had been as they rode.

"No doubt you've seen a turkey before, but they're wild and for the taking here. Back in England, the sumptuary laws make them cost dearly; in the colonies, instead of having them just for Christmas, we dine on them whenever God blesses us." He put the turkey at the back of the wagon. "I have a friend who keeps a flock on his farm. He clips their wings, so they can't fly, then drives them through his tobacco fields. They're good at eating worms off his plants."

She looked at the tom. Her hands came up and flew wide to indicate that she thought him to be of notable size.

"Aye, this fellow will make a few fine meals."

Sam had already slit the neck to bleed the turkey. Garnet crawled to the back and hauled the bird onto her lap. She pulled out the first few large feathers and set them aside. Looking up at him, she held one up in a silent query.

"Save the largest, but let the rest go. We've nothing to save them in, and a turkey left unplucked ends up having to be skinned to rid it of the feathers. The meat becomes all dry and charred in that eventuality."

She bobbed her head in acknowledgment and set to work at once as he went to get the flintlock. Inspecting his weapon carefully, her master came back and lifted it up a few inches. "How much powder did you put in?"

Too much powder would make it explode. Too little would be a waste. It was a reasonable question. She made him understand just how much and what steps she'd taken.

" 'Twas done as I would have. I've not seen a woman load a firearm ere this, and you did so correctly. Did you do it because I said I always kept her loaded?"

She nodded.

"And you've done the task ofttimes afore, haven't you?"

She bit her lip and nodded again.

"Garnet, I'm not upset with you. I'm near poleaxed, though. I've had a mother and a wife, and neither ever loaded a weapon. It never occurred to me that a woman might have gained that useful skill. Tell me this, though: If you load her again, how am I to know the deed is done?"

Garnet didn't even have to think. Setting the turkey aside, she took the flintlock from him, plucked out a single strand of her hair, and wound it three times around the trigger guard. Handing the flintlock back, she calmly resumed her work on the turkey.

"We will keep that as our signal. Aye, we will. 'Tis both clever and easy. As I grab the weapon, I'll know at once by feel without having to take my eyes from the target."

She nodded.

Samuel stooped and inspected the wagon. "I was hoping I didn't crack the wheel on that rut. The noise flushed out our supper, but I fretted that it boded ill for the wagon. 'Twasn't anything more than a dry stick in the bottom of the rut."

They went on, and Garnet quickly plucked the huge bird. By poking the largest feathers between fruit, she preserved enough to use as basting brushes. Being in the wagon's bed lent her an opportunity to take stock of the contents. Yesternoon, her master mentioned apples and grapes. Those counted as a small portion of what he hauled.

Spotty school attendance lent her enough skill to read simple words. Barrels bore chalked words. Garnet tilted her head and read. *Rye. Flour.* The next word was the longest. She studied it and felt a flare of happiness. *Cornmeal.* Cornmeal from the colonies cost dearly in England, and the few occasions when she'd eaten bread or mush from that grain left Garnet with a taste for more. She counted two barrels each of the rye and flour, eight of cornmeal. They must not eat wheat bread as much here.

The apples—what a boon! She'd be able to make pies and tarts aplenty. It would be good to dry as many as possible, too. The grapes were fresh, but they'd soon grow moldy. If the days stayed warm, she could dry them in the sun. Raisins would taste fine during the winter months.

Lettering on the staves of the single firkin read MO–LASS–ES. *Molasses!* But nine gallons of it? Brewers in the New World made rum from molasses, but surely nine gallons of the stuff wouldn't yield enough to make the effort worthwhile. Then again, what household would require an entire firkin of it?

Four jugs clanked and rattled against the molasses firkin. Garnet wondered about their contents. Just about anything could fill them, but if it were spirits, that could bode ill. A drunken man was a mean man. So far, Samuel Walsh had been uncommonly mild and kind. If he drank, that might change in an instant.

"Come up here, Garnet. I'd like you to see the meadow. 'Tis a lovely sight." He reached out a hand and helped her climb over and onto the seat. "Your hand is cold."

She snatched her hand back, then yanked his cloak over her lap and burrowed her hands beneath it.

Master Walsh pointed into the distance. "See there? My neighbor and I come here to hunt each autumn. A deer trail cuts directly through here, so we've gotten several. There's an earnest need for me to do some hunting before winter sets in."

She nodded.

"I have a small smokehouse. It hasn't much in it at the moment. We've eaten through most of our supplies, and they've yet to be replenished. I've been busy with the crops."

Pointing at the flintlock, then the meadow, Garnet struggled to come up with a way to make him understand her. She tapped her chest. Then her thumb and forefinger made a ring, and she pulled the circle across the air and closed it, repeating the action several times.

"You make sausage."

Pleased he understood her, she nodded.

"Venison sausage would taste fine. I'd be most appreciative of you making some."

Garnet bit her sore lip and gingerly reached down. She fleetingly touched the fabric of his britches at the worn knee but withdrew her fingers as if they had been burnt. Steeling herself with a deep breath, she then made a sewing motion.

"You'd make me buckskin breeches?"

Her head bobbed once again. She held up two fingers and branched her hands over her head to make a rack of antlers.

Samuel boomed out a great laugh. "You talk well with those hands, girl. Two deer to make the buckskins. I know how to tan hides. I already have one all cured."

She wrinkled her nose.

"Aye, the process stinks. I'll do so away from the house."

His house. I can ask about his house. Garnet shaded her eyes and pretended to look around, then sketched a shape in the air.

"You see a cabin."

She pointed at him.

"Ah. Where is my home? We'll travel 'til a little past noon. That'll be at the Mortons'. They're my nearest neighbors. Our homes lie about a mile apart."

She eased back and quietly watched the scenery. Other than the road, no sign of civilization existed. Back home in England, cottages and farms dotted the landscape. She hadn't traveled more than from her own village to her husband's, but that trip took only half a morning. She'd seen habitations aplenty during the transit, too. Garnet couldn't figure out a way to ask how late in the day they'd left the small town yesterday, but all of their travels since then carried them past untamed land.

This is called the New World. I thought it received that name because it was newly discovered. Maybe that's not so. Perhaps it's because coming here causes a person to start life afresh because it is all so different.

Sam was glad of the silence between them now. If there happened to be any game, sound would make it bolt. He'd mentioned the need to replenish the meat supply. Though Garnet might not speak aloud, she could make noise. She remained quiet, and he stayed vigilant.

Once past the meadow, Samuel looked down at Garnet and frowned. Her hand felt like ice earlier. Now shivers wracked her. He resisted the urge to touch the backs of his fingers to her forehead to test her for a fever. She happened to turn toward him and looked up. Her heat-flushed cheek told him she'd contracted a fever. Glassy eyes and chattering teeth reinforced his diagnosis, yet she did her best to smile bravely and straightened up.

Sam didn't have the heart to remark on her ill health. Instead, he pulled the heavy woolen garment she'd draped over her lap earlier. "Let's wrap you." He draped it around her slight frame.

Awhile later, the wagon drew up to the front of a farmhouse. A girl of middling school years ran up. "Heaven have mercy! Goodman Walsh, you've a woman with you!"

"God's blessings, Mary Morton. Go fetch your mother."

He eased away from Garnet. She'd fallen asleep again, and he'd tucked her close to his side in hopes of warming her sufficiently. She'd not been cold in the least, though. Once he got off the wagon, he gathered Garnet into his arms.

"Samuel!" Ruth Morton exited her cabin as she wiped her hands on the edge of her apron. "Mary told me you'd brought home a woman."

"Ruth, I fear she's ailing. I'll bear her to the barn so we don't take sickness into the house."

Ruth drew closer and parted the cloak so she could assess the situation. "Mary, you and Henry tote the tub to the barn. Fill it halfway with water from the pump. John, fetch the boiling kettle and bring it, carefully, mind you. Peter, fetch my bedgown and a blanket. Hubert, bring a towel and soap."

Hubert tugged on his mother's skirt. "Master Walsh said she's sick, Mama— not dirty."

"Yes, dearie. I know. But she can't sweat away her fever if dirt covers her."

"I'll fetch the soap!"

"And a towel," Ruth called.

Sam laid Garnet on the blanket Ruth spread on the barn floor. He thought to leave, but Ruth stopped him. "Wait 'til I bathe her face. If she rouses with strangers, she'll be frightened."

Her words made perfect sense. Samuel hunkered down and snatched the soggy cloth from Ruth. "Go ahead and start on her slippers and stockings." He gently swiped Garnet's face a few times.

"I've not seen such filth on a person before," Ruth stated in a hushed tone as she removed the girl's slippers. They were nearly worn through at the soles. "Dear me, she's even worse off than I thought."

Samuel shoved up Garnet's sleeves and swiped at her arms and wrists. "Cooling her will help."

Ruth struggled with the knot in the waist tape of Garnet's skirts. "Talk to her, Sam. I don't want her waking to think someone means her harm."

Samuel dipped the cloth again and rubbed it across Garnet's forehead. "Open your eyes, Garnet. Wake now."

Garnet remained alarmingly limp and silent.

Ruth clucked over Garnet's bodice. "Oh, such care she took making this. The buttonholes—she embroidered little flowers about them. I doubt I'll ever manage to salvage these clothes, Samuel. They're rags."

"If you're concerned about saving her clothes, am I to assume you're sure you can spare her life?"

"How she fares is in God's hands. She's half starved and in a deep swoon." Ruth sat back on her heels and thought for a moment. "I'm going to have you lift her so I can remove her bodice and loosen her shirt. Once that's done, you can leave. I'll sponge her off since she hasn't roused."

Ruth's plan seemed practical enough. Garnet would remain modestly covered. Samuel scooped Garnet into his arms and lifted her. She let out a whimper, and he immediately cupped her head to his shoulder and made a shushing sound.

"God bless her." Compassion whispered in Ruth's prayer. She looked up and gave him a quizzical look. "How did you come by her?"

He rasped, "I bought her in town. She cannot speak."

"You bought her?"

"Look how pitiful she is. Her owner was cruel, and I couldn't bear to leave her with him." He changed his hold to allow Ruth to unbutton the homespun waistcoat from the base of Garnet's throat down to a very narrow waist. The garment was a standard woman's article, simply and modestly made. But even with layers of clothing beneath it, Garnet still looked impossibly thin.

"Alas, Samuel, your heart is compassionate—"

"I confess, 'twas not just an act of mercy, Ruth. I'm hoping she'll stay so I can get Hester back from Dorcas. It grieves me deeply to have my daughter under her roof."

Ruth nodded. "She's a difficult one. Still, how are you to. . ." Her voice trailed off, and she gasped as the waistcoat came free and the back of the shirt beneath it sagged. "Oh, Sam!"

Chapter 5

He didn't mean to look, but he couldn't help himself. He reflexively held Garnet closer and glanced down. Ruth's hands shook as they unfastened the last few lacings, but the fabric stuck to ugly wounds. Garnet's back bore lash marks and bruises aplenty. For a brief second, she roused only enough to stiffen and whimper before her body wilted.

"Blessed Savior, have mercy," Samuel whispered in anguished prayer.

Ruth swallowed hard. "Rise up and hold her for me, Sam. I thought to leave her on the blanket and sponge her clean, but I must soak the shift to peel it from the stripes on her back."

"Aye, then. Be quick about this ere she rouses. I tell you, Ruth, I didn't know she was wounded. She bore her pain in silence." Sam tucked one arm behind Garnet's knees and rose.

Ruth removed each garment until the strange woman wore only her threadbare shift. Samuel supported Garnet's weight, but in no way did he help divest her of a single scrap of cloth. He wouldn't shame her or himself in such manner, so he kept his eyes trained on a dusty cobweb hanging from a nearby rafter.

"There now." Ruth moved away. "Lower her into the water. The tub's a little to your left and a pace and a half ahead."

The toe of his boot let him know he'd found the large wooden vat. Water saturated his sleeves as he gently folded Garnet and situated her in the tub.

"It'll take some time to soak the shirt away from her wounds. Send Mary in with more buckets of water. We may as well see to the girl's hair. You called her Garnet, did you not?"

"Aye. Garnet Wheelock. She's a widow. Sold to cover her husband's debts."

"Best you and Falcon pray, Samuel. By faith, I say only the Almighty can heal the wounds in the heart of a woman so miserably mistreated."

Sam exited the barn. The Morton children all crowded around to hear about Garnet. Sam heaved a sigh. "Mary, your mother requires your assistance. John and Henry, round up buckets. They'll need more water."

"Samuel!" Falcon, Ruth's husband, came from a nearby field with Hubert riding on his shoulders. "My son tells me you brought back a woman."

"He did, Father," John shouted. "But she's sick."

Mary gave John and Henry each a shove. "Hush and go fetch water. Father needs to speak with Goodman Walsh."

Falcon lowered Hubert to the ground and ruffled his hair. "I spied a few hens by the oak stump. Take Peter, and search for eggs."

"Peter!" Hubert scampered off.

Falcon's jaunty grin faded. "So the woman's ill?"

Sam nodded curtly. "A fever's taken hold. Ruth's with her. I didn't know when I bought her that she'd been whipped."

Falcon turned toward Samuel. "What, my friend, could have possibly motivated you to buy a bride?"

"She's not to be my bride." The very notion appalled him.

Falcon shook his head. "After years of rearing the children on your own, I fail to understand this."

Sam folded his arms akimbo. "My reason is plain enough. I'm not rearing my children; I'm rearing my sons."

"Ahh, Hester."

"I want my daughter back, and I cannot pry her from Dorcas unless I have capable assistance. I confess, after realizing Garnet's ill, I think perhaps I have lost my fair reason."

Falcon slapped him on the shoulder. "I doubt this. The hand of our Lord moves in unexpected ways. We should trust in His wisdom instead of your understanding. My goodwife will tend the girl with care."

Falcon's faith—both in God and his wife's skill—reassured Sam. "How have my sons fared?"

"They're fine boys. Hardworking. They missed you sorely, though. Your Christopher and my Aaron have done well, going to and fro your place each morning and eve. I sent Ethan with them this noon with instructions for the boys to divert water from the stream into your watering pond. I figure our flocks can graze in your pasture the next week or so."

Sam frowned. "My sheep haven't overgrazed, have they?"

"They ate no more than I expected." Falcon gestured dismissively. "Your land sustained my sheep when I took my grain to the mill. I daresay our flocks could double in size and still have sufficient pasture. I see you have a turkey in your wagon."

"My trip turned out to be far more productive than I expected. I've apples and grapes to share."

"I'll not turn down either. 'Twill be good to enjoy them."

Samuel heard laughter and pivoted. "Christopher! Ethan!"

His sons rounded a bend of trees. At the sound of his voice, they ran into his outstretched arms. At thirteen, Christopher was a copy of his father. Tall and broad, he would soon be a man. Ten and already stretching past the phase where he was nothing more than knees and elbows, Ethan showed the same promise.

Samuel hugged them both, then stated matter-of-factly, "I've brought a woman home. Her name is Widow Wheelock. She's ailing, but as soon as she recovers, she'll help us greatly."

Christopher asked, "Are you going to marry her, Father?"

Falcon chuckled. "You can't fault him, Samuel. All will wonder the selfsame thing."

"They'd do better to mind their own business than to plot out my life." Sam gave his sons a steady look. "I bought the widow so we can bring Hester home."

Falcon peered over Sam's shoulder and raised his brows as Mary emerged from the barn and approached them.

"Father, Mama's rubbing the lady's hair dry. She directed me to tell you the woman's fever is because she's hurt, not because she bears disease."

"She's hurt?" Ethan scratched his elbow.

Sam didn't want to explain. "Goodwife Morton's seeing to the widow. You boys go gather your belongings." As the boys walked away, Sam and Falcon turned and headed to the barn. Falcon called out, and Ruth softly bade them enter. Sam strode to the edge of the blanket and hunkered down. "How does she fare, Ruth?"

Ruth finished wrapping the towel about Garnet's hair and whispered in a pained tone, "No one ought ever be so mistreated."

Falcon rested his hand on her shoulder. "She won't be again."

"She's not roused at all. Perchance she ought to remain here for a time."

Samuel's face tightened. "I understand you mean her well, but she's been bought and sold twice already. To finally awaken and discover herself in yet another household will only make matters worse. I'll take the boys and go on home with her."

Ruth chewed on her lip for a moment. "I suppose you can keep watch over her whilst Christopher goes to Dorcas's and fetches Hester."

Sam shook his head. "I'll need to fetch my daughter."

Falcon nodded. "A wise decision. For all her sour talk, Dorcas benefits from keeping your daughter. With Hester carding wool, Dorcas is able to spin far more. She'll be loath to let Hester go."

"The decision isn't hers to make. Hester's my daughter. She's coming home."

"Your resolve is clear." Falcon addressed his wife. "Dear, Sam offered us some apples and grapes. Go see to having the children carry in whatever Sam spares us. Mary can stay with the widow whilst I empty the water into the garden."

Ruth rose. "Come, Samuel. We'll prepare a place in your wagon. Feed her broth until I pay a call in a day or two. Mind you, give her nothing more than broth or hasty pudding. Curds and whey are acceptable, as well. She's too care-worn to take in much else."

"I'm thankful for your skill." They reached the wagon. He looked at the apples and grapes. "I'll leave a basket of apples and most of the grapes for your family. The grapes will spoil ere Garnet's healed sufficiently to dry them."

"I'll take just a few apples and thank you for the grapes. In a few days, I'll come to call and help Garnet preserve apples. 'Twill provide an excuse for me to come, so I'll tend her back again then. She'll be able to stay seated whilst we work on the apples afterward."

Ruth called to one of the children. It took no time at all for her to fill the baskets they brought from the house with grapes and apples. She took Christopher and Ethan's blankets and formed a bed for Garnet.

Falcon came out of the barn with the little widow in his arms. Samuel barely kept from gaping. Completely washed and clean, Garnet wore a white linen bedgown. His cloak wrapped about her at least twice over. Fever painted bright red flags across her cheeks. Even so, her finely carved features relaxed with sleep into a rare prettiness. Without caked-on mud and grease, her hair took his breath away. Her name made perfect sense now, because her tresses were a deep, rich red.

Ruth fussed with the cloak as Falcon put Garnet in the wagon.

"Falcon, you're blessed to have such a good woman to wife."

"I know. I think it a shame you've not yet found another woman for your hearth."

"I cannot imagine marrying again. It would not be a good union."

Ruth cast her husband an exasperated look. "The topic's come up before and will yet again. For now, take pity on this woman and let Sam take her home. Sam, put her abed and keep her there. If the fever stays high, you know how to brew willow bark."

"I will."

"Go with God."

———

Garnet woke and slowly studied her surroundings. She lay in a jump bed, propped up by several pillows. Half-drawn bed curtains kept the heat radiating from a low fire in the hearth. Hazy memories of a little girl singing to her and a man giving her sips of water filtered through her mind. The last thing she clearly remembered was plucking a turkey as she sat at the back of the man's wagon. The man—his name was Wa-something. *Walter? Wallace? Walsh. Yes. Walsh. Am I in his home?*

She couldn't bring herself to stay abed at all, let alone in a stranger's home. Garnet pushed off the thick coverlet and swung her legs over the side of the bed. She felt a little dizzy, but that passed soon enough. A neatly made trundle poked halfway out from beneath the bed. Nicely enough, it acted like a step for her. She paused a moment again as dizziness assailed her, then shoved the trundle in the rest of the way.

Her master's keeping room looked spare. Aside from a few trunks and the cupboard, it held only the bed, a table, and benches. As homes went, this one wasn't cluttered, but it certainly wasn't clean, either. Many of the things Garnet expected were absent. No herbs hung on the ceiling pegs to dry. Neither did many vegetables dehydrate on shelves, racks, or pegs. The posts for drying apple rings lay barren. The clarified hide that served as a window wore such a thick coat of dust, no light filtered in.

Worried her master might enter when she wore only a nightdress, Garnet searched for something to lend a little modesty. A length of cloth lay draped over a peg, so she helped herself to it, tying it into a petticoat of sorts. With a towel for a shawl, she looked passably covered.

The fire burned too low in the large stone fireplace. Garnet added another log and checked the pot that simmered over the flames. The broth inside held no flavoring save the remainder of what she suspected to be the turkey Samuel had shot on their travel homeward. A few stale crusts of bread lay sprinkled across the tabletop. She dusted off the far end of the table, helped herself to a bowl, and soon had corn bread ready to bake. After putting the cast-iron pan over the fire, Garnet took one of the carrots and a turnip, chopped them, and added both to the broth.

"You're up!"

Chapter 6

Garnet turned and smiled at the young girl she faintly remembered. The little dark-haired beauty stood in the doorway, clutching a basket of eggs. "Father says you must rest yet. I am Hester."

Garnet wet her lips and lightly shook her head. She looked down at her ridiculous outfit and plucked at it, then smiled at the girl as her brows rose in question.

"Papa says Goodwife Morton has your overgarments. She's to come today. You'll like her. She has a merry heart and will be glad to see you're better." She put the basket down and smoothed her apron. "I'm to go gather feathers. You'll not get me into trouble by doing much, will you?"

Garnet gave her a smile and shooed her away. Waves of weariness washed over her, but she couldn't very well lie back down. Instead, she sat at the table, took up a knife, and very carefully peeled all of the candle wax from the candlesticks into a small plate. She felt terribly weak, but she desperately wanted to be useful. Moments later, a shadow fell over her.

"Good morrow, Garnet Wheelock! You'll not recall me. I'm Ruth Morton—Samuel Walsh's neighbor to the south. I hope you'll be my friend, as well as my neighbor."

Garnet rose as the woman began to speak and curtsied.

"Oh, don't fuss with that. Sit down. Better yet, you ought to lie down. I didn't expect you to be up. You still belong abed."

Garnet didn't want to be quarrelsome, but she shook her head.

Ruth smiled. "I'll have to trouble my mind now whether to leave you the overgarments you wore, for I fear to do so will enable you to stay up. We want only good for you."

Her face was so preciously kind that Garnet felt something deep inside start to crack. Something about Ruth's steady blue eyes and soft voice made her feel so vulnerable. All she'd endured suddenly loomed up and nearly overwhelmed her. She found herself clasped to a soft, ample bosom, rocked, and crooned to as if she were but a babe.

When Garnet's weeping drew to a conclusion, Ruth simply brushed a kiss on her forehead and whispered, "A good cry is ofttimes what a body needs most to return to health."

Abashed, Garnet nodded and went to get the pan of corn bread from the fire.

She stirred the broth and couldn't help making a face at it.

Ruth twittered. "I oft wonder that Sam and the children don't get the dwindles. He cooks only the most basic of necessities. Christopher chars meat over the fire when he must. Little Hester just came home, and I fear she's too small to trust much near the fireplace."

Garnet nodded in acknowledgment. Not wanting to ridicule her benefactor for the lack of staples in his home, Garnet still needed to know about the food supplies. She pointed to the ceiling. The meager supply of herbs and vegetables spoke for itself.

" 'Tis harvesttime, and there's a need to dry and put up. You've actually a well-planted garden, and God was generous this year. Samuel left the grapes at my farm. I've set them out to dry in the sun and charged my sons to keep the birds away from them. We'll share the raisins betwixt our homes. In a day or two, I'll return, and we'll preserve your apples."

Garnet found herself smiling at the woman.

"Here, now. Let me see to your marks."

She knows about them?

"Don't fuss," Ruth said gently. "Someone mistreated you, and 'twas to his shame—not yours. Christ was whipped, too—and we know He was innocent."

This woman wants to be my friend. How blessed I am that You've given me her, Lord.

Ruth Morton smiled. "If I'm pleased with how you're healing, I'll allow you the overgarments. I fear, should I not, you might be seen gardening in a bedgown!"

Garnet smiled.

Ruth took care of her back, helped her dress, and chattered the whole time. "Samuel Walsh is a widower. His wife's been in her grave about four years now. The only man I know who's kinder than Samuel is my husband, Falcon." Ruth laughed. "I'm partial to Falcon, so the comparison is a compliment."

Garnet smiled, then held out her hand and drew imaginary stair steps in the air, then flipped both hands palm upward and raised her brows.

"Children?" Ruth reached up and adjusted the clout covering her hair. "Samuel has three. Two sons and little Hester. All three are well behaved."

Garnet gestured again.

"Yes, the dear Lord has blessed Falcon and me. We have four sons and a daughter. There were two more children, but they returned to God's bosom. Have you had children?"

Garnet shook her head.

"I'd planned to make corn pone and split pea soup while here, but I can see you've already seen to the meal. Rest, Garnet."

Garnet waved to encompass the entire keeping room.

Ruth laughed. "I can't deny that much wants doing here. Samuel is a kind man, though. He wouldn't expect you to work for a while yet. Plenty of time lies ahead for you to put your hand to tasks."

Though she opened her mouth, no sound came out. Garnet wanted so badly to talk to Ruth Morton. The love of God shone in her kind eyes.

"Sam told me you're mute, yet you speak in your sleep."

Sadly, Garnet hitched her shoulder. She didn't understand the malady, either.

"Mayhap the Lord is permitting you this trial to increase your faith. Some religious orders practice silence." Ruth smiled. "When God is ready, He'll give you back your voice. Betwixt then and now, we'll manage. Now I'm going to take my leave. I'll be back day after next. Rest up, because I aim to have us dry apples and make applesauce. 'Twill be a busy day."

Ruth gave her a hug and paused ere she stepped over the threshold. "When the boys stayed with me, they brought over the milk each day. I churned butter aplenty and tucked some in your springhouse."

Garnet hurried over to the doorway.

"Oh, you've not gone outside yet? Come." Ruth took her arm and led her off to the left. "The stream here flows with sweet water. Sam built a springhouse off to the side so you can keep butter, milk, and eggs even during the hottest part of the summer."

After looking at the clever setup and feeling a spurt of gratitude that she wouldn't have to haul water far at all, Garnet looked back at the house. She shot Ruth a startled look and held up two fingers.

"Aye. The boys sleep on the second level. 'Tis a common arrangement in these parts. The entrance is on the other side and can only be reached by a ladder. Winters are bitterly cold. This way, the fire's heat remains down in the keeping room. If memory serves me correctly, Sam cut a trapdoor in the floor so the upstairs can take on some heat before he sends the boys to bed."

Tapping her temple, Garnet smiled.

"Aye, 'tis clever. I'll be back day after tomorrow."

Garnet dipped another curtsy. Ruth had called her a friend and been exceedingly kind, but Garnet knew Samuel was not only master of the house but her master, as well. She would thank him for rescuing her and for his kindness by serving his family with diligence.

Samuel plucked a weed and stood back up. "God's blessing on you, Ruth."

"I've just come from visiting Garnet. She fares well enough."

"Fie! She needs rest yet."

"You'll not see it of her. Already, she's made corn bread and worries over the harvest. She was modest when I tended her. What do you know of her?"

Sam knew Ruth was no gossip. Her interest stemmed from Christian charity. He leaned on his hoe. "I know nothing other than her name and that she's a widow. I'm heartened to hear you think her health's improved."

"The girl has a ways to go, but time will solve that."

"It bodes well that she's modest. I've never seen sadder eyes, but the cause is unknown to me. Sorrow of all kinds can dim the spirit in such a way."

Ruth tucked her hands into the pocket of her apron. "The marks on her back bode ill. Have you considered that she may be with child?"

Necessity made such frank talk acceptable. Still, Samuel squinted at the horizon. "I've no way of knowing. Time will tell. Hester shares the jump bed. Any offspring won't be mine."

"Samuel Walsh! I would have never supposed that to be the case!"

He gave Ruth a grin. "You might not, but others can be quick to judge and slow to think. I appreciate the faith you carry for me."

"Hear me: I know you too well to think otherwise. Her overgarments are in tatters. If you still have Naomi's old things, I'm sure Garnet would not take offense if you offered them."

"They're in the barn. I'll fetch them."

Ruth looked down at the rich earth and said softly, "Just because they're the same clothes doesn't mean the woman wearing them will take on the same temperament. I probably ought not speak ill of the dead, but memories of your wife..." Her voice died out as she shrugged.

Sam nodded curtly. He'd been careful not to speak of his wife. The memories were unpleasant at best. His sons didn't need to hear tales of a shrewish mother, and they'd been young enough to be unaware of Naomi's worst qualities. Sam refused to lie about her, so silence was the best he could manage.

"I meant you no insult, Samuel. I intended to give reassurance, not to gossip."

Sam shifted his weight. "Truth is the truth. I didn't for a moment question your motive. You and your husband have been stalwart friends. 'Twas a merciful thing you said, for I confess, I hesitated to fetch Naomi's clothing for that ridiculous fear."

"You couldn't help it, Sam. Your memories are painful ones."

"There are those who would fault a man for living by feeling instead of faith." He cleared his throat.

"You? Lack of faith? Oh, Sam! You've acted wisely. A man shouldn't plunge back into the river when he almost drowned in it."

His face and ears burned. As a man with children, his family rated higher on a level of need than did a single man. Twice, though, he'd refused bridal candidates. The first time, the woman's father asserted he expected Samuel to give over Christopher in exchange. The second had been last summer—but Sam recoiled from the very notion of taking the offered thirteen-year-old bride.

Ruth took her hands out of the pocket of her apron. "Who knows? Mayhap you waited because the Lord had Garnet in store for you."

He stared at Ruth, and his voice went rough. "Put aside that thinking here and now."

Ruth laughed. "Now, Sam, there's no need to get riled. You've brought your daughter home and have a woman there."

"I'll move my bed to the attic to still any wagging tongues and quench wild imaginations."

"You'll do no such thing—at least not yet! The trundle is decent enough until Garnet has recovered. If Garnet's fever returns, Hester is too small to go outside and climb up a ladder in the pitch-dark of night. Clearly, these are uncommon circumstances. With the bed curtains closed between the trundle and the jump bed, along with little Hester there, propriety is maintained."

"It's a temporary arrangement. As soon as I'm positive she's fully recovered, I'll join my sons in the loft."

"You've thought it out. I agree with the plan. For you to stay in the keeping room would make others believe you're fostering an attraction."

He scowled. "Widow Wheelock is comely, but her character is yet a mystery. I know nothing of her. I've not even heard her voice other than in the garbled mutterings of a fever."

"You might think to have the reverend pray over her. That she talks in the night means her heart is sorely troubled. No doubt, he will pay a call to see her. The elders will demand it."

"I assumed it to be the case. They'll see her on the Sabbath."

"Best you be sure to give her Naomi's cap. Her hair is a thing of beauty and will be cause for comment. She's not vain in the least, but others will find it less than plain. To have an attractive widow under your roof will likely wreak havoc."

Samuel mulled over Ruth's words for the rest of the morning. At midday, he went to the cabin for lunch. Corn bread awaited him, fragrant and still warm. Hester met him in the doorway, her eyes twinkling. She whispered excitedly, "Just imagine! She fixed up the broth!"

A bouquet of mustard and sweet cicely poked out of a small crock on the table. A generous bundle of the same lay off to the side on one of the trunks. Herbs and flowers hadn't been brought into the cabin since Naomi died four years before—and then they'd been for use and never to simply add charm to their abode.

In deference to the small woman who had fallen fast asleep on the bed once again, Sam silenced his sons as they entered the house. They sat down, and Samuel ladled up the soup. His mouth began to water. A few sliced cabbage leaves floated along with the carrot and turnip bits. The broth was thickened with something to give it body, and bits of seasonings that teased his memory lent a toothsome aroma to the steam rising from the pot. Best of all, dumplings floated on the surface.

"Did she make this, or did Ruth Morton?" Ethan demanded to know in a hiss of a whisper.

Hester smiled and giggled as she pointed to the small occupant of the jump bed. "She did."

As Christopher reached to help himself to even more, Samuel checked his arm and inquired, "Did she partake of any, Hester?"

"Aye. Only the tiniest bit."

Samuel let go of Christopher's arm and let him have more. "She eats very little."

"She's not much larger than Ethan," Christopher decided, staring at the small form on the bed. "Are you sure she's all grown up?"

Samuel hadn't thought to ask her age. One didn't ask such a thing, but under the circumstances, it was an understandable question. Christopher counted thirteen winters, and he'd wish to marry in another three or four years. He was coming to the point that young bucks noticed women. Still, Samuel had held her and knew she was not in the bud but in the bloom of her life.

"Mayhap when she awakens, we can discover more of her."

They finished eating and went back out. Samuel returned to the house past sunset. Hester sat outside the door and churned butter. "Father, we've been busy!"

"Is that so?" He paused and relished the happiness lighting his daughter's face.

Her head bobbed in rhythm with the knocking paddle. "The lady took me for a little walk. We gathered milkweed and twisted it. She told me it'll serve as candlewicks."

"She's talking?"

"With her hands," Hester said in a blithe tone. "Ethan caught fish. Three fish. The lady is making them for supper."

"So that's what smells so good."

Garnet lightly fried the fish in butter and sprinkled fresh dill over them. She also sliced, fried, and seasoned potatoes. A salad of freshly picked dandelion greens filled up the remainder of the space on the pewter plates. Christopher poked Ethan in the side and mocked, "It's about time you caught good-tasting fish!"

"What is this?" Samuel looked at an odd thing in the center of the table.

"You'll never imagine, Father. We looked about, and there are only a few tapers left. Widow Wheelock scraped the wax from the candlesticks and melted it on a plate. She dipped mullein leaves in it."

Sure enough, as supper almost ended and the room got dim, Garnet lit the tip of the leaf, and it acted just like a candle.

"You're clever, Garnet. I've not seen such a thing. I'll have Ethan gather rushes from the stream on the morrow. They make good light, too."

She nodded and got up to clear the table.

"Garnet, Hester will clear the table. I need you to sit back down. I'll ask you about yourself. Ethan, fetch your slate for us."

Garnet hesitantly sat down.

"Without a formal introduction, we've done well thus far," Samuel moderated. "But the time has come to discover a bit more about you. Forgive my lack of manners, but I wish to know your age."

She held up all ten fingers, then closed her hands for a second before holding all of them up again.

"Twenty. The man I bought you from said you were sold to pay your husband's debts. Am I correct in presuming your husband died?"

She nodded.

Obviously, she was remembering something painful. Samuel gave her a few moments. "When the time came that your mourning was over, did you hold an understanding with someone to become his wife?"

She decisively shook her head.

"I am Samuel, as I told you. I am nine and twenty. My wife died four years past. Christopher is thirteen; Ethan, ten; and Hester is five." He felt it necessary to impart that information so she'd have a chance to collect herself. Judging by her wide eyes, short, quick breaths, and tightly clasped hands, Garnet was rattled. He should have told her about his family as they traveled. She must have been frightened, coming into an unknown situation. Just because she couldn't speak didn't mean that she didn't communicate.

"I should have thought to spin yarns about the children on our journey. You'll learn of them soon enough, though. They are good children and most often do their chores willingly. I've not had much trouble from them and do not anticipate that you shall, either. Nevertheless, you've my leave to bid them do whatever chores you deem necessary."

Her lips parted in surprise, then pressed together as she dipped her head. Did she think he was teasing or ridiculing her? He barely grazed the back of her hand. "Heed me, Widow Wheelock. I redeemed you unto yourself. I've need of help and hope you will consent to stay, but I'll not have you to slave, nor will my children show you disrespect. Freedom is a right in this land. I'll not hold with denying it to another."

He saw the shock in her face and tried to continue as if he'd not said anything to surprise her. To make an issue of her emancipation would be more of an emotional drain, and he wanted to discover as much as possible about her past.

That, in and of itself, was going to be hard enough.

Her hands shook as she took the slate he placed in them. He fought the urge to steady them. Instead, he wove his fingers together and rested his clasped hands on the tabletop. "Are you able to read and write?"

She held her thumb and forefinger apart.

Samuel stated softly, "A little. That's better than I could have hoped. If you'd care to learn more, mayhap I could teach you in the evenings. Without speech, you need some way to talk. I understand you've not spoken to anyone since your ship landed, yet you do in your sleep. Won't you speak to us now?"

Her lower lip quavered pathetically, and she captured it between her teeth. He hadn't noticed until now that her front teeth overlapped ever so slightly. That small flaw was strangely endearing. Tears slipped down her cheeks, and she closed her eyes to dam them in.

"I'm a patient man. When you're ready, you'll speak. Until then, we'll get by. You seem much at home on a farm." He spoke in a carefully modulated tone, trying to elicit information without fraying her composure more than necessary. "I take it your family farmed?"

She nodded jerkily.

"Well and good. Indeed, that is well and good! We are in sore need of a woman's help and influence. Believe me, your knowledge and skills will be more than welcome. My little Hester could be merry to have a lady friend."

Garnet looked over at the little girl and gave her a ghost of a smile. Samuel knew that smile cost her dearly. She was obviously grief-stricken, yet she cared enough about a child's feelings to try to set aside her own hurts for a moment.

"Because you now abide with us, I fetched Hester home. My wife died the year after bearing Hester. Dorcas—my wife's sister—has kept Hester for me since then."

Hester gave Garnet's arm an exuberant hug. "I like you. And I know you like me. Aunt Dorcas is sour as unripe berries."

Samuel cleared his throat.

Hester shot him a surprised look. "Aunt Dorcas always says it's not gossiping if what she tells is the truth."

"It's not a lie if you're telling the truth," he said slowly. "But if your reason for telling a truth is to make someone else think badly of another, then you've stooped to gossiping."

Hester beamed at him. "Then I wasn't sinful, Father. I was telling Widow Wheelock a happy truth. She is kind and cares nicely for me. It is a good change."

Garnet gave Hester a smile and pressed a trencher into her small hands. Hester headed for the swill bucket to scrape off the scraps. The young widow arched her brow at him.

Samuel cast a look at his precious little daughter, then measured his words carefully. "I owe Dorcas a debt of gratitude for the safety she afforded Hester. Dangers abound, and I couldn't mind her adequately on my own. Hester is capable of helping about the house and assisted Dorcas in many ways."

Garnet's brow puckered. Since she sat with her back to Hester, she crossed her arms in a huglike fashion and rocked from side to side.

Samuel answered her with a curt shake, then forced his voice to sound positive. "As Hester said, 'tis clear your heart overflows with affection. Having her back and knowing she will flourish under your care—'tis undoubtedly a heavenly reply to countless, diligent prayers."

Her eyes misted, and she again crossed her arms and made a silent pledge to cherish Hester.

"You have my gratitude." He paused, then pressed on. "What do I need to know about you? Did you leave any children behind?"

Garnet shook her head, and he let out a gusty sigh of relief. "Good. Very good. I've noticed you pray. Is this of habit or of heart?"

Her hand went to her bosom and patted over her heart. Suddenly, her features twisted with revulsion. She shoved away from the table and inched backward.

Chapter 7

Samuel turned around to see what elicited such a strong reaction from Garnet. He saw nothing out of the ordinary. A bit of movement caught his eye. A field mouse scampered along the edge of the room and darted toward the broom. He turned back and realized Garnet's gaze remained pinned on the creature. "'Tis naught but a field mouse and a babe at that, Garnet. Chris, grab the broom and sweep him out."

Garnet opened the door, and Sam thought it helpful of her; but as Christopher started to nudge the mouse, Garnet lost all color and shuddered dramatically. The tiny rodent scampered toward freedom, and Garnet let out a wail. She spun around and raced outside.

The dark swallowed her when she was a few feet away, but her terrified screaming made her easy to track. For one so sick and weak, she moved with astonishing swiftness. Samuel chased after her and tackled her in the middle of what had recently been his cornfield. Even though small and pitifully frail, she fought him wildly—kicking, scratching, and hitting with panicked desperation.

"Garnet! Garnet!" He tried to calm her, but she'd spiraled completely out of control. Samuel hated to strike her, but he knew no other way. He slapped her cheek, and her screaming halted in the middle of a shrill note. She sucked in a shocked breath, then broke into body-wracking sobs.

"Garnet, Garnet." He wrapped her up in his arms and rocked her in the field of dirt and cornstalks. Her hands fisted, clenching his clothing in tight balls as she pressed her cheek to his chest and wept. He pulled her closer still and murmured wordless sounds of comfort. It tore at him to witness her raw horror. He'd failed to appreciate the depth of her fear, a mistake he'd not make again.

"Father?" Christopher shuffled close by. He held one of her candle leaves.

"Light us back, son." Samuel stood and cradled her in his arms. Wrenching sobs still shook her tiny frame all the way back to the house. Hester stood in the doorway, gnawing uncertainly on her knuckles.

Christopher patted Garnet's arm. "It's gone. I got rid of it."

Sam ordered softly, "Hester, you'll aid me with Garnet. Boys, you'd best wait outside." Hester silently helped him tuck the woman in bed.

Garnet finally reached the point of total exhaustion. Her tears and energy spent, she lay facing the wall with a dull look that carried hopelessness and heartache. Sam gently smoothed back her hair. "Hester, curl beside her here in the bed. The widow needs the warmth of another's presence and caring."

Samuel tucked his daughter in and watched as she turned and wound her arms around Garnet and nestled close. "We'll love you, Garnet," Hester whispered in her soft, pure voice. "You can be here with me and Father and Christopher and Ethan. All is well now."

Garnet gave no reaction.

Sam stooped and pressed a kiss on Hester's crown. "Well said. You cuddle and find the peace of a sound rest."

He stepped outside afterward and stared up at the stars. He sought a second of solace from heaven, but it was slow in coming. Christopher somberly stated, "Mama cried like that once."

Ethan didn't remember his mother. "She did? When?"

"When Grandmother died."

"Did she scream like the demons had her, too?" Ethan asked, his voice shaking with fright.

"Nay." Samuel drew his son close to his side and gave him a reassuring squeeze. "I was there to hold and comfort her. She wept every bit as hard, but she was not alone in her grief."

Christopher kept a bit of distance and tried to act like a young man. He cleared his throat, and his voice barely cracked as he said, "Garnet has no one. Not a soul."

"True. I've no idea what transpired with Garnet, but 'twas something too terrible to let her mind and soul find peace."

Ethan looked up at him. "Father, she has us."

"Aye, that she does, but she barely knows us at all. God, alone, will have to be her comfort until she gains a trust in us."

The boys each recited their scripture for the night, went to the privy, and climbed the ladder to their bed. Samuel went out to the barn and opened a small chest that contained Naomi's clothes. Without discussing the matter, she'd bartered his best ram to obtain a French brocade for her bodice and a length of fancy wool for her skirts. Staunch friends that they were, Falcon Morton and Thomas Brooks both lent him their rams that season. Memory after bitter memory swelled. Samuel tamped them down, grabbed the garments, and shut the chest with notable force. If the Widow Wheelock didn't need the clothing so desperately, he'd have gladly left them tucked away forever.

Sam slipped back into the keeping room. To his relief, Hester and Garnet lay curled together in a warm knot. Hester seemed more than content, but the firelight illuminated Garnet's face. Judging from the expressions flickering there, she suffered troubled dreams.

Unable to change that, Samuel drew the bed curtains closed to keep them warm and provide modesty. He prepared for bed, then pulled the trundle out for himself. The trundle measured far too small for him. Constructed for a pair of small children, it was less than restful for a big man.

That fact didn't matter. Garnet kept him awake with her restless cries. In her sleep, she sobbed and mumbled more pitifully than she had even at the height of her fever.

"Lord most high," Samuel prayed quietly, "take pity on your daughter Garnet. You, alone, know what she's endured. Grant her peace of mind and a tranquil heart."

Garnet surfaced from her sleep in slow degrees, with different things registering one at a time. She was warm. Her back stung. Something felt strangely out of place. She opened her eyes and gasped.

A large hand rested over hers on the pillow.

Garnet tried to pull away, but that hand curled about hers, and the callous thumb rubbed her palm. "Shh," a deep, slurred voice bade from the other side of the bed curtain.

Her gaze traced from the hand, to the thick, hair-sprinkled wrist, down to the muscled forearm that disappeared between the split of the closed bed curtain. Master Walsh honorably stayed on the trundle, yet he'd sacrificed his comfort and sleep to give her consolation.

Garnet wasn't sure what to do. Part of her wanted to accept the strength and caring her master offered. On the other hand, a woman of virtue could scarcely allow herself to be in such a compromising position. She made a small sound of protest and tried to slide free of his hold.

"Garnet, rest awhile where you are. You're safe. Daybreak isn't far off."

His tone was so inviting, so mellow that it was impossible to defy his quiet command. She sighed and rubbed her cheek against her pillow. As Samuel Walsh patted her hand, she coasted back to sleep.

The cockerel crowed. At the first rusty sounds the bird made, she came alert. Heat filled her cheeks when she had to disentangle herself from her master's hand.

"Garnet," Samuel ordered, "remain abed whilst I dress. There's no cause for anyone to be overset."

Samuel's bland voice calmed her tremendously. It was his home, and she— she was his rightfully purchased slave. Even so, he'd treated her with respect and great compassion.

Was it just a dream, him telling her that she was free? It was hard to tell fact from fancy anymore. Everything blended in a muddle. Whatever her station in his house, Samuel Walsh seemed to be a godly man. He had not taken advantage of her. That said much of his moral fiber.

In mere moments, the solid sound of him stomping each foot into his boots let her know he'd finished dressing, but a rustling sound ensued.

"Widow Wheelock, hold fast to the bed curtains. I aim to push in the trundle."

He'd made the trundle bed? What manner of man was he, to perform such a mundane, domestic chore? Garnet couldn't answer him, so she simply did as he bade. The trundle scraped a little as he shoved it beneath the jump bed.

"I've placed my wife's clothing upon the table for you. Wear them in good health. I'll go milk the cow. You'll have some privacy." The door opened, then shut.

Garnet crept out of the bed and tucked the covers back over little Hester. Garnet looked down at her tattered clothes. She'd slept in them—a reminder of how she'd panicked the night before. Shame and revulsion washed over her.

I can't waste time regretting what's past. I have to forge ahead and prove myself now.

The luxurious quality of the clothing her master left on the table stunned Garnet. She could scarcely imagine wearing such fine garments. The blue brocade bodice looked fine enough to be worn by the queen's own ladies-in-waiting. The skirts were wool—of mingled blue and green threads—but far more voluminous than a farmer's wife normally wore. With a farthingale beneath them, his wife would have been outfitted elegantly enough to be seen as a woman of consequence in London. The apron was made of finest linen. Never had Garnet owned clothing of this quality, and what she did own bordered on immodest due to its sad condition.

She quickly changed, then knelt at the fire and added just enough wood to bring it to a cooking level. Wood took time to chop and carry. She didn't want to make any more work for the boys. Already familiar with the food supplies on hand, Garnet started corn mush for breakfast. Once she had that underway, she took the larger pot and filled it with a chopped onion, some garlic, half a dozen peppercorns, water, and peas. By nuncheon, she'd locate wild thyme and sage to add to that hearty soup.

Ethan brought in milk, and Christopher filled the wood box. Those light chores done, they all sat down to eat. After asking the blessing, Samuel added milk to his mush and stirred it. He'd given her clothing a long look, then turned away.

He must have loved his wife dearly to have provided such finery for her. *If seeing me dressed in her clothing is painful, then it would be best for me to change back.*

"Ethan, you're to gather rushes and reeds today. Christopher, you're to stack the cornstalks so they'll finish drying. Another thing: I've seen several hares."

"I'll set snares." Christopher reached across the table, scooped a generous heap of butter with his spoon, and plopped it atop his mush. Grinning at Garnet, he said, "I'm partial to roast hare."

She smiled at his boldness. Ruth Morton had mentioned the Walshes hadn't eaten well in years, and the zeal with which they dug into what she'd prepared made it clear her master and his sons would gladly devour whatever she set before them.

Garnet listened as Master Walsh directed each of the children with their duties. The chores he set out were common enough. She wondered if he was doing this more for her benefit than theirs. Still, it was good of him to let her know how the family operated. She needed to hear what was already set to be accomplished so she could fill in the other areas.

"Widow Wheelock, we are grateful to you for the meal. 'Twas tasty enough, but I'll thank you to remain abed this day. A sickness near took you to the here-after, and it cannot be permitted to return."

She took up the slate they'd left on the table from last night. Laboriously, she wrote, *I am well.*

He smiled at the way she underlined the last word. "You are spirited, if not completely hale. I fear you will overdo."

Her face scrunched; then she shook her head and used the same gesture she'd used back on the road—of blowing on her hands and a bubble floating away.

Samuel chuckled. "You're right; we have little soap left."

She tapped herself.

"No, no. Soap making will have to wait. You've not enough strength to endure that task. Given a fortnight, I've no doubt but that we'll have soap from your hand. You'll need to save lard up to make it, regardless."

"I'll help make it," Ethan offered. "I've helped Goodwife Morton."

"We'll speak with Ruth Morton. Mayhap you women will labor together over that chore. For this day, Garnet, I'll still thank you to—" He halted midsentence and looked at the message she wrote on the slate.

Work to noon, then rest.

The pleading look she gave made him chuckle. "Very well."

As soon as Hester and she were alone, Garnet changed back into her own clothing. It made no sense to wear such finery as she cleaned this abode. Then, too, mercy demanded she not wear her master's wife's clothing since the sight of it caused him pain.

Garnet paused in the doorway and watched as Christopher stacked the cornstalks so they'd finish drying. His father worked in a distant cornfield, plow-ing under the stubble. He'd mentioned he needed to do so to restore the soil. Ethan tromped by with an armful of rushes.

Without Hester here, I imagine Master Walsh and his sons all slept in the keeping room. I cannot continue to usurp his bed. Something must be done, but it isn't for me to determine exactly what. Mayhap, if I air out the bedding, that will nudge him into changing the arrangement.

Garnet beckoned to Ethan. She wrote on the slate, and he laughed. "You want me to throw my bed out?"

Garnet caught the mattress as he tossed it down. As she emptied the ticking, Hester hopped from one foot to the other. "Aunt Dorcas did this, too. I always tied the old corn husks so we could feed the cookfire. Would you have me do that?"

With Hester occupied, Garnet shook out the empty mattress ticking, hung it over a fence, and beat out more dust.

It was obvious from the state of the mattress that the attic desperately needed cleaning. The dirt dislodged when she cleaned the attic would spoil the keeping room in an instant. Best she start up on the second story, then move downstairs later. She took rags, water, and a corn-husk broom up and attacked the attic.

Because the ladder was outside, no room was wasted with a staircase indoors. Both the floors boasted a full measure of usable space. Pegs protruding from the rafters indicated that food and drying once took place up there, too. Since the pegs all stood empty, Garnet set to dispersing a wealth of cobwebs with the broom. She treated the walls with the same vigor, then almost punished the floor to dislodge all of the dried mud.

Mindful of her promise to limit her time, Garnet went down and took the eggs from the morning gathering and whipped up some custard.

As Hester licked the spoon, her eyes brightened. "Are you going to bake it in a pumpkin? Ruth Morton did that once, and Father relished it."

Though unsure as to what a pumpkin was, let alone the peculiarities in using one as a cooking container, Garnet didn't have the heart to deny Hester's request. She nodded.

"I'll go choose the pumpkin!" Hester dashed out the door and returned in a few minutes holding a bright orange squash as big as her head. "I'll scoop out the inside and wash the seeds if you cut it open. I like to eat the roasted seeds."

Pumpkins, turkey, and corn. Virginia Colony provided remarkable food. Garnet filled the hollowed pumpkin with the custard she'd made, then set it inside a cauldron and poured a few inches of water around the edge. Once she hung it over the fire, she picked up a long spoon and prepared to stir the soup.

"I can do that!"

Garnet waggled her forefinger back and forth.

Confusion puckered little Hester's face. "Aunt Dorcas had me stir soups and such."

Women often got nasty burns. Appalled anyone would allow such a small child near a fire, Garnet fought to hide her reaction. Instead, she pointed to the corn husks Hester had tied together and smiled.

"You want me to tie the rest of the husks." Hester plopped back down and set to work. Her nose wrinkled; then she giggled. "Your soup smells better than these old things."

A wink of agreement set Hester into another set of giggles. Garnet added a little more water to the soup and set aside the spoon. She wanted to add thyme and sage, but with no supply of herbs in the house, she feared she'd have no spices whatsoever. A quick walk around the outside of the cabin allowed her to see where an herb garden had once been. Left untended, the patch was a huge tangle, but she didn't fret over that small fact. One quick look assured her she'd have ample caraway, dill, rosemary, fennel, marjoram, basil, thyme, sage, and savory. For the time being, she took just enough to flavor the soup.

Satisfied that the attic now rated as habitable, Garnet dragged the empty mattress ticking up the ladder. Ethan followed her. "There's a pulley we can use to draw up the baskets of corn husks."

Fatigue pulled at her as she finished stuffing the mattress. Garnet watched Ethan scramble down the ladder, and then she gestured to her mouth, rubbed her tummy, and pointed toward the field.

"You want me to go fetch Father and Christopher for nuncheon?"

She nodded, so he dashed off.

"Are you certain she wanted us to eat?" Christopher asked as he dried off his hands. He and his father exchanged dubious looks. Garnet hadn't taken any of the food from the fire. The keeping room smelled wonderful.

"We'll ready the table," Samuel decided. "Widow Wheelock might have stepped out a minute."

Hester set the table as he took the food from the fireplace. Garnet didn't show up. Samuel began to ladle the soup. The bowls were full, and Garnet's place still stayed vacant. "Hester, go to the privy and assure us that the widow fares well."

Hester giggled and ran out of the cabin. A few minutes later, she came back, but her face was sober. "The widow isn't there."

Chapter 8

Christopher rested his elbows on the table. "Do you think she ran away again, like she did last eve?"

"I cannot say. You children eat. I'll look for the widow. She's much too weak to go far." Samuel rose. He gave the pumpkin custard a longing look and sternly demanded, "Leave some of that for me. I've not had such a treat in a long while."

He went out and looked at the ground. Christopher's and Ethan's shoes left a definite imprint. Hester's tiny footprint stood out clearly, as did his own large ones. The other prints had to belong to Garnet. Samuel followed them, but they led to the springhouse. After following a few more tracks to the garden, he became more confused. He headed toward the stable to saddle up his horse, but he had no clue as to which direction Garnet had taken.

"Father! Come!" Hester ran up to him and threw her arms about his thighs.

He hugged her automatically. "What is it?"

"She's here! She was here all along!"

"Oh?"

Grabbing her father's hand, she put a finger to her lips and led him to the attic ladder. "Go see. She looks so peaceful, Father. We didn't have the heart to waken her."

Peaceful didn't begin to describe her. Garnet had fallen asleep on the boys' freshly aired and filled corn-husk mattress. Sam's brows furrowed at the sight of her in her rags. Why had she changed back into such pathetic wear? He'd almost praised Garnet for looking handsome this morning—but 'twasn't fitting to do so. He'd gladly praise her cooking and how she treated his children, but a man oughtn't make personal statements if he didn't intend to court a woman. Nonetheless, he'd instruct her to wear Naomi's clothing hereafter.

Samuel took a blanket and covered her. She burrowed into the pillow. The action dislodged her cap, causing her glorious hair to spill freely across the bed. His fingers absently threaded through her mane, and he smiled softly. She'd kept her word, at least in part. She'd worked 'til midday, then rested. The smudge on her cheek told him that she wasn't yet ready to quit her labors.

Sam looked about the attic and caught his breath. It looked as it ought to—which was, sadly enough, something it never did anymore. Nary a speck of dirt, a web, or a stray feather could be seen. Indeed, the loft smelled fresh, and the boys' few possessions hung neatly on pegs. A woman's touch made a difference. He descended the ladder and went in to eat the soup. It tasted excellent, but the pumpkin custard truly got his attention.

"I'm thinking I'm glad we grew lots of pumpkins this year," Ethan declared with relish.

"You'd best see to weeding the garden," Samuel admonished his son as he served a goodly bit of custard onto his plate. The aroma of it made his mouth water. "After the garden is done, you and Christopher are to gather up the crockery and jars. Hester, you help them wash and dry all of them. We'll be needing to put by all of the vegetables and apples."

Ethan stared at his father's plate. His eyes shone with greed. "Might I have a little more custard ere I finish my labors?"

Samuel took a taste. "It is enough to tempt a body, isn't it?" He grinned as all three children nodded enthusiastically. "I confess the same weakness, but the widow will see no reward for her labors if we all have more. Be satisfied with your first helping—she will share the remainder at supper with us. It will be good for her to witness your thankful smiles."

After lunch, Sam went back to plowing the field. He'd cautioned the children to allow the widow to sleep. She'd accomplished far more than he thought possible and clearly worn herself out with the effort.

This morning, he'd decided the time had come for him to move up with the boys. Witnessing how weak Widow Wheelock was made him reconsider. Tomorrow, Ruth Morton would come over and they'd preserve apples. Even with Ruth's help and her daughter's assistance, such labor would still wear out the widow. Garnet would need a full day afterward to recover. Only she wouldn't rest. After the way she bargained to work half of today, Samuel knew she wouldn't be guilty of sloth.

Sunday. He nodded to himself. It seemed appropriate for him to move his bed on the day of rest. They'd go to worship this week. Missing church last week on account of Garnet's fever couldn't be helped. But this Sunday, after the service, he could tote the mattress from the trundle up to the chamber he'd share with his sons.

The breeze carried Hester's laughter. Sam delighted in it. "Lord, You've been faithful. I called upon Your name and asked You to bring my daughter home to me. You prepared a way and have mercifully increased the blessings so my sons will know the gentleness of a woman's care. I would never have imagined my prayers would be answered in this manner, but Your wisdom and mercy abound."

He plowed two more furrows, turning the stubble into the rich soil and praising God for His provision. Sam paused at the end of the field and wiped his brow with his sleeve. As he turned, his eyes narrowed.

"Samuel Walsh." A tall, sallow-faced man approached and nodded curtly.

"Erasmus Ryder." Sam wondered at the arrival of Dorcas's husband. The man had no reason to cease his labor early and come calling. "I trust all is well with you."

"We fare well enough. My goodwife tells me she's running out of wool."

The purpose of the visit fell into place. In years past, Dorcas and Erasmus claimed the shearing as payment for keeping Hester. As Sam's flock increased, Dorcas claimed that Hester was growing and it took more to keep her; thus the Ryders still took all of the shearing. Dorcas was known for her fine weaving, and the skill proved to be lucrative for her. Sam knew full well that even taking Dorcas's time and skill into account, the profit she made off his sheep's fleeces paid several times over what it cost for them to feed Hester. Since Hester wore hand-me-downs from Mary Morton, Dorcas hadn't had to clothe her. Nonetheless, creating ill will when his daughter lived under the Ryders' roof would be foolish indeed.

Only Hester no longer lived there. Samuel stood in silence, waiting for Erasmus to make him an offer on the wool.

Erasmus folded his arms across his chest. "'Tis round the time you fall-shear your sheep."

"Indeed. But plenty wants doing. I'll get to it anon."

"Dorcas has need of the fleeces soon." Erasmus cast a look toward the house, then added, "And you owe it to us."

Irritated by that comment, Samuel widened his stance. "The day Hester went to abide under your roof, you took the spring shearing. Dorcas has received the entirety of my fleeces in advance twice each year for the seasons to follow. The only indebtedness I hold is of gratitude."

"You would cheat us?"

"I'm an honorable man." Sam stared him in the eyes. "I gave over all of my wool in the years Hester lived beneath your roof. You've often boasted about how much Dorcas's cloth brings in. I've met my obligations fairly."

Erasmus glowered at him. "Best you reconsider. Taxes and tithe will come due."

"I cannot deny that is true."

"You'll need my tobacco. You cannot pay in wheat or corn. Nothing but Virginia tobacco is accepted, and you have none."

The exultant tone grated on Sam's nerves. He chose not to raise tobacco. It depleted the soil, and he considered smoking of the plant to be a distasteful habit. Nonetheless, he refused to be coerced. He wrapped his hands about the handle of the plow and shrugged. "I've always paid you full-market value for the tobacco required for my taxes and tithes. Thomas Brooks is a good friend to me, and he also grows tobacco."

"This is no way to treat family," Erasmus growled.

"I agree. Had you made me an offer on the fleeces, I would have struck a deal with you—a deal which took into account that Dorcas is my children's aunt. As it is, you tried to make an unjust claim."

Chin jutting forward, Erasmus rasped, "Reconsider. Once I walk away, I'll not deal with you again."

"I hold no agreement with you about buying your tobacco. You're welcome to sell it to any buyer, just as I am free to make arrangements with another grower. Indeed, Brooks has expressed how eager he'd be to have some of my cornmeal."

"You'll regret this, Samuel Walsh."

"Begone, Erasmus. I'll pretend this conversation never occurred."

"Remember it." The lanky man shook his finger at Sam. "Remember it well. You'll live to rue the day you crossed me."

Chapter 9

The scent of apples still filled the keeping room. Scores and scores of apple rings dried on pegs and strings all about the cabin. Apple peels steamed dry in shallow trays near the fire, and two crocks full of applesauce lined the wall near the table. A barrel with straw-packed apples sat in the springhouse.

Garnet stood in the doorway and waved good-bye to Ruth and Mary Morton. Hester slipped her sticky little hand into Garnet's. "Come back again soon. Widow Wheelock and me—we had fun."

"'Twas a good day," Mary said. "But school starts again in a week."

Hester let out a little squeal. "I'm to go to school this year! Please, let's work together next week so we get everything done first!"

"I'm sure we will, Hester." Ruth waved. "We'll see you at worship on the morrow!"

The next two Sundays, Garnet enjoyed fine sermons. If only she could raise her voice with the congregation, though. When they sang hymns, she longed to join along.

A couple of weeks flew past. While the children were at school, Garnet tended a variety of chores and sometimes met with Ruth so they could work together. Garnet found contentment in her new life.

The next Saturday evening, Samuel watched as she exchanged the water she'd soaked beans in all day. "Ruth must have told you about our custom of eating baked beans on Sunday."

Garnet added molasses and a little salt pork as she nodded. Tomorrow's meals would be curds and whey, baked beans, and pumpkin custard—all prepared with a minimum of labor tonight. She placed the bean pot in a spot she'd chosen. By setting the pot of beans near the fire all night, they'd be ready to eat on the morrow and relieve her from cooking on the Lord's day of rest.

Pumpkins were odd squashes, but Ruth Morton had shown her countless ways to use them one morning while the children were all at school. Rings of pumpkin now took the place of the apples on the drying pegs and strings all about the keeping room, and Garnet pulled a pan full of roasted seeds from the fire. Garnet slid the pumpkin seeds into a bowl she'd set on the table.

"The meals you make are toothsome, and you've been quick to learn how to prepare and preserve the foods specific to the colonies," Master Walsh praised.

"You seem to enjoy cooking. What other things do you take pleasure in?"

She didn't have to pause to think. Garnet wheeled her finger vertically in the air, then pantomimed knitting.

"Spinning and knitting?" Master Walsh bolted to his feet. "Come with me, Widow Wheelock."

Perplexed, Garnet followed him out to the barn.

Master Walsh led her to the far corner of the structure and grabbed a hoe. He swung it in the air to banish thick cobwebs. "There."

Garnet leaned forward and clapped her hands for joy upon seeing a dust-covered spinning wheel. It was a smallish one made for spinning both flax and wool. She immediately thought about the sheep whose fleeces were heavy and of the small patch of flax.

"No doubt, it requires cleaning and the works are in wont of oiling, but we can see to that. Where's. . .there!" He located a tiny chest, blew the dirt and straw from the lid, and handed it to Garnet. "Carry that back to the house. I'll bring the spinning wheel."

While he painstakingly disassembled the spinning wheel over by the hearth, Garnet gathered rags. "Once I clean this and oil the wheel axle, it ought to serve well." Sam tested the leathers holding the bobbin and flyer. "The maidens are straight, and the mother-of-all is in fine condition."

She paused and watched as he deftly removed the flywheel. The firelight illuminated the beautifully turned spokes.

Sam laid the wheel on the table. "Flat as can be—I worried it might have grown warped. . . . The drive band is filthy. Can it be washed?"

Garnet inspected the dirty linen strip and nodded. Washing might alter its length, but she'd be able to adjust the tension to account for that.

"I'll set to work on this whilst you take stock of what's in the chest. If something is missing, we'll need to replace it ere the weather turns."

Garnet opened the chest. A pair of sewing needles, a paper of pins, and a daintily painted porcelain thimble rested in a small wood tray, which she removed. Three sets of knitting needles lay there along with a half-dozen balls of yarn. Then Garnet's heart leaped. A recorder rested in the bottom. Hands shaking, she drew out the instrument and offered it to her master.

He shook his head. "I put it out in the barn for good cause. Neither Christopher nor I could coax any pleasant sounds from it. Are you able to play?"

Rubbing it on her sleeve, Garnet tried to decide what to play. After blowing through the recorder, she took a deep breath and started playing.

Master Walsh perked up, and the children all rushed in. After she finished the piece, he chortled with glee. " 'Butter'd Peas' is one of Ethan's favorite tunes!"

Christopher poked his brother in the side. "One of his favorite dishes, too."

"Will you teach me how?" Hester reached over and touched the instrument.

"Father, I used to have a whistle." Ethan scanned the keeping room. "Where is it?"

"A flageolet." Master Walsh remembered. "I'll have to think on where it went."

Ethan smiled up at his father. "I'll clean the spinning wheel while you look."

"Mind you clean every last nook and cranny. Any dust will spoil the yarn Widow Wheelock will spin." He handed the rag to his son and turned his attention back on Garnet. "We'd appreciate a few more tunes, Widow Wheelock."

Garnet thought for a moment, then raised the recorder and played "Childgrove." "Argeers" followed thereafter.

Christopher took up another rag and helped his brother. "Please don't stop," he pled.

Garnet looked to her master. He'd been wandering around, looking for the flageolet in vain. "I confess, I cannot recall where I put it. You've scoured every corner of the house, Widow Wheelock. Have you not seen it?"

She shook her head.

"What does it look like?" Hester tossed one of her plaits over her shoulder.

"It's smaller than the recorder Widow Wheelock is playing." Christopher scrunched his nose. "Wasn't it white?"

"No, it was pearwood." Furrows plowed across his father's brow. "The holes were brass."

"Is it a lot smaller?" Hester held her hands out so they were only six inches apart.

Christopher scrubbed one of the spinning wheel's spokes. "That's far too small."

"Two of the sections are that size, Hester." Sam stared at the fire. "The third is about the size of my thumb."

"I think I know where it is!" Hester scrambled to the far side of the keeping room and climbed onto the table.

"Hester!"

"Here, Father! See?" She stood on tiptoe and touched what looked like pegs. "I thought they looked funny when we took down the apple rings and put up the pumpkin rings."

"Now, I remember. Ethan dropped his whistle in the trough, so I put it up to dry." Samuel Walsh stalked over and pulled his daughter off the table. " 'Twas not mannerly of you to climb on this. Wipe it down and give Widow Wheelock an apology."

Garnet scarcely believed her ears. The master of the house ordered his daughter to apologize to her?

Hester approached Garnet and barely managed to bob a curtsy ere she burst into tears. "I f–f–forgot my–myself. I'm s–s–sorry."

Garnet set aside the recorder and opened her arms wide. Hester burrowed in close and clung tight as Garnet rocked her. When her storm of tears abated, she whispered, "Please don't be wroth with me!"

Garnet kissed her brow and smoothed her hand up and down the child's back.

"Widow Wheelock is a kind woman." Master Walsh dabbed tears from his daughter's cheeks with the edge of his shirt. "She labors hard. Be sure you don't cause her additional work."

"Yes, Father." Hester wound her arms around Garnet's neck and gave her a fierce hug. "I'm so glad you're here. I'm so glad I'm here."

"Well and good. Now see to the task." Master Walsh relocated the drying pumpkin rings to other pegs, puffed air through each of the pieces of the flageolet, and put them together while his daughter wiped off the table.

"I'd be pleased to hear another tune," Ethan said.

"And you will—tomorrow." Master Walsh smiled. "Thomas Brooks is taking his viol to worship tomorrow. Think how lovely 'twill be for Widow Wheelock to accompany him on the recorder or flageolet."

Indeed, Garnet took both instruments to church the next day. She and Goodman Brooks played accompaniment as the congregation sang Isaac Watts's "O God, Our Help in Ages Past." Gerhardt's "Put Thou Thy Trust in God" came next. Though she couldn't sing the lyrics, Garnet thought of the words as she played. They suited her situation so clearly. She'd been reduced to nothingness; but God's strength sustained her, and He'd answered her prayers by placing her in the Walsh home.

> Put thou thy trust in God,
>   In duty's path go on;
> Walk in His strength with faith and hope,
>   So shall thy work be done.

Lord, I put my trust in You. Though all I owned, and was, were stripped from me, You have been my stronghold. You heard my prayers and placed me in the Walsh home. I give You my thanks.

When the music ended, Garnet slipped onto the end of the Walsh bench. The preacher set his Bible on the pulpit. "Before I pray, the schoolmaster is suffering quinsy. As a result, he cannot teach for the next few days. Word will be sent out when school is to resume." The reverend prayed, then read from the third chapter of Proverbs. " 'Let not mercy and truth forsake thee....' "

Garnet cast a quick look at her master. *He did just that—he's shown me great mercy.*

" 'Trust in the Lord with all thine heart; and lean not unto thine own understanding. In all thy ways acknowledge him, and he shall direct thy paths.' "

I don't understand all that has happened to me, but, Lord, You have a purpose. I trust in You.

After the service, Goodman Brooks called across the churchyard to them, "Hold a moment!"

"If you intend to talk about music, I'm sending Ruth to be part of the discussion," Falcon Morton announced. "There's nothing sweeter than the sound of her playing her dulcimore."

"Come then, Goodwife Morton." Goodman Brooks still held his viola de gamba as he approached. He then beckoned another man. "And you, Alex Smith. No one plays a fiddle more pleasingly than you." Ruth and Goodman Smith came over.

Another woman scurried up, as well, but something about how Samuel drew Hester close to his side struck Garnet as odd. He nodded politely. "Goodwife Ryder."

"Aunt Dorcas," all three of the Walsh children greeted in unison.

Instead of returning the pleasantry, the woman stuck out her hand, palm upward, toward Garnet. "That recorder was my sister's. By all rights, it should be mine now."

"No, it shouldn't." Master Walsh stepped up to Garnet's side.

Goodman Brooks shook his head, and in an excessively patient tone said, "Goodwife Ryder, all a wife owns belongs to her husband."

"Naomi owned her recorder ere she married." Dorcas tilted her head defiantly.

"Yes, she did," Smith agreed. "But upon marriage, two become one."

"Surely grief made you overlook that important truth," Ruth said in a kindly tone. "I recall you once played a cittern—and handily. It would be merry to add yet a different instrument to the group."

"Indeed. We'd have a quintet." Garnet jumped at the sound of the preacher's voice. He'd come over and now gave Dorcas a conciliatory smile. "I'm sure once you reflect upon it that you'll not begrudge Widow Wheelock playing the recorder. 'Tis a blessing for her to be able to give sound, if not voice, in worship."

Most of the congregation milled around; clearly they were eavesdropping.

A man stood behind Dorcas and rested his hands upon her shoulders. Hatred twisted his features as he looked first at Samuel, then at Garnet. "You cannot blame my wife. Walsh has given Naomi's clothing to his servant. My wife looks upon her, and her grief is renewed. For that woman to stand before the congregation and play Naomi's recorder is more hypocrisy than is to be borne. Know this, Parson: They sleep beneath the same roof. Furthermore, whilst the children are at school, Walsh and this woman are alone."

Chapter 10

Your implication is vile." Samuel stared straight back at Erasmus Ryder. "The widow and my daughter sleep in the keeping room; I sleep in the second story with my sons."

"There, then." Reverend Clark nodded his head. "Samuel Walsh is a man of sterling character. We've his word that naught is awry."

"If it troubles you to see Naomi's clothing. . ." Ruth Morton patted Dorcas's hand. "Mayhap you ought to give her some of the fine cloth you weave. I'll help her sew a new set of overclothes—though she probably needs no assistance. Christopher wears the shirt she stitched for him, and little Hester is charming as a chickadee in the new bodice the widow made from the scraps of her very own clothes. Still, if it grieves you to witness another wearing the clothing Naomi once wore, this arrangement will allow you to trade for your sister's garments."

"All of my cloth is spoken for. I cannot renege."

"I have no patience for this." Sam scowled. Dorcas would find fault in any bargain or solution. Garnet already labored long and hard. He couldn't imagine making her sew another set of clothing merely because Dorcas indulged in pettiness and greed. "Children wear clothing handed down because 'tis sensible. When someone perishes, other than the attire in which they are buried, any other garments go to others who can make use of them. So I've done, and no one should find fault in it."

"You buried my sister in nothing more than a blanket!"

Samuel stood in silence. He didn't need to defend himself or his actions.

"Father?" Christopher gave him a beseeching look.

I was wrong. Though I needn't defend myself, I cannot allow my children to believe I dishonored their mother.

Falcon cleared his throat. "My goodwife and I were present at the time. Given the circumstances, Naomi—"

"Given the circumstances?" Dorcas gave Falcon a withering look.

"Your mother caught fire whilst preparing breakfast," Samuel said softly.

A slight gasp escaped Garnet. She immediately took Ethan and Hester by their hands and led them off.

"I knew she got burned." Christopher still looked confused.

"I wrapped your mother in a blanket to put out the flames." Samuel wished his son didn't have to hear this. He chose his words carefully. "Her burns were severe. The very morning of the accident, she went to her Maker."

"In nothing," Dorcas snapped, "more than a burned nightdress and a blanket."

"Her pain was great, Christopher," Ruth said. "I sat with your father at her bedside for half the morning until she slipped away. We buried Naomi gently. Dressed as she was in her nightdress and the quilt she favored, she looked peaceful. She'd gone on to her eternal rest."

Christopher nodded slowly. "Thank you, Goodwife Morton, for being a friend in my mother's time of trouble. Aunt Dorcas? Surely my mother would be gladdened that someone in need received her clothes."

Reverend Clark smiled. "Well said, lad. A godly woman's heart is full of charity."

Unwilling to allow the Ryders any further opportunity to upset his son or promulgate falsehoods, Sam said, "I bid you all good day."

"Good day," the others said—all save the Ryders who turned and walked away.

Falcon said, "Christopher, since there's to be no school on the morrow, I plan to send Aaron to chip out salt blocks in the morn. If perchance your father needs more, my son would be glad of your company and help."

"Father?"

Resting his hand on his son's shoulder, Sam said, "I'll send Christopher over with the wagon. He recently spotted a salt vein."

"If the boys bring me salt, as well, I'd be willing to spend the morrow on a trip to the coast." Brooks grinned. "A good-sized sturgeon would feed us all many a meal."

"The last time he did so, Reverend, the fish he hauled back was enormous." Ruth slipped her hand into Falcon's. "You'll have to come for supper."

"Aaron and I will fetch even more salt." Christopher's eyes glittered. "Reverend Clark, you weren't here yet. The last time Goodman Brooks brought back a sturgeon, he found it necessary to behead the creature and chop off the tail just to fit the body diagonally in his wagon!"

"I'd be pleased to have such a fine meal." Reverend Clark grimaced. "The best that can be said of my cooking is that 'tis warm."

"There's always a place at our table for you," Ruth said.

"The same can be said for my household." Sam and Christopher walked back toward the wagon. On the way to church, Garnet had shared the seat with Samuel. Now, she'd climbed into the back with Ethan and Hester—due, no doubt, to Erasmus's base accusation. Sam tamped down the urge to order her onto the seat. After nuncheon, he'd speak with her privately.

"You said—" Chris's voice cracked, and he coughed into his hand to cover the embarrassment. "You said I'd drive the wagon on the morrow."

"Indeed." Sam clapped his son on the back. "In fact, you'll drive us home today."

Wisdom dictated he sit beside his son on the bench. Still, Sam didn't want to have everyone in the churchyard believe he allowed Ryder's crudity to leave any taint. He stood by the side of the wagon and squinted at Hester's bodice. "If my estimate is correct, you could take the lacing from that and use it to play cat's cradle on the trip home."

"Widow Wheelock taught me how to play that." Hester immediately started to pull the lace free.

"She's teaching us many things," Ethan hastened to say.

Christopher climbed up onto the seat. "I'll be sure to bring home sufficient salt for you, Widow Wheelock. With all the pickling and salting and drying you've been doing, you'll need more."

Garnet smiled at Chris.

Sam thought of all the herbs, vegetables, and fruits she'd been preserving and drying. "Thanks to her industry, your belly won't just be warm and full this winter. 'Twill be tasty fare we enjoy."

Ann Stamsfield's giggles filled the air as her husband drove by them. She called back, "Anything would have to be an improvement, Goodman Walsh!"

Upon taking his first bite at nuncheon, Christopher looked across the table. "Widow Wheelock, Goodwife Stamsfield teased Father that anything would be better than his cooking. Since you've come, the stirabout in the morning is never burned, and I've not had a single bellyache."

Samuel waggled his spoon at his son. "Your cooking was no better. For mercy's sake, Widow Wheelock, please be sure to teach Hester how to make such fine food. One of these days when a man takes her to wife, he will be thankful for the kindness."

"I'm thankful now." Ethan eyed the pumpkin. "Especially for that custard."

"Eat the rest of your nuncheon, son. No sweet until you've finished what's already on your plate."

Four times in the past two weeks, Garnet had made pumpkin custard. Ruth had also shown her how to make pumpkin muffins and pumpkin pie. While many of the pumpkins sat out in the field curing, those without a stem attached wouldn't keep well. On the day Ruth and Garnet made soap, Ruth taught her to cut those pumpkins into rings to dry.

"Father." Hester swallowed a bite. "Is it work to go on a walk and gather?"

"It would depend on what you gather and why you took the walk. If your brother went on a walk to set snares and collect the creatures they'd captured, that would be work. If you went for a stroll and found a patch of flowers that made you happy, then gathering them to share God's beauty on our table would be fine."

"Any plant out there, the widow can find a use for. Many uses. On Sundays, if she takes me for a stroll and the flowers are pretty on the table that day and she can use them the next day, is that work?"

"Each person must examine his own heart and submit to the Lord. It isn't for me to judge what another feels is acceptable to God. I must live as He gives me light. Widow Wheelock has shown a love for the Lord and great kindness. I trust she would act in accordance with what she knows in her heart to be right."

In keeping with it being the day of rest, neither Garnet nor he could busy themselves with ordinary chores. After they'd enjoyed the custard, Sam rose. "Today's fair, but it won't be long ere we deal with the cold. Why don't we all take a stroll to the stream? You children may wade."

His children hopped up and bolted out the door.

Sam picked up the slate. "Come, Widow Wheelock. Christopher swims like a fish, and Ethan manages to paddle around well enough to enjoy himself, but I worry for Hester."

Garnet made a shooing motion with her hands.

"Come along with you." Sam used the tone and expression he used when his sons bordered on being stubborn. Garnet's cheeks flushed, and she bowed her head—but she started toward the door. Samuel followed close on her heels, then shut the door behind them. "There's a spot I've always taken the boys to. 'Tis wider and more shallow than where we fetch the water by the house, so 'tis a better place to allow them to frolic. Ethan and Hester can enjoy themselves quite safely. This way."

Reaching the stream took no time at all, but Samuel led her almost fifty yards farther downstream. He sat on a log he'd placed there long ago and patted the spot beside him. "We can watch the children from here."

Garnet smiled at the sight of Ethan kicking water at Christopher. She started toward the stream, but Samuel halted her. "Sit. We need to talk."

Wariness painted her features. Slowly, she sat on the log—almost a yard away.

"Erasmus Ryder holds a grudge against me. In his anger, he insinuated you and I have...sinned."

The widow's cheeks blazed; then suddenly the color drained away, and her lower lip quivered ever so slightly before she bit it. Her hand shook as she reached for the slate. Slowly, she formed the letters and gave it back to him. *I will leaf.*

"No! Absolutely not."

The saddest smile he'd ever seen lifted the corners of her mouth as her head bobbed up and down.

"There's no reason at all for you to leave and every reason to stay. You've made my house a home, and because of your presence, Hester is with us. I've been desperate to bring her home. After seeing how Dorcas and Erasmus behave, surely you wouldn't want her to return to them."

Garnet looked horrified at the thought.

"As you heard Dorcas say, she and my wife were sisters. The truth is a bitter one: I was young, foolish, and lonely. In a matter of one slim week, I met and married Naomi. Eight years we were wed, and not a single day passed without strife. Naomi was the mother of my children, and I will not speak against her. Suffice it to say, I will never again marry."

That same sad smile crossed her features as she tapped her breastbone and shook her head.

"You are a widow and were sold to cover your husband's debts. Are you telling me 'twas not a happy union?" Her expression was more eloquent than words. "It grieves me to know your marriage brought you no contentment. If you remain, you won't have to marry just to keep a roof over your head and food in you."

Her eyes fluttered shut, and she let out a silent exhalation, then looked at him. Gratitude gleamed in her eyes, turning them silver. Her lips moved, forming *Thank you.*

"Before you thank me, I would be honest with you." He rubbed his sweaty palms on the knees of his worn breeches. "There's no doubt in my mind: Erasmus will be a thorn in our sides. He tried to sully your virtue and damage my reputation. Alas, I expect him to persist."

Her lips twisted into a wry smile, and she shrugged.

Glad that she had the courage to put up with the bedeviling they'd inevitably suffer from the Ryders, Sam dared to ask what he'd hoped for since the day he bought her. "I granted you your freedom, and so you are free; yet I ask you now, Garnet Wheelock, to give me your promise to remain here as a valued member of my family."

She pressed her hands together.

"Would you have me pray, or are you asking for time to pray, yourself?"

She scooted off the log and cast a look at the distance.

"Aye. Go and talk with the Lord. It is fitting to seek His wisdom in all things." Garnet disappeared behind a grove of trees, and Samuel turned his attention on the children. Ethan handed Hester a little boat he'd made from a bit of bark and a leaf. She squealed with joy and set it in the water. As it started to float, she wrapped her arms around Ethan's waist and hugged him. By the time she looked back, her boat had drifted out of reach. She let out a cry and started to go after it. For an instant, Samuel started to rise.

Christopher grabbed Hester by the waist and twirled her back onto dry land. "Let's go make more!"

Seeing Christopher attend Hester allowed Sam to sit back down. Garnet showed wisdom in seeking the Lord's will. Sam rubbed his hands on his knees again. *I'm never anxious, yet I'm even more nervous than when I asked Naomi to wed me. Naomi was a stranger to me; the widow abides beneath my roof and has proven to be of excellent character. She is kind beyond telling and holds great affection for the children. Surely that will sway her to make this commitment.*

But what if she doesn't?

The eighty-fourth Psalm ran through his mind, and he recited it aloud. " 'For the Lord God is a sun and shield: the Lord will give grace and glory: no good thing will he withhold from them that walk uprightly. O Lord of hosts, blessed is the man that trusteth in thee.' Father of light, You have blessed me richly. I place my trust in You. If it be Your will, press upon the widow's heart how desperately we need her. Be my family's shield against Erasmus's plots. Safeguard us and be the sunlight that illuminates the path we are to follow. In Christ Jesus' name. Amen."

"Father!" Hester beckoned him. "Come make boats with us!"

Sam gathered several leaves, twigs, and bits of bark, then went and sat at the edge of the stream. Hester plopped into his lap, and Sam enveloped her in his arms. Hester didn't stay long. She hopped up and set the next boat a-sail. Pleasure rippled through Sam as he watched his children frolic. Finally, he stood. "It's time we went home."

Garnet sat over on the log. One look at her expression, and Sam's heart fell.

Chapter 11

I promiss. Garnet had written the words because deep in her heart she knew God wouldn't have brought her across the ocean and put her through all of her trials without having a purpose. During her prayer, a sense of certainty filled her that His intent was to allow her the joy of children and a family without ever having to wed again. In the three weeks she'd been with the Walshes, she'd been provided for and treated with kindness and respect. Even so, Garnet didn't believe in making promises lightly. Writing those two words committed her, and she felt the gravity of her vow as she waited for Master Walsh.

"Look!" Hester pointed. "Widow Wheelock wrote us a message! What does it say?"

Ethan ran ahead, but Garnet kept her gaze on Master Walsh. "I promise," Ethan read aloud, and relief transformed his father's features.

"What do you promise, Widow Wheelock?" Christopher's brows furrowed, momentarily making him look exactly as his father had on other occasions.

"I asked her to give us her word that she would remain here." Joy radiated from Samuel, and he scooped Hester into his arms. "Because of your promise and generous spirit, Garnet, my family is together, and my daughter will learn how to keep a happy home. We are all beholden to you for all you have done and will do."

"And I'll help you." Hester hooked one arm around his neck and twisted toward Garnet. "We can garden and cook, and whilst you spin, I can card wool. Aunt Dorcas set me to that task every day."

"That's a fine plan." Samuel tickled Hester's tummy. "I suppose I ought to shear the sheep on the morrow, then."

"But I was to go get salt," Christopher said.

"And so you will. I'll accompany you to the Mortons', and after Falcon and I shear his sheep, we'll come here and do ours. I'm sure Goodwife Morton would be amenable to sharing a chore with Widow Wheelock. You and Aaron bring the salt here, and we'll all preserve the fish together."

Garnet wiped the slate and wrote as quickly as she could, *Ruth asked preecher to supper.*

"Yes, she did." Samuel shrugged. "Henry, John, and Peter Morton could give the message to the reverend, then walk over here to fetch Ethan. Ethan, you may use the wheelbarrow so you boys can go gather beechnuts, butternuts, walnuts, and acorns. Until the Morton boys arrive, I want you and Hester to go pick the last of the beans and peas."

They all walked back to the house. Ethan lifted the recorder from the table and handed it to Garnet. "Would you please play a tune?"

Garnet thought a moment, then began to play the simple notes.

Samuel Walsh sat by the hearth and cuddled his daughter close as he began to sing, " 'Praise God, from whom all blessings flow. . . .' " The fierce tenderness of his hold and the sincerity of his voice touched Garnet deeply.

The next day, Garnet heard Master Walsh singing that same hymn as he set out toward the Mortons'. Garnet set to work at once. She wanted to accomplish several tasks ere Ruth arrived.

Just past midmorning, Ruth arrived. She barely scrambled down from her wagon ere she dashed off and purged her stomach.

Garnet dampened a rag, knelt beside her, and blotted her friend's face.

"Don't fret over me. I'm not sickening." Ruth managed a wan smile. "I told Falcon this morn that we're to be blessed with another child. The first months, my stomach puts up a fight."

Empathy flooded Garnet. She'd always been hale, but when her husband had gambled away all they owned, hunger drove her to eat food that must have been spoiled. She hadn't recovered from that ere they put her aboard the ship and seasickness plagued her.

Ruth took the rag and passed it over her own face. "Don't look so worried, Garnet. The time I carried Mary, I was sickest of all. Since the nausea is bad again this time, I'm hoping the babe will be a girl."

Fleetingly running her hand across Ruth's tummy, Garnet frowned. She couldn't feel so much as a tiny hint of a babe.

"No, I won't show for a few months yet. By then, the sickness will cease. It only lasts the first few months."

Garnet rose and helped Ruth stand.

"Samuel made me promise that you'd nap after nuncheon." Ruth let out a small laugh. "In truth, 'twas a promise easily made. Whene'er I'm carrying, fatigue nigh unto overwhelms me at midday."

Staring at Ruth, Garnet couldn't respond.

"I won't feel quite so guilty resting since you will, too. Garnet? Garnet!"

Everything inside her started shaking, and no matter how hard she tried, Garnet couldn't draw a breath.

"Here. Come here now." Ruth tugged her over a few yards and leaned her against the split rail fence.

"Mama? I brought you water." Mary held out the dipper.

"Nicely done." Ruth took it. "Take Hubert and Hester with you and go a-gathering. We'll need herbs aplenty when the fish arrives."

"Is the widow ailing again, Mama? She's wan as can be."

"Off with you, Mary. Do my bidding." Ruth pressed the dipper to Garnet's mouth. "Sip this. We must talk."

Having carried many children, Ruth asked some piercing questions and pressed one of Garnet's hands between her own. "You carry a life within you. You're shocked, but things will work out. By my reckoning, you have almost five months to go—that's time aplenty for you to get used to the fact and prepare."

Misery swamped Garnet. As a little girl, she'd dreamed of her future. She'd marry a man who cared for her, and they'd have babes to cradle. Her dreams came to naught but nightmares. Her husband had given her nothing but heart-ache and a babe he'd not be around to support.

And what will Samuel Walsh say? Surely, when he asked me to stay, he didn't anticipate I'd have a child.

The rest of the morning passed in a blur. Accustomed to marshaling her sizable family, Ruth took over and organized chores for the children and kept Garnet busy.

"We finished faster than we expected."

Samuel's voice made Garnet spin around.

"I confess," he said as he put the spring-back shears on the table, "'twas the thought of eating a tasty nuncheon that spurred Falcon and me to shear his flock so quickly."

"You'll have wool aplenty to spin this winter." Falcon gave his wife an affectionate pat.

"Father!" Henry burst through the doorway. "We just brought back our third wheelbarrow full of nuts!"

"Bring back a fourth; then you may eat." Ruth shooed him away and tugged on her husband's hand. "Come, Falcon." A moment later, Ruth shut the door, leaving Samuel and Garnet alone in the keeping room.

Samuel gave Garnet a quizzical look. "Ruth's behaving oddly. Do you suppose 'tis because she's increasing? Falcon told me they will be blessed with another child."

Slowly shaking her head, Garnet took up the slate. She bit her lip, gathered all of her courage, and wrote down a few words.

I have babe to.

For a moment, Sam stared at the slate and felt a bolt of sheer anger. *I had everything planned. This will ruin it.* Sam tore his gaze from those stark words and looked at Garnet. "You're with child."

Eyes wide and glistening, she nodded and swiped away the first message.

I can't tell whether she's happy or devastated. The first noontime Ruth came to call, she inquired if this might be a possibility, yet I banished it from my mind. 'Twas foolish of me.

Garnet caught her lower lip between her teeth. Laboriously, she scribed, *You want me to lea—*

"Give me that." Sam yanked away the slate and set it on the mantel. Curling his hands around her upper arms, he pivoted. "Sit, Garnet."

She sank onto the bench and clenched her hands in her lap. Though he'd considered her already pale, all color bled from her face.

"Am I to take it that you've just realized your condition?"

Her head bobbed a jerky affirmative.

Naomi resented carrying our children. She made life miserable because she— He caught himself. *I cannot compare Garnet to her. Garnet is a different woman and has displayed nothing but a sweet temperament.*

"This changes nothing." As Sam voiced those words, resolve built within him. "No, it doesn't." He rested one knee on the bench and tilted her face up to his.

The cloudy tint to her eyes testified to her confusion and concern.

"Neither of us counted on this eventuality, but the Lord chose to quicken a life within you, and we bow to His wisdom." Though he spoke the truth, it sounded harsh. Sam couldn't honestly say this development pleased him, but the widow oughtn't be made to feel guilty. He cleared his throat. "Widow Wheelock, you promised to stay and help my children. I make that same promise in return. I will provide for your child as I would for my own."

Tears spilled down her cheeks.

Sam couldn't tell the cause of her tears—relief? grief? delight? But he had no right to ask such personal questions. Having the babe would strain her. She was not yet fully recovered from her ordeals. A thought shot through him. "Garnet, 'tis a difficult question I pose you, but I would know: In the time since your husband died, has any man forced himself upon you?"

She shook her head.

"So your husband sired the babe." Relief flooded Samuel. The Almighty had spared her that horrific burden. "You will continue to abide here, and we'll pray the Lord gives you succor in the months ahead."

Her narrow shoulders straightened. Garnet wiped away her tears, and determination painted her features. She took up the slate and wrote, *This changes no thing.*

The very words I spoke to her. Samuel nodded once with great emphasis. "This alters nothing whatsoever." In his mind, he agreed completely, but his heart called him a liar.

With all of the children at the table, nuncheon passed quickly and without any further discussion of the pregnancy. As soon as he finished his bowl of stew, Samuel rose. "We've sheep to shear."

Falcon stood. "And you have three more than I. We'll have them done by the time Brooks arrives with the fish."

Once they were out in the barn, Sam let out a heavy sigh. "Ruth told you?"

"Aye." Falcon said nothing more. They set to work, but instead of the jocularity they'd enjoyed that morn, the men remained silent. Finally finishing the last ewe, Falcon said, "Even with Brooks fetching the sturgeon, I need to replenish my smokehouse. What say you to us going hunting?"

"Venison would suit me."

"After that turkey you shot, Ruth's been after me to get a few."

"It made for good eating."

Falcon leaned back and studied Sam's face. "Left to your own devices, you or Christopher would have burned it o'er the fire. You might think to dwell on the improvements in your life now that the widow is here."

"The problem with sage advice is that 'tis easier to give than to live. Nonetheless, Hester is home. For that, I'll endure—"

Ruth cleared her throat loudly.

Sam wheeled around. Ruth wasn't alone. The shattered look on Garnet's face told him she'd heard his thoughtless words.

Chapter 12

The first shot downed that stag," Samuel Walsh said. "Widow Wheelock is the one who loaded my flintlock. Her red hair about the trigger reminded me so. She ought to take some credit for the fine venison we'll all be eating."

Garnet pretended she hadn't heard him. She'd rinsed the tripe thrice, making it suitable for casing sausage. Ruth and Mary both chopped the bits of meat left over after Sam and Falcon both butchered their bucks.

"I can tell you fattened your swine with milk and corn. 'Twill be tasty," Ruth said. "Are you sure you want to share the pork?"

Garnet nodded emphatically.

"You know venison sausage alone tastes gamey. The hog was of great size, and adding the pork to the sausage will improve it." Sam stared at the bucket of dill, fennel, onion, and garlic Garnet had washed, dried, and minced. "Adding Widow Wheelock's spices will make for an excellent flavor."

Garnet walked in the opposite direction and added more tansy to the steaming pots of water. The smell kept flies away from the butchering. If only there were a way to keep Master Walsh away. *He spoke his mind to a friend, and I heard the truth. Surely he cannot believe fulsome praise will make me forget the truth. I am here by his sufferance.*

Slaughtering a hog at the same time they dressed two deer made for a long, wearying day. Garnet appreciated Ruth's help, but even more, she needed her presence. Trying to do all of this alone with Master Walsh would have been impossibly awkward.

By the day's end, venison, sausage, and ham joined the fish hanging from crossbeams and pegs in the smokehouse. Garnet and Ruth boiled the tongues and fried the livers, and both families ate together. Afterward, Samuel went to the Mortons' so he could help suspend the meat in their smokehouse. Garnet fell asleep with thanksgiving—not only for the providence of plentiful food, but also for Samuel's temporary absence.

The next afternoon, Garnet inspected the meat and assured herself it was curing well. Nothing looked spoiled. She added another handful of hickory chips to the fire.

"It's hot in here." Hester wrinkled her nose. "It doesn't smell pretty like when you cook."

Garnet forced a smile and led the little girl from the smokehouse. While the children were at school in the mornings, Garnet strove to complete tasks too difficult for Hester. By keeping the simpler chores for when the little girl came home from school, she managed to make Hester feel both cherished and helpful. With the schoolmaster sick, Hester followed Garnet like a little shadow. Garnet loved her chatter and companionship. After Garnet latched the smokehouse door, they picked up their buckets and started toward the house.

"Ho, now. What have we here?" Reverend Clark dismounted and pointed toward Hester's pail.

Beaming, Hester swung her pail from side to side. "Widow Wheelock never walks out without returning with herbs for cooking and healing. The herb garden was a fright, but we've reclaimed it. She's teaching me plant lore."

"That's a fine thing." The parson scanned the yard and asked, "Where's your father?"

"On the other side of the barn, sir. He's scraping a deer hide." Hester popped up on tiptoe and added, "He shot a big buck."

"So I heard. Your brother Christopher also helped bag some fine turkeys. I was most grateful to receive one, as was your schoolmaster."

Hester threaded her small hand into Garnet's. "The widow and me—we've been busy. She's teaching me how to salt and pickle and cure all sorts of things. We spent yesterday making sausage. Did you know that adding pork to the venison makes for a better sausage?"

"Indeed."

Hester continued to chatter. "The smokehouse is full now."

"God be praised for His bounty." The parson looked at Garnet. "Widow Wheelock, mayhap you could accompany me to pay a call on Samuel Walsh. Hester, take the widow's bucket along with yours and go bind the herbs for drying. I'm sure Widow Wheelock will be pleased to come back to the keeping room and see how industrious you've been."

Unsure as to why the parson had come, Garnet accompanied him toward the barn. It would be fitting to welcome him to their nuncheon table, but she would leave that to Samuel. In the past two weeks, they'd accomplished much about the farm. They both labored diligently, but a strain existed between them.

Her shock about her maternal condition gave way to a mix of wonder and sadness. Though Garnet would never marry again, God had chosen to give her a child of her own. 'Twas a gift beyond imagining—but Samuel considered her babe an encumbrance. She'd vowed to remain here, and her word was her bond. Samuel promised to provide for the baby—more than Garnet could do on her own—but a child ought to be cherished, not just tolerated. Emotions and concerns bundled into a knot in her stomach. Just yestereve, Garnet decided her inability to speak had turned out to be a blessing in this situation.

"Samuel Walsh."

Sam looked up from the hide. "Reverend Clark. Welcome."

"So Ethan is of an age where he's helping with deer hide." The reverend smiled at Ethan. "You're on your way to manhood."

The sound of the ax made him turn to the side. "I see Christopher's chopping more firewood. A good thing, too. Winter's on its way."

Sam rose and wiped his hands on his thighs. "That's a fact. My winter wheat is already sown."

"The wind carries a decisive chill. Mayhap we ought to take Widow Wheelock into the barn, out of the cold."

Garnet tensed. Until now, she'd believed this to be a social visit. Clearly, it wasn't. The parson quite deftly had managed to ascertain where the children were, then asked Samuel and Garnet to come away from them for a private conversation.

As they entered the barn, the parson halted. "Is that a cheese ladder?"

"Aye. The widow's been making use of the overage of milk. As you said, the wind's stronger. She asked me to move the ladder inside so the cheese won't be tough. Widow Wheelock, when the reverend takes his leave, perchance could you allow him some cheese?"

Garnet nodded.

"You work together well." The parson looked from Garnet to Samuel and back again.

"The widow is unafraid of labor. She puts her hand to any task quite willingly."

Samuel's praise would mean far more if he didn't keep referring to me as "the widow." He does it apurpose, too. He means to remind me and all others that I am set apart from him.

"It is rumored that you are with child, Widow Wheelock."

She gave the parson a startled look.

"Word reached Goodwife Ryder. She's gathered a handful of others and approached me, saying Hester needs to be removed from this unwholesome place and returned to her care."

Samuel bristled. "Hester is staying here. Dorcas and Erasmus are angry at me and seek to cause strife."

"I supposed that might be so after the incident in the churchyard, but there is still the—" The parson shot a look at Garnet. "The other matter."

"The widow bears her husband's child." Sam's tone held a definite edge. "When the babe is born early next spring, 'twill be evident the gossipmongers were wrong in assuming I'm the sire."

"The Ryders wasted no time in spreading tales. Until spring comes and your point is proven, it would be best for Hester to—"

"No!" Sam's eyes burned with fury. "My daughter is not a pawn to be moved about in some game."

Reverend Clark picked some lint from his sleeve. The seemingly casual action didn't fool Garnet in the least. He looked at Samuel. "It defies the natural order of things for a woman to be alone—especially when she is with child. Four of the men in the congregation have reminded me of that fact and stated they are willing to wed the widow."

Clenching her teeth, Garnet shook her head.

Samuel's eyes narrowed. "Not a whit do I care for what others may say or wish. The widow has vowed to remain to assist my household, and I promised to provide for her and her child. The arrangement suits us."

The parson remained silent for a few minutes. "The Bible exhorts us to abstain from the very appearance of evil. The arrangement, which suits the two of you, sets a poor example for the children. The Lord Himself said it was not good for man to be alone and thus He created Eve. By keeping Widow Wheelock here, you rob some other man of the God-given need to be complete."

The parson's features pulled. "I confess, I hoped to answer the issue by way of the fact that the woman was bought; therefore, she is your indentured servant. When Goodman Brooks told me that you bought her as a bride and hold such papers, I lost the ability to justify your reason to keep a woman here without wedding her."

Samuel bristled yet again. "Thomas Brooks asked for her?"

"He did so out of mercy. Alan Cooper was boasting to him that he'd decided to place a claim on her. Thomas said if you'd not wed Widow Wheelock, he would."

A wave of revulsion washed over Garnet. She'd seen Alan Cooper at church. He stank of libation and leered at the women. Brooks had shown great kindness in trying to spare her such a match.

"You've backed me into a corner." Sam's face darkened. "The only way I'm to keep this woman here is to wed her. If I fail to do so, you'll remove Hester from my home?"

"I would not, but the council has the power to do so."

"Ryder is on the council." The muscle in Samuel's jaw spasmed.

"He is." Reverend Clark paused, then added, "The council is to meet regarding the matter tonight. I hoped to appeal to you ere it came to that."

"I stand by my word. I promised Hester she is home to stay, and I vowed to provide for the Wheelock child. If marriage is the only way for me to do so, then I have no choice. We will wed."

Garnet watched as the men shook hands. *Once again, I'm bartered in marriage. Samuel is bleak. He doesn't want me, yet he spoke for us both.*

"I'd normally conduct the marriage on Sunday after the sermon, but waiting is unwise."

"Ruth and Falcon can witness the marriage." Sam finally looked at Garnet. "I'll hitch the wagon whilst you gather my children."

My children. Before they'd discovered she was with child, Samuel always said "the children." Ever since, he'd referred to them as his—a potent reminder that she and her babe were outsiders.

She held out her left palm and walked two fingers across it.

"No. We'll ride." Impatience tainted his voice. "It's faster, and we'll get this over with at once."

Sam didn't say a word on the drive over to the Mortons'. It turned out that Falcon was at Thomas Brooks's. Ruth sent Aaron to go fetch him. Still, Sam remained utterly silent.

"Mary, you and Hester go gather some pretty flowers. A bride deserves beauty on her wedding day." Ruth tugged Garnet toward the house and called back over her shoulder, "Let us know when the men arrive."

Ruth shut the door, then let out a mirthless laugh. "If I don't miss my guess, Sam didn't propose—he ordered."

Folding her arms across her chest, Garnet nodded.

Dipping a rag into water, Ruth said, "Falcon did the same with me. He later told me he wouldn't allow me a choice because he feared I'd refuse." She handed the soggy cloth to Garnet and urged her to freshen up. "I reminded Falcon that I could have spoken my denial when asked to speak the vows. Can you believe he'd not thought of that?"

Ruth barely paused to draw in a breath as she swiped the cap from Garnet's head and started to run a brush through her hair. "I'll bet Samuel hasn't thought of that, either. Then again, you can't speak. They'll allow you to nod your head. Hear me, Garnet. 'Twill be a sound union. Other than my Falcon, there's not a finer man in all of the colonies. You and your child could do no better.

"Mary came home from school yesternoon saying Erasmus Ryder was congratulating the Cooper man on finding a wife. Now I know why. I'm not sure whether it's a sin or not, but I'm relishing the fact that their scheme failed. No, now that I think of it, it can't be a sin. King David was a man after God's own heart, and he wrote many a psalm in which he delights in how the wicked are laid low."

She teased out a snarl and continued to brush Garnet's hair. "This marriage will protect you from such scheming men, and that is good. Better still, you and Samuel make a fine team. Yes, this marriage is right, no matter which way I look at it."

Lord, what am I to do? The day we learned I'm with child, Samuel changed. He said he'd endure anything to keep Hester home, and so he's being pushed into a marriage he resents. I don't want it, either. How are we to abide beneath the same roof in harmony?

"Do you, Garnet Wheelock, give your consent to wed and freely enter into the covenant of holy matrimony?"

Clutching a handful of flowers, Garnet stood at Sam's side. For the first time, he realized she'd been herded into this, too. He'd been so desperate to shelter Hester that he'd been blind to the fact that Garnet was caught in the same trap. His blood boiled at the thought of Cooper trying to wed her. No woman ought be bound to such a sot.

Reverend Clark held *The Book of Common Prayer* and had already made opening comments concerning the church and holy matrimony. Never before had Sam paid any attention to the fact that the reverend always ascertained publicly if the bride and groom were willing.

The corners of Garnet's mouth tightened, and her shoulders rose with the deep breath she took.

Agree, Garnet. Though not pleased, I'm at least willing. He stared down at her, silently entreating her to grant approval for the ceremony to continue.

Chapter 13

The color of Garnet's eyes darkened to a pewter gray as her head dipped and rose in a nod—tiny as it was.

"Fine then," Reverend Clark responded. "Samuel, repeat after me. 'I, Samuel, take thee, Garnet, to my wedded wife. . . .'"

Samuel not only repeated the words but carried on without any prompting, "to have and to hold from this day forward, for better for worse, for richer for poorer, in sickness and in health, to love and to cherish, till death do us part, according to God's holy ordinance; and thereto I plight thee my troth."

Reverend Clark turned to Garnet. "As you cannot repeat after me, place your hand upon Samuel's. I'll place my hand atop yours, and with each phrase, you can signal your vow by squeezing."

Small calluses roughened the tips of her fingers and her palm. Garnet was no stranger to hard work, yet her hand felt impossibly small compared to his. Sam noted that her hand remained steady. She squeezed with the reading of each phrase until Reverend Clark read, "to love and to cherish."

Sam had rushed through his recitation, stating the words by rote. With each phrase requiring Garnet's attention, Sam felt the full impact of the vows. Softly, he murmured, " 'Tis sufficient that we care for each other in Christ Jesus, Garnet."

Never before had the simple closing of a hand carried so much meaning. Relief poured through him. When the time came to greet his bride, Sam barely grazed her lips with his.

"Father?" Hester tugged on his breeches. "Is she my mama now?"

Garnet stooped down and nodded as she opened her arms.

Hester threw her arms around Garnet's neck. "Chris! Ethan! I have a mama!"

Christopher chuckled. "So do we, you silly goose. She's our mother now, too."

Garnet kept hold of Hester as she straightened up. Hester's little legs wound around Garnet's still-evident waist. Ethan wrapped his arms around Garnet's hips.

"Now there's a fine sight." The parson smiled.

Sam pulled Hester from Garnet and set her down. "You must be careful. You're a big girl, and the wid—" He caught himself. "Your mama's deserving of special consideration."

"I made hasty pudding this morn." Ruth turned slightly to keep the wind from catching her apron and sending it into a wild flutter. "Hester and Mary can come help me dish it up."

"Come, Mama!" Hester tugged Garnet's hand. "Isn't this merry? We're celebrating!"

Thomas Brooks slapped Sam on the back. "You've a goodwife now. Little Hester's delight bodes well. Though the timing is poor, I'm to call you to the council meeting this eve. I've already asked Falcon to be present, as well."

"But it's his wedding night." Christopher flushed brightly after his outburst.

"I'll attend," Sam said as if his son hadn't mentioned that awkward fact.

As soon as they partook of the hasty pudding, Sam loaded his family into the wagon and headed home. After he lifted Garnet down, he traced a finger down her cheek. "You're pale."

She hitched a shoulder, then slid from his reach. Taking that hint, Sam turned to his sons. "Chris, unhitch the wagon. Ethan, you're to return to work on the deer hide. Hester—"

His daughter stood in the wagon by the edge. Crooking one arm around his neck, she rested her forehead against his. "Father, I get to stay with you forever and always, don't I?"

"Yes, poppet."

She whispered, "Aunt Dorcas told me I'd have to go back. I don't want to. Mama lets me lick the spoons and has me do fun things. We walk out and gather herbs together, and she let me help her oil the eggs and store them so we'll have plenty come winter."

Sam rubbed noses with his daughter.

Hester giggled, then whispered in his ear, "I'm going to card lots and lots and lots of wool. Aunt Dorcas always wanted wool, so I think that'll please Mama—don't you?"

"I'm sure she'll be happy with any help you render." Sam set her down and nudged her toward the house. Glancing at the length of shadows, he had about two hours ere they supped; then he'd go to the council meeting.

Adding another log to the carefully banked fire in the smokehouse, Samuel looked about. Scores of sausages hung from crossbeams. His mouth watered at the thought of enjoying those in the coming months.

Lord, Your bounty fills the root cellar, this smokehouse, and the pegs in the house. I thank You for Your generosity. I thank You, too, for good friends who surround me and keep me from the snares of the wicked. You've returned my daughter to me. That, most of all, matters to me. As for my wife—I confess, Father, that I've married in haste. I failed to seek Your will. I'm tardy in coming to You, but I ask Your blessing on our union. Amen.

Chores kept him busy until Hester called, "Supper's ready!"

Ethan met him just inside the door. "We're having bubble and squeak for supper!"

Looking at Garnet as she finished frying the meal, Sam said, "I'm partial to that."

Ethan grinned. "It really does bubble and squeak, Father. When you tried to make it, it didn't do that. Mama's carrots and cabbage didn't grow limp, and the pork is in fine, thin ribbons instead of funny chunks."

"We are blessed that God has sent her into our lives and home."

The children chattered through dinner, and Sam didn't silence them. Garnet deserved to hear how they welcomed her into their hearts. Then, too, it covered the strain between the two of them. As soon as he finished, Christopher announced, "I'll go saddle Butterfly for you."

"No need." Sam pushed away from the table. "I'll walk."

By the time he arrived at the meeting, both Thomas and Falcon had joined him. The parson opened the meeting with a prayer; then Erasmus Ryder announced, "In the interest of time, I think it best that we address the most pressing issues first. In keeping with Christian charity and familial obligation, my goodwife and I will take back her niece, Hester. Not only that, but Ethan and Christopher should come, as well."

"My children are going nowhere."

Erasmus pointed his finger. "You, Samuel Walsh, cannot deny the woman beneath your roof is with child."

"She's a widow," Thaddeus Laswell said. "Her husband could have sired the babe."

"Not with her belly still so flat," Erasmus shot back.

Alan Cooper rose. "Even though she be with child, I would take the woman to wife. The reverend has preached on how Hosea married Gomer, knowing full well she was a harlot."

"I doubt any other man would be so accepting." Erasmus spoke so quickly that Sam knew they'd scripted out this little performance. "I'd have us resolve one last matter whilst Walsh is before the council. He's cheated me of wool and coin for my tobacco. I went to him in private, but he refused to part with what he owes me, so I now seek recompense."

"Walsh," Fred Stamsfield said, "how do you answer this charge?"

"I'm grateful for the opportunity to set matters straight, Goodman Stamsfield." Sam looked about the room, making it a point to look each council member in the eyes. "I appreciate Goodman Laswell for crediting the right man for siring the babe. I can state with a clear conscience that I've known but one woman thus far in my life, and 'twas within the sacred bond of marriage."

Sam paused to allow that declaration a moment to sink in, then continued. "As for the widow's condition—indeed, she does not outwardly appear to be with child, but for understandable reason. She was dreadfully ill when I bought her, so she'd lost much flesh. Come spring, when she delivers, those who have misjudged her morals and mine will realize how they've wronged us."

Laswell combed his fingers through his beard. "My goodwife made mention after the first Sunday the widow attended church that she looked exceedingly frail."

"Ample proof that I should wed her." Cooper puffed out his chest like a bantam rooster preparing to spar. "The widow needs to rest, and she cannot do so in a home where three children require attention."

"I'll be sure to mention your kind concerns to her, Goodman Cooper." Samuel couldn't suppress a smile. "I fear it's misplaced, though. This very noon, Garnet Wheelock became my wife."

"That's not possible!" Cooper shot to his feet. "Banns weren't posted or read."

"We all know Samuel has been free to marry. He's been a widower for years now. Since he bought the bride, any reasonable person would understand marriage might well ensue. As for the woman. . ." Reverend Clark shrugged. "Widows are shipped here with the clear understanding that they marry. Samuel possesses legal paperwork, which declares her free of any encumbrances. She's accompanied the Walsh family to services for the past four weeks. I deemed that sufficient declaration of intent on her part, as well."

"I witnessed the marriage," Falcon said.

"As did I," Thomas said. "Though I, myself, would have considered taking such a fine widow as my own wife, I respected Walsh's claim."

"Reverend Clark would not have gone against his good conscience and officiated improperly," Stamsfield said.

"But by law, a widow must be delivered of her child ere she marries again," Alan Cooper snapped. "Isn't that right, Dickson?"

"You were willing to overlook that matter and wed her," Laswell mumbled.

The son of a judge, Dickson had more knowledge of the law than most. His brows beetled as he pondered the situation. "Such laws are in place with specific intent. A man's rightful heirs ought to be his own flesh. Since Samuel has two sons, the addition of a babe would not pose a challenge to their status. In this instance, the pregnancy posed no impediment to marriage."

Falcon snorted. "This whole meeting is an affront."

As head of the council, Dickson turned to Erasmus Ryder. "You cannot fault a man for keeping a woman to whom he's not married beneath his roof, then fault him for wedding her in the next."

"They weren't wed when I called a meeting," Ryder pointed out. "My concern was for my niece and nephews."

Sam seriously doubted the veracity of his brother-in-law's assertion, but he chose not to dwell on it at the moment. Clearly, his children would remain in his keeping. "With those matters settled, I challenge Erasmus Ryder to state his claim against me so I can clear my name."

Erasmus folded his arms akimbo, and his eyes narrowed. "I went to you to collect on debts you owe me, and you refused payment."

"This is a serious charge," Dickson said. "Honorable men discharge their debts. What do you say Walsh owes you?"

Erasmus rested his hands on the table and leaned forward as he enunciated each word with hatred. "Fleeces and cornmeal."

Dickson turned back to Samuel. "Goodman Walsh? How do you respond to this?"

"In the past, I've bartered cornmeal for Ryder's tobacco in order to meet my tithe and tax obligations." Sam hitched his shoulder. "I made no commitment to him to do so this year, and as he's known for growing good-quality Virginia tobacco, he's able to sell it elsewhere."

Dickson drummed his fingers on the tabletop. "How, then, did you meet your tithe and tax obligations?"

"I dealt with Thomas Brooks."

"That makes no sense," Dickson mused aloud. "Surely you would have garnered a more favorable exchange with Ryder since he is family to you."

"Not so." Sam looked at Erasmus and revealed, "Ryder always demanded and received fair market value from me."

"A crop costs me the same to grow no matter who buys it," Erasmus said. "And Walsh just told you all my tobacco is of the finest quality."

"Have you since sold the tobacco you assumed Walsh would buy from you?"

The question barely left Dickson's mouth ere Erasmus spat, "I'm no fool. Of course I did—but I had to journey to do so, and the trip cost me four shillings."

"You cannot hold me at fault for the assumptions you made," Sam said. "And there's not a man here who doesn't incur costs for the business he conducts. I had to travel a day and a half each way to the gristmill, and the miller takes one-sixth of the milling as his portion."

"What about the fleeces?" Ryder's head took on a defiant tilt.

"Shearing is done in spring," Parson Clark frowned. "How can you still owe Ryder wool now?"

"My flock is longwool. I shear the sheep both spring and autumn. The day Dorcas and Erasmus took my Hester to live with them, they took my spring shearing, as well. Since then, each spring and autumn, they've claimed the fleeces as the cost of keeping her for me."

"Your flock has increased by half again in that time." Thomas Brooks shook his head.

"And," Erasmus countered, "the child has grown, as well."

"You sought payment for minding the welfare of your own niece?" Reverend

Clark's voice reflected disbelief.

"Women are scarce, and their time's valuable," Alex Smith stated in Erasmus's defense. "Had Samuel hired someone to mind Hester, it would have cost a pretty penny."

"But had I done so," Sam stated wryly, "you would have brought me before the council and removed Hester from my home. Tonight is ample proof of that."

Smith sighed. " 'Tis true. No matter which route you chose, someone could find fault."

"My goodwife always passes our Mary's clothing down to Hester. Her shoes, as well." Falcon arched a brow. "Ryder, was it such a burden to feed one small child?"

"None of this is your concern, Morton," Alan Cooper rasped.

"Nor is it yours, Cooper," Samuel said. He then looked at the council. "But I state it clearly here: My sheep average slightly over fourteen pounds of wool apiece each year. Multiply that by eighteen, and 'tis abundantly clear my daughter's needs posed no hardship on the Ryders."

"Eighteen? But that's your entire flock." Falcon gave Samuel a puzzled look. "Dorcas took Naomi's loom and your spring shearing that year, so I assumed all along that she shared the profit of her weaving with you. Has she not?"

"No."

"Why should she? She does all the labor, and she minded the girl." Erasmus pointed at Samuel. "And you've sheared your sheep again but not given over the fleeces."

"If," Dickson said slowly, "the fleeces were first taken the day Hester went to abide in your home, then he's paid—and dearly, I might add—in advance."

"But who among us would ask payment for watching kin?" Disgust painted Thomas's face. "At the outset, Ryder said Christian charity and concern motivated him to seek the care of Walsh's children. I'm thinking greed, not charity, is behind all of this."

"My goodwife spins yarn aplenty and knits our wear." One of the newer settlers plucked at his doublet as if to illustrate his point. "We were told looms are forbidden in the New World. Mother England is to receive all raw materials and send them back as bolt goods."

"At a cost none can afford," Brooks muttered.

Dickson let out a sigh. "Reverend Clark, almost a score of years ago, we met o'er this very issue. By sending all our wool, flax, and cotton to England, we doomed our citizens. The cost of the cloth they sent back was so dear that none could afford to clothe their family and blanket their beds.

"Throughout England, families own looms and weave homespun. As we are all English citizens, that same right ought to belong to us, as well. Surely the law was intended to ward off the start of industrial development here when other endeavors are more important. The council voted if someone wove for family or for charitable means that then the spirit and heart of the law were met."

"Thank you for that explanation, Goodman Dickson." The parson nodded. "Christ admonished us to render unto Caesar what is Caesar's and unto God what is God's. By paying taxes and tithes, you fulfill His instruction. I am not a scholar of the law. What I would say is that each man is responsible before the Lord for his family's needs and conduct."

"It occurs to me," Smith said, "that Goodwife Ryder has gone beyond simply providing for her family's private need and uses the loom as a business enterprise."

Dickson turned to Smith. "A point well made. One we need to address."

"The solution is plain enough." Falcon gestured toward Samuel. "Sam was generous to allow Dorcas the use of the loom these many years. Now that he's wed, the loom rightfully belongs back in his household. I'm sure his bride has need of it."

Erasmus let out a roar. "Now see here!"

"I, for one, agree." Stamsfield looked about the table. "What say the rest of the council?"

Erasmus fumed, "You overstep your authority in seeking to interfere with family affairs."

"Citing familial concern, you brought me before the council, Goodman Ryder." Sam folded his arms across his chest. "Once the matter came to this assemblage, you implicitly agreed to abide by the council's decision—just as you expected I would have to."

"This would rob me of coin!"

Sam stared at him. "You worry about money. I came to fight for my family."

Chapter 14

G arnet sat at the spinning wheel and kept her hands busy. Unsettled by the day's events, she tried to reassure herself that she'd done the right thing by marrying Samuel. Compared to Alan Cooper, her groom was a prince. From the day Samuel had purchased her, he'd treated her with respect.

But he doesn't want my child.

She lost the rhythm of pressing the pedal and pulling on the fibers.

"Mama?" Hester set aside the carding brushes. "Will you walk me to the privy? It's so dark."

Christopher whispered something in Ethan's ear as Garnet led Hester outside.

When she and Hester returned, Sam stood in the open doorway. He looked years younger as he smiled. "God went before me. All is well."

Garnet slipped past him and busied herself at the spinning wheel once again. Hearing all went well for him pleased her. Sweet Hester had used every opportunity to call her "Mama" all afternoon, and relief filled Garnet in knowing the council hadn't broken the little girl's heart.

"Mama and me—we've been keeping each other company, Father. I'm carding the wool, and she's spinning it. Look how much we got done!"

Samuel leaned against the edge of the stones that formed the fireplace. "Hester, you've nigh unto filled that basket with carded wool, and it's rolled in such a way that it stays straight. Mind you, I'm not much of a judge of these things, but it all looks excellent to me. And look at your mama's bobbin. She spins with a deft hand, don't you agree?"

Hester beamed her agreement.

Ethan shifted from one foot to the other. "Father?"

Samuel ruffled Ethan's hair. "Yes?"

"The wid—I mean, Mother made Christopher a new shirt and a bodice for Hester. We're curing that deer hide so she can stitch you buckskin breeches. Will the cloth she weaves be for a shirt for me?"

Samuel's smile faded. "I cannot say. Her babe will require blankets and swaddling clothes. Those needs most likely will come ahead of your desires."

"Oh." Ethan's mouth drooped.

Resting a hand on his son's thin shoulder, Samuel said, "Take a lesson from this. As a man, you must sometimes put aside your own desires for the sake of another's needs. Not a one of us gets everything he wants in life. You must learn to be satisfied with your lot."

Every last word her new husband uttered drove a stake of pain through Garnet's soul. He'd not tried to be diplomatic in the least. Samuel Walsh was keeping his promise to make sure her child would be provided for—but at what cost? It wouldn't take many such comments to turn his children's hearts against the babe.

Christopher stretched and pretended to yawn. "It's bedtime."

Ethan brightened. "We have a surprise for you!"

"I want to tell it!" The carding brushes clattered from Hester's hands onto the floor. "I'm not a baby anymore."

"So she's moving upstairs with us," Ethan chimed in.

The spinning wheel stopped, and the yarn broke as Garnet heard their announcement.

"Ethan and I snuck the mattress off the trundle and toted it up the ladder whilst Mama took Hester out to the privy." Christopher stood straight as a lance. "I'll listen to their scripture verses tonight so you don't have to trouble yourselves with us."

"Actually, Chris, I'm going to need your help." Samuel's voice started out at a croak and quickly normalized. "Goodman Laswell is to arrive soon."

"Why would he come at night?"

Garnet wondered the same thing.

Samuel folded his arms across his chest. "He and some other men are bringing over the loom."

"You bought a loom today?" Ethan gaped at his father.

"No, no. Long ago, I bought it for your mother. Your aunt Dorcas borrowed it. Now that we have a woman, we'll have need of it again." He looked at Garnet. "Since it's so large, I thought to put it in the barn until you've spun enough to weave. Does that meet with your approval?"

Garnet nodded her head while promising herself she'd work diligently so she'd soon have use of the loom and make sufficient for a shirt for Ethan, as well as clothing for her baby. With that on her mind, she joined the ends of the thread together and started the wheel in motion.

Her thoughts spun as fast as the wheel, leaving her slightly dizzy. *I need to spin each morn and eve, and at any other moment I can spare. I've yet much to preserve. Ruth offered us some of their pears. Drying pears will take a few days' work, but 'twill be well worth the effort in the dead of winter. I could trade her cheese for them.*

Cheese—by the beginning of next month, the cow will go dry. Since Samuel slaughtered the hog, I've not had to pour the excess milk into the swill and have been able to make more wheels. Cheese keeps well, and from what Samuel said, most around here don't make cheese. Instead of buying it from the northern colonies, they could purchase it from us.

A big, strong hand halted the spinning wheel. "Garnet? You were lost deep in thought. The wagon bearing the loom has arrived. They took far less time than I expected." The children ran outside, but Sam didn't immediately follow them.

"Garnet, I would have you know that Goodman Dickson insisted upon the loom coming to us this very night. Erasmus Ryder was sorely vexed that his wife would no longer be permitted to weave for profit. To assure that no damage came to the loom, the men of the council went together and have brought it hence."

She'd used the slate to write to the boys earlier in the evening. Garnet lifted it from beside her stool and wrote, *Give cheese to thank?*

"That's a fine notion. Bring a knife with you. We'll cut one of the wheels and give each man a share."

Moonlight assisted the men in the yard; by the time they moved the loom inside the barn, Garnet and Ethan had lit four oil lamps. Christopher dragged a chest, a crate, and a pair of barrels away from a wall to make sufficient space for the loom.

Garnet counted seven men, but she'd already given the parson a small wheel of cheese that afternoon, so she selected a fair-sized wheel and cut it into sixths as the men carefully set the loom out of the way.

"Felicitations on your marriage, Goodwife Walsh," an older man said as he turned around. He reared back. "Bless me, is that cheese?"

Garnet nodded.

"Aye. My goodwife asked me to be sure you men received our thanks for your help this eve." Sam motioned to her.

Following his direction, Garnet approached the eldest first, then gave each man his portion. Reverend Clark grinned. "I've already enjoyed some of your delicious cheese, Goodwife Walsh. The flavor went especially well with an apple."

"You've a goodly supply of cheese there." One of the men gave Samuel an assessing look. "I'd not be averse to bartering for some."

"I'd gladly deal with you, as well," another said.

"Garnet and I will discuss the matter."

The eldest looked perplexed. "How can you discuss anything when she's mute?"

Someone else let out a bark of a laugh. "I have yet to meet a woman who couldn't make everyone know her mind."

"My goodwife is exceedingly expressive with her gestures, and she also writes on a slate." Samuel moved to stand beside her. "But I speak for us both when I thank you all."

The men took their leave, and Garnet headed back toward the house. Christopher tried to steer Hester to the opposite side of the house.

"Mama has to plait my hair so it won't tangle whilst I sleep." Hester slid her hand into Garnet's.

Relieved to stretch out the time before she and Samuel were alone, Garnet nodded. Once in the keeping room, she ran the comb through Hester's dark hair over and over, then divided it into three sections and plaited it.

Sam pulled the stool over to the middle of the room, stood on it, and pushed up on a section of the ceiling boards. Ruth had been right—a door existed there. "Chris," he said, " 'tis silly for Hester to go outside and climb the ladder when I can lift her from here."

Hester wrapped her arms about Garnet. "This is the best day of my life! I have you for my mama, and I'm grown up enough to be upstairs."

As Sam lifted the little girl up to Chris, Garnet headed back to the spinning wheel. Wood scraped; then the segment thumped into place, leaving her alone with her groom. Garnet fumbled with the carded wool and hastily started spinning.

"The children ought sleep well tonight. They've stayed up far past the time they usually go to bed."

Garnet didn't look up. She merely nodded.

"I planted very little flax this year—something I now regret. As you like to spin and knit, more flax would have allowed you to make linen and linsey-woolsey." He went on to identify some items he felt the farm needed and what he felt could be bartered away. Finally, he decided. "The hour grows late. Cease spinning, and we'll retire."

Pulling back the covers on the bed, he cleared his throat. "It's been four years since Naomi passed on."

Garnet shuddered.

"I tell you this because my nightshirt fell to pieces awhile back. 'Twas beyond redemption, so I—" He halted and gave her a stunned look. "Here I am, confessing I've no nightshirt, yet I'm sure you must have returned Ruth's nightdress to her. What have you been wearing to bed?"

Heat enveloped her. Garnet didn't want to confess she'd been sleeping in a petticoat.

"None of that now. Blushing is for maidens." He towed her toward the door. "Grab the lamp. We'll find something that will suffice."

They ended up in the barn, and Samuel knelt by one of the boxes Christopher had moved to create space for the loom. "I've been remiss in offering these things to you. Here." The leather hinges of the box crackled as he opened it. "It's been so long since I had a female under the roof that I no longer recalled the feminine things a woman desires."

Garnet peered over his shoulder. He pushed a hairbrush off to the side. Next, he took out a pair of stockings that would help keep her warm during the winter months. The stockings Garnet currently wore were carefully darned but so threadbare they wouldn't last much longer.

"Ah. Ruth made this for Naomi." Insubstantial as air and prettier than a handful of snowflakes, the shawl he removed would be for fine occasions and church. Surely it wouldn't keep her warm. Sam studied it a moment, then nodded. " 'Twill serve you well whilst you suckle your babe."

Your babe. Though he'd not emphasized the word, his meaning still came through. Garnet rested her hand over her waist, as if to protect the child she carried.

Oblivious to her concern, he set aside a rabbit-fur muff and a cape of two tones of blue. Tails of fabric from two smallish folded squares were likely aprons. Sam then lifted a yellowed-with-age nightdress from the bottom of the trunk. It unfolded, but as he held the garment over the trunk, the hem stayed clean. "As I recall, the aprons and this belonged to Naomi's mother. She was a smallish woman like you."

Garnet mouthed, *Thank you.*

Sweeping everything back into the box, Sam said, "I'll carry this chest in for you. Mary Morton used to stand on one of similar size. Falcon built it to raise her up to the table so she could help her mother with cooking. Hester enjoys being at your side. This will enable her to assist you."

Garnet held the lamp as Sam carried the box back to the house. Every step demanded her courage. *We married out of necessity, but he is trying to provide for me. Cecil drank himself under the table at our wedding supper. Compared to that, this is a vast improvement.*

A movement caught Garnet's attention.

"Garnet, open the door latch."

Samuel's words barely made it past the pounding in her ears. A scream welled up.

Chapter 15

S am dropped the box and whipped around. Garnet's shrill scream wavered in the crisp night air, but he saw no danger. "Garnet—"

She shuffled back.

Sam grabbed her with one hand and the lamp with his other. Garnet tried to twist away. He blew out the flame and hastily thumped the oil lamp down on the box while still manacling her wrist in an unyielding grip.

Another scream welled up and burst out of her.

Sam squinted in the direction she was staring and saw nothing more than a rat scurrying away. *But 'twas a field mouse that caused her to panic that other time.*

For a small woman, she fought his restraint with astonishing might. Sam clenched her wrist more securely and yanked her against himself. Wrapping his other arm about her shoulders, he dipped his head so his mouth would be next to her ear. "Garnet. Garnet, 'tis gone. It's gone now. All gone. It ran off."

Terror left her stiff, but Sam counted that as a vast improvement. She'd ceased screaming and no longer tried to break free from him.

"You're safe. Hear me, Garnet. 'Tis gone." He turned loose of her wrist and wrapped his other arm about her in an unyielding hold.

She whimpered a single word, shuddered, and swooned.

Sam swept her up, carried her into the keeping room, and laid her on the bed. Flames from the hearth gave a soft glow to the room, yielding light and warmth, so he left her only long enough to pull in the box and lantern, then latch the door.

Help. She'd finally spoken, and the word was a plea wrought with nothing short of terror. *Help.* Admittedly, beady-eyed rats weren't welcome, but why would she hold such fear of a common rodent?

He pulled off her mobcap, then removed her slippers and stockings. Her stockings—they'd been mended in so many spots, 'twas nothing short of astonishing that they stayed together at all. *I'm glad there are stockings in the box I gave to her.*

Sam sat on the edge of the jump bed and chafed her hand. "Garnet? Garnet."

Slowly, her eyelids flickered open. At first, confusion clouded her eyes, but just as quickly, fright filled them.

Her panic tore at him. Clasping her hand firmly between his, Sam said, "You're safe. I promise; you're safe. 'Twas outside, and it's gone." Reassurance flowed from his mouth, and the fright slowly faded from her face, only to be replaced by vulnerability.

He held fast to her hand with one of his, but traced her lips with his other fingers. "You spoke, Garnet. God gave you back your voice."

She said nothing.

Lord, what am I to say to reassure her? Put words in my mouth.

Trailing his fingers through her hair, Sam let out a slow breath. "The day Naomi died, Ruth packed that box. I slammed on the lid and took it out to the barn. I've said the marriage was not a happy one. In truth, 'twas miserable. Keeping Naomi's possessions locked away was my way of putting the bad memories behind me. Now that I've opened the chest and gone clear to the bottom of it, I've found the memories no longer hold sway over me."

Garnet lay perfectly still.

"Something happened. It must have been terrible for you to sacrifice your ability to talk just to tamp down the memory. Just as you stood with me as I opened the lid to the chest, now I'll stay with you. Open your mouth and give voice to the fear. You asked for my help, Garnet. God gave you a gift by returning your voice. Don't turn away from it. Use your voice now, and we will lift the lid on the box of your fear. Once we get to the bottom of it, you'll be free."

Her lips quivered.

Sam continued to hold her hand and stroke her soft hair. "Help. That is what you said to me. You saw something—"

Her whole body went rigid.

Sam cupped her cheek and bent closer. "It was outside. We're inside."

A broken sigh poured out of her.

"On the day you left England, did you still have your voice?"

She nodded.

"Yes. Say yes, Garnet."

"Yes." The single syllable sounded tentative and raspy.

"Well done." He studied her by the fire's light. "The voyage was harsh. The man I bought you from said of the dozen brides, only five survived."

She seemed to shrink right before him. "Chained." Her eyes squeezed shut, yet her hand gripped his with desperation. "Together."

The first word chilled him to the marrow of his bones; the second left twin streaks of anger and disgust through him.

An ugly sob wracked her. "They died."

Sam pulled her into his arms. The horror he felt in knowing what happened didn't begin to compare with what she'd endured. From her reaction to the rodents, Sam knew what would come next. Holding her securely, he echoed her words. "They died." She shuddered, and he knew how cruel it was to push her—but 'twas also essential. Until she finally purged her mind of the gruesome memory, she'd not break free from the terror that enslaved her. Cradling her head to his shoulder, he said, "They died, and the rats—"

A keening wail tore through her. Words tumbled out between her sobs. "Storm. . .rats! Screamed. . .no help. No help."

Garnet wept and wept. Finally, she slumped against him.

" 'Tis over now, Garnet." He kissed her brow. "Sleep."

She fell headlong into sleep, and Sam tucked her in. He kicked off his boots and removed his doublet but decided to stay in his shirt and breeches. It wasn't much of a wedding night, but it wasn't much of a marriage, either. After a time, he crawled into the bed.

In the still of the room, the fire glowed and occasionally sparked. Night sounds intruded, and there were the occasional odd bumps from the children up in the loft. Then Garnet made a choking sound.

He opened his eyes at once. "Garnet, give me your hand."

Biting her lip, she tried to silence her weeping.

"Garnet, your hand—yield it over to me. If you are fearful of me, please attend and know there is no cause. If you are saddened, then take the comfort a friend offers."

A small, work-chapped hand slid timidly across the mattress. He engulfed her hand in his. Hers was too thin by half and shook. Samuel noted both facts with a measure of dismay. He whispered in a deep rasp, "Slumber now, Garnet. No harm shall come to you in my care. I vow it."

He held that hand until it went limp from her falling asleep. Still, he let it rest on their corn-husk mattress and covered it with his own big, capable hand. Should she awaken, there would be that sign of his concern for her. He should have gone to sleep straight off, for he was markedly tired, but something had happened that made it impossible. He'd caught himself just a breath away from kissing the backs of her fingers.

A blast of cool air awakened Garnet. She blinked. *Why am I on this side of the bed?* Memories of the previous day welled up. She gasped and turned her head in time to watch Samuel shut the door.

He glanced at the bed and smiled. "So you're awake." Setting the milk pail on the table, he chuckled. "Ethan laid snares yesternoon all by himself. He'll be impossibly proud of himself when he checks them."

Realizing she was dressed beneath the bedclothes, Garnet slid from the mattress and made the bed.

Warm, heavy hands touched her shoulders and turned her. "It would be wise for us to discuss bartering. Our neighbors will all know of your fine cheese and want to trade for it. What say you?"

Garnet nodded.

"Give voice to your thoughts," he urged quietly.

Last night hadn't been a dream? Had she regained her ability to speak? Garnet hesitated, then whispered, "Breakfast?"

Her husband smiled. "I'd ask you to make stirabout. I always burned it, but yours carries a fine flavor. What do you add to it?"

"Molasses or honey." She moistened her lips. "More honey? Rice?"

"The Carolina Colony grows rice aplenty. Laswell has connections to someone from there. Obtaining rice will be easy enough. As for honey—I'll ask Falcon. Last year, he found a stump brimming with honey. Not only did Ruth have honey to trade, but beeswax, as well."

"Ruth." Garnet felt a wave of warmth just from thinking of what a dear friend her neighbor had become. "Want her to have cheese. Generous."

"Are you telling me to be generous in the barter, or are you saying Ruth is generous?"

Garnet caught herself as she started to nod. "Both."

Samuel chuckled.

Since he was in a good mood, Garnet hesitated to ask the next question, but it still needed to be asked. "Owe any debts?"

"Not a one." He rubbed his forehead. "I've grown lazy about knowing what foodstuffs we have on hand. Since you took over cooking, all I've done is enjoy the meals and not paid attention to our supplies. In addition to honey and rice, what have we need of?"

"Oats?"

"Much as I like your stirabout, I should have anticipated that answer. Dickson grows oats. He has two indentured servants who help considerably, but men rarely trouble themselves over domestic chores. Betwixt your cheese and soap, I estimate Dickson will strike a deal quite gladly."

"Crocks of cheese." Her voice sounded funny, but Garnet continued on. "Sheep's cheese. In the springhouse."

His brows rose. "As much as Hester chatters, I'm surprised she didn't tell me all about that venture."

"Made it while children are at school."

He looked at the pegs in the ceiling and shook his head. "Your industry surpasses imagination." His gaze fell to her belly, and his tone went flat. "I suppose it's a good thing. The last days before having a babe, women slow down. You'll be abed for a solid month after delivering, too."

Garnet turned away and started breakfast.

Samuel rapped his knuckles on a tin pan as he did each morning to wake the children. "Up with you!" he announced.

The door to the second story slid open. "Hester left her shoes down there last night."

"Hurry! I have to go to the privy!"

Garnet located Hester's shoes as Sam reached up. "Hester, cease your wiggling and giggling, and I'll bring you down." As soon as he had her in his arms, Sam turned his daughter and snuggled her as if he'd never held anything more precious. "Don't fret over shoes, Garnet. I'll just carry her this morn."

Once he stepped out the door, Garnet set Hester's shoes on the crate. The soft thump echoed the heaviness in her heart. *He'll cherish his own children, but he'll merely tolerate mine. Lord, I don't know what to do.*

Chapter 16

As he carried Hester back into the house, Sam tugged on her braid. "Something special happened."

"You got married!"

"Yes, well. . .that's right, I did." He shut the door and bent to set her down.

"And now I got a mama."

He nodded.

"Mama does that, too—nods her head." Hester danced from one foot to the other. "That means you are the same. That's why you got married. Schoolmaster Smith said things that are alike belong together."

"You need to get dressed. It'll be breakfast time soon, and then you'll be off to school."

Once they all gathered around the table, Sam bowed his head and prayed. "Most loving Father, we thank You for the bounty You've bestowed upon us. Thank You, too, for the special gift You brought last night. Be with my children at school today. Let them be attentive and return home safely. Amen."

"What special gift?" Hester asked as she grabbed her spoon.

Christopher choked and turned crimson.

"The loom—remember?" Ethan plopped a dollop of butter on his stirabout.

"Actually, I wasn't referring to the loom, though I'm glad to have it back." Sam motioned to Garnet. "Why don't you tell them about it?"

"I'll get my slate." Ethan popped up.

Garnet reached over and stopped him. "No. Thank you."

"You talked!" Christopher half shouted in surprise.

"Oh no." Ethan slumped down. "Now Aunt Dorcas is going to want the recorder back because the wi—because Mother can sing at church."

"She can't have it, can she, Father?" Christopher rested his elbows on the table. "If we got the loom back, that means the council believes anything that belonged to Mother belongs to. . ." Christopher cast a look at Garnet.

"Mama," Hester supplied. She beamed. "Mary Morton calls her mother 'Mama,' and I always envied her. Was it sinful for me, Father? I wanted my own mama. Now I have one."

"One of the commandments exhorts us not to covet." Sam looked at his bride. "We are to be satisfied with our lot in life. Life rarely brings you what you want."

To his dismay, Garnet slowly nodded.

Over the next three weeks, everyone stayed excessively busy. Just as the creatures hoarded food for the winter, so everyone labored to extract each last morsel of food from the earth. Neighbors arrived in hopes of bartering for Garnet's cheese. Ruth Morton came over thrice a week with the excess from her cow, and Thomas Brooks sent his along, as well. They'd agreed that half of the cheese made from their milk would belong to them; the other half was Garnet's.

"Garnet?" Sam cleared his throat. "Goodman Dickson is here. He'd like some cheese."

Garnet sat at the spinning wheel and continued to work. "Deal with him as you will."

"Is there aught you need?"

"I've flax and fleeces aplenty. I trust you to do what's best."

"Very well." She'd been strangely remote since their marriage. Just yestermorn, he'd seen her placing her palm on her belly, measuring the small mound that finally testified to impending motherhood. She'd not known Sam was there, and the strained look on her face warned him not to make his presence known. Garnet chose not to say much of her former husband other than he'd shown a weakness for both spirits and cards. The day the sheriff arrived to take him to debtors' prison, he'd keeled over dead. She never spoke of the babe. Sam took his cue from her and didn't, either.

Sam left her in the keeping room and went back to the barn.

"So what does your goodwife name as the price of her cheese?"

"She left that to me. What do you offer?"

They settled on the payment of a small, tin-punched lantern. As Dickson prepared to leave, he squinted at Sam. "Has it occurred to you that your goodwife hides away in your keeping room? The only time I see her is at worship."

"She's spinning much of the time. In truth, it puts me in mind of a bird lining the nest ere the young come."

The old man chortled softly as he swung up into his saddle. "Just so. Goodwife Morton isn't finding a need to prepare for her babe—but she's very early on yet, and she's already been through this seven other times."

Sam handed him a wheel of cheese. "Aye, 'tis the truth. Garnet's on her first."

As Dickson left, Sam cast a look back at the cabin. *This babe will be her first, and if things continue on as they have, 'twill be her only. I've no one to blame but myself. Whilst we exchanged vows, I told her 'twas sufficient that we care for each other in Christ Jesus.*

I've always been a man of my word.

Sam bleakly walked toward the nearest field. All about him, the land struggled against the coming winter. Soon life would go dormant, only to burst forth in spring. Garnet would give birth in spring, too. But the only yield she'd ever have would be another man's child.

"Mama, I can't put my arms all the way 'round you anymore." Hester stood on tiptoe and tried once more just to prove her point. "See?"

"Enough of that." Sam shed his cloak and hung it on a peg by the door.

His curt tone of voice made it clear he wanted no reminder of her condition. Garnet tried to hide her sadness. It wasn't right for the children to be caught in the middle of the strain. She straightened the clout covering Hester's hair. "There. Now get back to practicing your letters."

"I'll write my whole alphabet for you." Hester skipped over to the table and picked up her slate. "Ethan, why do you look so sour?"

Garnet braced herself for his answer. Thus far, the children had remained oblivious to the tension between her and Samuel. Try as she might to keep the problem a secret, Garnet knew the time would come when she couldn't shield them from the fact that their father didn't want her child.

"You do look sour," Sam said to his son.

Using his slate pencil to scratch the back of his hand, Ethan let out a gusty sigh. "I'm supposed to figure out how much of a hogshead eight firkins is."

"You can do that." Sam headed toward the table. "It's a fractional problem. There are nine gallons in a firkin. How many gallons in a hogshead?"

As they worked on the arithmetic, Garnet sat by the fire and carefully stitched together the buckskin breeches she'd been making for her husband. Though supple, the leather was difficult to pierce with the needle. Samuel desperately needed these new breeches, though. She hoped to finish them tonight.

Christopher burst through the door and ran toward the hearth. "A huge buck is out where the vegetable garden was!" He reached for the flintlock. "Hurry, Father!"

"No, son." Samuel looked across the keeping room. "Our smokehouse is full. It would be a waste to slaughter the beast when we're not in need of meat. Never take something you cannot use."

Is that how he thinks of me? He bought me because he'd get Hester back from the Ryders. He married me to keep her and the boys. He took me because I suited his needs.

She pushed aside the buckskin and stood. The room tilted crazily.

"Garnet?"

Blinking, she turned and wondered how Samuel got from the other side of the table to her. He curled his hands around her upper arms as she said, "I'm going to add a log to the fire."

"Christopher, see to that." Sam exerted pressure on her arms. "Sit back down. You cannot rise of a sudden like that."

Melting back onto the stool, Garnet tore her gaze from her husband to Christopher. The boy moved the logs about in the fire with an andiron, then added another log. "Thank you, Chris."

"Is she faring better, Father?"

"I'd say so. Her color's come back." Sam studied her, and Garnet couldn't look away. " 'Twas just a passing affliction. Sometimes when a woman moves too swiftly, this happens." One at a time, his fingers released her arms until his hands hovered close but didn't touch her. "Have a care in rising."

Garnet nodded slowly. As her husband walked back toward the table, she lifted the buckskins back into her lap. *Mayhap I'm being unfair to him. He's shown me nothing but kindness.* It took forceful pushing with the thimble to force the needle through the leather. Garnet shoved it through yet again. *Truly, Samuel treats me well. But what about my child?*

He'd refrained from saying a word about the baby. In the midst of this episode, he'd never once referred to her condition.

"Christopher, have you completed your lessons?" Sam looked up from Ethan's work.

"Aye, I have. I'm to recite Reverend Michael Wigglesworth's 'The Day of Doom' on the morrow."

" 'Tis a long poem. Are you confident?"

Chris stretched to his full height and launched into the fiery passage, putting notable feeling into the piece. When he finished, Hester shivered. "That was scary!"

"Well done," Garnet praised.

"Indeed." Sam's voice held full approval.

"My stomach is growling." Ethan wiggled on the bench.

"You ate two bowls of stew at supper." Christopher folded his arms across his chest. "Just because you snared the hares doesn't mean you have to eat all of them by yourself."

Hester giggled. "Soon Ethan's belly will be as big as Mama's!"

"My hares were plump, but they'd never get me to that size. I'd have to eat a—"

"Silence yourselves." Sam scowled. "If you cannot speak respectfully, hold your tongue."

Ethan's teasing grin twisted into a stricken expression. He'd been told to be silent, so he couldn't say a word. His eyes begged Garnet's forgiveness. Confusion painted Hester's face.

Garnet smiled at them. They'd not meant any disrespect. Still, it would be wrong to disagree with Samuel in front of them. She bowed her head and set to stitching again.

Sam dragged a stool over, stood on it, and opened the ceiling hatch to the upper story. He hopped down, dusted off his hands, and pushed the stool against the far wall. "Chris, come with me. We need to bring in more wood. The weather's turning."

Ethan pushed away from the table. "I'm finished solving the problems. Shall I come along?"

"Put on your cloak." Sam reached for his own as he gave the order.

"I. . ." Ethan puffed his cheeks full of air and let it out in a slow, loud blow. "I left my cloak at school."

"You're ten, Ethan. Fast becoming a man." Sam shook his head. "You cannot indulge in such irresponsibility. The night's too cold for you to be out for more than a few minutes. Your brother and I will have to leave you behind and do this chore without you."

"I'm ready," Christopher said as he fastened the horn button at the throat of his own cloak.

Sam and Christopher went outside. Garnet finished the last stitch in the breeches, knotted her thread, and bit off the excess. She set her work aside and put towels on a stool close by the fire.

"Mama, why did you do that?"

"Rain is on the way. Your brothers might get wet when they climb up the ladder to go to bed. The towels will dry and warm them."

Ethan stared at the fire. "So you think it's going to rain, too?"

"Aunt Dorcas always said she could tell when it would rain. She could feel it in her bones." Hester's face puckered, and she used the tip of her finger to erase something on her slate.

"I don't feel it in my bones," Garnet said as she scooted the towels a little closer to the fire, "but I trust your father. He's very knowledgeable about the land and weather."

Hester let out a moan. "I can't fit the whole alphabet on here."

Garnet studied the carefully written letters. "You've scribed quite a few and nicely. I'd rather see you do your best work than to hurry through. You don't want to get into a habit of being messy."

Ethan wrinkled his nose. "Schoolmaster Smith read from *Poor Richard's Almanack* today. Benjamin Franklin said, ' 'Tis easier to prevent bad habits than to break them.'"

"Exactly. Very nicely said, Ethan. Hester, it's time to be thinking of putting you to bed."

"Will you please take me to the privy?"

"Of course, I will." Garnet slipped into the double-toned blue cape. Though Hester was afraid of the dark and didn't go out alone, something in her voice let Garnet know her little daughter wanted to say something. "Here." She buttoned Hester's cape and tickled her little nose.

Contrary to her usual giggle, Hester remained somber. She waited until she'd finished in the privy, then stood in a weak moonbeam and gave Garnet a woebegone look. "Goodman Morton tells his goodwife that she is fat and sassy. Mary laughs and says it is good when a woman's belly grows big."

"It's a sign that all is well." Garnet chose her words carefully. "Sometimes we pray together and give the Lord our thanks. Other times we whisper our prayers when we're alone. So it is when a woman is with child. Some feel free to celebrate with everyone. Others think it more fitting to be private."

"Oh." Hester slid her hand into Garnet's. "But it was just us, in our own home. No one else heard us say anything about how big your belly is."

"Even so, you must honor your father." As soon as the words exited her lips, Garnet felt a bolt of conviction. *It's my place to honor my husband. I've been sulking instead of thanking the Lord for His provision.*

"Yes, Mama. I will."

They returned to the house, but the keeping room was empty. A few minutes later, Sam and Christopher pulled a sledge to the cabin and started carrying in armloads of wood. "I meant to stack wood on the side of the house, but the weather's gotten ahead of me."

"But you brought gracious plenty," Garnet said. "Thank you." A minute later, she walked to the door and peered out. "Samuel, where's Ethan?"

"Isn't he in the house?"

"Not unless he went to bed."

Sam carried in another load of logs. "Chris, climb up and check on your brother."

A minute later, Christopher stuck his head down through the hatch. "Ethan's not up here."

Chapter 17

S am!" Garnet grabbed his hand and yanked as if her horrified tone hadn't already garnered his attention. "The water buckets are gone!"

"Ethan!" Sam broke away from Garnet and ran toward the stream. "Ethan!"

Christopher sprinted alongside him, shouting for his brother.

One bucket sat on the shore. Moonlight tipped small ripples in the water, but Sam couldn't see Ethan. "Lord—my son!" Sam cried out in anguish as he jogged along the water's edge, searching.

"Father!" Christopher pointed.

Sam dove into the water. Half a dozen powerful strokes took him to his son. Ethan's head bobbed above the water, but Sam clutched him and headed for shore.

Ethan spluttered and coughed—the sweetest sounds Sam had ever heard. "I have you. I have you." Sam lifted Ethan into Chris's waiting arms, then pulled himself out of the cold water and onto land.

"Ethan!" Panic lent an edge to Garnet's voice.

"We found him," Christopher shouted.

"Wet, but well," Sam added as he grabbed Ethan from Chris's arms.

"Lord be praised!" Garnet huffed breathlessly as she reached them. "Here." She swept off her cape and stood on tiptoe to try to envelop him and Ethan in its folds.

Sam stepped back. "Put that back on out here. It'll only get wet, and the last thing we need is for you to sicken again."

It seemed as if it had taken forever for him to run to the stream and reach Ethan. It took no more than a blink but that they were inside the keeping room once again.

"Mama, I did what you told me to." Hester peeked down at them from the hatch door. "Here."

"Good girl!" Garnet caught Ethan's nightshirt as Sam grabbed Hester and lowered her to the floor. "Ethan, get out of those wet things and put this on. Samuel, I finished your buckskins. You change, too."

Sam ignored her order and yanked off Ethan's sodden shirt. Garnet immediately enveloped Ethan in one of the towels.

"Sam, there's another towel to the left of the fire."

He grabbed the towel and started to rumple it through his son's hair. Garnet made an impatient sound. "Samuel, dry off. I'll take care of him."

"He's my son!"

Garnet jerked backward into the spinning wheel, but Christopher grabbed her ere she fell. The spinning wheel toppled over. The clattering sound it made as it tangled with the andirons didn't cover an ominous crack.

"Oh, dear." Hester's little voice whispered in the utterly silent keeping room.

"Are you all right?" Sam stared at his wife.

She nodded and turned away.

Christopher righted the spinning wheel. One of the spokes stuck out at an odd angle, the beautifully turned wood now cracked. "Goodwife Stamsfield's wheel is missing a spoke," Christopher said in an appeasing tone. "She claims it still works fine."

"Father, you're going to wear my hair off my head!"

Sam forced a chuckle and stopped rubbing Ethan's hair. "Change into your nightshirt."

Christopher shot a look from Garnet to him and back again. Worry dug furrows on either side of his mouth. "I'll bring in some more logs while you dry off, Father."

Reaching up, Garnet took a small bundle of herbs from a peg. By the time Sam dried off and had donned his new buckskins, she was setting cups on the table. "Hester, please fetch the honey."

Hester did so, then stood upon the box and asked, "What did you brew?"

"Bee balm tea. Do you like how it smells?"

"It smells pretty. Aunt Dorcas made lots of chicory tea." Her little nose wrinkled. "I didn't like it."

Christopher came back inside, his arms full. "These are the last logs from the sledge, and not a moment too soon. It's starting to rain."

"Some tea will warm you up." Garnet drizzled honey into the teapot, stirred it, and filled cups. "Here you are."

Sam frowned. "Garnet, there are only four cups."

The saddest smile he'd ever seen sketched across her face. "Ruth mentioned I oughtn't drink bee balm."

How she managed it, Sam wasn't quite sure. The mattress from the trundle barely fit through the hatch, but Garnet and Hester now huddled on it beneath a blanket whilst Ethan and Christopher climbed into the jump bed. Sam wanted to draw his wife aside for a private conversation, but with the children underfoot, he'd not yet managed to do so. Now it was too late.

"Garnet, are you warm enough?"

She nodded. "Be sure to keep Ethan bundled up. I don't want either of you to take a chill."

Giggles spilled out of Hester. "Mama! How did you do that?"

Ethan propped up on one elbow. "What did she do?"

"She has her arms 'round me, but her tummy bumped on my back like someone knocking on the door."

"It's her baby." Christopher gave the explanation in a matter-of-fact tone.

"It's not fair." Hester sat up. "How come Mama's baby isn't my baby, too? Mary said her mama and father share their baby with everyone in the family."

"That's different. Aunt Dorcas—"

"Hush, Ethan," Christopher hissed. "She was wrong about the recorder and about the loom. I—"

"Have you spoken to your aunt recently?" Sam fought to keep his tone even.

"She brought us cookies. After school," Hester said.

"And she said she'd bake us cookies when we decided to come live with her," Ethan added.

"Why," Sam gritted, "would you go live with her?"

"Because," Hester said, "she said Mama's not really our mama and when she has her baby, she won't care about us anymore."

"Well, she's wrong." Garnet's voice rang with certainty.

Hester continued. "I know. Aunt Dorcas was wrong about other things, too. She said I'll always be her baby, but I told her I'm a big girl now. I go to school and sleep upstairs."

"The only place you're going is to sleep." Sam strove to contain his temper. "Hester, lie back down."

Hester flopped down and squirmed beneath the covers. A second later, she whispered loudly, "Mama? Will you make a girl baby? I want a sister."

"The Almighty will decide what to give us." From the way the blanket moved, Sam knew she'd pulled Hester closer and kept an arm around her. "Know this, Hester. You are very dear to me. When the baby comes, God will add love in my heart so there's plenty for everyone."

"Add?" Glee bubbled out of his daughter. "Like when Schoolmaster Smith does the plus instead of the take-away sign!"

"So put your mind to rest." Garnet's head came off the pillow so she could look up at the jump bed. "Our Lord let us keep Ethan so we can all be together. No one can pull us asunder."

"Like when you married Father," Ethan said sleepily. "What God hath joined together, let no man pull asunder."

"But Aunt Dorcas is a woman."

"She's married, Hester," Christopher reasoned. "In God's eyes, a man and a woman are one. They become a team—like two horses pulling a wagon instead of just one."

"When I married your father, I knew he had three fine children in his wagon." Garnet spoke very softly. "When we wed, you became mine."

"I'm glad." Hester snuggled into the pillow.

"Me, too," Sam said. He waited for Garnet to react, but she didn't.

Chapter 18

The door opened, and Garnet looked up. Christopher stepped inside and shut the door behind himself. "The cow's gone dry."

She forced a smile. "I've been expecting that to happen."

He held up a basket. "I gathered the eggs."

"Thank you. Breakfast is ready." Garnet didn't ask about his father. Sam hadn't gone to bed at all last night. He'd sat before the fireplace, brooding for the longest while; then he took his cloak and went outside. He'd not come back. She didn't know where he was.

"Since we're having stirabout," Ethan asked between bites, "what are you going to do with the eggs?"

"Do you think, perchance, you could fetch me a pumpkin from the barn ere you leave for school?"

"I'm done eating. I'll get it now!" Ethan raced out the door. A few minutes later, he returned with a good-sized pumpkin. "Father is busy. He doesn't want you out in the barn."

Garnet pretended that news didn't wound her. Instead, she thanked Ethan for the pumpkin. A few minutes later, she stood in the doorway and waved as the children set off for school. Once they were out of sight, she shut the door and drew in a deep breath to steady herself.

It took no time at all to clean up from breakfast, and she set to making the pumpkin custard Samuel liked so much. It would take the last of the cream she'd stored in the springhouse. She slipped the two-toned blue cape around her shoulders and fetched the cream.

On the way back to the house, Garnet made a point of not looking at the barn. *Lord, I've been too busy looking upon my husband instead of keeping my eyes on You. I let discontentment come into my heart when I should have been praising You for all You've given me. Starting right now, I'm going to rely upon Your promise in the Bible that if I seek You first, all of the other things will be added unto me.*

She went back into the keeping room. As she poured the custard into the pumpkin shell, Garnet inhaled deeply. The fragrance of the mixture was pleasing.

I'm like the eggs. I was broken and was beaten, but God added sweetness to my life and set me in a new place. The heat—it's like a refiner's fire. I have to trust Him that all will turn out well in the end.

As she stirred up the fire, the door opened. "Mama?"

"Chris!"

"I've sent Ethan and Hester on with the Morton children. I came back because a few things need to be said. First, I'm glad you're our mother now. Father speaks well of others and won't speak ill of anyone. He speaks not at all of my mother. My memories of her are of her being quarrelsome, so I've followed Father's example and not said anything, either."

"I'm sorry, Christopher."

"That was in the past, and nothing can alter it." He puffed out his chest. "I'm not going to school this morning because I'm going to go to Uncle Erasmus, man-to-man."

"No." Samuel pushed the door wide open. "You're not."

———

Sam clapped a hand onto Chris's shoulder. "I'll put things in order. You belong at school."

Christopher looked at Garnet. "I meant what I said—I'm glad you're our mother." He left and shut the door.

As soon as the latch slid closed, Garnet turned back to the fire and lifted a cauldron.

"That's too heavy for you." Sam strode over and took it from her. He spied the pumpkin inside and gave her a long look.

"I used the cream I had left in the springhouse. It'll be the last pumpkin custard."

Sam lifted the cauldron onto the hook over the fire. "We'll all enjoy it, just as we appreciate all you do." He took Garnet's elbow and led her over to the table. "Sit. I need to speak with you."

She sank down onto a bench, but Sam felt too restless to join her. Instead, he paced toward the jump bed, turned, and approached her once again. "I spent the night in deep thought and prayer. I must speak some harsh truths."

Her face grew grim.

"I wed you because Erasmus forced me to in order to keep my children—or so I thought. But I gave him credit when 'twas not his. God brought you here before Erasmus Ryder thought up his schemes. The Lord merely allowed those schemes to unfold because He can redeem good from wickedness.

"I've spent years now rearing my sons. Protecting them—I do it naturally. Last night, you said when you'd wed me that my children became yours. 'Twas a bittersweet truth I pondered o'er most of the night. Sweet, because memory after memory came to mind of how you've shown your love for them—the praise you gave Christopher for driving the wagon so smoothly, the glee on Ethan's face when you call him over to lick a spoon, and the way you hold Hester's hand in yours as you walk."

"I love your children."

"I know. The bitter part of this is hard for me to confess."

Garnet sat a little straighter. Her hands—the way they moved to try to cover her belly—wrenched his heart. Sam straddled the bench and put his hands atop hers, and she gave him a startled look.

"I'd be lying to say I was happy to learn you were with child. It came as a shock to you, too. You've not said a word about this babe, and I tried to respect your silence by giving you time to accustom yourself to its arrival. Last night is the first time you've acknowledged you're carrying a life. You said God would add love. When the times comes, I have faith that He will fill you with love for this little one."

"He already has." Beneath his palms, he felt how she gently stroked her thumbs back and forth over the child she carried. "I'm blessed to have him."

Sam sat for a while and let that sweet truth fill the silence. Finally, he took a deep breath and looked at her earnestly. "In truth, I've worried I could not love this babe. 'Tisn't flesh of my flesh." The wounded look in her eyes tore at him. He hastened on. "But then I realized Naomi never gave her heart to our children; you have. 'Twasn't the blood tie that mattered. Then, too, there was Joseph. Joseph didn't sire Jesus, yet the Lord put His Son into Joseph's caring. God put your babe into my care."

"You promised to provide—"

"And a beggar's promise that was. It ate at me all night long." He reached between his shirt and doublet and pulled out what he'd worked on. "This is from the spinning wheel. The wood split badly, but I glued it back together. 'Tis smooth and probably stronger now than the other spokes."

Garnet looked confused.

Sam turned the piece so she could see what he'd done. "Look here. I carved a heart on it. I've not used words that will be lost in time. I carved this here, and it is past time I spoke to you of my love. Since you came, I've been so relieved that Hester is home and life has gone well, I didn't stop to recognize the truth. You filled my home with happiness. Not only that, Garnet—somehow, you filled my heart with love."

Sam placed the spoke in her hands and curled his fingers around hers. "We were both broken souls when God glued us together. Together, we are whole. God willing, we will have as many children together as there are spokes on your spinning wheel—but this is to remind you always that my heart is yours, and I will cherish this first child you carry."

Tears filled her eyes, making them glisten like just-polished silver. "Samuel, I bless the day you bought me. That day, you spared my life and gave me hope. Today, you've given me your heart, but I give mine in return. I love you, and my only regret is that there are only twelve spokes on that spinning wheel!"

Epilogue

H ere's your book, Mama."

"Thank you, Hester. I know I saw a recipe in here for pigeons." Garnet flipped through *The Art of Cookery, Made Plain and Easy*. It was the first book Samuel bought for her when he was teaching her to read better, and she treasured it.

"I can scarce believe Ethan netted this many pigeons. Hasn't he read *Poor Richard Improved* where Benjamin Franklin says, 'Kill no more pigeons than you can eat'?" Hester put the last handful of feathers into a bucket and laid a cloth across the top of it so they wouldn't blow away.

"Here we are, 'Pigeons in a Hole'." Garnet struggled to rise, and Hester pulled on her arm to help. "Thank you. Let's get these made."

Hester led her into the keeping room.

" 'Take your Pigeons, season them with beaten Mace, Pepper and Salt; put a little Piece of Butter in the Belly,'" Garnet read aloud. " 'Lay them in a Dish and pour a light Batter all over them, make with a Quart of Milk and Eggs, and four or five Spoonfuls of Flour; bake it, and sent it to Table. It is a good Dish.' It does sound tasty, don't you think?"

"Yes, but Father's going to be so eager to have the pumpkin custard that he probably won't notice anything you put on the table before it." Hester lifted five-year-old Prudence onto the small chest. "You did a nice job washing your hands, so you may help us cook."

Eight-year-old Molly set aside her sampler. "Mama, I finished stitching the alphabet. Do I get to help cook, too?"

"First have a care that you put the needle back in the case. Christopher was sore mad when he stepped on the last one you lost."

"I already did." Molly looked at the pigeons. "It's good Ethan netted so many. Those look dreadfully small. Is it greedy if I eat one all by myself?"

"You and Prudence will share one." Garnet smiled at Hester. "I expect we'll have a few guests by supper time."

"Oh, merry!" Prudence clapped her hands. "It's been forever since you and Goodwife Morton and Goodman Brooks played music for us all!"

"Prudy," Molly gave her little sister an exasperated look. "That's not what Mama meant."

Prudence's lower lip stuck out in a pout. "I like Goodwife Morton.

Why can't she come?"

Hester let out a trill of laughter. "She'll be here, but she's coming to help Mama."

"Mama, we'll help you." Prudence copied Molly and put a nubbin of butter inside a pigeon. "Father told us to be sure to help you lots."

"And you—" Garnet went silent as the next contraction hit.

Prudence turned to her. "Did you forget what you planned to say again?"

"She's probably thinking about how we need more butter. This is the last of what we have."

Garnet let out a shaky breath. "Yes, well, I suppose I'll take care of making more butter." She sat in the rocking chair Sam and Christopher had made for her right after she'd had Molly. "Ethan put the cream in the churn just awhile ago."

Having read how Benjamin Franklin devised an attachment that went from his wife's rocking chair to the butter churn, Samuel delighted in finding the diagram and making one for Garnet.

As she set her chair in motion and thereby started churning butter, Garnet smiled at her daughters. "Molly and Prudence, while Hester puts the pigeons in to bake, the two of you go on out to the garden and fill a bucket with peas, then sit in the shade and shell them."

"I like buttered peas," Molly said.

Ethan leaned against the doorjamb. "So do I. Mama knows it's my favorite song."

"Silly!" Prudence giggled. "We're talking 'bout supper."

Still wearing a rakish smile, Ethan looked at her. "I remember the last time you made pigeons. They tasted—"

Garnet held her breath and rocked a little faster as the next pain washed over her.

Ethan's grin fled as he bolted straight up. "Does Father know?"

"No." Garnet barely managed to squeeze out that word before the pain crested.

"'Course Father doesn't know we're having buttered peas." Prudence scratched her little nose. "Mama just decided."

Hester set the pigeons to bake, then decided. "You girls can go to Aunt Dorcas's house to pick the peas."

"Let's hurry! Christopher gives us piggyback rides!"

Ethan grabbed two-year-old Jane. "I'll take them over and fetch Biddie Laswell." He lifted Prudence. "Molly, I'm racing you. I have longer legs, but my arms are full."

Hester shook her head as they left. "Ten years ago, I wouldn't have dreamed I'd be glad to send children to Aunt Dorcas's."

"No one is beyond the love of God." Garnet smiled. "Your father was wise enough not to revile the Ryders when they wronged him." Erasmus hadn't changed his heart until he lay on his deathbed, but Dorcas had committed her heart to the Lord and her hands to doing good deeds. She couldn't manage the farm, so when Christopher married Mary Morton, Dorcas had invited them to her place. Instead of tobacco, wheat and corn now filled the fields.

"Garnet," Sam called from the yard.

"Yes?"

He dashed through the door and took a good, long look at her. "Hester, go fetch the midwife!"

"Ethan already said he'd bring back Biddie Laswell."

Sam didn't look reassured in the least. He cleared his throat. "Jane came so fast that Biddie didn't arrive in time. Go fetch Ruth Morton. Stay there and watch her little ones."

"Yes, Father."

He shook his finger at Garnet. "I should have figured out why you sent Andrew and Titus over to the Mortons' today."

"Samuel, you're the one who said they could go with Falcon and Thomas to pick out a sturgeon." Garnet bit her lip and rocked faster. When the contraction ended, she muttered, "I'm not going to be able to help salt down the behemoth when they return."

"I can do that, Mama."

Samuel started washing his hands. "Hester, enough talk. Make haste and fetch Ruth." He dried his big, capable hands and came toward her. "Let's put you to bed."

Garnet shook her head.

"What are you looking at?"

She let out a shaky breath. "The spinning wheel. A child for each spoke, remember?"

"Yes, but—"

"Chris, Ethan, Hester, Andrew... Remember how disappointed Hester was that she didn't get a sister when I had Andrew, then Titus?" Her voice died out as the next pain washed over her.

Sam let out a strained chuckle. "You made up for that with Molly, Prudence, and Jane."

Garnet reached over and held fast to his hand. "Bartholomew and Anne." They'd lost those two in their infancy.

"We loved them for the time the Lord granted them to us." Sam cupped her cheek. "God has blessed us again with this little one. Think on that."

Her hold on his hand tightened. As the pain subsided, Garnet rasped, "A child for each spoke. There's not one little one this time, Sam. Biddie told me 'tis twins."

"Twins!" His flummoxed expression wore off; then he rasped, "And you waited until now to tell me?"

"You hover and fret each time my days are accomplished and I'm to have a babe. Had we told you, you'd have been impossible."

"We've not prepared for two babes!"

"I have." She scooted to the edge of the rocking chair. "The butter will have to wait."

"This is no time to discuss churning butter! We need a second cradle." While he fretted, he helped her rise.

Garnet leaned into his warmth and strength. "They've shared a womb, Sam. They'll share the cradle just as happily." Another pain started, but the sensation shifted dramatically.

Sam swept her into his arms and laid her on their bed. "Ruth—"

"Won't be here in time." She gasped and grabbed for him. "These babes are coming faster than I thought!"

Fifteen minutes later, Sam wrapped their second baby in a blanket and sank onto the edge of the bed. "Healthy sons. Both of them. God be praised."

"Indeed, He's blessed us." Garnet accepted her other baby from him. "Two more things, though."

"What?"

"Take the pigeons out of the fire in about five minutes."

"I can do that. What else?"

"Either you explain to Hester why we now have more boys than girls, or you'd better figure out how to add another spoke to the spinning wheel!"

CATHY MARIE HAKE

Cathy has been married for twenty-eight years to the man she met at church when she was thirteen. They make their home in Southern California and have two adult children, two dogs, and countless books. Cathy is an RN who specializes in teaching Lamaze, breastfeeding, and baby care.

Spinning Out of Control

by Vickie McDonough

Dedication

This story is dedicated to my coauthors,
Cathy Marie Hake and Susan Page Davis.
Cathy took an interest in a wannabe author
and helped make a dream become a reality.
Sue, a stranger when we first started work on this collection,
soon became a critique partner and dear friend.
I love you both and appreciate all the help you've given me.
You're a blessing from God.

Chapter 1

Virginia, 1803

M—marry you?" Amy Rogers clutched her carpetbag to her chest and stared at the lanky wagon driver sitting next to her. Was he addlebrained? The roughest day of her life had just taken a turn for the worse.

Marry me. To wed, one had to take on a husband, and that was not something she wanted to do, especially not a stranger she'd only met an hour ago. Still, she didn't want to hurt the man's feelings after his kindness to her, but she couldn't encourage him.

"I truly appreciate your driving me from Stewart's Gap to my cousin's farm at no fee, but. . ."

"I know it's kinda spur of the moment to ask you to marry me, ma'am, but I have a little time before I needed to be back at the livery." Hank Foster pulled on the reins to stop the big horses in front of their destination. " 'Sides, I figure it don't hurt none to ask. Just thought I'd beat the rest of the single fellers to the punch. Once they see the likes of you, they'll all be heading out this way, hoping to court you."

Mr. Foster had skipped the courting part and gone straight to the marrying part. Amy shook her head. Even if she wanted a husband, she wouldn't marry a man who smelled like horse dung. Refusing his filthy hand, she held tightly to the side of the wagon as she clambered down on shaky legs. She might be desperate, but not enough to marry a total stranger. Not yet, at least.

The thin man dressed in faded baggy overalls tipped his hat. "I reckon I'll give you a little time to settle in and think on things. I'll come callin' in a few weeks. G'day, Miss Rogers." He hopped back in the wagon, clucked his tongue, and jiggled the reins. With a shake of their heads and a unified snort, the two large horses pulling the wagon plodded forward, harness jingling.

"No, wait!" Couldn't he get it through his head that she wasn't interested?

He gave a smile and friendly wave as he turned his team back toward town. "See you in a fortnight."

Clutching her carpetbag, she turned to face the weathered porch and willed her heart to stop its frantic pounding. Rejecting Mr. Foster had been simple compared to what she had to do now. How could she ask a cousin she hadn't seen in years for sanctuary?

Cousin Kathryn Walsh's log cabin looked smaller than Amy had expected. Perhaps Kathryn wouldn't want a cousin she barely knew living under her roof. As a child, Amy and her mother had twice visited Kathryn's parents at their large home in Richmond. But now her parents were gone, and Kathryn was her only living relative. If Kathryn couldn't—or wouldn't take her in—she had no idea where she'd go or how she would survive.

Taking a moment to collect herself, she tilted her head back and studied the second story of the log cabin. It looked as if it consisted of only a single room. A ladder with dead vines entangled around the rungs leaned against the south wall. Above it was an opening covered with a colorful bear claw quilt. The space looked just big enough for a person to climb through. The house had seen better days, but the smell of wood smoke spiraling from the tall chimney beckoned her. Though it was well past noon and the sun still shone overhead, the cool spring weather chilled Amy to the bone. Her stomach churned, whether from hunger or nervousness she wasn't sure.

Taking a deep breath and hugging the carpetbag to her chest, she hopped up the porch steps, the wood creaking under her weight. Her whole future depended on her cousin's generosity. If Kathryn wouldn't take her in, Amy didn't know what she'd do.

She lifted her trembling hand and knocked. While she waited for a response, she glanced over the property. A good-sized log barn and a smaller structure that looked like a little house were set off to the left. The house had a broken pane in the lone window. Someone had stuffed a rag through the hole to block the wind. Several chickens clucked and pecked around the outside of the barn, searching for their dinner. Though she couldn't see it, she caught a whiff of a hog nearby and lifted her hand over her nose. At one time, this was probably a nice farm, but it looked as neglected as a child's swing in the heart of winter.

Amy removed her gloves, hoping for a louder knock. She pounded on the door and winced when a splinter pierced her knuckle. Why was no one answering? Someone had to be home or there most likely wouldn't be a fire burning inside.

Tired, hungry, and determined to get out of the cold, Amy reached for the latch at the same time the door jerked open. A small black man with curly gray hair stared at her, eyes wide. He blinked, and then a big, gap-toothed grin replaced his worried frown. "Oh, praise the Lawd. Praise the Lawd. You jes' come right on in. Miz Kathryn, she needs you real bad."

Amy wasn't sure who the old man thought she was, but if Kathryn needed help, she would gladly come to her cousin's aid. She stepped inside and found herself in a large room that was a kitchen on one side and parlor on the other. The man took her bag and set it behind the front door.

"This'a way." He motioned toward a large opening in the wall to her right, and Amy stepped forward. Inside was a smaller room containing two beds. Her cousin lay writhing on the larger bed, fully with child.

"I'll jes' leave you with Miz Kathryn and go ask the Good Lawd to watch over her. You jes' let me know if'n you need any wood or water or anything." He hurried toward the doorway. "You give a holler when Mizzy Beth wakes, and I'll tend to her. I go pray now."

She watched the little old man hightail it out of the room like a cat with his tail on fire. His time spent in prayer might be put to better use going to town for a doctor than beseeching a God who didn't answer petitions.

Amy squelched the panic that made her want to swoon. She wondered who Missy Beth was at the same time she noticed a small lump lying under a quilt on the tiny bed in the corner of the room. A smattering of dark hair peeked out from the top of the colorful cover. Kathryn had a daughter.

"Ahhh!" Kathryn twisted sideways. One hand pressed up against the wall above her head while her other hand pushed against her rounded stomach. "Do I—do I know you?"

Fingers of fear wrapped around Amy's heart at Kathryn's pained expression. Was she having a troublesome birth? Taking a calming breath, Amy laid her gloves on the small table next to the bed and shrugged out of her wool cape. A chair sitting along the wall squeaked as she dragged it closer to the bed and laid her cape across its back. She wrung out a cloth lying in a bowl of water and laid it across Kathryn's forehead.

"I'm your cousin, Amy Rogers from Boston. I'm here to help you." *And perhaps you'll help me.*

Amy's stomach growled, and she pressed her hand against it, pushing away the desire to have her own need for sustenance met. She'd gone a full day without food. Going another hour or two wouldn't kill her. Her own problems seemed trivial to helping her cousin at the moment.

Stay calm. The last thing she wanted to do was to tend another sickbed, especially after the way things turned out last time. Wringing her hands, she looked at her cousin and summoned all her remaining strength. "Shhh, you just relax now."

After a moment, Kathryn's stiff body sank down into the bed as her pain seemed to lessen. A soft smile relaxed the tension around her pale lips. "Cousin Amy—how did you know I needed help?"

Amy twisted her hands in her lap. "I didn't. Actually, I came seeking help from you—but we can talk about that when you're feeling better."

Kathryn's blond hair, darkened with sweat, spread out against her pillow like strands of damp flax. Her nightcap lay askew on the unused pillow to her right, making Amy wonder where Kathryn's husband was. Why wasn't he helping her?

Her cousin breathed in and out, as if trying to force herself to relax. Amy had never had a baby—never had a husband for that matter—not that she wanted one.

She couldn't help wondering how long Kathryn had been suffering. At least she was calm enough now, thank goodness.

"It's too soon for the baby to come, Amy. It shouldn't come for at least another month." Kathryn reached over and gave Amy's arm a squeeze as she wondered how Kathryn could possibly get any larger with child. Amy wished she could flee out the door and run to the nearest neighbors' for help. Was there something special to do for a baby that came too early? Could it even survive? Suddenly, Kathryn's grip tightened. "Oh! Here comes another birth pang—"

If Kathryn squeezed any harder, Amy thought surely her fingers would pop off before the birth pain had passed. If not for Kathryn's grip, Amy thought she might bolt out the door, even though she had nowhere else to go.

Gritting her teeth, Amy tried to ignore her aching hand and concentrated on helping her cousin. Oh, if only she'd been allowed to help some of her married lady friends in Boston with their birthings then perhaps she'd know what to do, but the older women had insisted that an unmarried girl had no business attending childbirths.

"It's ta–king too long. Should have come by now—" Kathryn arched her back and groaned a sound unlike anything Amy had ever heard a woman utter.

Fear snaked around her chest and threatened to suffocate her. She glanced at the door. She could walk out and just keep walking. But no, she couldn't leave Kathryn to suffer alone.

Be brave. Tears blurred her eyes. "What do I do? How can I help you?"

"You can't. Just wait—"

After what seemed like hours, the pain lessened, and Kathryn relaxed again. "Oh, my back hurts."

Amy stood. "Can you roll onto your side? I could rub your back for you."

"I'll try." Kathryn removed the cloth from her head and wiped her face, and then with great effort, she wobbled onto her side. She grabbed her husband's pillow and hugged it to her chest. After a few moments her labored breathing returned to normal. "How's your family, Amy? It's been so long since we've heard from you."

"Shhh, we can talk later. You need your rest now." Amy gently eased onto the side of the bed and pressed her fist against Kathryn's lower back. Sweat drenched her cousin's clothing. "We need to change your gown."

"After the baby comes."

Amy moved her fist in little circles against her cousin's lower back.

"Ummm. . .that feels good." Kathryn heaved a deep sigh. "How are your parents?"

Amy wasn't sure what to say. She didn't want to upset her cousin further. "How are yours?"

"Oh. . .Momma and Father died of cholera several years back."

"I'm sorry for your loss." Amy winced and squeezed her eyes shut. So much for not upsetting Kathryn. "Both my mother and father are gone, too. Mother died from a bad heart two years ago, and Father—well, he died several weeks ago."

"I'm so sorry."

Both women remained quiet as Amy continued to massage her cousin's back. After a few minutes, Kathryn's body stiffened and her breath quickened. Her legs writhed, and she whimpered like an injured animal. Even though the muscles in Amy's arm ached, she continued to press her fist into Kathryn's back, hoping to give her cousin some relief. Suddenly, Kathryn swatted Amy's arm. "D–Don't touch me."

Clenching her hands in her lap, Amy sat back confused. Had she pressed too hard?

After a couple minutes, Kathryn rolled onto her back again and her breathing slowed. "I'm sorry. I don't mean to yell at you."

Leaning forward, Amy brushed her cousin's damp hair out of her face. "Don't worry about me. Just tell me what I can do to help you."

A tear trickled down Kathryn's cheek. "I—I don't know. Ben should have been back with the doctor by now. Something's wrong."

"Shhh, don't worry. I'm sure Ben is just fine. He's your husband?"

Kathryn's golden eyebrows lifted, and a soft smile tilted her thin lips. "No, Ben's my husband's younger brother. Micah is my husband. He's been gone so long. . ." She closed her eyes. Damp blond lashes brushed her pale cheeks.

Wondering why Micah Walsh had gone off and left his pregnant wife, Amy retrieved the washcloth from the other side of the bed, rinsed it in the water, and then placed it on Kathryn's head again. If she thought it would do any good, she'd petition God on her cousin's behalf. But praying hadn't worked when her mother had taken ill, so why should it work now?

After another hour of Kathryn's struggling, the little lump on the child's bed moved. Amy watched intrigued as a young, rosy-cheeked cherub wriggled out from under the quilt and sat up. Dark brown hairs had pulled free from her braids and stuck out all around her head. The little girl yawned and rubbed her eyes, then suddenly glanced at the bed, as if she'd just remembered her mother. Seeming satisfied that Kathryn was still there, the child's gaze traveled past her mother to Amy. Brown eyes, much like Amy's cousin's, widened in curiosity.

"Good afternoon. You must be Elizabeth. I think they call you Beth."

The child's concerned gaze darted between her mother and Amy. She wondered if the girl wanted to be at her mother's side but was afraid to move any closer to the stranger in the room. Beth glanced around her bed and under her pillow then pulled a rag doll wearing a blue dress from beneath the quilt. She hugged it to her chest.

Kathryn moaned, and Beth's worried gaze darted between her mother and Amy. The past half hour, Kathryn had been so tired that groaning was about all she could do. Amy feared for Beth. She shouldn't witness her mother's pain.

Standing, she stretched and pressed her hands to her back, which ached from hours of traveling in bumpy wagons. Beth scooted to the far corner of the little bed and eyed her warily.

Amy wished that old man had told her his name. She was surprised Kathryn owned a slave, though she probably shouldn't have been since her cousin's parents had owned several house slaves last time she visited there.

She crossed the small sleeping area and went into the big room. The combination parlor and kitchen held three large wooden rockers and a smaller one that circled a braided rug covering the wooden floor. A three-foot-high stack of wood sat next to the inviting stone hearth. A large pot hung over the flames, though Amy hadn't noticed the aroma of anything cooking in the air. Had the old man come in and fixed supper without her even noticing?

Her stomach growled, reminding her how long it had gone unattended. She walked over and peeked in the pot. Hot water. Disappointed, she glanced around and saw a partially cut loaf of bread. She tore off a hunk and shoved it into her mouth, savoring the fresh flavor. Cooking utensils lay jumbled in a small wooden crate. Jars of green beans and canned fruit lined a shelf.

Shaking herself, she headed for the front door. She could study the house later, but right now, she needed to find that old man and get back to her cousin. She jerked the heavy door open, and before she could step off the porch, the man hurried toward her. He must have been sitting inside the little house and watching out the window. *Bless his heart.*

"Beth is awake now. I think it would be best if she didn't have to watch her mother suffer."

"Yes'm. Yes'm. That's jes' what I was thinking. I'll take Mizzy Beth to play in the barn. Never seen a youngster what liked animals as much as that one." He hobbled up the porch steps, as if the effort pained him.

Amy stepped back to let him pass, though in a normal setting she would have been expected to stand her ground and force him to go around. "Beth is leery of me. Of course, she has no idea who I am."

The man paused and scratched his hairline. "Who did you say you was?"

Amy grinned. "I never said. You hustled out of the cabin faster than the British left America after the war. I never got a chance to tell you."

His whole body shook with a wheezy chuckle. "I knowed the moment I laid eyes on you that you had a good heart and would help Miz Kathryn, no matter who you be."

"I'm Kathryn's cousin. Amy Rogers."

The man doffed his cap. "A pure pleasure, Miz Amy. I be Jonah." He smiled then motioned for her to enter before him. She stepped inside, her eyes readjusting to the darker interior.

Jonah. That was it? A single name. No other explanation. The old man was much more talkative than Amy remembered the slaves being at Kathryn's folks' house. Ignoring her curiosity, she hurried back to her patient's side.

Jonah shook his head and twisted his worn cap in his hands. "Mistah Ben should have been back a long time ago, Miz Kathryn. That doctor, he must've been off doctoring somewheres else."

Amy's gaze darted to the old man. Would she have to deliver this child herself? Surely Jonah wouldn't be much help when it came to birthing a baby.

"I hope you're wrong about the doctor, Jonah." Kathryn offered him a weak smile. "Thank you for watching Elizabeth."

The girl must have slipped to her mother's side after Amy had gone for Jonah, because she now snuggled on the bed with Kathryn. Beth gave her mother a sweet kiss and hug. "Go see horsies, Mama?"

Kathryn's face tightened with pain. "Yes—baby."

"Come along, Mizzy Beth. Them horses is a waitin'."

Unaware of her mother's struggle, Beth giggled and shinnied off the bed. She trustingly took Jonah's hand and looked back over her shoulder, giving Amy a curious glance.

"There's a pot of hot water on the fire, if'n you've need of it." Jonah nodded toward the fireplace. He took a brown cape off a peg behind the door and tied it on Beth's shoulders then secured a cap over her long, dark hair. Amy wondered if the girl's hair color resembled her father's. Jonah and Beth stepped outside, and Amy secured the door shut.

"Amy! The baby's coming."

She scurried back to Kathryn's side. "What should I do? I—I never helped birth a baby before."

"Help me—sit up."

Kathryn pressed against the bed but was too weak to push herself up. Amy lifted her skirt and slid onto the bed. She hoisted up the exhausted woman and propped the two pillows behind her.

"Thank you." Kathryn laid her head against the wall and moaned softly. After a few moments rest, she drew her legs up. "Towels. Water."

Amy hurried into the parlor and found the towels on the table. Using a notched piece of wood, she swung around the iron arm holding the pot until it was no longer over the fire. She snagged a ladle hanging next to the hearth and scooped some water into a wooden bucket. Quickly, she unlaced her French bodice, removed it, and pulled an apron from her travel bag. She tied the apron over her chemise, wishing she could take away her cousin's pain.

Why did women have to suffer so much to bring a child into the world?

On a whim, she grabbed the knife lying on the table, along with the towels and bucket of water. Amy rushed back into the sleeping room and nearly stumbled. A tiny baby lay motionless on the bed. Tears blurred Amy's eyes. She'd never seen a brand-new life before.

How amazing! One moment Kathryn had one child, and in another moment, she was the mother of two. The perfectly formed infant had ten tiny toes and fingers and a cute little nose. Awestruck, Amy couldn't move. It was almost enough to make her believe in God. But shouldn't the baby be moving?

"Knife." Uttering the single word seemed to sap Kathryn of all her strength, but it pushed Amy into motion.

"I have it." She set the bucket on the chair and bent over the bed.

"Tie the cord tight—two places—'bout a thumb's length apart, then cut in between."

Amy winced. Wouldn't such a feat hurt the baby?

"Hur–ry. Cut it."

Swallowing her fear and apprehension, Amy found two pieces of ribbon lying on the bedside table. She tied them tightly around the baby's cord about an inch and a half apart; then she snipped the cord in half. The baby girl jerked—perhaps from the touch of Amy's cold hands—sucked in a deep breath, and then wailed a warbling cry 'til her face turned red. It was the most beautiful sound Amy had ever heard. Almost lovely enough to make her want to marry and have her own child. But to have a child one must have a husband, and Amy never wanted to experience what her own mother had been through.

She toweled off the infant then laid the baby on her mother's chest, as Kathryn gave her daughter a proud but weak smile. Amy stuffed the spare pillow under the baby to help support it, then helped her cousin untie her chemise so she could nurse her child.

Heat rose to Amy's cheeks as Kathryn lifted the baby to her breast. Her gaze darted away, then back to mother and child.

While the baby learned to suckle, Amy tended Kathryn. She wiped her cousin's brow then turned back to tend the bed. Her heart plunged down to her toes at the dark stain on the bedding. Should there be so much blood after a birthing?

"Promise me." Kathryn's voice was a mere whisper. "Take care of my girls."

"What?" Amy glanced at her cousin, a sense of impending doom filling her. Kathryn's face looked as pale as Amy's mother's had right before she died. Her gray, sunken eyes sent a saber of fear straight into Amy's heart.

"Care for Micah, my girls. Please—"

Amy sat beside Kathryn and lifted a trembling hand to brush her cousin's hair from her face. "No, sweetie, you'll do that yourself. Just as soon as you get some rest—" Her voice broke, choked off with emotion. *This can't be happening. Why now? I just found you again.*

"Micah must name the baby." She placed a gentle kiss on her daughter's blond hair.

"Yes. Of course. If that's what you want."

"He didn't know." Kathryn closed her eyes and tears ran down the side of her nose.

"Know what?"

"Micah. I didn't tell him."

Amy's heart pitched. "You didn't tell Micah about the baby before he left?"

Kathryn barely nodded then gazed down at her daughter. Amy wanted to ask why she hadn't told her husband she was with child. And where was this missing husband? He was just like her father. Never there when she needed him. Were all men the same?

"Stay, Amy. Care for my family."

Tears blurred Amy's vision and stung her eyes. Her throat tightened, making it hard to talk. "Yes. I will. Now don't you fret."

Stay with me, Kathryn. I know nothing about caring for babies.

Kathryn's lips turned up in a soft smile then straightened, and her arm slipped off the pillow onto the bed. Amy grabbed the baby to keep her from falling to the floor then cuddled the tiny newborn child.

She raised a trembling hand to her cousin's mouth and felt nothing. Not a single breath. A tear tickled her cheek as she touched Kathryn's neck, just under her chin. No heartbeat. Amy sucked in a sob and cried for her dead cousin. She cried for this nameless, motherless child. She cried for Beth and Micah. And she cried for herself.

Chapter 2

Micah Walsh's chest swelled with thankfulness to God. He'd been gone from home six weeks longer than he'd planned because of a lengthy illness and several unusually heavy snowfalls that trapped him on the far side of the Appalachian Mountains. Winter had refused to yield to spring, but here on the east side of the mountains, in the foothills, the temperatures had warmed and spring had won the battle.

He smiled, knowing he was almost home. Just another few hours and he'd be back on his land—land that had belonged to his parents and grandparents, even before America was a free nation. Land his family had shed blood to keep.

His heart ached to see his beautiful wife and daughter. Had Beth grown much in the five months that he'd been gone trapping? Was she talking better? Would Kathryn welcome him home?

His city-born wife had not adapted to farm life as he had hoped. While their newlywed love carried them the first year, things had gotten worse recently, and Kathryn had grown more dissatisfied. He hoped with all the furs he was returning home with that he could barter and make life a bit easier for her. He'd prayed all these months that God would heal their relationship and show him how to be a better husband.

His thoughts drifted to his farm, and his mind raced with all the things he could do with the money he'd get from the four mule loads of furs that trailed behind his horse. He hadn't wanted to leave his family for so long, but two years of lean harvests necessitated such a drastic venture. He hoped Kathryn understood. She'd acted strangely during the final days of his preparation but never once complained about him leaving. She had probably dreaded his being gone so long.

It wasn't as if he'd left her alone. Jonah was there. And Ben. Micah had decided it was time for his younger brother to take responsibility and care for the farm while he was gone, so he'd left him in charge. Ever since their parents died and left the farm to Micah, he'd had trouble with Ben. His seventeen-year-old brother said since he didn't inherit the farm, he saw no reason to work on it like a slave. Ben didn't know that Micah planned on splitting the farm, just as soon as his little brother showed he was man enough to care for his half. Micah heaved a deep sigh. He figured leaving for a few months would force Ben to step up and handle things.

"I sure hope I didn't make a mistake."

Micah reveled in the greenness of the Shenandoah Valley after months of looking at gray skies, white snow, and barren trees. Reining his horse to a stop he marveled at the colorful wildflowers and trees starting to bloom. Rusty snorted and pawed, anxious to be on his way, but Micah held him steady. The afternoon sun warmed him, and a choir of birds chirped their cheerful tunes.

To Micah's right, a patch of dogwoods was shedding its pink and white flowers in favor of bright oval green leaves. The tiny purple flowers of the blue-eyed grass stretched their faces toward the sun. "Ah, Lord, thank You for the beauty of Your creation."

He nudged his horse forward, feeling a tug as the lead rope attached to the first mule pulled taut against his leg. The tired mules were not happy to move away from the tender green feast at their hooves. After several hee-haws of resistance, the overloaded quartet reluctantly plodded forward.

Micah smiled. Tonight he'd hold Kathryn close and nuzzle her sweet-smelling hair—but he should probably take a bath first. She'd be proud of his success, though less acceptable of how he currently smelled. As soon as he cashed in his furs, restocked the pantry, and bought a few fripperies for Kathryn and Beth, he would find the best broodmares in the area and buy a dozen or so. He'd finally realize his dream of raising horses.

Tobacco and cotton were popular crops and had made many Virginia farmers wealthy, but Micah refused to raise them. Unlike most of his neighbors, owning another human just didn't sit right with him. He'd never owned a slave, but he couldn't afford to hire the workers needed for either labor-intensive crop. He grew corn and wheat, though two years of above average rainfall had caused most of his crop to rot. But that was in the past. He couldn't shake the feeling that this year's crop would be a good one, providing Ben plowed the fields and started planting as he was supposed to.

Micah whistled a jolly tune. Life was good. He kicked Rusty into a trot, anxious to be home.

Around midnight, his horse nickered and picked up his pace. Amazingly, even after months away, the faithful animal knew he was home. A short while later they stopped in front of the barn, and Micah studied the area. The full moon cast a warm glow, but Micah couldn't tell if things had changed much.

He dismounted and stretched out the kinks in his back, happy to know he wouldn't have to spend tomorrow on the back of a horse. After unsaddling Rusty and putting him in his stall with a fresh manger of hay, Micah unpacked his four mules and put them in the pasture. He stashed his furs in a hidden storage area below the barn then headed for the cabin with a wide smile on his face. He couldn't wait to see Kathryn's expression when she realized he was finally home.

Opening the door quietly, so not to wake anyone, he slipped inside, crossed the room to the fireplace, and poked the ashes. They flickered and sparked bright orange. He tossed on some kindling, because once Kathryn knew he was home, sleep would flee and she'd want to hear all about his trip. The kindling sputtered and sparked, then flamed to life. Standing, Micah laid his arm on the mantel and watched the flames dance and grow, sending its wave of heat over his tired, cold body. The faint aroma of fresh-baked bread tantalized his senses. It was so good to be home again.

Amy froze, straining her ears for any sounds out of the ordinary. Something had awakened her. Perhaps it was just an animal prowling around outside. After a month on the Walsh farm, she still wasn't used to the country sounds. It was all so much different from city life in Boston.

She sat up in bed and listened for Missy. Some nights the baby slept straight through, which was a good thing because Sookie, the wet-nurse slave Ben had borrowed from a neighbor, slept like a hibernating bear on her floor mat. If Missy did awaken, Amy would get up and change her, then wake Sookie.

The slave girl had hardly said a word the whole time she'd been at the Walsh farm. Amy's heart went out to her, and she'd tried hard to make friends, but Sookie preferred keeping to herself. Perhaps she was still grieving the loss of her young husband and child. Ben had told Amy how Sookie's husband had been injured while working and died after his wounds had gotten infected. Then Sookie's baby was born too early to survive.

Amy rubbed her eyes, sorry that the young woman had endured so much pain. Was it hard for Sookie to nurse Missy? There wasn't much Amy could do about that, but she could be more diligent in trying to make friends with Sookie.

Amy yawned and felt around on the pillow for her nightcap. The ribbon that secured it kept coming untied. She didn't like wearing the crazy thing anyway. Finally, she gave up her search.

She lay down again and thought about all that had happened the past month. How her life had changed. In a way, it was a relief her father had finally passed on. She no longer wondered when he'd come home or if there'd be food on the table. Kathryn had left behind a good-sized root cellar filled with a bounty of vegetables and fruit. The smokehouse still held some meat, and Ben was a decent hunter, when she could get the stubborn lad to go hunting. He was sweet, with a willful streak, and at seventeen, he was only two years younger than she.

Some nights it was a relief to see him head off to his room upstairs. At times, he wore her down more than the two little girls put together.

Beth was finally warming to her. At first, the three-year-old only wanted her uncle or Jonah to handle her, which made getting her dressed in the morning an ordeal.

Amy yawned again and relaxed against the pillow. A smile tugged at her lips as she thought about their numerous conversations about Missy's name. Ben wanted a modern name like Charlotte or Henrietta. Jonah preferred something biblical such as Dorcas or Martha. In the end, they just called her Missy, just like Jonah called Beth, Mizzy Beth—only Missy didn't have a second part. Amy wondered if the child would ever have a real name, since it had been Kathryn's wish for Micah to name her. It seemed Missy's father had abandoned both girls for good.

And wasn't that just like a father? To be unreliable and irresponsible?

Perhaps he had run into some kind of trouble while trapping. For the girls' sake, she hoped not. She flipped onto her side. Perhaps she wasn't being fair to Micah Walsh. But then again, what would he say when he found out that Kathryn had died because she wasn't skilled enough to save her? Would he toss her out of his home without a second thought?

Her eyelids lowered of their own accord. Amy didn't want to travel down that road again. She'd endured more than her share of guilt. At least she had cared for Missy, and the child was thriving.

Amy yawned. Morning would come soon enough, and she needed her rest. Jonah had agreed to clean and fix up an old spinning wheel she'd found in the corner of the barn. In the morning, she'd bring it up to the house, and if time allowed, start spinning some flax.

As she relaxed and her body grew limp, she heard someone drag a piece of wood off the pile and drop it into the fireplace.

Amy bolted upright, wide-awake. Someone was in the house. Her heart stampeded. Tossing aside the quilt, she slid off the bed and tiptoed to the doorway. During the day, a colorful quilt hung over the opening between the sleeping room and the parlor, but at night, they needed the warmth of the fire, so she left the quilt pulled aside.

Eerie shadows danced on the walls from the growing fire. Jonah and Ben never came inside the cabin once they'd gone to bed. This must be an intruder. She'd give her life to protect the girls, though she hoped it wouldn't come to that.

Fishing around in the dark, she groped for the musket she knew sat in the corner. She'd told Ben she had no need to learn how to load the confusing weapon, but now she wondered if she'd been wrong. Her hand landed on the cold metal, and her fingers tightened around it. Ever so slowly she lifted it up then clutched it to her chest.

Gathering her courage, she peered around the doorway. Her heart leaped to her throat. She smelled the bear of a man before she saw him. And he looked just like a grizzly bear with that thick fur coat and long hair. He stood warming his hands at the fire.

For a moment, she considered screaming. Ben would hear her through the opening in the roof that allowed heat to his room upstairs, and he'd be downstairs in an instant—provided he woke up. But then her hollering would most likely awaken the girls, and they'd be frightened. She almost wanted to ask Jonah's God for help.

But it was up to her to protect Kathryn's sweet babies—and she was up to the task.

Ignoring the chilly floor against her bare feet and clutching the musket like a club, she tiptoed toward the intruder. Her hands shook, and her knees almost gave way. Surely the man could hear her heart ricocheting in her chest.

Think of the girls.

As she moved closer, the man's odor grew stronger. How in the world could he live with himself?

Four more feet.

Three feet.

Please don't turn around—and please don't let me kill him.

Amy lifted the musket and swung with all her might. For once she wished that she were taller than five and a half feet. The weapon connected with a *thud*. The wide-eyed man turned his bearded face toward her, the flames of the fire illuminating his cheek. Her heart pounded like a blacksmith's hammer. She stepped backwards, tightening her grasp on her weapon. His questioning gaze latched onto hers for a split second, and then his eyes rolled upward. His knees buckled, and he dropped to the ground in front of the fireplace with a loud *thump*.

Chapter 3

Micah clawed his way through the darkness and pain, focusing on the dancing light in the distance. He blinked, and a fireplace took shape. His fireplace. He rolled onto his back, hoping to ease the throbbing in his temple, and waited until the room stopped spinning. Reaching up, he touched his forehead, wincing when he made contact with something moist. He pulled his arm back and looked at his fingers.

Blood?

How had he managed to trap in the mountains all winter and not get injured, yet as soon as he stepped foot inside his home he got smacked upside the head?

At the sudden thought of an intruder in his cabin, he forced his sluggish body to a stand. A wave of nausea washed over him, and he grabbed hold of the mantel to steady himself. If someone wanted him dead they'd had plenty of time to accomplish the task while he was unconscious. Confusion worked its way through his dizziness and pain.

Opening his eyes, he scanned the room, instantly regretting having moved. After a moment, he tried again, and his gaze landed on a musket pointed straight at his heart. Catching his breath, he eased his gaze up to his captor. A wide-eyed waif with messed up hair and dark eyes stared back at him.

He squeezed his eyes shut, then opened them to make sure he wasn't seeing things. On second glance, he realized a woman—not a youth—stood before him in her nightgown and bare feet. Who was she?

The fire beside him flickered and popped. A bead of sweat trickled down his temple. He needed to shed his bearskin coat before he passed out again, but he was afraid to let go of the mantel. It was difficult to believe that a woman so small could pack such a wallop.

He loosened his belt with his free hand and dropped it to the floor. His heavy coat spread open, and he shrugged his shoulder out.

The woman took a step back. "Just what is it you want?" The musket in her hand shook, proving to Micah she wasn't as confident as she sounded. She tossed her head like a wild filly. "There's some bread under that towel on the table. If you're hungry, take it and get out."

Micah clenched his jaw as anger and concern surged through him at being told to leave his own home. Where was Kathryn? His gaze darted toward the inky blackness of the sleeping room and back to the woman.

Her gaze followed his, then returned back to him. "M—my husband will be back any time now. You'd best get out of here before he does."

Micah noticed she kept her voice down—probably so as not to wake whoever was sleeping. Fear and concern fought their way to the top rung of his emotions. Where was his family?

Three steps brought him to the table. The woman's eyes widened even more. Light from the fireplace danced around the shadows darkening her face. He had to get that musket before she fired it at him. He took another step in her direction, and she suddenly swung the musket around and waved it over her shoulder as if she were going to club him again.

"Don't come any closer."

He had no desire to fight a woman. A Bible verse darted into his mind: *"A soft answer turneth away wrath: but grievous words stir up anger."*

"I don't mean you any harm." Micah held up his hands as if in surrender.

When she didn't respond, he pulled out a chair at the table and dropped into it. He could easily overpower this woman, but he didn't want to get shot if the musket happened to have powder and ball in it. He sank his head into his hands and pressed on his forehead, hoping to make the aching cease. After a moment, he reached for the towel covering the bread, yanked it off the loaf, and dabbed his forehead. The fragrant scent of fresh bread just about did him in. Pushing his thoughts away from food, he concentrated on the stranger and asked, "Just who are you? And where's my family?"

Micah heard the woman's sharp intake of breath. When she didn't respond, he glanced up, wondering why she had gasped. She'd backed up clear into the corner by the front door and held the musket across her chest.

"Look," he said, his patience wearing thin, "I don't mean you any harm. I'm just hurt and confused." Micah ran his hand across his thick beard. No wonder the woman appeared half scared to death. He probably looked and smelled like some kind of mountain man. "I'm Micah Walsh. This is *my* house. Where's my wife?"

————

Amy pressed against the front door, wishing with all her being she could open it and run outside, away, anywhere but here. It didn't matter if it was chilly outside or not. Anything would be better than telling Micah Walsh his wife was dead. Would he blame her? Send her packing? And she had clubbed him unconscious! Amy faced him with remorse.

Did it matter if he held her responsible? He couldn't blame her any more than she blamed herself. There should have been something she could have done to save Kathryn. The doctor—once he had finally arrived that awful day—told Amy it wasn't her fault. He didn't even think he would have been able to save her. He'd said, "Sometimes it's meant to be this way. God wanted to call Kathryn home."

That manner of thinking confused Amy. Her own mother's doctor had said something similar the day her mother died. Amy still didn't understand why God hadn't spared her. She'd been the only person who'd ever loved Amy. Blinking back tears of longing for what couldn't be, she lifted her head to face Micah Walsh.

Somehow she had to find it within herself to tell him about his wife. If only she were braver. And on top of everything, she'd wounded him. Perhaps she couldn't help him with the pain in his heart, but she could treat the wound she'd inflicted—and it would give her time to work up her courage.

Amy set the musket in the corner by the door then moved over to the table. Before he turned in each night, Ben made sure there was a bucket of fresh water inside, in case anyone wanted a drink. Micah sat at the table with his head in his hands. He looked exhausted. But she had a feeling he wouldn't be sleeping anytime soon.

With a tug, she pulled the bread towel from his hand and dipped a clean end into the bucket. "Turn toward the fire."

He lifted his head and raised an eyebrow. She trembled at his closeness and tried to ignore the question in his gaze. The chair squeaked against the floor as he turned it toward the fireplace. Amy didn't want to touch this man. She'd spent the last month both worrying about him and despising him for leaving Kathryn. But he hadn't known that his wife was with child. Would he still have gone trapping if he had?

Even with the glow from the fire shining on Micah's head, it was too dark for Amy to see well enough to doctor his wound. Taking a twig of kindling, she stuck it in the fire and lit the wall lantern closest to the table.

Micah blinked at the brightness and glanced at her. Amy looked down and felt the skin on her face tighten with embarrassment. She was standing next to a stranger, and she was dressed only in her nightgown.

"Oh!"

She darted around the table, tiptoed into the sleeping room, and grabbed her bed jacket. Tying it shut, she checked on the children. She could barely make out Beth's bed but could hear the girl's soft breathing. The baby's bed was dark in the shadows on the side of the room where Sookie slept. Though Amy couldn't see little Missy, she knew the child would let her know when she'd awakened. Amy eased out of the room, hoping Sookie's soft snores would hide any noises she made. She dropped down the quilt to cover the sleeping room doorway and made her way back to Micah.

His arms rested on the table, and he'd laid his head down. Amy swallowed back regret for clubbing him so hard. She'd known she would only get one chance to take down such a big man, so she'd used all her strength.

I was protecting the children.

Amy picked up the damp cloth, wondering again how badly she'd hurt Mr. Walsh. She expected he'd be demanding to know where his wife was, but he'd only asked the one time. Perhaps he sensed something was wrong.

She reached out her hand then yanked it back. The only men she'd ever touched had been those helping her out of a coach or wagon. She couldn't even remember ever touching her father.

Heaving a deep breath, Amy reached forward and lifted a dark thatch of hair off Mr. Walsh's forehead. Her heart stumbled at the sight of a long cut. At least it was a narrow enough wound that it should heal fine without her having to sew it up. With quick work, she wiped off the blood, applied some medicinal salve, then wrapped a cloth around his head and tied it.

Other than wincing a few times he'd said nothing. Now that she was done, he looked up at her with tired eyes. "How's Beth?" The words came out in a soft rush.

"Sleeping." Amy turned away, hoping he wouldn't see the pain in her gaze. She looked up at the ceiling, wishing she could petition Jonah's God for help. How could she tell this man about his wife?

Amy took a step away from the table. She needed to soak the towel in cold water before the blood set. As she moved forward again, a tight fist clamped around her wrist. Water sloshed out of the bowl, splashing her bedclothes and splattering on the floor. Her heart nearly leaped from her chest.

"Tell me," he said, his voice low and gravelly. "What happened to Kathryn?"

Micah knew in his heart that something was wrong. He'd seen the fear and apprehension in the woman's eyes. She looked like a spooked filly with a wolf on her tail. He wasn't a wolf, but she had no way of knowing.

A deep uneasiness settled in his spirit when she'd avoided his questions about Kathryn. His wife wasn't here. He knew that much. All during the time the woman tended his wound, he'd prayed. Prayed for his family. At least little Beth was safe in her bed. Perhaps Kathryn was out, helping a neighbor. Yes, that had to be it.

The chair across from him screeched as she pulled it away from the table and sat down. He didn't want to look into those sympathetic eyes, but her gaze held his for several moments before she broke the connection.

With a shaking hand, she smoothed her hair down then swiped at her eyes. "I don't know how to tell you."

Fear clutched Micah's heart. "Just say whatever it is. Please."

Like a flittering hummingbird, she looked at him and then away. "Kathryn died. Right after I arrived here."

An ache of loss lanced his being. "No. It can't be true." He leaned his head against the chair and stared up at the ceiling, fighting back tears. If only he hadn't left perhaps. . .

"Oh Lord, please, no." Tears stung his eyes.

His and Kathryn's marriage hadn't been the best, but he loved her. He knew in his heart the well-to-do city girl had married him—a country farmer—to spite her parents. But it hadn't mattered to him. He loved her, in spite of her persnickety ways at times.

Numb with shock, Micah wiped his burning eyes. How long had this woman been staying here, caring for Beth? Where was his brother? And Jonah? What else had changed in the five months he'd been gone?

Micah shoved to his feet, ignoring the spinning room. He took a feeble step toward the sleeping room. Perhaps Kathryn was actually snuggled safe in their bed. Weaving sideways, he took another tentative step. Why had this woman hit him so hard? And just who was she? He'd never seen her before.

Halting, he faced her. "What's your name?"

He saw her delicate throat move as she swallowed. "Amy Rogers."

Micah closed his eyes and contemplated that name. Why did it sound familiar?

"I'm Kathryn's cousin, from Boston."

From the sleeping room, he heard something that sounded like a lamb's bleating. It rose in intensity. Then the quilt covering the sleeping room doorway flipped aside, and his daughter padded out in her nightgown, rubbing her eyes.

Beth!

Micah's heart jumped. Oh, how she'd grown. At least an inch. He needed her in his arms, comforting him. He needed to comfort her.

Beth looked around, and when her eyes landed on him, they opened wide. She cast a frantic glance at Miss Rogers.

Kneeling, he opened his arm. Beth loved to run to him and then be tossed up in the air. "Come give me a hug, Punkin."

His daughter cast him an inquisitive glance; then her eyebrows dipped together, and she started moving forward. But instead of running to him, she made a wide arc around him and ran to the stranger, wrapping her arms around the woman's lap.

If his heart hadn't already broken at the news of Kathryn, it did just then.

Beth doesn't know me.

"Missy is crying, Mama."

Mama? How dare Miss Rogers allow his daughter—Kathryn's daughter—to call her Mama! Tightening his fists and clenching his jaw, Micah watched the woman kneel and give his daughter a hug. His blood boiled. He wanted to yell and express his anger at this intruder, but he couldn't make a stink about it with Beth there. As he looked at his daughter, his fury melted like a candle set too close to a fire.

"Beth, dear, this is your father. He's returned home." Miss Rogers's kind tone calmed the storm brewing inside him.

Beth gazed up at him with wide, curious eyes. She studied him then shook her head like a little schoolteacher. "Nuh uh. Him's not Papa."

Miss Rogers's eyebrows dipped down as if she might believe the child.

Micah stood, holding on to the back of a chair for support. "I assure you I am Micah Walsh. Just call Ben or Jonah if you don't believe me. They are still here, aren't they?"

The woman stood, holding Beth in her arms, and nodded.

"Them's sleeping," Beth said. "But Missy waked up."

Micah heard the noise in the bedroom getting louder and recognized it as a baby's cry. He glanced at Miss Rogers's hand. Perhaps he should think of her as Mrs. Rogers. She wasn't wearing a wedding ring, but then not all married women did. Micah rubbed at his heavy beard, suddenly realizing why Beth probably didn't recognize him. At home he rarely wore a beard, preferring to be clean-shaven. In the morning he'd remedy that.

Struggling with all the emotions surging through him, he watched Mrs. Rogers give Beth a drink from a cup then gently press the girl's head down until it rested on her shoulder. Oh, how he wanted to hold his daughter. To have her rest against *his* shoulder. His fingers tingled with anticipation.

"Let me put Beth back to bed and get the baby. Then we can talk."

Her waist-length fawn-colored hair swished back and forth as she carried Beth back to bed. It was rather plain compared to Kathryn's golden tresses.

He blinked at the stinging in his eyes. How long had his wife been dead? Why hadn't he sensed it? And why had Ben allowed this stranger to come in and care for his daughter instead of a neighbor?

Overcome with weariness and grief, Micah crossed the room and flopped down in his rocking chair. He ran his hand through his long hair. How could Kathryn have died? She was perfectly fine when he left. Did she have an accident? Get sick?

Micah thought again about how Mrs. Rogers had allowed Beth to call her Mama, and indignation coursed through him like a raging river. Of all the nerve! The child had a mother and needed to be reminded of her—not allowed to forget.

He stormed to his feet and paced the room. This was his home. Beth was *his* daughter. And this woman had to go!

Enjoying her sweet baby scent, Amy jiggled Missy against her shoulder, took a strengthening breath, and went back into the parlor. Her heart ached for Micah Walsh. She'd seen the devastation in his expression when Beth ran to her instead of him.

Her nose wrinkled at the pungent blend of male odor, wood smoke, and that furry thing Mr. Walsh had been wearing. Would he take offense if she put his bear rug out on the porch?

No, better not give him another reason to be angry with her.

Missy fussed but didn't scream. Amy knew the baby would be all right for a few more minutes—long enough to get her changed—but she would need to nurse soon. Sookie would have to feed her in the sleeping room if Mr. Walsh lingered.

As much as she'd fretted over his abandoning his wife and children, she'd never once considered what it would mean to her when he returned. Where would he sleep? If he wanted his bed back, she and Sookie would have to find someplace else to bed down. But where? They couldn't very well stay in this small cabin if he was here.

Amy barely glanced at the back of the pacing man, relieved not to have to see his upsetting expression again. She eased into a rocker, unwrapped Missy, and then quickly changed her. Pressing the infant to her shoulder, she stood, waited for Mr. Walsh to pass by again, then set the wet diaper in a bucket near the front door. Missy's warm lips and little tongue rooted around on Amy's neck, looking for a midnight snack, and her sweet baby breath stirred something maternal inside Amy as it always did.

Mr. Walsh pivoted suddenly, half scaring Amy's wits from her. Missy squeaked when Amy jumped back, pressing her shoulders against the door, to put some space between her and Mr. Walsh. He stepped closer. Anger and pain formed creases across his brow. The agony in his eyes made her want to take his hand and comfort him. Instead, Amy swallowed hard and tightened her grasp on Missy. She couldn't fault him for hurting. He must have loved Kathryn more than she thought he did.

He ran his hand through his hair then grabbed hold of his nape. For a moment, his eyes softened a speck. "Look, Mrs. Rogers. . ." Sighing, he looked away.

Odd. . .why did he think she was married?

"I appreciate all that you've done for Beth. But I'm home now, and I can care for her." He stepped back, walked over to the mantel, and leaned against it, facing the fire.

Amy's heart quickened. What did he mean? She licked her dry lips as Missy let out a frustrated squeal. "I don't understand."

He turned; his steady gaze revealed no compassion. "Come morning, I want you to take your baby and go home. My family needs to be with me, and you need to leave."

Chapter 4

Micah leaned down against the ax handle and wiped the sweat from his brow. Through the trees he could just barely see Ben struggling with the plow horse as they walked back and forth cutting rows into the dark soil. The fields should have been plowed weeks ago. What had his brother been doing the past five months?

Pulling himself back to his work, Micah eyed the huge stacks of wood spread out all around him. In spite of the cool morning, his shirt clung to his moist skin. No matter how hard he worked, he couldn't forget that he hadn't been there for his wife when she needed him most.

Ben explained how Kathryn had died in childbirth while he scoured the countryside, searching for the doctor. Ben blamed himself for not finding the man more quickly, but the doc had been out at a farm twenty miles the other side of the settlement, tending a boy who'd been wounded in an accident.

Micah rubbed the back of his neck. Missy was *his* daughter, not Miss Rogers's. Why hadn't she told him that first night? Not that he'd given her a chance. He could still remember how her face had paled when he told her to leave his home. And she hadn't left yet—even after three days.

As if in betrayal, his stomach rumbled at the fragrant odors of ham frying and bread baking. He didn't want to like her cooking. And he'd never tell a soul that it was much better than Kathryn's. At that thought, grief washed over him anew.

Turning, he sat on the stump that he used for chopping wood. He twisted the ax head, making little circles in the dirt. Why hadn't Kathryn told him she was with child? He'd asked himself that question a hundred times.

He hadn't even held his daughter yet. He couldn't bring himself to touch her. It wasn't her fault her mother died in childbirth, but still, he felt no connection with the baby. Perhaps if he'd been here when she was born and had heard her first cry. For all he knew, Missy could be an orphan Miss Rogers had taken in. But that kind of thinking was just plain dumb.

" 'Bout time you took yo'self a rest." Micah looked up to see Jonah shuffling toward him. "You been downright hard on yo'self ever since you come home."

Micah huffed a breath. "Not hard enough by half."

"Now don't you be blamin' yo'self for what happened to Miz Kathryn." Jonah shook his head, leaned against his cane, and eyed him with a narrowed gaze.

Micah fought the urge to squirm like a schoolboy. "Why not? It *is* my fault. I should have been here with her."

"No, it ain't. Miz Amy, she done felt the same way, but the doctor told her it weren't her fault. Weren't nothin' she could'a done that she didn't do."

Ben had told him the same thing, but it still didn't soothe Micah. He couldn't help wondering if *Miss* Rogers—as he now knew her to be—had done all she could to save Kathryn. There was no point thinking that way since she had no reason not to help his wife. And as young as she looked, she probably had never attended a birthing before.

"The Lawd moves in strange ways sometimes. We cain't know how come He took Miz Kathryn home to be with Him."

Micah stood and set a log on the tree stump. "I don't want to hear that, Jonah." He still couldn't understand why a loving God would allow his wife to die and leave behind a newborn babe. Ever since he'd become a Christian four years ago, he had faithfully served God. Why did God desert him in his time of need?

Jonah lifted a gnarled hand. " 'Member back when you done buyed me and set me free? Well, I couldn't understand that. How come God used you to free me but left behind all them other colored folks?"

Micah shook his head. "I can't explain it. I just did what I thought God told me to do."

"You sure could'a used that money fo' somethin' else."

Micah laid his hand on the old man's shoulder. "You've been a good friend to me, Jonah. I've never regretted helping you. After all, you helped me become a stronger Christian. I just wish I knew how to handle this situation."

Glancing up, Micah saw an eagle soaring high in the sky. It drifted behind a cloud and disappeared for a moment, then came back into view. Behind him, birds dueled each other in song, and afar off he heard one of his mules braying. Life went on. But not Kathryn's. It wasn't fair.

"We's all gotta learn to fly above the storms like that eagle."

Micah glanced down at Jonah and saw that the old man had gazed upward, his countenance glowing. Jonah knew how to soar above his problems. The man was always happy and spouting something about God, even though he couldn't read the Bible.

He'd learned a lot from the old black man and would forever be grateful. Still, this was the toughest trial he'd encountered since he gave his heart to God. He wasn't sure his faith could withstand the assault. A man never expects he might one day be a widower with two young children to raise before he turns twenty-five.

Micah raised the ax and brought it down with a swift stroke. Half of the log spiraled down to the ground and the other half stood in place.

"You gonna let Miz Amy stay? She ain't got no place to go." Jonah peeked up at him from the corner of his eye.

Sure, go ahead and heap on more guilt.

"Why doesn't she have a home? She's rather young to be on her own." He moved the half section to the center of the stump.

Jonah shook his cane, as he often did when riled. "Her no-good pappy up and died. Left her with his gamblin' debts. After she done sold their house, there was barely 'nough left to get her here."

"How come she came here?"

"Weren't nowhere else fo' her to go." Jonah rubbed his thumb and forefinger together. "We's her only kinfolk. Family should stay together."

Micah heaved a sigh. He didn't want to think about what the ex-slave hinted at. The truth was he needed Miss Rogers to care for the children, though he didn't want to need her. And he'd never forget her big brown eyes shining with tears when he'd told her she'd have to leave. Now he understood why she had been so reluctant. . .she had nowhere else to go.

He sliced the log in half again then tossed it in the thigh-high pile. He might as well let her stay. She was a decent cook, kept the house looking better than he'd seen it in ages, and she loved his children. That much was obvious in the way she hugged Beth, fixed her hair, and tried to keep the little rascal clean.

And she was so gentle with Missy. Even though the wet nurse kept the baby fed, Amy was always holding the child in one arm and working with the other.

Missy.

He had yet to hold his daughter. It didn't seem like she belonged to him. He never got to watch Kathryn's stomach swell or feel the unborn babe kick his hand. He'd missed so much.

"You gonna stand there a-lollygaggin' all day, or you gonna answer me?" Micah blinked at Jonah. "What?"

"I asked if you gonna let Miz Amy stay." Jonah lifted his eyebrows, showing Micah the whites of his eyes.

For the first time since coming home, he nearly chuckled. The little old man barely reached Micah's shoulders, and he didn't look one bit ferocious—just bug-eyed. Micah deliberately grabbed another piece of wood, waiting for Jonah to start shaking his cane again. For some reason, it always tickled him.

Without fail, the old man shifted his weight and lifted his walking stick in the air. "Now you listen here. You needs to do the Christianly thing. The Bible says—"

"She can stay." Micah grinned at the surprised look on his friend's face, which turned into a wide, gap-toothed smile.

"I knowed you'd do the right thing."

From her spot beside the cabin, Amy barely kept from clapping her hands and squealing. He was letting her stay!

She backed around the corner of the cabin and did a little jig. Perhaps all her hard work cleaning and cooking her best foods had paid off. Not that she was trying to sway him.

She stilled and looked into the nearby woods. Or perhaps he just wanted a servant that he didn't have to pay for. Disappointment strangled her joy. Perhaps Micah Walsh knew when he had a good thing.

But then, why did it matter, as long as she had a roof over her head and food. That's all she needed. The affection she received from Beth and Missy was a bonus. And Ben and Jonah liked her. She'd just have to stay out of Micah Walsh's way and try to please him with her work.

Peeking around the corner again, she saw Jonah hobble off and disappear around the other side of the cabin. Mr. Walsh picked up a giant log with one hand, set it on the stump, then lifted the ax over his head and whacked the wood in half. His long, dark brown hair flipped down over his eyes, but he brushed it back then tossed the firewood in his ever-growing pile. With the weather warming, she couldn't figure out why he thought they needed so much fuel. She pressed her hand to her chest. Did he perhaps think she used too much firewood?

His cotton shirt stretched tight against his shoulders as he reached for another log. Once he'd cleaned up and shaved, she realized her cousin's husband was a fine-looking man.

He swiped his forehead with his sleeve then began unbuttoning his shirt. Amy touched her hands to her warm cheeks and stepped back. Shame on her. She had no business spying on Micah Walsh. For three days, she'd despised him and thought him an ogre for telling her to leave. Each day, she expected him to force her to go, but he hadn't. Perhaps he was still shocked at finding out Missy was *his* daughter.

"Mama! I'm hungwy."

"Oh!" She'd completely forgotten why she'd come outside until she heard Beth's call. Straightening her apron, she plowed around the corner and ran straight into a solid wall of sweaty flesh.

"Watch it—" Micah Walsh's calloused hands grabbed her upper arms at the same time her hands landed against his damp, unbuttoned long johns top.

"L–Let me go." She jerked her hands back.

"Whoa. Hold your horses." He stepped back and raised his hands in surrender. "I was just trying to steady you."

Amy hiked up her chin. "I'm perfectly steady. Thank you very much." She folded her arms to hide her trembling hands. "I—I just wanted to tell you dinner is ready. Could you please tell Ben?" Without waiting for an answer, she turned and started back to the front of the cabin.

"Wait. There's something I need to tell you."

Amy halted at the soft rumble of his smooth, deep voice. Had he changed his mind about letting her stay? She closed her eyes and took a strengthening breath before turning. Already, he had buttoned his shirt and put his hat back on.

His lips tightened as if he didn't like what he was about to say. Amy's heart nearly stopped beating. His glorious blue-green eyes closed for a moment then opened again. He looked straight at her as if taking her measure.

"I've decided you can stay."

Amy gasped. "Truly?" She'd heard him tell Jonah, but having him tell her face-to-face made it real.

He nodded. "Jonah tells me you've no place to go. Besides, you're a fine cook and good with the children."

She just knew she was beaming. That was the first time he'd complimented her in any way. "I—uh—thank you. I don't know what to say."

"Don't say anything. Jonah talked me into it."

"Oh." Why should she have expected more? After all, she was partly responsible for his wife's death. She wouldn't take charity. Lifting her chin, she looked him in the eye. "I'll work hard. You won't have to worry about the house or the children or your meals. I thank you for your kindness. You won't regret it."

Micah's eyes widened. She knew that was the most she'd said to him since she beaned him in the head.

"Ma—ma! Sookie and me's gonna start eating." Beth wasn't one to be patient.

Micah's eyes narrowed. "There's just one rule you have to abide by if you want to live here."

Amy's heart fluttered. What rule? What would he expect of her?

He pressed his lips into a straight, white line, and a muscle in his jaw ticked. "I don't ever want to hear Beth call you *Mama* again."

Chapter 5

"What?" Confusion stormed Amy's mind.

"You heard me. I don't want Beth calling you *Mama*." Micah stood with his hands on his hips, glaring down at her. His striking blue-green eyes, which she imagined resembled the color of tropical waters, now looked more like a stormy, green sea.

Amy wrung her hands. "I've corrected her nearly every time she says it, but she keeps doing it. I didn't want to punish her for it. I figured in time she would quit." She looked away then back at him, knowing her cheeks were flaming. "She thinks I'm her new mama, because God took the other one away and brought me on the same day."

He blinked, and his dark brows dipped together. Even with his saddle-brown tan, his cheeks and ears turned bright red. "Uhhh. . .sorry. I assumed you encouraged her."

"I wouldn't do that."

"All right. I'll talk to Beth." Micah rubbed the back of his neck. "I reckon we ought to go eat before she downs all the biscuits. You know how she loves them." His mouth tilted up in a soft smile.

Amy nodded and turned, pressing her hand against the side of the cabin for support. She wasn't sure if her trembling knees would hold her. Was it his sudden apology or his smile that made them go weak?

"I'll holler at Ben."

Relieved to be free of his imposing presence, Amy looked over her shoulder and watched Micah stride toward the field where Ben was plowing; then she hurried around to the front of the cabin. Beth had left the door ajar, so Amy pushed it open and went inside, enjoying the homey scents of fried ham and fresh bread. Sookie had finished setting the table and was already seated next to Jonah.

It still amazed Amy that the Walshes allowed their slaves to dine with them. She'd never heard of such a thing before, but it did make things easier, and in truth, she was thankful for Sookie's presence, especially in the evenings when the men lingered around the fireplace, rocking in their chairs and talking. They usually stayed until Beth went to bed; then Jonah shuffled off to his little house, while Micah and Ben went upstairs to sleep. Amy was glad there wasn't an inside stairway. To get to their bedroom, the brothers had to go outside and climb the ladder. It was an odd setup, but she was happy to have at least some privacy.

Using a towel, Amy opened the oven and pulled out two golden loaves of bread. She breathed a sigh of relief that they weren't burnt, considering how long she'd dawdled outside.

Micah entered the cabin, removed his hat, then hung it on one of the hooks behind the front door and ran his hand over his damp hair. He was in desperate need of a haircut, but she hoped he wouldn't ask her to do it, because she didn't want to be that close to him. The man flustered her way too much, considering she'd never been around men before, other than her father, and he hadn't been home all that often. Amy turned back to fetch the gravy off the stove.

The front door banged against the wall as Ben plowed inside. Amy jumped, nearly splashing hot gravy on her wrist. When Missy started crying, she set down the bowl and scowled at Ben.

"Next time you come in the house, do it a little slower and quieter," Micah ordered.

Ben stopped and looked at his brother. For a moment the two stared at each other; then the boy nodded. Amy knew it was hard for Ben to no longer be the one in charge after doing so for the five months Micah had been gone. In a way, she empathized with him, but at least his brother was still alive and had returned home.

Chairs scraped against wood as the men seated themselves. Sookie sliced the bread, laid it on a plate, and set it on the table, while Amy retrieved the green beans and sliced ham. After dinner they would divide a warm rhubarb pie. Amy crossed into the bedroom to check on Missy, but the baby had already fallen back asleep with her thumb in her mouth.

"Mmm-mmm, sure smells good." Ben reached for a slice of bread as Amy sat in her chair, but Micah grabbed his sleeve.

"Wait until we've said grace." Red stained Ben's cheeks, and he looked down as Micah bowed his head and said a quick blessing.

Ben snagged a slice of bread, slathered butter on it, and took a bite before anyone else could get a slice. Amy bit back a chuckle. By the time he quit growing, she imagined he'd challenge his brother in height, though she doubted his shoulders could ever measure up to the breadth of Micah's.

"Did you ride over to Jed Hanby's earlier, like I told you?" Micah glanced at Ben as he tore up his bread then spooned gravy over it.

"Yep." Ben spooned a generous serving of green beans in his trencher and then grabbed a large slice of fried ham before passing the platter to his brother.

"And?" Micah's dark brows tilted upward.

"He agreed to the deal. Said he'd swap Sookie for your two three-year-old mules, and he sent over her papers. They're upstairs in our room. I already told Sookie 'bout the deal."

Micah glanced at the young black woman, whose soft smile curved her lips.

Amy nearly choked on her ham. Micah *bought* Sookie from Mr. Hanby? He'd traded the life of a human being for two mules? She glanced at the slave girl, who sat staring into her plate—smiling? Was she happy to be sold? Was her old master so cruel that she was happy to belong to the Walshes?

Sookie rarely talked, and when she did, it was never about her past home. How could a human being own another person? Having grown up in the North, Amy had had little exposure to slavery, and it made her stomach churn.

"After you finish plowing, round up the milk cows out in the pasture and put them in the barn." Micah glanced over his coffee cup at Ben.

Ben's eyes narrowed. "And what are *you* going to be doing?"

They reminded Amy of two rams in a field, butting heads and vying to be the leader.

Micah stared at Ben until he looked away. "I'm taking a load of furs into town to sell so I can get supplies. Then I'm going to ride over to Sam Sutton's to look over some broodmares he's selling."

"That Sam, he's got some mighty fine hosses." Jonah looked from brother to brother.

"I like horsies, Papa." Beth grinned then licked off the white milk moustache covering her top lip.

Micah had a stunned expression on his face. For a long moment he stared at Beth, making Amy wonder what he was thinking. Beth had been frightened of him at first, because she didn't recognize him, but once he had shaved and cleaned up, she quickly started warming to him. This was the first time Beth had called him *Papa*.

Amy looked around the quiet table. No one ate, and they all stared at Beth. The young girl didn't seem to notice but sat there tearing the crust off her bread. She glanced up, as her thin eyebrows dipped. "I don't like da bwown part, Papa. But I like bwown horsies."

Micah chuckled and started eating again. Silverware clinked against plates, and eyes twinkled. Amy enjoyed being a part of this family. If only Kathryn were here.

———

Micah and Ben rode out of town after selling a mule load of furs. He'd wanted his brother to stay behind and work, but Amy had gently suggested it would be good for Ben to get away from the farm for a bit. And she'd been right. She had also hesitantly hinted that it would be wise to have someone with him rather than riding all over the countryside alone with a wallet full of money. He reached up and patted the bulge in his jacket to make sure it was still there. He had enough money to make at least one of his dreams come true today. The wagon-load of goods Hank Foster eagerly agreed to deliver when he returned Micah's mule would please the womenfolk.

For one so young, Amy Rogers had a lot of good qualities. She was wise, patient with the girls, a good manager of his home, and she kept herself looking tidy most of the time.

"Sam's got a nice-looking bay mare you might be interested in."

Micah looked sideways at his brother. "Yeah?"

Ben nodded. "She's fast. Won the Winter Harvest race last November. Don't know if Sam would part with her though."

Rusty edged into a rough trot, but Micah pulled him back to a walk. "Tell me about Miss Rogers."

Blinking, Ben gave Micah a curious glance. "Amy? What do you want to know?"

He shrugged. "Where's she from? How old is she? How come she's running our home?"

Ben peeked out of the corner of his eye. "Didn't Jonah tell you 'bout her?"

"A little. But I want to know more."

"Why?" Ben's question held a suspicious tone.

Micah strove for an air of nonchalance. "She's taking care of our home, watching over my daughters." He shrugged again. "I need to know if I can trust her."

Ben snorted a laugh. "Good grief, don't you think she's proven she can be trusted? I mean, she's been caring for things over a month now and came in after Kath—"

Micah felt his brother's eyes on him, but he didn't turn to look at him as grief threatened to overcome him.

"Sorry."

They rode in silence for a while. As Micah rocked in the saddle and listened to the rhythmic clopping of the horses' hooves, he blinked back tears. Nothing could bring Kathryn back. He'd always have fond memories of their time together—some better than others, but he had to move on. Often, he'd wondered if having more of his family around would have helped Kathryn.

A generation or two back, this area was swarming with Walshes. But all of the others had either moved south or west to the frontier, except for Ben and him.

He should have tried harder to help Kathryn. Micah shook his head. He couldn't let the guilt of not being a better husband weigh him down. Nothing could change the past. He had a farm and a family to take care of and needed to look to the future. Turning his face away from Ben, he wiped his eyes.

"Amy's from Boston. Used to visit Kathryn's home with her mother when they were children. Guess she's had it pretty rough lately," Ben said.

Micah remembered Jonah saying something about Amy's father deserting her and her mother, then returning when he was dying, expecting Amy to support and tend to him. He despised men who didn't care for their families. But then, hadn't that very thing—providing for his family—been the thing that separated him and his wife?

"There's Sutton's turnoff."

Micah glanced up and had to short rein Rusty to keep from missing the trail. Excitement quivered in his belly. How many years had he dreamed of being able to buy some mares and start raising horses? Anxious, he sucked in a deep breath and urged Rusty to go faster. Ben took up the challenge and kicked his horse into a gallop.

They raced down the trail, neck and neck. Micah grinned, enjoying this lighthearted moment with his brother. When they'd been younger they'd had fun together despite the seven years separating them. Ben had always been Micah's shadow, but his big heart and impulsiveness often got him in trouble. Like the time when he was four and brought home some black-and-white kittens. Only they hadn't been kittens, and the mama skunk hadn't appreciated him stealing her babies. Micah couldn't help chuckling. Ben had smelled like skunk for days afterward. It wasn't too funny then, since he had shared a bed with his brother, but it was now.

Two hours later, Micah and Ben were headed home. Micah led a frisky bay mare, and Ben herded eight more mares and a gelding behind her. Sam had said the other horses would follow the bay like sheep to a shepherd, and they had.

He still couldn't believe his good fortune. Sam Sutton told him since he'd reached his seventieth birthday, he needed to cut back some and had given Micah a great deal to buy out his remaining stock. Sam had kept only two horses—a roan saddle horse and his prize stallion.

The mares had already been bred, so Micah's herd should nearly double early next year. Sam had also offered him a low fee to breed the mares in future years. Yes siree, God had smiled down on him today.

As Micah rounded the trail and his cabin came into view, he saw that Hank Foster was just arriving with his wagon of supplies. Micah's chest swelled. It felt great to have his debts paid off and to be able to buy things his family needed.

Family. That thought startled him. When had he started thinking of Amy as family? She *was* actually—even more so than Jonah. Still, she wasn't family in the same sense that Kathryn had been. And she never would be. For now, the girls needed her, but down the road. . .well, he'd tackle that bear later.

Hank let out a low whistle. "That's some right nice horseflesh you got there." He pushed his floppy hat back on his forehead and stared at them. "I see Sam Sutton sold you his prizewinning mare. You must be a fancy talker to get him to part with her."

Hank Foster was one of the most talkative men in town. Micah knew better than to take his bait. If the livery worker got started yakking, it would be dark before he quit. Nodding, Micah rode past the man as Hank pulled his wagon to a stop near the porch steps.

The front door banged open, and Beth ran outside squealing with Amy close on her heels. "Horsies! Bwown horsies!" Micah smiled as his daughter bounced up and down, her brown eyes twinkling.

The bay mare jerked her head and snorted at the sudden noise. "Whoa, girl." He tightened his hold on the mare's lead rope until her head almost rested against his leg. Glancing to the porch, he noted Amy's arm around Beth, holding the child against her skirts. With his daughter safe, he nudged Rusty toward the pasture ahead where Jonah waited with the gate open.

Hank jumped from his wagon seat to the ground, tugged off his hat, and held it in his dirty hands. "Afternoon, Miss Rogers. I told you I'd be back. Have you decided to marry me yet?"

Micah jerked back so hard on Rusty's reins that the horse squealed and reared up. The bay mare beside him danced about, upset by the lead horse's actions. Rusty pranced in a circle, and Micah had to rein him back. He didn't want to miss Amy's response. How could she consider marrying Hank Foster? Oh, sure, he could be a likable enough fellow, but he was dumb as a stick.

With Rusty finally under control, Micah glanced at Amy. Her dark eyes shone wide against her pale skin. Would she agree to marry Hank? Micah couldn't help wondering if he'd expected too much from her—worked her too hard. Now that she had a chance, would she leave him and the girls?

Chapter 6

Micah awoke with a start, his heart pounding. He rubbed his eyes and shook off sleep as he listened for what had awakened him. He heard a scuffling sound, then the quilt covering the open doorway flipped back. Moonlight rushed through, along with the cool night air and the sounds of night critters. Ben's silhouette crawled in through the opening. He sure got up a lot at night.

"Where you been?" Micah asked, his voice gravelly. A drink of water would taste great, but he didn't want to climb down the ladder to get it. Morning would dawn soon enough.

"Where do you think I've been?" Ben crept across the room, removed his boots, and dropped onto the bed.

"You're going to have to quit drinking so much water at night, boy." Micah knew his brother hated to be referred to as *boy*.

"Don't call me that! I grew up while you were gone." As he crawled beneath his quilt, Ben mumbled something under his breath that Micah couldn't quite make out.

"Yeah, well, you're not there just yet." Micah rolled over onto his side. He hated to admit it—and he wouldn't admit it to Ben—but his brother was indeed a young man. Micah just wished he would act like one.

"What's that you said?"

"Nothing. Go back to sleep." Micah fluffed his pillow and settled down, hoping to catch another hour's sleep. As when he'd first gone to bed, his mind drifted to Miss Rogers. He shouldn't have worried that she might up and marry Hank Foster. Her expression when Hank asked her to marry him alternated between embarrassment and shock.

Micah recalled how Beth had started fussing and clinging to Miss Rogers's skirts when she thought the woman might be leaving. Miss Rogers stooped down, hugging the child and glaring over Beth's shoulder at Hank. The foolish man just wouldn't take no for an answer. Said he figured he'd give her a little more time to get used to the idea. He climbed back in his unloaded wagon and rode off, hollering that he'd see her soon.

Micah remembered the relief that had flooded through him. *Thank You, Lord, for bringing Amy Rogers here, just when we needed her. Bless her, and let her be happy here. Help me to be kinder to her. It's not her fault that Kathryn is gone. Forgive me,*

Father, for taking out my hurt on her.

Heaving a sigh, he rolled onto his back and stared up at the black ceiling. Somehow, he had to stop feeling guilty that he hadn't been here for Kathryn. And even if he had been, he wouldn't have had any idea how to stop her bleeding. The doctor had assured him nothing could have been done.

Fully awake, Micah pulled on his clothes and boots and tiptoed across the room. Ben's heavy snores rattled off the walls. It seemed his brother could sleep anywhere these days. Micah had found him dozing in a stall in the barn with the shovel he was supposed to be using to muck out the stall lying in his lap. One morning, Micah had come in for breakfast and found Ben at the table with his head down on his arm, sound asleep.

He climbed down the ladder, wondering if he'd been working his brother too hard. In his grief, had he taken out his anger on Ben, too? He didn't think so, but still, he'd try to do better. He was thankful Beth had finally warmed up to him and now treated him the same as before he'd gone trapping, but he couldn't yet bring himself to touch the baby.

Why can't I hold her?

Not awake enough to sort out his emotions, he opened the barn door and smiled as his animals greeted him with a soft nicker or a *moo*. The one animal missing was a dog. Every time he mentioned getting Beth a puppy, Ben complained that the farm already had enough critters to care for. Ben used to love dogs. Odd how people could change.

Two hours later, after milking the cow and caring for the other animals with Jonah's help, Micah entered the house for breakfast. Fragrant smells wafted around the warm room, making his mouth water and his belly beg for sustenance. Bleary-eyed, Ben sat at the table leaning on one hand, with his clothes and hair disheveled. He yawned as Micah pulled out his chair and sat. Sitting to the left of Ben, Jonah glanced at him then exchanged a look with Micah. Did the old man know something he hadn't told Micah?

For the first time, Micah wondered if perhaps Ben was going out carousing with some friends late at night. Had he gotten mixed up in something while he was gone?

He couldn't ever remember Ben being so tired at breakfast. He'd just have to watch his brother and see if he was involved with some scallywags. *Please, God, I pray he isn't.*

"I washed up like Amy tolded me to, Papa." Micah looked down to where Beth stood smiling up at him. She stepped onto the rung of the chair and brushed a sweet kiss on his cheek. His gut clenched. A child's unconditional love was a wonderful blessing. A blessing he was missing out on with Missy.

"That's a good girl, Beth. I'm happy that you obeyed Miss Rogers." He scooped up his smiling daughter and hugged her.

Beth's little hands patted his shoulders then she pushed back. "Her name is *Amy*."

"It's not proper for children to refer to adults by their first names." Though his voice was gentle, he gave Beth a no-nonsense look.

"What about Jonah and Sookie?"

Micah chuckled at Beth's response. Obviously his daughter had outsmarted him. Both Jonah and Sookie kept their expressions straight, but their eyes danced with mirth.

"That's different."

"How?"

Ben sucked back a chuckle, and Micah eyeballed him with a glare.

"If you don't mind, I prefer Amy to Miss Rogers." Her voice was soft, gentle, just like she was. Micah wouldn't admit it out loud, but he'd forced himself to think of her as Miss Rogers so he could maintain a proper distance—but it was too late.

"See! *Amy*, not Miss Wogers." Beth's eyes gleamed with a triumphant twinkle.

Micah exhaled, knowing it was time to surrender. "All right, you may call her Amy, but only because that's what *she* wishes."

"Pardon me." Amy leaned past him to place a plate of bacon on the table. As she pulled back, his eyes locked with hers. He smiled, purposing to be nicer. Her thin brows dipped and dark eyes clouded with confusion. She darted away, like a startled doe in the woods.

Remorse weighed him down. He remembered how short he'd been with her the past few weeks. He owed her an apology. Fine example of a Bible-believing man he'd been.

Sookie put the eggs and biscuits on the table then sat next to Jonah. Micah remembered her shy thank-you the day before when he had freed her and offered to pay her to stay on and continue wet-nursing Missy and helping Amy. At least he'd done something right since returning home. He wondered if he ought to tell Amy that he had freed Sookie, but then he figured that Sookie would tell if she wanted to.

"I wanna eat on your lap." Beth scooted off her chair and onto his legs then picked up his fork as if the matter were settled. He would enjoy holding her while eating but didn't want to start something he'd have to deal with at every meal.

Gently he removed the fork from her little fist then hugged her. "That would be nice, Punkin, but you need to eat at your own place. You're a big girl now and don't need to be held while eating like baby Missy does."

That seemed to satisfy her. She slipped off his lap and onto her chair, tucked her napkin in the neck of her dress, looked around the table and declared, "I'm a big gool."

Jonah and Sookie chuckled. Even Ben woke up enough to smile. He took a big swig of his coffee then yawned again and scratched his head.

Micah glanced at Amy to see if she'd noticed Beth's antics. Amy stood next to the worktable spooning some strawberry jam from a jar into a small bowl. Even though she'd been cooking breakfast, the kitchen remained tidy. Loaves of uncooked bread sat in their tins, rising on the kitchen's worktable, and a pot of beans was already soaking for the evening meal. Amazing. After Kathryn had cooked, the place always looked as if a cyclone had rumbled through. Having grown up with servants, she never quite adjusted to caring for a house. She'd tried though.

He looked across the table into the parlor. The whole house was orderly and clean. Of course, Amy did have Sookie to help, but then again, they also had Missy to care for besides Beth.

Amy set the jam on the table, removed her apron, and sat next to Beth. Micah said grace; then they started passing the platters laden with food. His mouth watered. He'd never eaten this well when Kathryn had cooked. More times than not her bread had sagged in the middle and had been doughy inside. Her bacon was always burnt, and her cornmeal mush lumpy.

A shard of guilt pierced his chest, causing almost a physical pain. He shouldn't be comparing the two women.

"I—uh, hope you don't mind that I asked Jonah to clean up that old spinning wheel I found in the barn." Amy's gaze darted to his; then she concentrated on spooning food into Beth's trencher.

Micah glanced across the room to where his mother's spinning wheel sat in the corner. It looked polished and at attention like a soldier awaiting orders. Warmth flooded him at the memory of nights by the fire in this house when he was a boy, watching his mother spin wool or flax. She often spun while rattling off math problems for him to decipher. The fact that she could do more than one thing at a time had amazed him.

His grandmother had originally given the spinning wheel to her eldest daughter, but when Hester went west with her husband, they left it behind, hoping to one day return for it and a visit. Only that never happened. Micah's mother had been thrilled to become the new guardian of such a family treasure.

Did he mind Amy using his mother's spinning wheel? Kathryn had never shown an interest in it. She had always managed to barter and not have to do the work herself. His heart warmed to have the spinning wheel in the house again. "No." He looked at Amy. "I don't mind if you use it."

Her lips curved up and her eyes gleamed. Knowing he'd put that smile on her face did odd things to his insides.

———

Was she imagining it, or was Micah being nicer to her? Was his attitude toward her changing? He'd certainly been pleasant at breakfast, almost as though he was pleased with her cooking and her bringing in the spinning wheel.

He'd even asked her to call him by his first name, like she had. That thought tickled her insides. She'd wanted to call him Micah for a while now, but he had seemed to want to keep things formal between them.

Amy crossed the room and studied the old spinning wheel. She would have understood if he hadn't wanted her to use it, since Jonah had explained its heritage. She stroked the odd spoke with the heart etched out, wondering what it would feel like to have someone love you so much that he'd engrave a heart in wood as a symbol of that love.

She jumped when the door banged open and hoped it didn't cause Beth to get out of bed again. The girl had a hard time going down for a nap and often gave excuses for getting up before she finally went to sleep.

"I'm not avoiding Missy. I just don't know much about tending for babies," Micah said to Jonah as both men entered the cabin with an armload of wood. He glanced at her, closed the door with his booted foot, then crossed the room and dropped his load in the woodbin, just as Jonah had done.

Sookie glided into the parlor with Missy on her shoulder. "Miz Beth is takin' her nap, and lit'l Missy done finished her lunch and is ready to play."

Amy sighed, relieved all the noise hadn't disturbed Beth. They all needed a few moments without the active child racing about. How did those women with six children manage?

"There's no time like the here and now." Jonah peered up at Micah then glanced at Missy.

Micah lifted his dirty hands. "I can't touch a baby. I'm filthy."

"There's water in the basin for yo' to clean up."

Amy rather enjoyed watching the little old man stand up to brawny Micah. Even though they were of different races, Jonah seemed more like Micah's good friend than his slave.

Micah sighed and looked at his daughter then back at his hands. In the weeks that he'd been home, he had yet to hold the child. Amy wondered if he blamed Missy for her mother's death. She took the baby from Sookie. "The washing is ready to be hung up."

"Yes'm. I'll tend to it right away." Sookie lifted the latch on the door then went outside.

Amy checked herself and called out the door, "Thanks for your help, Sookie." She didn't ever want to become accustomed to treating Sookie and Jonah like mere slaves. She wished she felt confident enough to speak to Micah about the issue of slavery but knew that would have to wait until they were more comfortable with each other, if that time would ever come.

Amy smiled at the sweet baby. How could anyone not love such a happy, little thing? Missy squirmed; then her mouth formed an *O*, and she cooed out a greeting. Amy's insides warmed as if she'd drunk a cup of hot coffee on a cold morning.

"All right, I'll hold her after I wash."

Amy glanced up, surprised at Micah's announcement. Her heart soared with relief that he was finally acknowledging his second daughter.

"God's been telling me I haven't been much of a father to Missy. I need to do a better job." Micah pivoted and splashed in the water basin.

Was he embarrassed by his surprising confession? Amy studied his wide shoulders, so different from her father's slim, bent form. Had God really spoken to Micah about Missy? Amy's mother often said God had spoken with her, but Amy could never understand how a being you couldn't see or hear could speak to you. Jonah, too, was quick to tell her how he conversed with God. Imagine a Holy Being who talked to His children.

Micah approached her. He dried his hands on a towel then tossed it over one shoulder.

"Praise da Lawd. This surely be a happy day." Jonah's wide smile could have fueled a dozen lanterns.

Micah dropped into his rocking chair then looked at Amy, as if for encouragement.

"She's a sweet girl. Has an even temperament. I suspect she won't be as rambunctious as Beth when she's bigger." Amy's arm shook, both in anxiety and happiness.

The corners of Micah's lips curved up in a gentle smile, and his eyes took on a faraway look. Was he remembering Beth as a baby? When Amy stepped toward him, he looked her way again, and her heart thundered in her ears. Would he reject his child? She knew what it was like to be rejected because she'd been born a female instead of a male.

Please God, if You're really up there, let Micah Walsh fall in love with Missy. She deserves a father.

Amy could feel Micah's hands tremble as she passed him his daughter. The baby studied him with wide blue eyes. Her fuzzy hair stuck straight up like the down of a duckling.

"She has blond hair—like Kathryn's." Micah stroked Missy's head as if he were touching something rare and valuable.

Amy didn't miss the awe in his comment. Had he not looked closely enough at his daughter before now to know her hair color? She wanted to be angry at him for his neglect, but she couldn't be as she watched his face transform from trepidation to pride. His eyes shone, and he blinked back tears. A smile pulled at her lips that she couldn't hold back. Joy flooded her heart. Perhaps this baby wouldn't grow up with a father who despised her.

The love in Micah's expression was evident. She glanced up to see tears coursing down Jonah's face. He nodded with his head in the direction of the door, and she followed.

Peeking back at Micah as she and Jonah slipped out, she heard him say, "Hello, Melissa Kathryn Walsh, I'm your father."

Tears stung her eyes as she shut the door. Melissa. Had he given the baby that name so they could still call her Missy as a nickname?

"Glory hallelujah! Thank you, Jesus." Jonah hopped down the stairs then did a stiff-legged jig in the grass. He looked heavenward, and her gaze followed.

If there was a God in heaven, He'd truly worked a miracle this day.

Amy needed something to divert her from the heart-tugging scene inside, or she just might burst into tears. She decided now was as good a time as any to inventory the canned items in the cellar. She couldn't be certain, but she thought that some things had gone missing lately. But who could be taking them? Could a stranger be helping himself to their supplies?

Before she could go to Micah about the missing supplies, she had to be certain. She would rearrange things in her own system, and then if any were missing later, she'd know for sure.

———

Micah yawned in the dark. He forced his cramped body to lie still and to stay awake. If his brother was up to something, Micah was determined to figure out what it was. Ben tossed and turned on his bed.

Needing something to keep his mind active to drive sleep away, he thought about Missy. He'd been a fool to distance himself from her. She was just a little baby. It wasn't her fault her mother had died, though he knew at first he had blamed her. Did he need to blame someone for Kathryn's death so he wouldn't blame himself?

The pain of her being gone wasn't as raw as it had been last month, but it still hurt. If only he'd been here.

He shook his head. No. He couldn't keep thinking that. Jonah told him often that God works in mysterious ways. Well, it sure was a mystery to him why the Good Lord would take a young mother from her children. There had to be a reason, and he would trust God to reveal it one day.

He yawned and prayed for his daughters, for this year's crop, and for Ben. The thoughts in his mind grew thick and slower in coming, mixing with the inky blackness of exhaustion. His body relaxed. Perhaps he could rest for a few minutes. Perhaps Ben wouldn't get up tonight.

A loud *thump* startled Micah awake. He heard a scratching noise and realized Ben was climbing down the ladder. He shot up off his mat and grabbed in the dark for his boots, thankful he'd slept in his clothes. Peeking past the quilt that covered the opening to the room, in the moonlight he saw Ben disappear around the corner of the house instead of heading toward the privy. Was he going to the barn?

Micah had learned to move stealthily when trapping and glided down the ladder. He tiptoed to the side of the cabin and could just make out Ben's form heading into the barn. His heart pounded out a frenzied rhythm, and his stomach swirled with anxiety. What was Ben up to?

As he eased inside the barn, the familiar smells soothed him, but a shaft of light shone upward from the opening in the floor, increasing his anxiety. Downstairs, in the small room where he stored his furs, he could hear Ben's voice but couldn't make out what the boy was saying. Micah crept closer, hoping not to disturb the sleeping animals and alert Ben to his presence.

His heart thundered in his ears and all kinds of thoughts assaulted his mind. Was Ben stealing the remaining furs and selling them?

Ben was just fourteen when their parents died in an accident. Micah was already married with a pregnant wife to care for. He'd been grieving and knew he hadn't been as good a support to Ben as he should have. What did he know about raising a hurting, angry young man?

Holding his breath, he eased forward and leaned over to try to discover who was down in his hideout with Ben. Unable to see, he shuffled forward. A fine sprinkling of hay from the barn floor spiraled down. The voices went silent. Ben gasped and held up a lantern. He looked up with wide eyes, but beside him, Micah could see the whites of three more pairs of eyes set against the black backdrop of frightened slave faces.

Micah stepped back and grabbed his head, his thoughts swirling, mixing with a deep ache that knew no bounds. No. It couldn't be.

His little brother was a slave trader!

Chapter 7

Micah's heart sank to his feet. He placed both hands on the top rail of an empty stall and dropped his head between his outstretched arms. "Dear God, no."

The short prayer was all he had strength to utter. His whole body trembled. How could he have failed his brother so badly? Didn't Ben value human life?

"Micah! It's not what you think." Ben was right behind him, his voice begging Micah to listen.

He didn't want to hear his brother's excuses, but he stood, swiping at his eyes before he turned. A musket ball to his gut would have hurt less. Somehow he had to right this wrong. Had to make Ben see the error of his ways.

Taking a strengthening breath, he turned to face his brother. At least Ben had the sense to look regretful. From downstairs, he could hear the soft murmuring of the slaves. It sounded as if they were praying. They had no way of knowing he was an abolitionist and couldn't abide a man owning another man.

The lantern light shined upward from the cellar, illuminating Ben in an eerie glow. He paced and fidgeted as he always did whenever he was in trouble.

How would their father have handled this situation? If only their parents could have lived until Ben was completely grown. Micah had had so many responsibilities suddenly dumped on his twenty-one-year-old shoulders when his parents died that he'd barely managed to keep the farm up and running and keep his homesick wife from hightailing it back to her parents. He hadn't been the support his brother needed.

"Listen to me, Micah." Ben turned his pleading gaze toward him. "I know what you think, but you're wrong."

"No, Ben. You're the one who's wrong. How could you not know slave trading is a wretched, evil thing?" A wave of anger washed over Micah, replacing his initial shock.

"I am *not* slave trading." Ben spit out each syllable in staccato. His expression took on a determined hardness.

Micah blinked, confused by his brother's declaration. "Then why are there slaves in our barn?"

Ben looked at his feet and kicked at a clod of dirt, stirring up a cloud of dust that settled over his boot. "They're runaways. I run a safe house."

Micah barely heard the words. His mind churned. *Runaways.* Not slaves.

His heart soared, only to plummet again as he considered the staggering ramifications. Ben had brought illegal runaways onto their property. Slave catchers didn't care if they captured the right Negro; they'd take any that were handy. "Don't you realize how you've endangered Jonah and Sookie by bringing these slaves here?"

"I'm real careful, Micah. You've been back a month and are just now finding out."

"You've brought runaways here before?" Micah heaved a sigh. "How long have you been doing this?"

"About eight months."

Stunned, Micah leaned back against the stall gate. His horse, in the neighboring stall, stuck his big head over the railing and nickered. Micah reached out and patted Rusty. He needed the comfort of his old friend while he decided what to do with Ben and his dilemma. His brother had been helping runaway slaves since before Micah had left to go trapping. Unbelievable! They'd been right under his own nose, but he'd been too preoccupied to notice. Now he understood why his brother had been so opposed to getting a dog.

"If an irate slave catcher had stormed into the cabin, one of the females could have gotten injured. I can't believe you'd imperil the girls like this."

Ben puffed up like an old rooster. "I never put them in danger."

Micah took a step toward his brother, his ire growing. "Do you have any idea what slave catchers do to agents and safe houses when they're discovered?" Ben's eyes widened as Micah moved closer. "They don't care who they hurt. They burn houses, kill livestock, and I can't even say what they do to unprotected women."

Ben finally had the sense to back down. The concern in his eyes did little to soothe Micah. "I didn't think—"

"That's right. You didn't think."

"But you're an abolitionist. How can you not help them?"

Micah crossed his arms and glared at Ben. "I have too much to worry about trying to keep this farm afloat so we have food to last the winter and enough produce that we can barter for the things we need. I have a nursing baby and a three-year-old who don't have a mother. And a little brother who'd rather help runaway slaves than help his own brother work their farm."

Ben hiked up his chin. "It's not *my* farm. It's *your* farm."

Shoving his hands into his pockets, Micah stared at his brother. Beth wasn't the only one who'd grown while he'd been gone. Ben was only a few inches shorter than he now. His brother's face had lost that boyish look. How could he make Ben understand how he felt?

"As far as I'm concerned, the farm belongs to both of us."

Ben shook his head and kicked at a tuft of hay. "Pa left it to you."

"That doesn't matter. You were too young for him to leave part of it to you when he died. You'll always have a home here."

"It's not the same thing. You don't understand."

"I understand more than you think."

Ben glared at him. "No, you don't. You never trust me. Always think of me as the younger brother who never does anything right. Well, freeing slaves feels right. You could have at least given me the benefit of the doubt before you accused me of being a slave trader."

The animals in their stalls grew restless at the raised voices. They stomped, snorted, and moved around, tossing their heads. Ben was right. He *had* jumped to conclusions. That thought strangled Micah's throat, threatening to cut off his breath. Why had he believed the worst of Ben instead of trusting his good character? He needed some time alone with God to sort things out.

Glancing down in the hole, he saw three heads of black hair—two men and one woman. While he didn't approve of slavery, he wasn't sure if he was willing to put his family in jeopardy to help those runaways. He looked at Ben. "Just get them out of here as fast as possible—and don't bring any more slaves onto this land."

As he closed the barn door and headed back to the house, it struck him that he'd included Amy as part of his family when arguing with Ben. He had to admit he was growing fond of her. While he wouldn't classify her as a beauty like Kathryn, she was easy on the eyes—and kind, even when he hadn't treated her as he should have. Shame tightened his chest. He was a Christian and had done very little to show God's love to Amy. He climbed the ladder to the upstairs room, purposing to do better—with Ben and with Amy.

A river of excitement coursed through Amy as Micah drove the wagon into town. It had been nearly two months since she'd first come into Stewart's Gap looking for her cousin. The only dark cloud on such a lovely day was her fear of running into Hank Foster. Perhaps he'd found some other woman on which to turn his affections by now. She could only hope.

Amy could tell that Saturday in Stewart's Gap was as busy a day as it was in Boston. Many of those living on the outskirts of the town like her and Micah ventured in to stock up on supplies. Children ran up and down the dirt streets, playing hide-and-seek behind the wagons their parents were loading. A group of men stood lined up outside the barber shop, talking and laughing. The smell of fresh pastries from a bakery wafted on the morning breeze, making Amy's stomach growl.

"We used to have to travel over a day's ride to town." Micah glanced sideways at her. "About the time I was eight or so, a group of men started Stewart's Gap as a freight town."

Amy breathed a sigh of relief to not have to travel that far when they needed supplies.

"Can I have a pickle, Papa?" Beth squirmed on the bench seat between Amy and Micah.

"Bit early for that, isn't it, Punkin?"

Beth shook her head. "Nope."

Micah had wanted to leave her at home with Sookie, but Amy thought that caring for the two girls alone might be too much for the young slave woman. She didn't abide one person owning another, so she did whatever she could to make Sookie's life easier.

Amy glanced at Micah, the other reason she wanted to bring Beth. The long drive into town would have been uncomfortable without the child's constant chatter. Though he was treating her nicer these days, she couldn't imagine riding several hours alone with him.

Beth jumped to her feet, and Amy reached out to steady her as Micah stopped the wagon in front of the mercantile. "I have an account, so get what you need. Be sure you get some fabric to make summer dresses for each of you females, Sookie included."

His generosity touched Amy's heart. Had he noticed she only had two dresses? And those were getting threadbare. She'd taken one of Kathryn's dresses apart to make a new one for Beth, but she didn't feel right making one for herself.

Micah reached up to help her down, and Amy's heart jolted. She would rather get down by herself, but it would be discourteous to refuse his aid. Tingles tickled her fingers as she put her hands on Micah's broad shoulders. He wrapped his hands around her waist and lifted her up as if she weighed next to nothing then set her on the ground. Butterflies danced in her belly and her hands trembled. As much as she didn't want to admit it, she'd begun to care for Micah Walsh. Her initial opinion of him had been wrong. He was a kind man who loved his family with a passion and wanted so desperately to support them that he had left them in Ben's care and gone trapping for months during the winter to provide for them. It was much more than her own father had ever done.

"Lots of horsies, Papa!" Beth skipped around Amy's skirt until Micah took her by the hand. He knelt beside his daughter and gently held her shoulders until the girl settled and looked him in the face.

"Horses can be dangerous, sweetie. You know to stay away from them and to stay near Amy and me while we're in town."

Beth nodded. "So can I have a pickle, please?"

Micah smiled and brushed his hand down one side of Beth's head. "We'll see." The big man's gentleness stirred something inside Amy. She turned away and stared in the mercantile window. *I can't allow myself to have feelings for Micah. He's Kathryn's husband.*

She regained her composure, and her shoes tapped against the boardwalk as she followed Micah and Beth into the store. She inhaled the fragrant scents of spices mixed with dried meats, coffee, and pickles.

"Got your list?" he called over his shoulder.

Amy nodded and pulled it from her reticule. Besides cloth, thread, and a new needle, they needed coffee, sugar, and other staples.

"Mornin'." A plump woman dressed in blue gingham and an apron smiled and waved her hand in the air at Micah. "I do declare, we haven't seen you for a long spell."

"Good morning, Mrs. Maples. Everything fine with you and yours?" Micah tipped his hat and was rewarded with another wide smile from the store owner.

"Just fine as a new barrel of crackers."

Amy bit back a chuckle at the kind woman's odd comment.

"This is Amy Rogers, Kathryn's cousin. She'll be doing some shopping for me, so put whatever she gets on my account. I've got some more furs, and I'll settle up with Horace after I tend to some business at the livery."

Mrs. Maples's cheery grin disappeared, and her gaze darted everywhere but at Micah. "I was very sorry to hear about your wife, Mr. Walsh. Seems to me Kathryn had finally settled into life here."

Amy glanced at Micah to see how he'd respond. She knew the woman was just being polite.

"Thank you, ma'am. We all miss her."

As Micah turned to Amy, she noticed a muscle tic in his jaw. He never talked to her about Kathryn, so she had no idea if he was beginning to get over his wife's death or not. At least he'd become the father Missy needed, and now rocked her to sleep nearly every evening after Sookie nursed her.

"I need to go to the livery and get the horses reshod. Might take awhile if there are others already waiting."

"That's fine. It will take Beth and me a bit to pick out fabric and select supplies."

"If you get done and I'm not back, feel free to walk over to the livery. Beth loves to see the horses." An ornery grin twisted Micah's lips. "You want me to tell Hank Foster that you're in town and would like to see him?"

Amy's mouth opened, but no words came out. Surely he was teasing. Could he know how much she worried about running into Hank? The man wouldn't take no for an answer. Hank seemed to think if he asked her to marry him every time he saw her that she might finally give in. Well, she wouldn't. She had no desire to marry any man.

He laughed out loud, reached his hand forward, and nudged her chin upward, closing her mouth. "I'll take that as a no." Amy tried to ignore the fire-flies tickling her stomach at his touch.

Stooping down, he looked at Beth. "You stay with Amy and mind her. When

I get back, we'll talk about that pickle."

"Yes, Papa. I'll be good."

Micah stood, tipped his hat at Mrs. Maples and Amy, and then walked off with a satisfied grin on his handsome face. She ought to be upset at him for teasing her, but inside, she knew she'd enjoyed it. This was a side of Micah she hadn't seen before—a side she very much liked.

Amy glanced around for Beth, and her heart ricocheted in her chest when she didn't see the girl. She hurried to the door to see if Beth had followed Micah. He was halfway down the street, driving the wagon toward the livery, and Beth was nowhere to be seen. She turned back into the store, squinting to see in the dim lighting.

To her left, over on the next aisle, she heard some giggles and hastened in that direction. Beth sat on the floor next to the cracker barrel, hugging her dolly and playing with a cute little girl with bright red hair and light blue eyes. The child's pale skin looked stark white next to Beth's lightly tanned arms.

A woman with auburn hair and fair skin walked down the aisle toward her. "'Tis a good time our girls are having. Your daughter sure resembles you."

Amy blinked, startled at the woman's comment. Beth looked like her? She studied Kathryn's daughter and realized it was true. Both she and Beth had brown hair and brown eyes, though Beth's hair was darker, like her father's.

The girls pushed their dollies together in a hug, and the store filled with childish giggles. The woman smiled at Amy. "Looks like they've become friends. I'm Tierney Chambers, and that's my daughter, Sophie. She's four."

"Amy Rogers. This is Beth, my cousin's daughter."

"Oh, 'tis sorry I am." Tierney pressed her hand over her mouth. "You two favor each other so, I was sure you were her mother."

"Beth is as dear to me as if she were mine." Amy stepped past the girls and motioned Tierney to follow her down the aisle. "Her mother died last month giving birth to Beth's sister."

"Oh my. Forgive me for being so callous. My husband always tells me my quick mouth will get me into trouble."

Amy waved her hand in the air. "Think nothing of it. It was an honest mistake. I suppose Beth and I do look a bit similar."

Tierney nodded. "Aye, you do, for sure." She looked to her right and fingered a ready-made denim shirt, starched and folded.

"It would be so nice for Beth to have a child her age to play with. Do you live in town?"

"No, not so close. We just moved here from Pennsylvania about a month ago. My Sean wanted to try his hand at farming. We live a couple hours' ride south of town."

Amy gasped. "Truly? We live out that way, too."

"Aye?" Tierney's eyes sparked with excitement, and she touched Amy's arm. "Oh, 'twould be wonderful if we lived close enough to visit each other once in a while. We'll just have to make sure my Sean and your husband meet."

Husband. Amy doubted she would ever marry and certainly wouldn't have the good fortune of wedding someone like Micah. She looked away, so Tierney wouldn't see her embarrassment, then glanced down at the two youngsters prancing down the aisle and making horse sounds. A smile tugged at her lips as she watched Beth enjoying her new friend. "Yes, it would be nice for Beth to have a playmate, and I would enjoy talking with another woman, but this is my first trip to town from our farm. I'm afraid you'd have to ask Micah for directions."

"Micah? That fine-looking man who walked you into the store is your husband, I'm guessin'." Tierney's pine green eyes held no guile.

Amy's face warmed to think of Micah as her husband. That would never happen, even if she had dreamed it a time or two. She was sure her cheeks were rose red. "No, um. . .Micah is—was—my cousin's husband. He's Beth's father."

Tierney blanched. "Oh no, I've done it again."

Amy couldn't help but laugh at Tierney's devastated expression. A soft smile tugged at the other woman's cheeks, and soon they were both laughing. Both girls stopped their horseplaying and looked at them with wide, curious eyes, making the women laugh even harder.

Tierney pulled a handkerchief from her sleeve and dabbed it in front of her mouth. "Oh my, I fear Sean is right. I do have a big mouth."

Amy grinned. She liked this woman. She hadn't had a close friend since she was eight years old and played with Velma Wheaten, her next-door neighbor. In her heart, she hoped that Tierney and she could become good friends, even though they'd just met.

"Well, I should let you finish your shopping." Tierney dabbed at her eyes then tucked away her handkerchief.

"It was a pleasure meeting you, Tierney. Please, let's try to get together. I would enjoy it as much as Beth."

"Me, too. Perhaps if you finish gathering your supplies before Sophie's father returns, we could sit out front in the rockers and let the girls play."

"That would be delightful. I'll get busy then." Amy looked down at her crumpled list. It shouldn't take too long. Picking out fabric was the only thing that would take much time.

Half an hour later, Amy and Beth left Mrs. Maples to cut out the cloth Amy had selected and met Tierney and Sophie on the mercantile's porch. Amy leaned against the porch railing with her back to the street, while the girls sat on the edge of the boardwalk, eating pickles and swinging their short legs back and forth.

"Heard you was in town."

The blood began to pound in Amy's temples, and she stiffened. She'd recognize Hank Foster's voice anywhere. Had Micah been serious about telling Mr. Foster she was in Stewart's Gap? Tierney lifted her brows and gazed at Amy. Her eyes held the question she didn't voice. Amy swallowed and turned.

"You're lookin' mighty fine today, darlin'. You ready fer me to come courtin' yet?"

Mortified, Amy gripped the railing and forced herself to look down at Mr. Foster. How could she make the man understand she wasn't interested in him without being too harsh?

Before she could respond, a rider raced into town and passed them at full speed. Both women and Hank turned to watch him. The man yanked his mount to a quick stop, jumped off, and ran up to a group of men gathered outside the saloon. Seconds later, the crowd erupted into cheers. Amy watched as the men quickly splintered off in different directions. Cheers and whoops could be heard all over the town.

Amy's gaze darted to Tierney's. What could be happening?

Chapter 8

Amy sighed with relief as Hank drifted off toward a nearby group of men, probably to find out what all the ruckus was about.

Micah drove the wagon up near the boardwalk and called out, "Whoa." As he jumped down, his gaze captured hers, his blue-green eyes twinkling. He darted up the steps, grabbed her around the waist, and swung her around in a full circle.

Amy's heart ricocheted in her chest at being pressed up against his sturdy body. His coffee-scented breath warmed her forehead. What was going on?

He set her down and stepped back, looking both excited and a tad bit embarrassed. He scratched an ear that was turning a bright shade of red. "Didn't you hear the news?"

Amy glanced at Tierney, who stared back with a crooked grin, eyebrows uplifted, and arms crossed over her chest. Forcing her heart to stop its stampeding, she looked back at Micah and shook her head. "No. What news?"

Micah's charming grin made cornmeal mush of her insides. "The United States signed a treaty with France buying all of Louisiana—from the Mississippi River all the way to the Rocky Mountains. It more than doubles the size of the nation."

Excitement coursed through Amy. "That's wonderful!" She peeked at Tierney and saw a thin man with blond hair and a big smile hurrying toward her friend. He murmured something and engulfed Tierney in an embrace. Amy surmised he was her husband, Sean. Glancing back at Micah, she almost wished he'd hug her again. She never knew being in Micah's arms would be so breathtaking and make her feel so protected.

"Yes, it's fantastic news." Micah's eyes danced, and he looked the most unfettered Amy had ever seen. "I feel like celebrating. Let's get a bite to eat before we go home."

———

At dusk, hours later, Micah handed Beth's limp, sleeping form to Sookie, who carried her inside the cabin. He returned to the wagon and helped Amy down, trying to ignore the way his fingers tingled when he touched her. All the way home, as the sunset painted the sky a brilliant wash of pink, purple, and orange, he'd berated himself for his impulsive hug, even though he'd like to sweep Amy into his arms right now.

But it was wrong, wasn't it?

His wife had not been dead that long. How could he even look at another woman? He realized he still had his hands on Amy's waist and released her. He stepped back.

"Thank you for dinner, Micah. I've not eaten in a café in a long time. It was very good." Amy seemed to be studying the ground. Her shyness stirred a protectiveness in him that he didn't want stirred.

He cleared his suddenly husky throat. "Um. . .you're welcome. I'll go find Ben, and we'll get the supplies unloaded so you women can get to sleep. I'd leave it all out here in the wagon overnight, but the wild animals would get into some of the things."

"All right." Amy glided up the steps and into the cabin. Was that disappointment he heard in her voice?

He shook his head. She'd been happy—grateful—moments before, so why was she downhearted now? Womenfolk sure were hard to understand. He hollered for Ben then grabbed a box near the back of the wagon.

Why had he enjoyed hugging Amy so much? Simply because it felt nice being close to a woman again?

He leaned against the side of the wagon and stared up at the darkening sky. No, it was more than that.

He was grateful for all she'd done for him and his family. That's all. She could have found work elsewhere, but she'd stayed and cooked, cleaned, and cared for his daughters and the rest of them. Yes, Amy Rogers was a woman deserving of hugs, but he wasn't the man to be giving them.

"It was mighty nice of your Sean to offer to help Micah and Ben with the farming." Amy smiled at Tierney, ever so glad her new friend had come to visit. Though it was only their second meeting, she felt a strong bond with Tierney, unlike anything she'd ever experienced. Sitting on the porch, sewing squares of a quilt Kathryn had cut out, they could watch Beth and Sophie, who sat under a tree, piling their laps full of yellow dandelion flowers and clover blossoms.

The comfortable breeze cooled Amy with its gentle fingers as birds chirped high up in the trees. May was a wonderful time of the year. Everything seemed new and fresh.

"Think nothing of it. My Sean is as happy to be with other menfolk as I am to spend time with you. 'Tis a rare day to sit and talk with a friend."

Amy giggled, and Tierney peeked up from her stitching. "Do you suppose the men actually talk to one another? I mean, Micah is so quiet."

"Aye, Sean is quite the talker. Some men are just more quiet than others."

"I suppose. Ben *is* more talkative than his brother."

"How is it you came to be caring for two such fine men?"

Amy darted a gaze at Tierney, not sure if she was teasing or serious. Her friend's brow dipped down in concentration as she tied a knot and then started sewing together two more sections. Amy blew out a sigh then told her the story of her mother's death, her father's mistreatment and leaving her destitute, and coming to the Walshes to find Kathryn in childbirth.

Tierney stopped sewing and had tears in her eyes by the time Amy was finished. "Aye, I do remember hearing something about that now, but I didn't know who folks were talking about then since we were new to the area. 'Twas sad circumstances that brought you here, to be sure, but God works in mysterious ways. I saw how Micah hugged you back in town."

Amy's heart skittered, and she poked her finger with her needle. Sucking at the blood, she stared at Tierney, stunned at her comment. "That was nothing. He was just excited over the new Louisiana treaty."

Tierney grinned. " 'Twas more than that, and I'm sure you noticed."

"No." Amy shook her head. "Micah still mourns his wife."

"How long has it been since she died?"

"Three months, yesterday." Amy watched Beth and Sophie chasing each other around a tree. Oh, to be an innocent child again. But then, she would have had to live her life over and learn anew that life wasn't always good—rarely good. Her father taught her that.

"Aye, it hasn't been all that long at that. But a man needs a woman by his side. These days are often hard, and a man must do what's best for his family— especially a man with young children. He doesn't always have time to mourn properly. Maybe God brought you here to take Kathryn's place."

This time her friend shocked her so much that she couldn't look anywhere but her hands. Why would God want her—a waif from a poor family—to replace Kathryn? Wouldn't God want the children to be with their real mother?

"I see that mind of yours contemplating." Amy looked up and saw Tierney wagging a finger at her. "Don't try to figure it all out. You just need to understand that God is a God of love. He sees what we cannot, and His plans are far greater for us than we could ever imagine. Don't be afraid of marriage. Perhaps Micah isn't the man for you, but there are other good men in this world."

Amy licked her fingers and smoothed out the crease she'd scrunched into her fabric. She'd seen few good men in the world. But could it actually be true that God had a plan for her life? And could it perhaps include Micah?

Her breathing trembled at the possibilities. She'd already gone from despising the man to admiring him. Could love be in the future? It was too much to hope for.

"Why do you suppose Kathryn wanted a quilt with a house design on it?" Tierney asked. "There's even smoke coming from the chimney on that section I just pieced together."

Amy shook her head. "I don't know. I've never seen one quite like it before, but Ben told me it's the sign of a safe house."

Tierney set her stitching in her lap and looked up. "What's that?"

"A place where runaway slaves can find refuge. The agents who run a safe house clothe and feed the runaways, then help them to get farther north. A quilt with a cabin and smoking chimney design that's hanging in a window or outside on a rope is a sign of a safe house. In fact, there are other quilt designs that also have hidden meanings. In some places, a bear claw quilt means to follow the bear tracks over the mountain."

"That's quite interesting." Tierney studied the fabric in her hands.

"But surely it must be a coincidence that Kathryn had this particular coverlet cut out and partially stitched."

Tierney shrugged. Amy glanced up as Sookie stuck her head out the cabin door.

"The soup is nearly done, Miz Amy."

"Thank you, Sookie." The young woman disappeared back in the house. She'd asked Sookie to join Tierney and her, but Sookie had preferred to stay inside and work while Missy slept. Amy turned her attention back to Tierney. "It doesn't make sense. The Walshes wouldn't run a safe house *and* own slaves."

"Are you certain Jonah and Sookie are slaves?"

Amy blinked. "Well, yes, I'm sure. I even heard Ben talking about how Micah had bought Sookie from a neighbor. He traded her for two mules. Isn't that appalling?"

"Well, perhaps you are right. It must be a coincidence."

One thing she knew, if Micah were dealing slaves, she could never give her heart to him totally.

Beth and Sophie squealed and ran toward them. "Horsies comin'," Beth cried.

Amy squinted and peered down the dirt trail. Her heart dropped to her feet, and she popped out of her chair. "Oh no. It can't be."

Tierney turned around and squinted at the approaching wagon. She looked back with a mischievous grin and twinkling green eyes. " 'Tis your beau."

Heat rushed to Amy's cheeks. She spit out each syllable, "Hank Foster is *not* my beau," then gave Tierney a disgusted look.

Her friend giggled and called the girls onto the porch. They clomped up the steps, arm in arm.

"Sophie's hungwy." Beth looked up with a hopeful gaze.

"No, I'm not." Sophie shook her head, and her thin braids bounced back and forth on her shoulders.

"Yes, you are. You want some pie." Beth's comment and her vigorously nodding head almost made Amy laugh in spite of Hank Foster's nearing presence.

"Oh, I do like pie." Sophie's eyes lit up at the prospect of a tasty treat.

Amy peeked at her friend, and Tierney's eyes gleamed with mirth. Amy refocused on the girls. "How about if you have that pie after dinner? The bean soup is nearly finished cooking. The men will be back from the field soon, and then we can all eat dinner."

Beth's bottom lip poked out. Sophie noticed and followed suit, causing Amy to bite back a grin. *The little scamp.* "Go on inside, wash up, and see if Sookie needs help setting the table. We'll be in shortly."

Amy strode to the end of the porch and picked up a metal bar then ran it around the inside of an iron triangle Micah had made. The loud clanging sound always hurt her ears, but it saved her or Sookie from having to walk all the way out to the field to call the men in for mealtimes.

Movement near the barn drew her attention, and she watched Jonah hobble out of the barn where he'd been polishing the saddles and other leather tack. She heard a whistle in the distance to her right and saw Micah, Ben, and Sean heading her way. *Please hurry.*

Gathering her composure, she turned to face Hank Foster.

"Well, how do, buttercup?"

Amy wished she could turn into butter, drip through the porch slats, and hide in the darkness under the house. Why couldn't this man leave her alone?

Tierney seemed to be struggling to keep a straight face. She ducked her head and studied her stitches, but her eyes kept darting upward.

Hank climbed down from his wagon and started toward her. Amy moved back until she ran into the rough cabin wall. He tipped his cap at Tierney then hopped up the stairs like a young man ready to take his gal to her first social.

"You're sure a sight for sore eyes, darlin'. I been dreamin' on you 'bout every night."

Amy tried unsuccessfully to swallow the lump in her throat. Had she ever been so mortified?

Tierney stood and laid her sewing in the basket next to her rocker. "I believe I hear Missy crying. I'll go in and tend her and help Sookie get dinner on the table."

Amy sent her a don't-you-dare-leave-me-alone look, but to no avail. Tierney ducked inside without a word but peeked back around the door and sent Amy an amused grin. Some friend. Deserting her when she needed her the most. Somehow, Amy had to make Hank understand she had no feelings for him. But how?

"I got that load of lumber Micah wanted from the sawmill. Said something about building some stairs."

She had no idea what he was talking about but felt a small amount of relief that he hadn't ridden all the way out here just to see her. Her legs trembled. She wiped her sweaty palms on her dress. Confrontation was not one of her strong points. She had learned just to stay out of her father's way when he'd been drinking or was in a foul mood.

"You know, I hinted to the parson last time he rode through these parts that he might have to preach a wedding ceremony next time he made his circuit."

Horrified, Amy straightened. This was getting out of hand. "Now see here, Mr. Foster. I never said anything about marrying you."

"Call me Hank, darlin'." He shrugged. "I knowed it would take you some time to get used to the idea, what with you bein' new to town and all. If it ain't this month when the parson comes, next month will do."

Amy tightened her fist and wanted to scream. How could a man be so dense?

"I heared tell that Micah and his brother is slave trading." He pulled a stem of hay from his overalls pocket and stuck it in the edge of his mouth. He pushed his cap back on his head, revealing a receding hairline.

The man's total shift of topics made Amy feel as if she'd been turning around in circles until she was dizzy. What had he heard that gave him the idea Micah was a slave trader? She had been hoping that Micah would not be involved in trading *people*, but the evidence seemed to be showing different. *That could explain the missing food from the root cellar.*

She sagged back against the cabin. It was bad enough that he owned two slaves, but if Micah was trading them, Amy would be sorely disappointed. Still, she'd defend Micah and Ben as long as she was under his employ.

"What if they *are* selling slaves? It's not illegal." Immoral maybe, but in this issue, the law had failed to catch up with what was right and decent. Amy shuddered. She knew Jonah and Sookie had a good life here, but they were still slaves. They couldn't go where they wanted or do what they chose to do. How could a person live like that?

She herself had nowhere else to go, but if she wanted to leave, she could. She had the option of choice—even if she only had one choice at the moment. Marrying Hank Foster didn't even rank as a second option.

Hank sniffed like he'd been insulted. "I might like to get in on the action."

Off to her right, she heard laughter and the crunch of boots against the ground, and relief flooded through her. The droning of Ben's tenor voice relaying a story to Micah and Sean grew louder. The men rounded the edge of the cabin, and Micah's eyes pricked with interest as he spotted the wagon. Amy knew the second he saw Hank Foster, because his countenance changed instantly, and his dark brows drew together. His gaze darted from her to Hank and back. Amy wasn't sure why, but she thought Micah wasn't too happy to see Hank.

Did he worry that she might take Hank up on his offer and leave him without someone to care for his home and children?

Chapter 9

As he approached the cabin, Micah watched Hank Foster strut around the porch like an old rooster, just as the man did every time he was around Amy. Had he asked her to marry him again?

Not one to normally dislike a person, Micah wasn't sure what it was about Hank that bothered him so much. Perhaps he was simply afraid of losing Amy. He couldn't imagine how they'd get along without her. Not that Amy returned Hank's affections. She acted peeved rather than moon-eyed like the eye-batting, coy young women he'd seen at town socials before he was married.

Ben's prattling voice faded as Micah stared at Hank's lips to see if he could decipher what the man was saying. When Ben took a breath, Micah was certain he heard something about a parson. Concern tightened his gut.

Beside him, Sean Chambers laughed out loud at something Ben said. Micah had liked Sean the day they first met in town. The wiry Englishman was a hard worker and a good help today as they weeded and hoed a large section of the cornfield.

Sean had explained how he and his wife were new to the area and anxious to get to know their neighbors. Micah was glad that Amy and Tierney got along so well together. Amy needed a friend.

She worked hard taking care of his home and children. Thinking of how he'd watched her working at the spinning wheel after the girls were in bed last night made him realize he never saw her idle. If she wasn't cooking or doing washing, she sat sewing or spinning.

Yes, he'd be up a creek without Amy, and yet he thought he'd miss her gentle smile and soft voice even more than all the things she did to care for him and his family. Somehow she managed to control his wild daughter without raising her voice, unlike Kathryn, who had little patience with her feisty child. A soothing warmth seeped through him as he realized that he didn't want Amy to leave because he'd miss her. He had feelings for her.

Micah stopped in his tracks. *I can't have feelings for Amy.*

Ben looked over his shoulder, eyebrows raised. Sean also stopped and turned toward him. "Something wrong?" he asked.

Scrambling to avoid questions, Micah looked at the shovel his brother held. "I think I'll run down to the barn and put away the tools before dinner. We'll enjoy our guests and visit for a while before they have to leave, instead of returning to the field."

Something that looked like panic darted across Ben's face. "*I'll* put the tools up." He reached for Micah's shovel, but Micah pulled it away.

"No, you go ahead. Maybe Sean wouldn't mind helping you unload the lumber in Hank's wagon, so he can get started back to town." Micah lifted his brows in question to Sean.

"Right, chap, I'd be delighted to help ol' Ben." He handed his hoe to Micah and waited for Ben to do the same.

"But—" Ben glanced at the barn and back to Micah.

"No buts. The sooner we get that wagon unloaded and Hank on his way, the sooner we can eat."

Ben looked at the barn again then nodded his head and handed Micah his shovel. Micah wondered why his brother was so interested in the barn, but his mind was swarming with so many other thoughts that he shrugged off his concern. Ben smacked Sean on the shoulder and started into another tale, obviously enjoying having someone willing to listen to his stories.

Micah shook his head and glanced at Amy, who was staring at him. She looked confused. He wanted nothing more than to take his hand and smooth away the creases lining her lightly tanned forehead. Would her skin feel as soft as Kathryn's?

He kicked his shovel, and all three tools clanged together. Turning toward the barn, he berated himself for thinking of Amy in that way. If he didn't keep his emotions under control, he'd scare her straight into Hank's arms. And that was the last thing he wanted.

The barn door didn't squeal when he opened it this time, thanks to a generous greasing he'd applied to the hinges this morning. One by one, he hung the tools on the wall.

He paced over to Rusty's empty stall. In a few hours, he'd have to bring the horses in from the pasture where they were grazing. Leaning on the stall gate, Micah considered his feelings for Amy.

They'd taken him by surprise. He first noticed his attraction to her back in town the day he'd grabbed her and swung her around in his arms. Her small form tucked in his arms perfectly.

He lifted his hat and ran his fingers through his sweaty hair. So, what should he do now? Amy hadn't done anything to make him think she might return his feelings. Sure, when she smiled at him those saddle-brown eyes of hers gleamed, but then, she smiled at everyone.

He'd watched her cuddle Beth and coo to the baby. Amy had been rewarded with Missy's first real smile. She'd make a good mother someday. Actually, she made a good mother now.

By keeping her here, working day and night, was he being fair to her? If she worked in town she might meet someone better than Hank Foster, someone who might woo and court her.

Micah's gut twisted. He didn't want anyone wooing Amy. He knew now that he wanted that job. But was it right? To court a woman living under his own roof? To consider remarrying when his wife had only been dead three months?

Men remarried quickly all the time, especially those with young children. But was he ready? His marriage to Kathryn had been far from perfect. His citified wife never quite adjusted to farm life. Was it wrong to hope he might one day have a happy marriage?

Arguing with himself wasn't getting him anywhere. He knelt in the hay right where he was and lifted his gaze toward the barn ceiling. "Heavenly Father, show me what to do. Was there a reason You brought Amy here? Dare I hope that You've provided another woman for me—a woman to care for my family—and me? A woman who might grow to love me?"

He waited, but no answer came. Not that he expected a lightning bolt from heaven, flashing God's response. He'd just have to keep praying and seeking God's will.

In the meantime, he'd enjoy Amy's good cooking and her company, and perhaps they could get to know each other better. They'd kept their distance since they first met. He knew Amy was embarrassed and sorry for bashing him in the head. Now, it was kind of funny thinking of that pint-sized woman knocking a man his size to the floor. He chuckled and turned toward the barn door. Best he get back or someone would come looking.

He took a step and froze in place. Behind him, he heard a scuffling then a whimper. Pivoting around, he saw nothing out of the ordinary. Empty stalls lined with fresh hay awaited the horses' return. Saddles sat on blocks, awaiting their riders. Dust motes drifted lazily on the sunlight, sneaking through small cracks in the barn.

Ben wouldn't disobey him, would he? As Micah started to turn, a squeal erupted near his feet. His blood boiled at his suspicions. Taking two steps to the center of the barn, he stooped, lifted the hatch to the underground storage area, and blinked when a young black woman holding a toddler stared up, the whites of her eyes showing.

What had Ben done now?

Micah had a difficult time waiting until dinner was over and the Chambers family had gone home so he could confront Ben about the slaves in the barn. He'd gone back and forth, trying to decide what was the right thing to do.

All through dinner, Amy sent him questioning glances. Perhaps she wondered how he'd managed to send Hank on his way so quickly. After the wagon was unloaded, Hank had told Micah he needed to talk to him about something. Micah suspected it had to do with Amy but never gave the man a chance to explain.

He told Hank they had guests and would have to talk another day. Relief, like taking a dip in a cool creek on a hot summer's day, spilled through him as Hank drove away. At least for now, they still had Amy. But for how long?

He paced out back of the cabin near the chopping block, waiting for Ben. His brother said he'd promised to tell Beth a story before she went to sleep. He probably should have given his daughter a good-night kiss, but he had to get out of the cabin before he said something he'd regret.

Micah turned when he heard a shuffling sound behind him. Jonah moseyed toward him at a slug's pace. "Hollerin' at that brother of yours won't make you feel no better."

Blinking, Micah stared at Jonah, amazed how the old man could read him so well. "How did you know?"

Jonah's shoulders bounced on a wheezy laugh. "If'n there'd been an unlit candle on the table betwixt you and Ben, it would have flamed to life. I seen the way you was glarin' at him."

Everybody had probably noticed. He was sure Amy had. That might have been why the Chamberses hightailed it on home after dinner instead of sitting around and visiting. But then Tierney *had* said something about making it home before dark.

The cabin door slammed, and a few moments later Ben strode around the side of the house, looking as if he were ready for a fight.

"Be nice to him, Micah. That boy done did a good thing."

Micah jerked his gaze toward Jonah. Did his friend know what Ben was doing? Was Jonah perhaps helping with the runaways, too? Why did it feel as if his life was spinning out of control?

He fought cobwebs of confusion and the pain of betrayal. Had his old mentor and friend been helping Ben? Why hadn't Jonah said something before?

"I guess I know what you want to talk about." Ben crossed his arms over his chest and glared at Micah without flinching.

Micah lifted his chin, determined not to give in. "I told you not to bring any more runaways on this land."

"As you're so fond of saying, it's my land, too."

Ben had him there, but Micah wasn't ready to back down. "I've seen what slave catchers do to the slaves they find."

A gleam sparked in Ben's eyes, and he leaned forward. "All the more reason to help runaways."

Micah crossed his arms over his chest. "I've also seen them burn the cabin they found the slaves in, leaving a family with six children homeless and the father injured. That's my point. They don't care who they hurt. Do you want them to hurt Jonah or Sookie? Or maybe Amy or the children?"

"Of course not. But there's more at stake here than just our family. That woman in the barn ran away because her *master*"—Ben nearly choked on the word—"was fixing to sell off her baby as soon as it was weaned—just like he'd done with her husband and two other children. How would *you* like it if that was Beth or Missy being sold and you had no say in it?"

Micah forced that picture from his mind. "This isn't a game, Ben. People can get hurt. Die."

"I know that," Ben hissed through his teeth. "I'm not stupid."

Micah wondered if his brother was wrong on that account. Ben sure wasn't thinking clearly. Micah yanked his hat off his head and ran his fingers through his hair. While he was opposed to slavery, he didn't want to put his family in danger to help runaways escape. He'd already lost his wife. He couldn't lose anyone else.

"Come on, Micah. I'm good at this. It feels right to help these people."

Micah stared into his brother's blue-green eyes, so much like his own, and saw the sincerity there. His brother was asking for a chance to prove himself. As much as Micah disliked Ben endangering the family, he couldn't help but admire him for wanting to help these unfortunate people who had so little. His esteem for his brother kicked up a notch or two.

"Are you a conductor? Is that why you get up so often at night?"

A sheepish grin turned up the corners of Ben's mouth. "Sometimes, but I only take them a few miles then pass them off to a true conductor. I didn't want to be gone too long while you were off hunting. And with you home, I couldn't be gone too long, or you'd find out."

Micah wanted to rage at Ben for putting Kathryn and Beth in danger and then going off at night and leaving them with only aged Jonah for protection. But God had watched over his family, and now he was home and would protect them, with God's help.

"You can't fault that woman for wanting to keep her child."

"No, I don't." Micah looked at Ben. "But I need you to understand how much pressure I already have on my shoulders. It's not easy running a farm, raising and protecting a family, and now to have the worry of slave catchers coming here and hurting you or someone else."

"Sometimes God asks us to do difficult things," Ben responded, looking older than his seventeen years. "I have to be obedient to what He calls me to do, just like you do. It wasn't easy for us when you left to go trapping, but you had to do what you felt God was calling you to do, just like me."

Micah heaved a sigh. How could he fight God?—if this was truly God's doing. His brother's hopeful eyes begged for understanding.

He never remembered Ben being so dedicated to any other cause. He was scared half to death to think of his brother in such danger. But he couldn't protect Ben forever. Time to trust God to do that.

"All right, but I want you to be very careful. And I don't want slaves coming here too often. Only when absolutely necessary, and only for a short time. And keep them away from the cabin and Amy and the children. Runaways are desperate, and I don't want my family getting hurt. You understand?"

Ben's eyes sparked with excitement. "Thank you, Micah. I'll be careful. I always have. You won't regret this." Ben dashed off. He pumped his fist in the air and jumped, yelling, "Yeehaw!"

Micah grinned at his brother's youthful exuberance, but deep inside, he already regretted his decision.

Chapter 10

Happy to be away from the hot, steaming washing pot, Amy tossed Micah's freshly rinsed blue cotton shirt over the rope and straightened it. Beth trotted back and forth underneath the clothing strung out on the line between two trees. She neighed like a horse and waved her hands in the air.

"Look at me. I'm a horsie."

Amy smiled as Beth pretended to rear and then pranced off toward where Sookie sat under a tree, nursing Missy. Her heart pinged. *What would it feel like to hug a baby to my bosom and nurse it? To have a child totally dependent on me for life? My own child?*

Amy shook her head to force away the gripping thought. Unlike most women her age, she'd never before wondered what it would be like to be a mother. To have a child, she had to have a husband, and she'd never wanted that before.

Her gaze traveled back to Sookie. In a way, the young woman was lucky, but then again, she had lost her own child. Was it difficult for her to wet-nurse little Missy?

Sookie rarely spoke, except to Jonah. She went about her chores, content to hum and do her work, but she preferred not to socialize with Amy. That was a big disappointment. Amy had hoped they might become friends, but that was probably a foolish thought. On the other hand, Micah and Jonah seemed quite friendly with each other.

Shaking out Ben's shirt, she stared off into the distance, reveling in the happiness she'd found at the Walsh farm. Back home, she'd been happy when her mother was alive, though there was always the cloud of fear that her father would return and hurt her mother. Horatio Rogers had never hit his daughter, but Amy had grown up frightened of him and most other men.

She reached for Micah's spare long johns. At first, she'd been terribly embarrassed to look upon and handle the men's undergarments, but now it no longer bothered her. They were just clothes that needed laundering.

Spreading out the undergarment on the line, she considered how contented she'd grown. But how long could things continue as they had? She and Micah had settled into a comfortable rapport, though they didn't spend much time together. Micah was so busy with the farm that he was rarely around except for meals and the girls' bedtime.

She figured at some point Micah would want to remarry, and then where would she be? The cabin was far too small for another person. Already, she and Sookie shared a bed, having long ago tossed out the mat Sookie had first used for sleeping. Amy had no idea where Missy would sleep once she outgrew her crib. Beth's tiny bed was too small for both children.

Amy's thoughts turned to Ben. She worried about him. He seemed so tired lately, often nearly falling asleep at the dinner table. She hoped he wasn't sick. He'd become the brother she never had, and he had settled down quite a bit since Micah's return. As much as Ben complained about wanting to be treated like a man, Amy thought he felt relieved that Micah was the one in charge.

"Mighty purdy day we're having, ain't it, Miz Amy? Mizzy Beth sure is having a pleasurable time."

Amy peeked between Ben's shirt and the long johns to see Jonah's dark face, alight with his gap-toothed grin. She couldn't remember a time, other than when Kathryn had died, that he didn't have a smile on his face or was humming a song. What would it feel like to be so lighthearted?

"Yes, siree, the Good Lawd done painted one fine day t'day."

Glancing upward through the tall oak trees, Amy narrowed her eyes against the glare of the bright sky. Cottony white clouds drifted against the blue blanket. A hawk screeched then dove downward and swooped away with some poor critter in its talons.

"That's the law of nature. The strong survive and the weak don't. But with man, the Good Lawd, He gives us the strength we needs to get by."

Amy fixed her gaze on Jonah. He wasn't a big man like Micah. In fact he only stood an inch or so taller than herself, yet there was a power in him that emanated from inside. Was that what he was talking about? Strength from God?

If only she could have that surety. But how could she trust a heavenly Father she couldn't see when her own earthly father had been so vile? "I'm trying to figure God out."

"You cain't figure it all out. There comes a time you just have to believe."

Amy studied the bed of clover at her feet. "But it's so *hard* to believe."

"How come?" Jonah leaned against one of the trees supporting the clothesline. He pulled out his pocketknife and a partially carved stick and started whittling.

Amy glanced over to where Sookie had been sitting and realized she must have taken Missy inside. Beth sat near the porch steps digging dirt with a stick. With nobody else around, she told Jonah about her parents and how Horatio Rogers had left her and her mother to get by on their own—at least until the day he discovered he was dying. By then her mother was already dead, and Amy was sewing clothes and doing mending to put food on her meager table.

"You gotta fo'give yo' pappy."

"How?" Amy stared into Jonah's sympathetic eyes. She'd despised her father for so long, she had no idea how to be rid of the sourness it left in her like curdled milk. She viewed all men the same—until Micah and Ben proved her wrong. Tierney also helped her to realize that there are good men in this world, just as there are bad ones. "How do I forgive my father?"

"You cain't do it by yo'self, Miz Amy, you gotta let God help you."

"But how do I do that?"

"You start by surrendering yo' heart to the Good Lawd."

Amy picked at a hole in the sock she'd just retrieved from the basket. She needed to repair it before it got any bigger. She wanted to ask Jonah the question burning in her heart, but felt it rude. Still, she needed answers. "Is that how you handle being a slave? By surrendering your own desires to God?"

Jonah blinked then smiled his big, yellow-toothed grin. " 'Twas a day I did that. Got up ever' morning and asked God fo' the strength to do what He set before me. Fact is, I still do that. We all need God's help each day."

His forehead furrowed, and he rubbed his thumb and forefinger together. Then he looked up with gray brows lifted. "But don't you know I ain't a slave no longer? I'm a freed man."

Free? "But I thought you were a slave. How long have you been free?" Amy's mind blurred with confusion. That could explain how Micah and Jonah were such good friends. Though she'd personally known no white men who associated with slaves on social terms, it warmed her heart that Micah did.

"I been free ever since Micah done bought me from my last owner. First thing he done was to grant my freedom."

"Why do you stay here if you can go wherever you want?"

"Right here's where I want to be. Everybody I love is here."

Amy considered his comment. They were one and the same—everyone she loved lived here on this land.

"Sookie ain't no slave neither. Micah done set her free, too."

Amy blinked, trying to grasp what he'd said. She looked into the little man's dark eyes until he nodded. How could she have not known this? For months she'd misjudged Micah, and realizing her mistake made her feel ill.

She'd made a flagrant assumption that had allowed her to keep an emotional distance from him. What would she do since that barrier no longer stood between them? Living and working on the Walsh farm was all she had. It had become her home. She loved the children and everyone else residing there—even Micah. That last thought rooted her in place.

"Miz Amy, we all face hard times and good times. It's easy to love and follow God when things are good, but we need Him even more on the bad days. God is not like yo' father. The Good Lawd loves you and yearns for you to turn to Him. Don't shut out the Good Lawd. You needs Him—and He needs you." Jonah pushed away from the tree he'd been leaning on and ambled toward where

Beth played in the dirt.

God needs me.

That was something she'd never heard before. Why would He need her? It was something to contemplate.

God loves me.

Amy stared up through the trees to the bright sky above. The thought of the Creator of the world loving her warmed her insides, making her feel special.

If only she could be sure what Jonah said was true, she'd embrace it in a heartbeat. But she'd known so much disappointment that trusting and believing in Someone as good and loving as Jonah's God was difficult.

———

Micah stared down at Missy, asleep in his arms. Her fuzzy blond hair stuck straight up. One of the high points of his day was rocking her to sleep after Sookie nursed her every evening. Pink, bow-shaped lips darted up in a smile then relaxed, making him wonder what babies dreamed about.

He pushed up from the rocker with one arm and carried Missy to her cradle in the bedroom. Beth, who should have already been asleep, flipped over, watching him.

"Tell me another story, Papa."

He laid Missy down and covered her then turned to Beth. He took in her soft brown hair and mischievous brown eyes, and it stunned him to realize that Beth's coloring closely resembled Amy's. Dropping to the side of the bed, he considered that. A stranger walking down the boardwalk in town would most likely think Beth was Amy's daughter. Instead of feeling regret at that thought as he would have expected, his chest warmed with the idea. Amy would be a good wife and mother someday. Was it right of him to hope her eye might turn his way? Wouldn't she rather marry a younger man than be strapped with him, caring for his children and his home? The fair thing was to offer Amy her freedom—just like he had Jonah and Sookie.

That thought chilled him as if he had stepped from a warm cabin outside on a cold, snowy day.

"Papa, tell me a story." Beth's warm hand pushed against his leg.

Kneeling, he tickled her tummy, receiving a squeal and giggles from her. "Do it again." She lay with her arms over her head, waiting for him to repeat his actions.

Not wanting to stir her up so she couldn't sleep, he bent over the bed and applied a loud kiss to her soft cheek. "How about a butterfly kiss instead?"

Beth giggled and nodded, her eyes sparking with delight. Leaning down, he fluttered his eyelashes up and down on her cheek. Her sweet laughter sounded better to him than the wind rustling through a cornfield, lush and ripe for the harvest.

"Again."

Complying with her orders, he turned his head and kissed her with his other eye.

"Again."

This time he looked up and shook his head. "Time for all little girls to go to sleep."

Beth stuck out her bottom lip in a pout, but he ignored it and pulled the lightweight cover over her legs. He kissed her forehead and said, "Night, night, Punkin."

Neither of the women were inside, so he left Ben, who sat at the table looking through a catalog, to watch over the girls. Sookie sat on the porch in the rocking chair next to Jonah, stitching a gown for Missy.

"Where's Amy?"

"Down at the garden." Jonah nodded his head in the garden's direction.

Micah trotted down the stairs and around the back of the cabin and saw Amy standing outside the weathered gray picket fence that surrounded the patch. Her garden was just as tidy and orderly as the cabin. In fact, it resembled a finely planned patchwork quilt. Salad vegetables like lettuce and radishes had reached their peak growing season and were starting to fade, while turnips, potatoes, and squash were still leafing out.

Amy must have heard his approach because she turned around. She brushed her hands along her skirt, and then held them in front of her. Her thin eyebrows lifted in curiosity. Since he rarely sought out her company, he wondered what she was thinking.

He took a moment to survey the garden again then glanced back at her, hoping he just imagined that his presence made her nervous. "Might I have a word with you?"

She nodded. "Of course. I'm done here anyway. I wanted to see if there were enough greens left to make a salad tomorrow. With the sun setting, it's getting hard to see. Mind if we walk down to the creek?"

"That's fine." He opened the fence gate, allowing her to exit. Side by side, they veered past the cabin and toward the creek. He wondered how to say what was on his heart. Best just start at the beginning, Jonah always said.

"I should have done this a long time ago, but I want to thank you for how you took charge of the house and the girls after Kathryn died. I know I haven't said much about it, but I do appreciate everything you've done." He glanced sideways, sure now that it was a blush that colored Amy's cheeks.

"I didn't do all that much."

Surprised at her humility, Micah stopped and Amy did, too. He turned toward her, wanting to make sure she knew how deeply he was in her debt. "Yes, you *have* done a lot. I can't imagine what things would be like around here if not for you."

Her cheeks remained a soft rose color, and Amy glanced down. The evening breeze lifted and teased wisps of soft brown hair that had come loose from her bun, making him want to smooth them in place. Walking past her on the street, most men would think Amy plain. . .until she lifted those big brown eyes and stared into their souls. Hers was a gentle beauty of giving of herself to others. He didn't remember ever hearing her complain, although she *had* nagged Ben a time or two not to slam the door or to wipe the mud off his boots before entering the cabin.

When Amy peeked up at him through her thick lashes, Micah realized he'd been staring. He cleared his throat. "I think perhaps I've been taking advantage of you."

Something like alarm flashed through Amy's eyes. Micah rubbed the back of his neck, trying to figure out what he wanted to say. Sometimes he wished he was better with words. "You're so good with the girls. . .uh, that I just thought maybe you'd want to be a mother someday."

Amy's eyes widened even farther. If he hadn't felt so serious, he might have laughed at her expression.

"Well. . .o–of course I would. Someday."

"It's just that you work so hard here, you'll never have a chance to meet a beau. I was wondering if maybe you felt stymied here, what with all you have to do. I thought perhaps you would rather live in town."

Amy's mouth opened, but no words came out. Her eyes suddenly brightened with unshed tears. Micah knew his words hadn't come out as he'd planned.

"Y–you mean you want me to leave?"

Chapter 11

Amy's misery knotted her stomach and pinched her heart. She lifted her hand to her chest and stared out at the creek. The waters looked darker as the evening shadows grew. Crickets chirped, and nearby a frog croaked, oblivious to her pain.

What had she done wrong? Why would Micah cast her aside like a broken ax handle? Where would she go?

Micah lifted his hands in surrender. "Hang on, I didn't mean that at all."

She swatted at the tears trickling down her chin, then turned and lifted her gaze to his. His beautiful blue-green eyes looked pained. Frustration wrinkled his normally handsome face, and he rubbed the back of his neck in a manner that Amy had come to recognize as meaning he was perplexed or deep in thought.

"Amy."

Her heart skipped at the sound of her name on his lips. She wasn't sure when it had happened, but she cared far too much for Micah Walsh.

"I don't want you to leave. The fact is, I can't imagine how we'd survive without you. I just don't want you to feel like you're tied here if you desire to go somewhere else. You'd tell me, wouldn't you?" Micah's penetrating gaze begged for understanding. "I mean, if you weren't happy here? If I worked you too hard?"

She swallowed the thick lump in her throat, thankful that she'd misunderstood his meaning. He didn't want her to go! "I believe I would."

Micah's expression softened, and his eyes brimmed with relief. "Good. You can always be honest with me."

Amy wondered what he'd say if she told him about her attraction to him. She bit back a smile as she imagined the big man hurrying away without so much as a glance back over his broad shoulder.

"Now don't take me wrong here, but I want to pay you a little something for all you do. You can save the money or use it to buy fripperies or other things you need at the store."

The soothing warmth that had just flooded Amy melted away. He wanted to pay her like some servant? She didn't know why, but for some reason that cheapened things. Made her feel like paid help instead of family. She shook her head.

Micah held up his big hand. "I won't take no for an answer. I pay Jonah and Sookie, so it's only fair to pay you, too."

She crossed her arms over her chest, knowing he wouldn't understand how she felt. So much for being honest with him. "I don't want your money."

"Well, you're gonna get it." Micah shoved his hands on his hips. "It's not a lot, but it's yours to do with as you please. After I sell the next batch of furs, I'll give you three dollars for the months you've already worked and a dollar the first of every month from now on."

Amy blinked. She could do a lot with a whole dollar. Still, it would change everything. Shaking her head, she turned and walked back toward the cabin. Micah's warm hand on her shoulder pulled her to a stop.

"Please, let me do this for you. It's such a small thing when you've given up your whole life to stay here and help me. . . uh. . .us."

He had no idea that this *was* her whole life. She had nothing else. No home. No family. When she didn't respond, he moved around so he could face her.

His calloused thumb wiped her tears, sending a delicious shiver down her spine. "Is it such a hard thing for you to accept a man's gratitude?"

He didn't understand. How could he? He lived on the land his parents and grandparents had worked. Lived in the cabin his own great-grandfather built. Had a brother and children he loved, who loved him back. Micah Walsh had no idea what it felt like to have nobody. Nothing.

Still, she wouldn't inflict her pain on him. She would accept his gift, and maybe someday she'd have enough money to get her own place. One day when Micah no longer needed her. Without looking into his eyes, she nodded.

His sigh of relief blasted her in the face, and she smelled coffee on his breath. "Great. Good."

After a moment he brushed her hair back off her cheek and tilted her chin up. "I want you to be happy here. Are you?"

Frustrated by her tears, she wiped them on her sleeve.

"Why are you crying?"

She couldn't explain the swarm of emotions buzzing through her at his nearness. She didn't understand them all herself, so she surely couldn't explain them. "I'm happy."

Micah huffed. "You sure don't look it."

Amy ventured a glance upward. "You've been married. Don't you know by now that women cry when they're happy?"

He looked confused for a moment then understanding dawned. "Oh. Yeah."

"I've never been happier in my life than I am here. I love the girls and. . ." *You.*

She had to control her sudden realization that she loved Micah Walsh. "And?"

"Umm, I, uh. . .need to mix up the bread for tomorrow."

Dazed, Amy pivoted and hurried toward the cabin. It was so hard to remain coherent in Micah's overwhelming presence. A tumble of confused thoughts and feelings assailed her. How could she hide her attraction to him? She couldn't let Micah know how she felt, or he'd surely send her away.

She remembered the night she'd overheard Micah and Ben talking about marriage while she did the dishes. Ben had said he'd like to marry one day, but Micah said he didn't ever plan to wed again.

Suddenly, that dollar a month sounded like a tremendous blessing. If she could only hide her feelings long enough, perhaps she could save enough to start over somewhere else.

The thought was both exhilarating and distressing. How could she leave the children she loved? Leave Micah?

"They's here!"

Beth's excited shriek signaled that the Chambers family had arrived. The girl ran back outside, not even bothering to shut the door. Amy didn't mind though. The warm breeze helped circulate the hotter air inside where she'd been baking.

Using her sleeve, Amy wiped the sweat from her brow, grabbed a nearby towel, and covered up the apple crisp that had just finished cooking. Her mouth watered at the fragrant, apple-cinnamon scent and the thought of eating her favorite dessert. Gratitude for Micah's beaver pelts coursed through her. They had been able to trade for luxuries like cinnamon, nutmeg, and extra sugar, because it seemed every man in Boston just had to have a beaver fur hat.

She stepped onto the porch, and the cooler air felt wonderful to her moist skin. Tierney grabbed her husband's shoulders as he lifted her from the wagon. She looked up with a smile and waved. The hammering on the side of the house where Micah and Ben were building a stairway up to their room ceased, and they stepped around the side of the cabin and into view. Sean, an expert carpenter, had offered his services and brought Tierney and Sophie along to socialize while he worked.

The moment Sean set Sophie on the ground, she and Beth were off like racehorses, squealing and chasing each other in a wide arc around the wagon. The horses hitched to the wagon snorted and shook their heads, unused to two miniature people whooping and hollering. Micah snatched up Beth as she ran past, and Sean hurried to the front of the wagon to calm his team.

"Down, Papa. Gotta play with Sophie." Beth squirmed and kicked her feet, while Tierney took hold of her daughter.

"Beth, hold still and look at me." Micah's stern voice didn't allow for nonsense.

Not used to her soft-spoken father's rare scolding, Beth stopped moving and looked up with her bottom lip stuck out and trembling.

"You know, Punkin, that you don't run around hollering near horses. They're big and can get spooked and hurt you."

Beth nodded, her big brown eyes brimming with tears. Micah gave her a hug and said, "Good girl."

He set her down, and she ran to Amy, burying her face in Amy's skirts. She patted the girl's head. "Your father is right, Beth. You know better."

Not getting the sympathy she wanted, Beth moved over to Sophie. "We're going spwashing in the cweek."

Amy glanced at Micah, and he grinned.

The men slapped each other on the shoulder and asked how their crops were doing and how the hunting had been. Ben laid down his hammer and joined in the conversation.

"Girls will be girls," Tierney offered.

Amy turned and hugged her friend. "I can't believe it's only been a month since you were last here. Seems more like half a year."

" 'Tis a busy season."

Amy agreed and looked at her friend's beaming face. "Shall we go down by the creek? It's shady, and the girls can play in the water."

"Aye, sounds delightful."

Amy glanced at the porch where Sookie sat with Missy on her shoulder. The baby had finished nursing and now looked ready to play rather than nap. "Would you care to join us, Sookie? We'd love to have you come along."

The young black woman glanced away. "Oh no, ma'am. I's jus' gonna play with little Missy then sew on my new dress for a spell."

Amy knew it wouldn't do any good to try to persuade her. Sookie was a loner. "At least let me take Missy. That way you'll get more sewing done."

"That would be nice, ma'am. I'll jus' change her nappy and get her blanket." She stood and disappeared inside the cabin.

Tierney rocked back and forth, her gray calico skirts swishing around her legs. "I have a secret." Her eyes, the color of pine needles, danced with glee.

Amy took her hand. "Oh, do tell."

Her friend shook her head. "No, you'll have to wait till we're at the creek."

"Meanie."

Tierney tucked her hands behind her back and laughed.

Sookie returned and handed Missy to Amy. The cherub bounced in Amy's arms then laid an openmouthed, wet, sloppy kiss on Amy's cheek.

"Looks as if she loves you."

"And I love her." Amy smiled back at Tierney.

"I'll keep an eye on the stew while you're gone," Sookie said as she turned toward the porch steps.

Amy watched her go back inside the hot cabin, wishing Sookie would let

184

her guard down so they could become friends. Though Amy now knew that Sookie was free, she still acted as Amy imagined a slave would act. Only she was no longer a slave. If only she could help the girl somehow.

Down at the creek, Amy spread out Missy's blanket on the ankle-high grass and laid the baby down. The child pumped her feet and arms as if she wanted to go for a swim, her downy head bouncing. Amy wondered what their lives would be like when Missy started crawling.

Tierney plopped down beside her and started removing Sophie's shoes. Beth followed suit, trying to remove her own boots. After removing Beth's smock, Amy watched as the children, dressed in their undergarments, waded into the shallow water. There had been little rain lately, which was bad for the crops and garden but made the water the perfect depth for two little girls. They squatted down and squealed when the cool water wetted their bottoms. Tierney's soft laugh drew Amy's attention to her friend.

"So tell me your secret."

Tierney's eyes twinkled. "Sean and I are expecting again."

Amy rose onto her knees and threw her arms around her friend. "Oh, that's wonderful! I'm so happy for you."

"Aye, me, too. I didn't know if I could bear another child after losing Patrick."

A tremble raced through Amy, and she gasped. "You lost a child? When?"

" 'Twas after Sophie was born." Tierney stared in the direction of the stream. "I was with child on the ship ride to America, but the journey was so rough and the food so poor, me wee babe didn't survive. We named him Patrick, and he was buried at sea."

"Oh, Tierney, I'm so sorry." Amy blinked back the tears stinging her eyes and ached for her friend's loss. Why did life have to be filled with so much pain?

" 'Twas in the past, and God has seen fit to bless us with another child. 'Tis happy I am."

"Well," Amy ventured, her insides all a-jiggle with nervous excitement, "I have some news, also."

Tierney quirked up an eyebrow. Amy glanced at the girls to make sure they were all right. She plucked a leaf from Missy's hand before the baby could stuff it in her mouth. "I've been talking with Jonah."

"Have you now? And what does Jonah have to say?"

"He's been telling me about God."

Tierney sat up straighter, her eyes sparkled with excitement. Amy knew her news would please her friend.

"I've come to see that not all men are cruel like my father. In fact, I believe he's in the minority. Ben and Micah are both kind, gentle men. . .for the most part, as is Jonah. I've seen how kind Sean is and how much he loves you and

Sophie. My distorted view of men affected my ability to believe in God."

Tierney nodded. "Aye, 'tis often the way of things."

"I'm ready now." Amy clutched her fingers in her lap, hoping—no, knowing—she was making the right decision.

Tierney's brows dipped. "Ready for what?"

Amy inhaled a deep breath. "To give my heart to God."

Chapter 12

Amy snapped another green bean and dropped it in the bowl she and Sookie were sharing. Joy bubbled up in her heart as she remembered the day the previous week when Tierney had explained how to ask God to forgive her sins and come into her heart. Afterwards, Amy had given her heart to God. "Do you believe in God, Sookie?"

With eyes wide, Sookie stared at Amy then dropped her gaze back to her apron, which was filled with freshly picked beans. She grabbed several, snapped off the ends, and broke them in half.

"It's all right if you'd rather not talk about it." Amy hoped to make Sookie feel less intimidated. Trying to draw the young black woman into conversation was harder than catching one of the wild geese that frequented the creek area.

"I didn't use to." Sookie cast a shy glance Amy's way. "But Jonah, he's been yammering on about God ever since I comed here. Some of what he says makes sense."

Amy closed her mouth. That was the longest passage of speech she'd ever heard Sookie utter. Deep inside, she still hoped that one day they'd become friends. Maybe Sookie had to learn first that she was safe here.

"I know what you mean. Jonah has been spouting his gospel to me as long as I've been here, too."

Sookie's lips turned up in a shy smile. "He's persistent, for sure."

Amy peeked at Beth to make sure she wasn't getting into trouble. Relief flooded her to see the child asleep next to Missy on the quilt where she and Sookie sat. A crushed bean rested in Beth's open palm. The sun shone through the trees, leaving dappled shadows dancing on her cheek. Amy reached over and rescued the helpless bean, thankful the movement didn't awaken Beth. The feisty child had played until she dropped, as usual. Amy reached for another bean.

"I didn't want to listen to Jonah at first," Amy said. "But as I came to realize not all men are mean and cruel like my father, I began to hope what Jonah said was true. I guess my view of God was tarnished because of the way I looked at men. I never knew there was a heavenly Father who loves us more than we can imagine." Amy glanced at Sookie, surprised to see her staring back.

"Mm-hmm, I heared Jonah say that."

"Tierney says the same thing—and I believe it now."

Sookie glanced up again, surprise etched on her dark face. "You do?"

She nodded and smiled. "Tierney helped me to pray and ask God into my heart. Oh, Sookie, it feels so wonderful! I can't explain it, but I feel lighter. Happier."

"That be good, Miz Amy. You deserves to be happy. You work mighty hard to keep them men and children happy." Sookie shared one of her rare smiles and then focused on the pile of beans in her lap.

Amy breathed a mental prayer to God, thanking Him for the small breakthrough. It was hard to work side by side every day and not chat about things.

That evening, Amy closed the huge family Bible that had belonged to Kathryn. She yawned, pondering the words she'd read. She wondered how a man like Job could love God after all that had happened to him. It seemed to her that losing everything would make any man turn from God, but Job hadn't. She could relate well to him, having lost what little in life she held dear.

She yawned again and stood, clutching the heavy book to her chest. Time for bed. Sookie and the girls were already asleep, and soft snores could be heard from the bedroom. After putting away the cherished Bible, she stepped outside, thankful the weather was warm enough she didn't have to don her cloak for a final trip to the privy.

A few minutes later, she made her way back to the cabin. The half moon barely gave out enough light to illuminate the path. As she reached the back of the cabin, she stopped and leaned against it, staring up into the night sky. Since coming to believe in God, she felt closer to His creation and noticed things she never took time to notice before. As she stood without moving, the crickets once again began chirping. Far off, she could hear an owl hooting.

She never thought she could be happier, but once she asked God into her heart, it was as if a weight she never knew was there had lifted. The sky looked bluer, the flowers more colorful, and the love in her heart for Micah soared. She hadn't yet told him of her decision to serve the Lord. Micah was so busy, they rarely got to talk alone, and it didn't seem something she wanted to shout out loud.

Amy rubbed her hand over her heart. Why did it hurt to love someone? Or was the hurting because Micah didn't know she loved him? Standing well over six feet tall, his physical presence was impressive, but what amazed her was how he would get down on the floor and chase Beth around the table. The child's sparkling eyes and infectious laughter was sweeter than any treat Amy could bake.

And then there was *Micah's* laughter. She didn't hear it often, mostly when he played with Beth or joked with Ben. It warmed her insides like hot tea on a cold night. And his eyes. She'd never seen any blue-green eyes like his and Ben's. Too bad she had started averting her gaze from Micah's. If she didn't look into his eyes, he couldn't read the love burning there.

Jonah told her to give her burdens to God. Could loving someone be a burden? If that person didn't return that love, then yes, it could be.

Amy closed her eyes and prayed, asking God to show her what to do with these feelings for Micah Walsh that threatened to overflow like a flash flood. After a few minutes, a gentle warmth swept over her. She still didn't know what to do, but she'd try to leave it in the Lord's hands.

As she went around the side of the cabin, she saw a light flooding out the open barn door. Micah was probably working late. Dare she walk down there and talk to him?

She peeked at Jonah's cabin and saw that his lamp was already out. The old man preferred going to bed as the sun set, but she never could go to sleep that early. Looking up, she could see a light glowing behind the quilt covering the doorway to the room where Micah and Ben slept. The odor of freshly cut wood scented the evening air. Amy admired the new stairway up to their room. The men had done a fine job building it, but she wondered why they hadn't built a door while they were working.

Taking in a breath of resolve, she turned toward the barn. Moments alone with Micah were few and far between. Maybe she would tell him of her decision. She could talk to him and still hide her true feelings, couldn't she?

Peering around the door, she watched Micah working by lamplight at the far end of the barn. She tiptoed inside, admiring the fine picture he made with his muscles tightening his shirt across the back as he unloaded a heavy crate from the back of the wagon. The scent of horses, fresh hay, and leather greeted her. A nervous excitement tickled her stomach, and she couldn't keep what she was sure was a silly grin off her face.

Suddenly, she heard footsteps pounding toward her, and she instinctively ducked into the shadows beside the closest stall. A horse nearby nickered, but she hoped Micah would think it was greeting whoever was approaching.

Amy had spent many nights hiding in the shadows when her father had come home after drinking too much. She made herself as small as possible. Fortunately, the only lamp lit was the one on the other side of Micah.

The steps slowed as they neared the door, and Ben stepped inside the barn. "Found it." He held up something to Micah, but his body shielded the item from Amy's view.

"Good. The shirt Samson is wearing is in tatters."

Amy wondered who Samson was, and she now understood what had happened to all Ben's clothes. He'd given them away. She'd always wondered how he could lose something as important as a shirt.

"I don't know how I'm going to explain to Amy that I've lost another shirt. I mean, come on. How many shirts can a man lose? I'm down to two."

"After we sell this next batch, you can buy some new ones."

Amy held back a gasp at Micah's words. Tears burned her eyes. A batch of slaves? No. It couldn't be. Was Micah dealing slaves after setting Jonah and Sookie free? It didn't make sense.

She scooted forward, knowing the stall rails would hide her. Maybe she had misunderstood them.

"I'm thinking about taking this next batch somewhere besides Stewart's Gap. Mr. Maples said he had a glut at the moment so the price would be less."

Ben shook his head. "I thought he told you he'd take as many as you could send his way."

Micah shrugged. "You best give that to Samson, so we can get them on their way."

"All right."

Mr. Maples was also a slave trader? With her heart in her throat, Amy watched as Ben kicked away a pile of hay then bent over and lifted up a trap door she never knew was there. A faint light shone upward, then disappeared as Ben leaned over the opening. "Come on up here, Samson."

"Don't forget the door," Micah warned.

"Oh! Yeah." Ben pivoted, jogged to the barn doors, and closed them.

Amy held her breath, hoping that he wouldn't spot her. Fortunately, he turned away from her rather than in her direction. He strode back and held out the white shirt to a thin black man who'd crawled out of the hole. "Here. Put this on."

"Yassa. Thank ya, suh."

When the black man turned to slip his arm in the shirt Ben held out, Amy nearly gasped out loud. His back was covered in so many angry scars that she was hard-pressed to see a clear place on his skin. She shrank back against railings. Unshed tears scalded her eyes. How could one human be so cruel to another? It sickened her stomach. She held her fingers across her mouth. If she retched here, they would hear her.

When the nausea subsided, Amy peeked through the rails again. Samson had climbed in Micah's wagon and was lying down in what must be a false bottom, because he'd totally disappeared.

Another dark head popped up from the hole, and Amy watched a rail-thin black woman about Sookie's age climb up. Aboveground, she brushed hay off her faded dress. Ben motioned toward the wagon, and she nodded then climbed in and disappeared after a moment.

"Hurry him up, Ben." Micah opened a stall across the barn and led out one of his big horses. He tied the bay gelding to a hitching post then proceeded to strap on the harness.

Amy looked back at the hole as a teen boy hurried up the ladder. He gave Ben a haughty look then climbed into the wagon. After he was settled, Ben replaced some boards and threw in several bales of hay and some crates to cover them.

Slipping down to sit on the sweet-smelling hay, Amy rested her arms on her knees and laid down her head. Warm tears dampened her dress. Hank Foster was right about Micah dealing slaves.

Why God? Why does Micah have to get involved in selling slaves, just when I realize how much I love him?

Micah heaved a sigh of relief when he drove back into the barn. The morning sun shining through cracks in the walls bathed the barn with warm light and illuminated millions of dust motes dancing in the air. The big draft horses nickered and tossed their heads, eager to get into their stalls and eat.

Ben stopped pitching hay and leaned on the stall rail. "So, how did it go? Any problems?"

Micah yawned, glad to be back home. "Just fine. Whoa!" When the horses lumbered to a stop, he pulled the brake, set the reins down, and jumped off the wagon. "I passed the load to Hiram Addams at the Pennsylvania border and headed back home."

"See, I told you it was a piece of cake."

Micah glared at Ben. The only reason he'd delivered this group of runaways was to give Ben a break. They'd had slaves show up three nights in a row, and Ben had gotten little sleep lately. Amy kept asking him if he was sick. Micah rubbed his eyes. Now he was the one who'd gone without sleep and had no idea how he would make it through this day's work. "You might be more concerned if it was *your* wife and kids in danger."

Ben lifted a brow and smirked. "So Amy's your wife now?"

Micah's ears warmed. "No, I didn't mean that. It was a slip of the tongue."

"Uh huh." Ben started unhitching the wagon, and Micah headed for the woodpile. He could think better and stay awake if he was doing hard labor. Ben's comment rattled him more than he wanted to admit.

At the barn door, Micah stopped and looked back at his brother. "There's a doe in back of the wagon that needs dressing out. I shot it early this morning just past May's Creek."

He didn't wait for Ben's agreement or complaint but headed out into the cool morning air. He walked down to the creek and washed the blood off his hands from when he'd loaded up the deer. Then he splashed cold water onto his face, sending goose bumps racing up his arms.

Listening to the birds' cheerful chirping and staring out at the peaceful stream, Micah contemplated what he'd done. He'd helped illegal runaway slaves get to freedom in the North—and it felt great. But it meant leaving his family at night and putting himself in danger. Bringing home meat was just a cover-up, so Amy wouldn't get suspicious. So far it had worked, but sooner or later, she was bound to wonder why they always did their hunting at night.

Helping these runaways was taxing his resources. The pantry was less full than it had been, and he and Ben were starting to run out of clothes. Not to mention he was down to one quilt. He'd hung on to the quilt belonging to Kathryn's mother, thinking the girls might want it one day.

And Amy. He sighed. What to do about his feelings for her? Should he just come out and tell her he was falling in love? Was it too soon to think about marrying again?

He had no idea what her response would be. If anything, she was avoiding him more these days. Sometimes when she looked at him, his heart pinged, and he thought sure she had feelings for him, but most of the time, she barely looked his way.

Slipping down to the ground, he leaned against a tree. Maybe he'd sit for a few minutes and pray about things. It was times like these he wished his father were still alive to talk to. Well, he'd just have to ask his questions to his heavenly Father.

Chapter 13

Beth swung Amy's hand back and forth as they headed toward the barn. "I'm gonna find more eggs than you." The child grinned then started scanning the ground.

"Oh, you think you will, huh?" Amy enjoyed the little game she and Beth played each morning. Making a chore into a game ensured the child's cooperation.

"Yes." Beth tugged away and headed for the grassy area outside the barn where the chickens liked to roost. She moved aside the ankle-high grass with her booted foot as Amy had shown her. She stooped down and raised her arm, egg in hand. "Found one! Dat's one for me. None for you."

"I'll check inside the barn. Stay close, all right?" Amy squinted as she left the bright sunlight and moved into the dimmer light of the barn. She stood still, giving her eyes time to adjust; then she ambled over to the corner where Micah had tossed some loose hay. Some of the hens had claimed this as their roosting spot. Using a hay fork, she carefully flipped sections of hay until she uncovered a half dozen eggs. She laid them in her basket just as Beth's shadow preceded the child into the barn. Beth had an egg in each hand and the remains of another one running down the front of her dress. Amy sighed. More washing to do.

"I had me thwee eggs, but he scared me and I broke one." Beth looked down at her dress.

Amy walked out of the barn with Beth beside her and saw a man sitting on the seat of an empty buckboard. Her heart sank, just like the yolk that slid down the child's dress and plummeted to the ground. Hank Foster. Would the man never leave her alone?

He tipped his floppy, stained hat. "Howdy, darlin'. Been a long time since I laid eyes on your pretty face."

"Don't you put your eyes on Amy's face." Beth lifted a defiant chin and shoved her egg-filled fists to her hips.

Amy gritted her teeth, hoping the eggs wouldn't break.

"Huh?" Hank looked down at Beth and scratched his forehead.

Despite her anxiety, Amy tightened her lips to keep from laughing. She helped Beth set her eggs in the basket. "Take these up to the house."

Beth looked at her, eyes wide. "I gets to carry da basket by myself?"

Amy stooped and looked her in the eye. "Yes, but be very careful. We can't make custard without eggs."

Beth nodded and licked her lips. With care, she lifted the basket and held it with both hands against her chest as if it were a cherished treasure. She tucked her bottom lip between her teeth and took tiny steps toward the cabin. Amy watched her for a moment then turned to face Hank. "Why are you here?" She crossed her arms over her chest.

Hank hopped off the wagon seat and moved toward her. Amy wanted to step back but held her ground. She prayed he'd gotten over his desire to marry her. Even if Micah sent her away penniless, she'd never accept Hank Foster as a beau.

"I delivered a load of freight out to Henry Schmidt's place yesterday. It was late, so I slept in his barn. Thought I'd drop by and see you on my way back into town."

That explained the sprigs of hay sticking out of his hair and shirt pocket.

"Did you miss me?" Hank grinned, revealing yellowed teeth, and moved closer.

"I–I've been too busy to miss anyone."

"Ah, darlin', if you'd marry me, you wouldn't have to work so hard."

Her stomach somersaulted at the thought of what marriage would be like with this persistent, unwashed man. If only Micah were so attentive. Hank walked past her and into the barn.

"Micah around?"

Amy's heart thudded as Hank looked inside the barn. He walked over and opened the door to a small room where Micah stored some of his tools. Hank stepped inside, rattled something, and pounded on several walls. When he stepped back into the barn, he looked toward the back wall.

"Just what are you looking for? Micah wouldn't like you snooping around his barn." She didn't care for it either.

A sly grin replaced the dopey one that normally tilted his thin lips. "Don't think I ain't wise to what he's up to. I want in on the action."

Amy blinked. Was Hank after Micah's stash of furs? She had no idea where Micah kept them, unless it was down in the room belowground where he'd hidden the slaves. Glancing around, she looked for something she could use to shoo Hank out of the barn. Micah and Ben were so tidy that all the tools were hung up, either in the tool closet or toward the back of the barn on pegs. She wasn't about to venture any farther into the barn alone with Hank. He'd never done anything but express his desires as far as she was concerned, but then she'd never been alone with him before, except the day she arrived here at the Walsh farm.

"Don't play dumb with me, darlin'. I've heard by the grapevine that Micah's a slave trader. Gotta admit it did strike me odd at first, what with him being a churchgoin' man and all." Hank tugged up his too loose, stained overalls, which promptly drooped again when he let go. "The way I see it is, with you being his kin and all, when we get married, Micah and me will be kin, too. We need to keep his business in the family." Hank spat something out the side of his mouth, and Amy backed up.

Dear Lord, give me wisdom here. How had Hank learned about Micah's slave dealings? If Hank knew, then who else did? Slave trading wasn't illegal in Virginia, but it could be dangerous, especially if they were selling captured runaways. If the true owner found out, there could be big trouble, and people could get hurt. How could Micah endanger his family for a little extra money?

Hank moved toward her, a self-satisfied grin cocking his lips. "I've got a tad bit of money saved, and with what I can make helping Micah, we don't have to wait to marry. What say we tell him today? He's all for us weddin' up."

Too stunned to move, Amy's head swarmed with confusion. Micah gave Hank his permission to marry her?

Hank slid forward and took hold of her shoulders. "I've wanted you ever since that first day I laid eyes on you."

Hot tears burned Amy's eyes. The man she loved had given her to Hank? Were all those words about needing her just lies?

Amy stiffened, and a flicker of apprehension coursed through her when Hank touched her cheek with his dirty finger. His actions reminded her of how her father treated her mother, making her whole body shiver. "Now don't cry, darlin'. I know womenfolk get all teary-eyed just at the thought of a weddin', but we've got time for that later. How's about a little kiss for your future husband?"

When Hank's thin lips moved toward hers, Amy panicked. She shoved him away, but he grinned and grabbed her arm. "I like a feisty filly."

Her heart stampeded at the strength in his slight frame. Amy pushed his chest again, but he held her firm by her upper arms. One hand loosened and snaked around behind her, pulling her closer.

Both fear and anger knotted her insides. She'd seen her father force himself on her mother many times before they'd closed the bedroom door, and she'd determined it would never happen to her. Hank's expression darkened with emotion, and he leaned toward her. "I aim to have that kiss, Amy."

She turned her face, just as his lips came within reach, and he kissed her cheek instead of her mouth. He uttered an angry growl.

"No!" She cried out. Amy was just as determined that Hank Foster wouldn't be the first man she kissed. Her stomach burned with indignation and repulsion. With her arms crushed between her chest and Hank's, the only weapon she had was her feet. She balanced on one foot and hauled back with the other and kicked Hank in the shin. As he hollered and loosened his hold, she saw a shadow darken the doorway.

Amy fell backwards from Hank's quick release and landed on the dirt floor. Her wrist wrenched as she tried to break her fall. A wave of dizziness passed, and she heard quick footsteps and realized that Micah now had Hank in his steel grasp. Hank had suddenly turned into a limp rag doll.

"Just what do you think you're doing?" Micah ground out, his voice deep with anger.

"I—uh, she wanted a kiss. I was just obliging."

Micah's questioning gaze darted her direction. Amy shot to her feet. "That's not true. He forced himself on me."

Micah's eyes ignited with fury, and he faced Hank again. "I think you'd better leave before I do something I'll regret later." He released his hold on Hank's overalls, and the man plummeted to the floor.

Hank slowly eased to his feet. "Now hold on, Micah. No call to get upset. You know me and Amy are getting married. A man expects certain favors from his woman."

"I am *not* your woman." Amy hissed the words, making clear he understood. "I never agreed to marry you nor encouraged you one bit. Our getting married is some fantasy you've conjured up." She straightened and glanced at Micah. Something like relief passed through his eyes.

"Are you all right?" Micah's gaze caressed her face then scanned the length of her body. "You're not hurt?"

"I think I sprained my wrist, but other than that, I'm fine."

Micah moved closer and took hold of her sore arm. He gently massaged her wrist. Amy wanted to close her eyes and melt into his arms, but not with Hank gawking.

Micah eased his gaze away and glared at Hank, all the time rubbing her wrist. "Why are you here, anyway?"

Hank dusted off his overalls, not that it made any difference. Turning left and then right, he looked at the floor, then crossed the room and picked up his hat. "I want to do business with you."

"What kind of business?"

"Slave trading."

Micah gasped. He stopped rubbing Amy's wrist, his arm slid around her shoulders, and he pulled her to his side. Hank glared at him but didn't comment. Micah straightened. "I *do not* trade slaves."

A wry grin crept onto Hank's face. "Come on, Micah. The whole town knows about what you and Ben are doin' here. I want in on the action. I figure when Amy and I are married, you and me will be kin."

Micah's grip on Amy tightened, and she turned sideways, hiding her face against his solid chest. She was so tired of dealing with Hank. All she wanted was to stay right here, in the protection of Micah's capable arms.

"First off, you aren't marrying Amy. Second, she's not my kin. She's Kathryn's cousin. And third, I am *not* a slave trader. I never have been and never will be."

Amy so wanted to believe Micah, but she'd seen the proof with her own eyes. Could she possibly have misinterpreted things that night in the barn? Tears trickled down her cheeks, wetting Micah's shirt. He must be lying to keep his business a secret.

"I see the way of things. You want her for yourself."

At Hank's venomous words, Amy glanced toward him. His lips cocked in a disgusted sneer. "I never had a chance, did I?"

"You need to leave. Things aren't always what they seem." The tone in Micah's voice sent a shiver down Amy's spine.

Hank snorted a sound of disbelief and stomped past them. Micah turned, taking her with him so they could watch Hank leave. She heard the creak of the wagon as Hank boarded it and his angry, "Heyah!" The harness jingled as the wagon came into view. Hank turned it away from the barn, made a half circle, and disappeared from sight.

Amy's whole body trembled, whether from the ordeal or Micah's closeness, she wasn't sure. He wrapped both arms around her and pulled her against his chest. Tears gushed forth as she rested in his embrace. She knew he was only trying to calm her, but she wished that it was because he held affections for her.

His gentling shushing calmed her, and after a few minutes, she quit crying. Sniffing, she leaned back. She couldn't stand there all day letting Micah hold her. Well, maybe she could, but she was keeping him from his work.

He cleared his throat and looked down with concerned eyes. "You sure you're all right?"

Amy wiped her cheeks with the handkerchief she kept stuffed up her sleeve and nodded. "He was snooping around, and I didn't know how to get rid of him. Th–then he tried to kiss m–me." The tears started again.

Micah took her by the shoulders. "Please don't cry, Amy."

She swiped her eyes again. "I'm sorry."

"I'm just glad I showed up when I did."

"Me, too." Amy glanced up and looked at Micah's handsome face. His gaze darted down to her lips then back to her eyes. Her heart skipped a beat. Was he going to kiss her?

Micah rubbed his nape and looked at her lips again. Amy was sure she read longing in his gaze. He cleared his throat and stepped back. "I—uh, better go catch that mare. I was bringing one of the new horses up here from the pasture so I could start working with her."

Disappointment coursed through Amy. She wouldn't mind one bit sharing her first kiss with Micah, but she must have misread his expression. Still, she had to admit that he was more of a man than Hank. Micah would never force himself on a woman.

She watched him walk away, and it dawned on her that she hadn't even tried to hide her feelings from him. Had she scared him off? Was he repulsed that his housekeeper had fallen in love with him?

Sighing, Amy exited the barn. Micah mounted his horse and trotted off. This was going to be a long day. Maybe it *would* be better for her to leave. How could she stay here knowing Micah didn't share her feelings?

Chapter 14

Micah eased forward, cooing to the skittish mare that had taken advantage of his distraction. He'd been riding Rusty and leading the black horse to the barn when he saw Hank Foster trying to kiss Amy and jumped off, leaving the horses untethered. Anger had surged through him to see that man's hands on Amy. The fact that she might be a willing partner crossed his mind until he got close enough to see the fear on her face.

Hank was lucky. Micah wanted to knock the man crazy, but he yielded to God's convicting hand and just sent Hank on his way.

The black mare lifted her head and snorted. She must have gotten a whiff of the oats in Micah's hand, because she stretched her neck and used her big lips to scoop them up. He reached out and snagged her lead rope, causing the mare to jerk her head and try to rear. Holding tight, Micah crooned to her until she calmed down. Why couldn't women be as easy to handle as horses?

He climbed on Rusty and led the mare back toward the barn. Micah thought of Amy's big brown eyes staring up at him, shining with unshed tears. He'd almost given in to his desire to kiss her. And where had that thought come from? Thankfully, he'd been able to get out of the barn without embarrassing them both.

He remembered how his rebellious heart had responded when Amy was in his arms. She felt wonderful—different from Kathryn.

Thoughts of his deceased wife doused him like a bucket of cold water. Was he being unfaithful to Kathryn because he liked Amy?

Who was he kidding? He more than liked her; he had deep feelings for her. Yet, he couldn't admit he loved her, but when he saw Hank manhandling her, he'd nearly gone mad.

Clicking his tongue, he nudged Rusty into a trot. It was getting close to noontime, and Amy and Sookie would have dinner waiting. Nervous anticipation at seeing Amy again battled the hunger pangs in his belly. Who would think a grown man—a father no less—would be excited to see his housekeeper when he'd just seen her a short while ago?

"Where you been?"

Micah looked up at the sound of Ben's voice. He'd been so lost in thought he didn't even realize he was back home. "The mare got away, and I went after her."

Ben cocked an eyebrow then studied the black horse. "She doesn't look all that spunky."

"Maybe she's tired from her gallivanting." Micah pulled his horse to a stop and slid off.

"I'll take her." Ben held out his hand, and Micah gave him the mare's lead rope.

"Thanks." Micah led Rusty to his stall and dropped the reins.

"Saw Hank Foster on the trail heading to town. He didn't look too happy."

Micah uncinched Rusty's saddle, not sure how much to tell Ben. "He came to see Amy."

Ben pivoted, brows lifted. "Again?"

"Yeah."

"You don't think she harbors affections for him, do you?"

If Micah hadn't seen Amy's fearful expression when Hank held her, he would have wondered the same thing. But she made it clear that she had no feelings for the man. On the other hand, did Micah dare hope she held affections for him? When she looked at him after Hank left, there was something in her eyes that took his breath away.

"Besides, it's clear that Amy only has eyes for one man." Ben walked over and leaned his arms on the top railing of the next stall.

Micah's heart stumbled at Ben's comment. He looked at his brother, whose eyes twinkled as his mouth curved up in a lopsided grin. "Who?"

Ben blinked. "Oh, come on! Are you that dense, big brother? She's in love with me!"

Numb, Micah stared at Ben. Had he lost his heart to the woman his brother loved? Unable to face Ben's scrutiny, he turned back to Rusty, feeling as if a cyclone had blown away all his hopes and dreams. It was almost as if he'd lost Kathryn all over—only this time he'd lost Amy.

Behind him he heard a snort. Then Ben broke out in a gale of laughter. "You're so gullible at times."

Confused, Micah turned around.

Ben slapped his leg, and his blue-green eyes danced with mirth. "I knew it! Yep, I was right. You have feelings for Amy."

"And you don't?" Micah held his breath, hoping. He could never steal the woman his brother loved, no matter how much he cared for her.

"Well, sure I like her. When she first came, I was a bit addlebrained over her, but she's too old for me."

Micah realized he'd never asked Amy her age, but she couldn't be all that much older than Ben. "How old is she?"

"Almost twenty."

"That's not old."

"Depends on your perspective." An ornery grin tilted Ben's lips. "So what are you going to do, now that we both know you care for her?"

"Nothing."

Ben blinked, all traces of playfulness gone. "Why not? You going to wait around for someone like Hank to win her over? Not that she's that dumb."

It wasn't the first time Micah had considered such a thought. He didn't want to lose Amy, but was he ready to remarry?

"I know what you're thinking. But men remarry quickly when they have a family."

Micah stared at Ben. It was hard to believe his little brother was growing up. Finally. His words made sense.

"I think you ought to marry up with her before some other fellow stakes a claim and steals her away. It's obvious you care for her." Ben pushed away from the rails and crossed the barn.

Micah considered his words. He'd been praying what to do. Was this God's confirmation?

He'd married for love once, and it hadn't been what he'd expected. Kathryn never fully adjusted to farm life, and it created a breach between them that they had never gotten past. But Amy was different. She plunged into farm life as if she'd been raised on one. The girls loved her. His home had never been so clean or run so smoothly. He couldn't imagine life here without her. But was marrying her the right thing to do?

Missy's cries pierced Amy's ears. The poor thing must be teething, at least that's what Sookie thought. Having no experience with babies, Amy hoped that was all that was wrong with her.

"Missy's cwying too loud. I can't sleep." Beth sat up in her bed, her dark hair a mess and her doll in her arms. "Make her be quiet like Sophie."

Amy smiled. Beth had renamed her doll after Tierney's daughter. "I'll take Missy outside, so she won't bother you." Pushing up from the rocking chair, she glanced at Sookie, who was stirring a bowl of cornmeal mush for tomorrow's breakfast.

Sookie nodded. "I'll keep watch over Miz Beth."

Outside, Amy jiggled Missy on her shoulder and patted the child's back as the wailing continued. She was such a good little thing that it made Amy ache to know she was in pain. Amy hoped Beth wouldn't give Sookie too much trouble. With the sun setting later now that summer had arrived, it was harder to get Beth to go to bed at her regular time.

Amy followed the path to her garden. Often, in the cool of the morning, she worked it before the children woke up. Amy smiled. Beth liked to help her, but she was as likely to pull a healthy vegetable seedling as a weed.

A bright yellow butterfly danced from blossom to blossom. Studying the various plants, she made a mental note to pick cucumbers tomorrow. They'd soon have enough to make pickles. Her mouth watered. The ripe green vegetable beckoned to her, and she yielded to temptation. Holding Missy tight with one arm, she reached over the fence and tugged a small, ripe cucumber off its vine. A fresh fragrance scented the evening air as Amy wiped it on her apron and bit it in half, enjoying its crunchiness and fresh flavor that teased her tongue.

She shifted Missy down to her arm, and when the baby wailed again, Amy dabbed the cucumber across the baby's tongue. Missy wriggled, making it hard for Amy to hold her with one arm. Suddenly, the child stopped crying, scrunched up her face at the unusual flavor, and smacked her tongue.

Amy giggled at Missy's surprised expression. "Did you like that? Huh? Want some more?" Thankful for the quiet, Amy swiped the cucumber across the baby's tongue again. Missy smacked her lips and grinned, making Amy smile and her heart warm.

She loved this child so much. Amy couldn't imagine leaving the Walsh farm and never seeing Missy or Beth again. She'd found the home she'd always wanted. Only it wasn't her home. If she could stay here forever, she didn't think she'd ever ask God for another thing.

"Don't you think she's a bit young to eat cucumbers?"

Amy jumped at the sound of Micah's deep voice and soft masculine laughter. She'd been so engrossed in feeding Missy that she hadn't even heard Micah's approach. Glancing up, she noticed Ben and Jonah were with him. All three men smiled. Amy's cheeks heated, knowing they must have been watching her.

"That child's sure having a time of it." Jonah's gap-toothed smile illuminated his whole face.

Amy plopped the remaining vegetable in her own mouth and lifted Missy back to her shoulder. The baby fidgeted then let out a wail that Micah was sure to be proud of. Amy swallowed and looked up. "I was just walking Missy because she's keeping Beth awake."

"Mind if I walk with you?"

Her legs turned to liquid at the warm look in Micah's eyes. Could he possibly want to spend time with her? Or was he just concerned about his daughter?

Ben's lips turned up in an ornery grin, and he nudged Micah in the ribs. Micah gave him a scowl then held his arms out for Missy. Reluctantly, Amy handed over the child.

"Come along, Benjamin. I want to show you something." Jonah took hold of Ben's shirt and all but hauled him away.

Ben looked over his shoulder and waggled his eyebrows up and down. Amy wondered what he meant by that. Micah's brother could act so silly at times.

Micah started down the trail that led to the cornfield. Amy wasn't sure whether to follow or go back inside and help Sookie. She tried hard not to intrude on Micah's time with his daughter, since he had so little time to spend with the baby.

He stopped and turned her direction. "You coming?"

When she didn't reply, he nudged out his elbow in a silent appeal. Amy glanced over her shoulders to see if Ben and Jonah were still in sight and breathed a sigh of relief that they were gone. Moving forward, she tried to keep her hand from shaking as she looped her arm through Micah's. She knew he was just being polite, but she relished being alone with him, even with a fussy baby.

Micah led her down the trail, talking softly and cooing to Missy. When the cabin was out of sight, he slowed and stared at the cornfields. Amy wondered what he was thinking about.

"Looks like the corn's doing well. Not that I know much about it," she said.

Micah nodded. "We could use some rain though. You know, it's ironic. I lost the past two years' crops because of too much rain, and now I'm wishing we'd get some."

Had he asked her along merely to talk about the weather? Amy peeked up at Micah, noticing the muscle in his jaw twitching. The dark shadow of whiskers made him even more handsome in her eyes. Her heart ached with the desire to tell him how she felt, but she had no experience with men and didn't know if it was proper.

As Micah jiggled Missy, the child finally gave in to sleep. Amy sighed. It had been a long day, and she hadn't accomplished nearly as much as she'd hope because of Missy's fussiness.

Micah heaved a sigh and turned to face her, his expression serious. Amy's heart jolted. Was he unhappy about something?

"I've been doing a lot of thinking lately." Micah finally looked at her, making Amy's insides turn to pudding. "I realize we haven't known each other long, but I think we get along well."

Amy nodded, her mouth suddenly dry.

"I. . .uh, was wondering. . .if you'd consent to marry me."

Chapter 15

Amy's skin tightened on her face, and her whole body shook. Surely Micah wouldn't tease about something like marriage. She studied his steady gaze and knew he was dead serious.

"I—I know it's sudden." A quick look of panic stole through Micah's eyes, and he rubbed his neck with his free hand. "But you wouldn't have to worry about Hank Foster or some other yahoo asking you to marry him. You'd always have a home, and the girls love you."

But do you *love me?* she wanted to ask.

"I wouldn't ask you for a complete marriage. I mean—well, you know." Micah's ears turned a bright red, and he looked away. "It'd be more like a business deal."

Amy was sure her heart had dropped clear down to her shoes. He didn't want a true marriage? Well, maybe she didn't either—at least not if he didn't love her. But she'd have the home she'd always wanted and would never have to leave the girls. Would their love be enough? Was this God's answer to her prayers?

"Don't answer now. Just think about it. All right?"

There was only one thing about him that she couldn't abide—slave trading. She glanced at Micah, who fidgeted at her lengthy silence. *Oh, Lord, give me guidance.*

After a few moments, Amy lifted her chin. "All right, I will marry you—under two conditions."

Micah blinked. "What conditions?"

"That you quit slave trading, and you never go off and leave your family again."

Micah's lips turned up in a slow grin. "I'll do my best not to leave again, but on the first issue, you're going to have to trust me."

———

Amy lay in bed, listening to Sookie's soft snores. She still couldn't believe she had agreed to marry Micah two days ago. They decided not to tell anyone until they had all the details worked out.

She turned onto her side. The open window allowed a hint of light from the near full moon to illuminate the dark room. This would soon be her home, and she would be Amy Christine Walsh. Mrs. Micah Walsh.

Amy marveled at how far she'd come in a few short months. God had brought her here, healed her wounded soul, and given her a place to belong. She couldn't help wondering what Kathryn would think about it.

And she still didn't know what Micah had meant about trusting him concerning his slave trading, but she was willing to try. Maybe she'd misconstrued what she'd heard and seen in the barn that day.

The Virginia Commonwealth was now her home, and she loved it. No more frigid Boston winters. Her only regret was that she lived too far away to visit the ocean. But the beautiful Shenandoah Valley had stolen her heart with its lush greenery, its unusual Virginia bluebells that started out as pink buds and then matured into blue, bell-shaped flowers, and its colorful cardinals, blue jays, and flittering hummingbirds. Not to mention a quiet man who'd stolen her heart.

The front door squeaked as it opened, making Amy jump. The men never came inside after they'd gone to bed. Her thoughts skittered around for something she could use for a weapon if an intruder was in the house. Tossing off the covers, she sat up and listened.

"Amy." Micah's soft whisper filtered through the darkness.

She grabbed her bed jacket off the end of the bed, donned it, and tiptoed into the other room.

"I'm sorry to bother you, but I need your help." He'd turned up the lantern, and a soft glow illuminated the room.

Amy lowered the quilt dividing the two rooms so the light wouldn't awaken the others. "What's wrong?"

"Grab some bandages and your medicine supplies—and hurry."

"Why?"

"Just come on. You'll see."

Amy gathered what she needed, set the supplies on the table, and sat down to put on her shoes.

"We don't have time for that." Micah handed her the supplies; then he bent over and scooped her into his arms.

"Micah!"

"It's faster this way. Hold on."

Amy held tight to his neck as he jogged toward the barn. All manner of thoughts skittered across her mind, not the least of which was how good it felt to be so close to Micah with his arms holding her tightly. As they entered the barn, Amy saw a soft light shining on the far wall. When they came to the open door in the floor, Micah set her down.

"I don't want you to be afraid, but it's pretty ugly down there." He trailed his finger down her cheek, scattering her thoughts like chaff in the wind.

He headed down the ladder then turned to aid her. She handed him the supplies, which he passed to someone else, then made her way down, with Micah's hands on her waist. As her bare feet touched the hay-covered floor,

Micah steadied her and held on tightly when she turned.

Gasping, she lifted her hand to her mouth. A young black child lay on a cot in the downstairs room, his back bleeding. A Negro woman who looked to be Micah's age sat beside the bed, cooing to the child and rubbing his head. Ben stood against the back wall, looking pale.

Amy glanced at Micah. "What happened?"

"He was the plantation owner's whipping boy. Whenever the master's son disobeyed, Nathan suffered severe punishment." Micah motioned to the black woman. "Naomi is his mother. She finally took him, and with Simon's help"—he paused and motioned to a huge, quiet man sitting in the corner—"ran away, fearing her master would soon kill the boy."

"That's horrible!" Amy rushed to Nathan's side, unsure if she had the skills to help him. "I'll do what I can, but you might want to get Jonah. He knows things I don't."

"I'll get him," Ben offered. He scurried up the ladder and disappeared.

"Ben already got water." Micah nodded to a small table at the head of the bed.

Amy examined the boy. His back looked as if it had been cut open with a whip. Who could do this to a child? Tears blurred her eyes as she glanced at the boy's mother. "I'll do my best for Nathan."

Naomi sent her a soft smile and nodded. Amy squeezed water out of the cloth in the bowl and dabbed Nathan's back. She turned and looked at Micah. "I'm going to need more water and more light."

Micah climbed the ladder without responding. A few minutes later, he returned carrying another lantern. Jonah followed, and then Ben, lugging a bucket of water.

Amy worked feverishly, cleaning the unconscious boy's wounds. Jonah applied his special salve, and together they put on bandages. She wiped the sweat from her brow, even though the underground room was cooler than up above. Finally, she looked at Micah. He leaned against the dirt wall, eyes closed. She was sure he was praying.

Rubbing her back where it ached from bending for so long, she crossed the room and touched Micah's sleeve. His eyes opened; then he glanced at Nathan. She read the question in his gaze and shrugged. "I did my best for him."

His smile loosed a butterfly war in her stomach. "I know you did. Thanks. I should probably take you back to the house so you can get some rest."

Amy shook her head. "I'll stay with Nathan."

"Naomi and Jonah can look after him now. You need your rest, so you can care for the girls tomorrow."

Bone tired, Amy didn't argue but allowed Micah to guide her up the ladder. At the top, he lifted her again and carried her toward the cabin. She allowed her arm to rest along his neck as she contemplated what had happened tonight. Her heart ached, thinking about what Nathan had endured in his young life. He couldn't be more than six or seven. How brave and yet fearful his mother must have been to run away like she did.

Runaway.

The term slowly seeped into her weary mind. They were runaways. Big as he was, not even Simon had been in chains or tied up. Joy surged through her, making even her toes tingle.

When they reached the cabin, Micah set her down on the bottom step rather than the ground. As she stared at him eye-to-eye, she couldn't keep from smiling. Somehow deep inside, she knew his character wouldn't allow him to deal slaves.

Micah reached out and lifted her heavy braid off her shoulder and let it fall behind her back. She held her breath as he drew a calloused finger along her jawline. "I can't thank you enough for what you did tonight. You gave that boy a chance to live."

"So did you."

Micah's hands rested lightly on her shoulders. "What do you mean?"

"You're helping them get to freedom in the North, aren't you?"

Heaving a sigh that warmed her face, Micah lowered his hands off her shoulders and massaged her upper arms. "I didn't want you to know what Ben and I are doing. If someone like Hank Foster questioned you, I wanted you to be able to respond honestly."

"You were protecting me?"

"Yeah."

"I knew it in my heart. I didn't see how someone who believes in God could be a slave trader. You don't know how happy it makes me to know for sure."

Amy tossed her arms around his neck and laid her cheek against his. He stood there loosedarmed, as if in shock, then tightened his grip, crushing her against his chest.

"Amy."

Hearing his husky voice, she leaned back, barely able to see his features in the moonlight. Then his lips were on hers, full and warm. He tightened his hold on her, nearly squashing off her breath as he deepened his kiss. Her heart pounded a wild, staccato chant as she savored her first kiss.

Suddenly, Micah pulled back, holding her upper arms. His ragged breath matched hers. Her heart sang, keeping tempo with the chorus of crickets chirping all around them. Then Micah loosened his hold on her and let go altogether. She could feel his stare and wondered what he was thinking. His kiss was more than she'd ever dreamed it would be and ignited in her a craving for more. Now she understood the pull between man and woman.

"I. . .good night, Amy."

She touched her lips as he strode off, disappearing into the night shadows. Her heart was so light, Amy nearly floated up the steps and into the cabin, but she couldn't help wondering how her kisses had compared to Kathryn's.

Chapter 16

Micah strode back toward the barn, mentally berating himself for kissing Amy. He was the one who wanted to make this a business arrangement because he knew marrying Amy was the only way to guarantee her staying here. And he needed her.

She'd also be protected from men like Hank, who were only looking for a pretty woman to marry up with.

Guilt battled with the desire to go back and kiss her again. As he had prayed the past weeks, Micah felt sure it was God's will to ask Amy to marry him, but now he was confused. Was it fair to her? Sure, he cared for her, and she stirred a passion within him. He was a man, after all. But was it right to marry Amy, knowing he'd failed to make his first wife happy?

He'd taken Kathryn away from the city where she was raised and brought her to this rugged farm. She'd been in love and hadn't minded living there at first, but as time wore on, she became less content. He didn't want to make that mistake again. Did he have it within him to please Amy? Would she remain content in future years like she was now?

As he reached the barn door, he paused and looked heavenward. "Lord, if marrying Amy is a mistake, please make it clear to me. I can't marry and listen to my wife crying in the dark again. If Amy won't be happy here, show me, before I make another mistake."

Amy smoothed down the skirt of her new dress. Her insides quivered as she recalled Micah's compliment when he first saw her in the gold calico. He said the brown in the design made her eyes stand out. She hoped that was a good thing.

The wagon she was riding in hit a rut, tossing her against Micah's arm. Beth's giggle punctuated the quiet group.

"That was fun. Do it again, Papa." Beth bounced on Jonah's lap, where they sat in the back of the wagon with Sookie, who held Missy. Ben rode ahead of the wagon on his horse.

Micah's grin and shared glances sent shivers of delight charging a path through the goose bumps on Amy's arms. She smiled, remembering how excited the family had been when Micah announced at last night's dinner that he and Amy were getting married. The family had already planned to ride into town today for the annual July Fourth celebration, so she and Micah would tie the knot this afternoon in a small ceremony.

"Is Sophie comin', too?"

Amy turned on the seat, her knee bumping Micah's leg. "Yes, she is. Her mother is standing up with me at the wedding."

"I want to stand up, too." Beth bounced up and plopped down again.

Amy noticed Jonah's grimace. "You need to be still, Beth, or you can't sit on Jonah's lap. You're hurting him by bouncing."

Beth nodded, then glanced over her shoulder at Jonah and grinned.

Half an hour later, Beth crawled over the back of the wagon seat and sat by her father as Micah dropped Amy off at the store. He drove down the street toward the schoolhouse, which also served as the church, while she went inside the mercantile. Sookie and Jonah were up to something and didn't want her around for a bit. She suspected it had to do with whatever sat in the corner of the wagon, covered with a quilt. Since Missy was asleep, Sookie kept the baby with her, and Ben rode off, looking for some of his friends.

Cherishing a few minutes to herself, Amy went inside to see if she could find Micah a wedding gift. A bevy of scents greeted her as she stepped farther into the store. Four silver dollars jingled in her pocket—her pay for the months she'd worked at the Walsh farm. After handing her supply list to Mrs. Maples, she walked around looking at things she thought Micah might like.

Since she could sew well, she bypassed the ready-made clothing and looked at the pocket watches. Bright and shiny, they beckoned to her, but practicality won out, and she moved down the counter and looked inside another glass case. Several razors lay side by side, folded shut. The only time she'd come outside and caught Micah shaving, he'd been using a hunting knife. A razor wasn't a glamorous gift, but useful. Hoping Micah would be pleased, she handed over one of her coins and bought the razor and a sack of penny candy to share on the trip home, then pocketed both items along with her change and bid Mrs. Maples good day.

Nervous excitement tickled her stomach as she left the store and headed for the schoolhouse. In less than an hour, she and Micah would be married. She knew in her heart this was God's will and trusted Him that Micah would come to love her as she did him. Smiling at the thought, she ambled down the steps of the boardwalk, trying to take in everything going on around her. The whole town bubbled with excitement, and some folks had even decorated the outsides of their businesses in red, white, and blue swags. At the end of the street, she could see a stage with a group of singers on it, who were belting out "The Liberty Song."

As she approached the livery, she contemplated crossing the street but realized how silly that was. Hank Foster couldn't bother her now that she was getting married. She almost made it past the open doors, but Hank suddenly stepped out, blocking her path. Her heart nearly jumped to her throat.

"Howdy there, darlin'. I saw you come into town. 'Bout time you come to see me."

Amy glanced away, hoping to catch a glimpse of Micah. With the celebration in full swing, the streets swarmed with people driving wagons, walking, and riding horses. The town buzzed with conversation, almost as if it were a living being, but nobody was paying any attention to Hank and her.

He stepped closer. "I got somethin' to show you." He nodded toward the livery. "Won't take but a minute."

Amy shook her head. "I need to be somewhere. People are waiting for me."

"Let 'em wait. This'll only take a minute."

Hank moved between Amy and the street. She backed up several steps to get away, and suddenly realized her mistake as she moved into the shadow of the livery's tall roof. She sidestepped, hoping to dart past Hank, but he was too quick. As he moved closer, she reversed her steps again, blinking as her eyes adjusted to the dimmer lighting.

"Right over here." Hank pointed toward a stall in the corner where a mother dog lay with her litter of puppies.

Amy heaved a sigh of relief, and her pulse slowed. Perhaps Hank only wanted her to see the dogs. If she humored him, perhaps she could leave without incident. "Oh, how cute." She feigned excitement and stooped near the entrance of the stall. Hank stood close behind her.

"Thought maybe that little gal of Micah's might like a pup."

A fat black-and-white puppy noticed Amy's wagging finger and waddled toward her. Beth would love a puppy, but as long as Micah and Ben were helping runaways, they couldn't have a dog on the property. She patted the little female's head and giggled as it licked her hand.

As much as she liked the dogs, she had something more pressing to attend to. She stood and faced Hank, smiling. "They're adorable. I'll ask Micah, but I'm not sure he wants a dog. He's training some horses he bought, and a dog might be a bother."

"Well, I reckon you can ask him and see what he thinks. Since you're already here, would you mind having a look at a sick pup?"

Amy glanced back at the litter, but all five puppies looked perfectly healthy to her.

"Not there. It's in the tack room." Hank nodded toward a door in the back of the livery, which led to a dark room. "I separated it so the others wouldn't take sick."

Amy blew out a breath. She needed to get to the schoolhouse, but then again, the wedding couldn't start without her, and she hated the thought of a puppy suffering if she could help. "All right, but I need to be quick."

Hank held out his hand for her to precede him, so she turned toward the open door. She stepped inside the dim room and waited for her eyes to adjust. It smelled like the rest of the livery—of horses, leather, hay, and Hank. She lifted a hand to cover her nose.

Hank chuckled behind her, and she spun around. "Got you just where I want you. I reckon if you won't marry me, I'll use you for barter. Think Micah will cut me in on his slave trading in exchange for you?"

Amy felt the blood drain from her face. She'd always believed there was something not altogether right with Hank Foster, but even though she'd seen him fairly frequently, she didn't know him well and had hoped she was wrong.

"You can't keep me here against my will. And I told you, Micah isn't a slave trader."

"Maybe you don't know what is and what ain't."

She straightened and lifted her chin. "I know Micah. He's a God-fearing man who wouldn't want to prosper from another person's pain."

A wheeze of a laugh erupted from Hank, sending chills up Amy's arms. "I don't reckon you know him as good as you think you do. Word's all over town that he's dealing slaves."

Crossing her arms over her chest, Amy glared at Hank. "I don't suppose you had anything to do with spreading those rumors, did you?"

Hank's eyebrows dipped in a scowl. "Now there's no call to be unkind. All I wanted was a chance to make some money and marry up with you. But I can see you don't fancy me. I guess you've only got eyes for Micah. Maybe if he fancies you enough, he'll be willing to deal with me." Hank stepped forward, blocking the doorway.

Amy's body trembled. Her legs felt like mush, but she stepped back, suddenly falling over something behind her. She landed on her backside with a thud and glared up at Hank.

"I'll just leave you here to think a bit while I go down and have me some of Mabel Perkins's apple pie. Maybe if you get hungry enough, you'll see reason and be willing to talk to Micah for me. And don't go hollering at nobody, or I might have to do something to that dark-headed little gal you're so fond of."

He fiddled with a thick strand of leather, looping it through a knothole in the door and then through another hole in the wall. As he shut the door and tied it securely, leaving her in the dark, Amy's breath sounded in short, ragged bursts. Tears stung her eyes and her backside ached. How had she gotten into this mess? If only she'd crossed the street when she'd had that premonition. Had that been God warning her?

Something skittered across the floor, and Amy jumped to her feet. Streams of sunlight shone through the cracks in the wall and dappled the room with specks of light. An old table sat in one corner, covered in an array of papers, tin cups, and trenchers coated with dried food. A mass of cockroaches scurried across the trenchers and along the rim of the cups. Amy shivered and moved to the door. She shoved, and it rattled but didn't budge.

Leaning against the door, Amy stared up at the ceiling. "Oh Lord, please help me. And don't let Hank get his hands on Beth. Keep her safe, and show me a way of escape."

Chapter 17

Jiggling Missy on his arm, Micah paced in front of the schoolhouse and glanced at the sky. Amy had been gone nearly an hour and a half. Anxiety battled with common sense. Surely she had simply gotten distracted. The flowers Sookie had used to decorate the school as a surprise for Amy were already wilting.

Ben stepped up beside him and looked down the street. "Where do you think she is? You wouldn't expect a woman to be late to her own wedding."

"Perhaps she had to wait at the store. With all the people in town, there may have been a line."

"You don't suppose she got cold feet and left town, do you?" Ben chuckled.

A shaft of anxiety rammed straight to Micah's heart. Amy wouldn't up and leave, would she? Knowing the truth, he turned to Ben. "No. She would never leave without saying good-bye. You stay here and help with the girls. I'll go find her." He passed Missy to her uncle and stepped off the boardwalk into the dirt street, his gaze scanning the crowd.

As he entered the mercantile a few minutes later, he gave his eyes a moment to adjust to the dimmer lighting then scanned the crowded building. The aroma of coffee, spices, and all manner of things tickled his senses, but he didn't see the one thing he'd hoped to find. A wave of disappointment washed over him and his concern grew. When the last customer left, Micah stepped up to the counter.

"How long has it been since you last saw Amy Rogers?" he asked Mrs. Maples.

"Don't rightly know. Been purty busy here, what with all the folks in town. If I had to speculate, I'd say it's been well past an hour. She gave me her list—which I haven't had time to fill yet—bought a few items, then left."

"Did she say where she was going?"

Mrs. Maples shook her head. "No, just that some folks were waiting on her somewhere."

Micah thanked her, stepped outside, and studied the crowd. Here and there, people gathered at booths where the townsfolk sold food items, quilts, and hand-made goods, but he didn't see Amy anywhere. It would take too long to search the whole town alone, so he headed back to the schoolhouse.

As he crossed the street, he saw the Chambers's wagon pulling up in front of the small building. Tierney stood, holding her stomach. "Did we miss the wedding? We had a mare giving birth and couldn't leave until the foal was born. Where's Amy?"

Micah nodded hello to Sean, who'd not yet said a word, and reached up to help Tierney down. He set her on the ground then lifted his arms to Sophie.

"Where's Beth?" The little girl kicked her feet, anxious to be down.

"Inside with Sookie." Micah nudged his head toward the red building.

"Can I go see her, Mama?"

Tierney nodded, and Sophie skipped toward the schoolhouse door. After watching the girl go inside, Tierney turned to face him. "Is something wrong?"

Micah shoved his hands in his pockets, waiting for Sean to tie up the wagon and join them. When he did, Micah said, "I can't find Amy. She was supposed to be here an hour ago for the wedding. I dropped her off at the store and haven't seen her since."

"Perhaps she's shopping at the booths." Tierney gazed down the street, looking for her friend.

"That's what I thought, but I checked the booths when I went to the mercantile."

"We can help."

Micah nodded. "Let me get Ben, too. Sookie and Jonah can watch the girls."

After Ben joined them, they fanned out with Sean and Tierney going one way, and Ben and Micah another. Ben disappeared in the crowd to check the booths again, and Micah decided to walk around the outskirts of town. Amy had no cause to be there, but he had to rule out that she might have wandered out back for some reason.

As he walked, he prayed, hoping maybe she had just stepped inside a store and lost track of time. He passed the back of the restaurant just as Selma Spencer tossed out a bucket of water. Micah jumped back, and an arc of dirty, soapy water landed at his feet.

"Sorry 'bout that." The graying, heavyset woman gave him a toothless grin. "What'cha doing back here?"

"I'm looking for a friend. Amy Rogers." Micah described her.

Selma shook her head. "Haven't seen her."

"Thank you." Micah tipped his hat and strode off, determined to find Amy. He came to the back of the livery and stopped to jiggle the door handle. Most of the time, Hank kept the front and back doors open to allow a breeze to cool the inside of the livery. Micah stuck his ear to the wall and listened. He was certain Amy wouldn't come within a hundred feet of Hank's livery. When he didn't hear anything, he continued on, trying to shake the feeling that something bad had happened to her.

He continued praying, hoping he was wrong. Pain pricked his heart at the thought of someone hurting Amy. Fear gripped his chest. What if he never saw her again? What if she'd decided not to marry him and *had* hightailed it out of town?

He shook his head, knowing he couldn't give in to those negative thoughts. He recalled a verse that the minister had quoted last time he came to town: *Casting down imaginations, and every high thing that exalteth itself against the knowledge of God, and bringing into captivity every thought to the obedience of Christ.*

Drawing on the advice of scripture, he pushed aside his negative thoughts and continued his search.

Micah glanced around behind the saloon and still saw no one, though he could hear the ruckus of the crowd from Main Street. His heart ached that the town was making merry while Amy was missing. Where was she? Was she hurt?

If she was gone, she'd never know how he truly felt. How he loved her. Would it surprise her as much as it had him? He rubbed the back of his neck and knelt under an apple tree fully covered with tiny green fruit, not yet ripe for picking.

"Dear Lord, You know how I feel about Amy. How I've come to love her. She's selfless, always doing for others. Caring for the girls, for Ben—and me. She loves Sookie and Jonah as if they were her true family. I need her in my life. Need her love. Lord, I want to take care of her, so she never has to worry about having a place to belong again. Please keep her safe until I can find her. Help me tell her how I really feel and to be the husband she needs."

He stood, swiping his moist eyes. His heart felt lighter, but Amy was still missing.

As he continued his search, nothing looked suspicious or out of the ordinary. Several store owners had small homes behind their places of business, but they all looked as if nobody was home. Stewart's Gap had few celebrations, but when it did, the whole town and folks from the surrounding areas attended. He reached the final building and turned, walking past the end of town. He would search behind the buildings on the other side of the street then stop at the school and see if Amy had been located. He prayed she had.

Amy studied her prison in the dim light. Now that the morning sun had risen higher, it no longer shone directly through the thin cracks in the wall.

She had to find a way to escape. She shook the boards that made up the outer wall, but even though they looked old and weathered, they were secure.

Suddenly she heard footsteps outside and held her breath. Was it Hank, testing her to see if she'd cry out? Or was it someone who could help her?

Amy wanted to call out with all her being but couldn't take a chance. If it *was* Hank and he heard her, he might hurt Beth.

Leaning against the rough wall, she prayed, "Lord, help me. Provide for me a way of escape."

A shiver coursed through her body. Being locked in the dim room reminded her of the time she'd hidden in the wardrobe when her father had come home drunk. She crawled in behind the long dresses and sat as quiet as a mouse, not stirring no matter what she heard. She knew that when her father had passed out or left, her mother would come and find her. Only this time Mother wasn't coming. Maybe nobody was.

Tears burned Amy's eyes and trickled down her cheeks. How could her wedding day have turned out so awful?

Taking care not to get too close to the cockroach-infested table, she slumped down on the rickety chair, which groaned under her weight. Sniffing, she brushed her sleeve across her eyes. "Lord, please send me help."

She laid her hands in her lap, hoping to get more comfortable, and her elbow bumped the bulge in her pocket from the bag of candy. A peppermint would taste good and help soothe her upset stomach. As she removed the bag from her pocket, something fell out and thudded against the floor.

Leaning over, Amy stared at Micah's wedding present, and a slow smile tugged at her cheeks. "Oh, thank You, God!"

She reached down and grabbed the razor she'd bought for Micah then turned toward the door. She flipped open the metal blade and started sawing at the leather that held her captive.

"Dear Lord, thank You for not letting me buy that pocket watch."

Chapter 18

Micah returned to the schoolhouse, hoping and praying Amy would be there. He took the steps three at a time then pushed his way through the door. Hopeful faces turned his way, but when they saw he was alone, each person's expression saddened.

"No luck, I guess?" Ben asked.

Micah shook his head.

"Me neither."

Tierney approached carrying Missy, with Sean close on her heels. Jonah stood and slowly crossed the room to join them. Micah was glad Sookie had Beth and Sophie occupied, drawing on slates with chalk.

"What now?" Sean looped his arm around his wife's shoulders.

"We search again—and keep searching until we find her. Talk to everyone you meet and ask if they've seen her." Micah tried not to let his anxiety show. He had to believe someone must have seen Amy.

"Nearly the whole county is in town today. You want us to question everyone?" Ben asked.

Micah sighed, knowing that was impossible. "Has anyone seen Hank Foster? I can't help feeling he's behind this."

Ben nodded. "He was eating pie at Mabel Perkins's booth awhile ago."

"I saw him watching the horse race," Sean said.

Micah rubbed the back of his neck. "Well, let's search again. I'm going to check out Hank's barn. He had the back of it locked up tight, but I want to get inside. Ben, you and Sean take opposite sides of Main Street and check again. Where's the minister?"

"Said he had to visit a sick couple, then he'll be back." Ben put his cap on and started out the door. Sean followed.

Micah adjusted his hat so the afternoon sun didn't shine in his face and block his view. Amy was somewhere in Stewart's Gap—and she needed his help. He could feel it.

Amy ignored the blister on her finger and continued sawing on the leather that Hank had used to tie shut the tack room door. Just a little more and she'd be through. With each sweep of the razor, she thanked God for providing a way of escape.

The blade zipped through the final thread, and the door swung open on a loud groan. She closed the razor and pocketed it. A sense of exhilaration surged through her, making her hands and feet tingle. As a child, there had been nothing she could do to help herself except hide. But as a woman, with the Lord's help, she was free.

She jogged through the quiet barn toward the muffled sound of the townsfolk's celebration. When she reached the livery doors, she gave a shove, but they didn't budge.

"No!"

Hank must have locked them from the outside. She turned, intending to check the back door, but heard the bar being lifted on the other side.

Hank!

Her gaze darted from side to side, searching for a place to hide. While Hank made his way back to the tack room, she would slip out into the crowd and get away. She rushed into an open stall and pressed herself against the wall, hoping he couldn't see her in the shadows.

The door crept open, allowing more light inside. The large silhouette of a man filled the triangle of light. Amy's heart pounded such a ferocious rhythm she was sure Hank would hear it.

"Hank? Anybody here?"

Her breath caught in her throat. "Micah!" she managed to squeak.

"Amy?" Micah rushed inside, and then she was in his arms, being crushed in a bear hug. "I've been looking everywhere for you. What happened?"

"Hank locked me in the tack room. I just managed to get out when I heard you rattle the door and thought it was him."

"I'm so sorry. I never expected he'd do something like this. He's always been harmless. Why didn't you holler out? Someone would have heard you."

Amy pulled out of his arms and wiped her eyes. "He threatened to hurt Beth if I did."

A muscle tightened in Micah's jaw, and then his eyes closed. "I'm so glad you're all right."

When he opened his eyes, his gaze took her breath away. "I was so worried you had left town, or that something bad had happened. You have to know that I love you, Amy."

She swallowed the lump that was suddenly stuck in her throat. A giddy joy surged through her, making her limbs weak. Micah loved her! No man had ever loved her. She threw herself into his arms. "Oh, Micah. I love you, too!"

His lips met hers in an urgent kiss that threatened to turn her bones into pudding. If not for his crushing hold, she was sure she'd slip down into a puddle on the dirt floor. His breath quickened, and he deepened the kiss, taking her breath with it. Amy had never known such joy, except for the day she gave her heart to God.

Finally, Micah pulled back. "Amazing."

Amy felt a shy grin tug at her mouth. "I agree."

"I hate to leave here, now that I have you all to myself, but we need to let the others know I found you."

Amy nodded and was glad when Micah kept his arm around her shoulders and held her tight against his side. She marveled at how different things seemed, knowing that he loved her.

She blinked against the bright light as they stepped outside. The town's celebration continued as if nothing had happened.

Micah stiffened, and she looked up to see Hank stomping toward them with an angry glint in his eyes. She tightened her grip on Micah's waist, wishing they could be rid of Hank Foster for good.

"Ben!"

Amy jumped when Micah yelled at his brother. Across the street, Ben looked up and smiled then jogged toward them.

"Go get the constable."

Ben's dark brows dipped at Micah's order, but he turned and ran down the boardwalk.

Hank straightened. "You and me's got business, Walsh."

"I don't imagine we'll ever do business again. You kidnapped my bride."

Hank scowled, and his gaze darted back and forth from Micah to Amy. "Aww, I didn't harm her. I just wanted to make you see reason and let me in on your slave dealings."

Amy felt Micah stiffen again. She'd never seen him truly mad and couldn't help the anxiety that made her stomach churn. Would Micah harm her in his anger, like Amy's father had hurt her mother?

Micah kept his hand securely on her shoulder, and with relief, Amy realized his wrath was directed at Hank, not her.

Ben and the constable jogged toward them, and Amy relaxed a smidgen.

"What's the problem here?" the constable asked.

"He's dealing slaves, and I want in on it," Hank whined.

The constable eyed Micah. "That right, Walsh? I didn't figure you to be a slave trader."

Micah shook his head. "No, it is not correct. But for some reason Hank thinks so. He kidnapped Amy and threatened my daughter as a way to try to sway me into working with him."

The constable spat a stream of tobacco juice at Hank's feet, and Ben chuckled when Hank leaped backwards. "You do that, Hank? You took this woman against her will?"

"I didn't hurt her none." Hank kicked the dirt and shoved his hands in his pocket. "I'd have let her go. I just wanted Micah to pay attention to me and cut me in on his business."

"There's no law against slave trading in Virginia, but there are laws about kidnapping. I'm gonna have to lock you up, Hank."

Amy watched Hank wilt. The constable took Hank's arm and dragged him off into the crowd. Ben accompanied the law officer, holding Hank's other arm. She sagged in relief.

Micah turned to face her. He ran his hand down her cheek, and she closed her eyes at his gentle touch. "That feels nice."

"Good, I plan to do it often."

She lifted her lids to see a twinkle in the blue-green eyes she loved so much. Micah leaned forward and kissed her right there with half the town watching.

Some men let out a couple of whoops, making Amy giggle.

"Do you feel like going ahead with the wedding today? Or would you rather wait until the preacher comes back to town next month?"

Amy stuck her hands on her hips and stared up at the man she loved. "Micah Walsh, you are not getting rid of me that easily."

Micah's grin tickled her insides. "All right then, let's get hitched." He held out his arm, she looped hers through it, and they headed for the church.

———

Amy wasn't certain how much longer her trembling legs would support her. First they had shaken from the fear of being locked up, and now from the nervous excitement of her wedding.

"Do you have a ring?" the minister asked Micah.

"Yes." Micah released her hand, reached into his trousers pocket, and pulled out a silver ring that bore a small ruby.

He held it up, and Amy's heart beat double-time. She was relieved to see it wasn't the same ring Kathryn had worn.

"Place the ring on her finger as a token of your love and commitment."

Micah's steady gaze sent shivers of delight charging through Amy's body. He slid the ring on her finger then smiled, making her heart stampede.

"In the name of God Almighty and the Commonwealth of Virginia, I pronounce you husband and wife."

Amy stared up at Micah—her husband. She'd never expected to marry, not after watching the way her father treated her mother. She'd never wanted to be dependent on a man, until she had gotten to know Micah.

The pastor cleared his throat. "Uh-hem. This is the place most folks kiss."

A spark ignited in Micah's eyes, and he waggled his eyebrows up and down. Amy giggled but felt like melting into the floor. She wasn't used to being kissed, much less in front of her friends and family. Before she could fret more, Micah pulled her closer and leaned down, claiming her lips.

Behind her Ben shouted, "Yahoo!"

To her side, Amy heard Tierney murmur, "Praise be to God."

Finally, Micah released her but kept his arm around her shoulders. Good thing, because her legs still refused to behave as normal. Cheeks aflame, Amy looked into the smiling faces of her friends and family.

The minister lifted his hand toward the crowd. "Folks, I present to you Mr. and Mrs. Micah Walsh."

Instantly, Ben was on his feet and moving toward them. "Welcome to the family, Amy." He gave her a quick hug and a peck on the cheek, then backed up, his ears a bright red.

Tierney was at her side, embracing Amy in a warm hug. "I knew he loved you," she whispered.

"How?"

"It was written all over his face. I'm glad his mind and heart finally figured it out." Tierney leaned back, smiling.

"Me, too."

Jonah stood on the outskirts of the group, next to Sookie, who held Missy. Amy slipped from Micah's side and past Ben to stand in front of the black couple. "Thank you so much for bringing the lovely flowers. I'm sorry that my delay messed up your surprise. Still, your kindness means a lot."

"It weren't nothing." Sookie hugged Missy and stared at the floor.

Jonah beamed his gap-toothed smile at her. "I knowed the day I set eyes on you that the Good Lawd had something mighty special planned for you."

"How did you know?"

He patted his chest. "I just knew in here."

Micah stepped beside Amy and pulled her against his side. "I'm hungry, wife. You ready to go eat?"

Amy wasn't certain she could eat a bite after all the day's excitement, but she nodded. She felt a tug on her skirt and looked down.

"Can I call you Mama now?" Beth looked at her with hopeful brown eyes.

Amy glanced at Micah. His eyes dulled for a moment then sparked back to life. "That would be fine, Punkin." He reached down and lifted Beth in his arms. "You hungry?"

His daughter nodded. "Can I have a store-bought pickle?"

Micah grinned and looked at Amy. "Ever heard of a child who'd rather have a pickle than candy?"

Amy smiled. It warmed her heart that Micah agreed to let Beth call her *Mama*. Imagine, in one day she'd gone from being a kidnapped victim to a wife and mother. The Lord sure worked in mysterious ways.

Chapter 19

Amy crossed the cabin and stood close to Micah. She twisted her hands together, her face a mixture of fear and anger. "When I agreed to marry you, you promised not to go off and leave us."

Micah glanced at Sookie's back. She sat at the table, rolling out biscuits. "Let's take this discussion outside."

With Missy on her hip, Amy stormed out the open cabin door, stomped down the porch steps, and marched along the path that led to the creek. He followed, wishing he knew what to say to calm her. She'd finally confessed to him how her father left her mother and her without food or support for weeks and months at a time. In spite of Amy becoming a Christian, she still feared being deserted.

But with Ben down sick, that left only him to see the latest group of slaves across the border. He didn't want to leave her any more than she wanted him to, but he needed to help the slaves move on to the next safe house.

So far, in spite of them both confessing their love, their marriage had remained chaste—and it would until he could finish the new cabin he was building for Sookie. If he didn't have to leave, he probably could have completed the new cabin in a day or two. Jonah was helping, but the old man moved slower than a caterpillar. Micah had prayed for patience, but he was a twenty-four-year-old newlywed who longed to be with his wife.

Amy stopped so fast, he nearly barreled in to her. She spun around. "You promised."

He held up his hands in defense. "No, I never promised I wouldn't have to leave. That's unreasonable. But I do understand your fears. I can't promise I won't ever have to go away, but I can promise that I'll always return."

Amy studied him, as if to see if he was being truthful. He ran the back of his hand down her soft cheek, and she closed her eyes and leaned into his caress.

"I don't want you to go, Micah."

"I know, but I'll only be gone a day. You can be assured I will hurry home."

A bird flittered in the trees overhead, chirping a cheerful tune. The water rippled along in the creek. The sun stretched its fingers through the trees and touched Amy's cheeks. Missy bounced in her arms, oblivious to the tension surrounding them. Love for his family swelled in Micah's chest.

The baby opened her mouth and gave Amy a slobbery kiss. His wife's lips lifted in a reluctant grin.

"I think Missy has the right idea." Before Amy could object, he swooped down and planted a kiss on her soft lips. He started to pull back, but Amy tugged on his shirt, pulling him to her again. Joy burst within him, and he honored his wife's wishes, kissing her until his breath was ragged. A sharp tug on his ear brought him back to his senses. "Ow! You little scamp." He reached for Missy and tossed her in the air.

Amy smiled, though her eyes still looked sad.

"How could I not hurry back when I have so many women here, longing to kiss me?"

His wife laughed for real this time, making his heart sing. "Besides, I have a cabin to finish so I can sleep in my own bed again."

Amy's eyes widened, and her cheeks turned scarlet. Micah chuckled, put his arm around her, and headed back to the cabin.

Tears stung Amy's eyes, and she fought them back so she could see through the darkness. The wagon Micah was driving disappeared down the road into the black night. Though it looked empty, except for some wooden crates in the back, she knew the wagon carried a precious cargo of two young black men who'd run away from their cruel slave master. She could still hear the soft jingle of the harness and creak of the wagon, but even that was fading against the backdrop of night creatures. She knew the importance of Micah's mission but dreaded seeing him leave.

Her fears were irrational—she knew that. But they still assaulted her. If Ben hadn't taken ill from all the unusual food he'd eaten at the town celebration, he'd be taking the runaways instead of Micah. In her heart, she knew what they were doing was honorable, but she was still afraid.

She yawned, bone tired after working hard and being upset with Micah all day. Somewhere nearby she heard a creature's feral growl and darted back inside the cabin and closed the door, leaning against it.

The tears came in earnest then. Why did he have to leave her? They weren't even a true man and wife yet. She never thought she'd want to give herself fully to a man, until she fell in love and married Micah. Now she might never have the chance.

Helping runaways was dangerous work. Micah had promised they would cease the work as soon as someone else in the area could take over. With a wife and young children, he didn't need to be putting his life in danger.

Amy crossed the room and dropped down in one of the rockers. The faint light from the lone lantern cast eerie shadows on the walls. She wished Jonah were here to quote her some scriptures and make her feel better. As a new believer, she had not yet committed many Bible verses to memory.

Her thoughts drifted back to her childhood. The only two times in her whole life that she'd been truly happy were when her mother's sister had sent money and she and her mother had gone to visit Kathryn's family in Richmond. If only they had stayed there, like Kathryn's mother had begged them to. But Amy's mother wouldn't abandon her husband, even if he *had* abandoned her.

Tears dripped down Amy's cheeks. Knowing Micah wasn't upstairs left her with an ache in her heart. She'd never known such longing. He'd only been gone a few minutes, and she craved to be held secure in his strong arms and to feel the warmth of his lips on hers. If she'd ever doubted that she loved Micah, she was now certain.

But he'd left her—just like her father.

Still, he hadn't left without provision. Just this morning he'd shot and plucked a turkey. They had enjoyed the delicious meat at dinner. And she had her garden, and she wasn't alone. Ben was already on the mend, though not up to traveling yet. She also had Jonah, Sookie, and the children to keep her company.

Yes, Micah had left, but he'd be back. His final kiss had branded her heart and proved where his affections lay.

But the months of being fatherless and having to beg for food were weeds with roots that ran deep.

Amy leaned over with her face in her hands. "Oh, God! Help me."

She cried until she felt she had no more tears. What it came down to was trust. She had to choose to trust God and trust Micah. It *was* unreasonable to expect her husband to be home every night. Situations were bound to arise when he would have to be away for a time.

As Amy prayed for herself and Micah, a warm calm relaxed her body. She leaned back in the rocker and stared at the ceiling.

"Okay, I give up. I will trust that Micah will be true to his word and will return tomorrow eve. Lord, help me cast aside the negative thoughts that only cause me turmoil. I'm safe here. Father is gone and can no longer harm me. And Micah isn't Father.

"Thank you for sending Tierney and Sean to help me learn that there are good men in this world. Please watch over Micah and bring him home safe."

She yawned and pushed up from the chair, feeling as if she'd been in a war. In the bedroom, she silently slipped under the sheets. Though she still missed Micah, her heart was at peace. She closed her eyes, dreaming of what it would be like to be in her husband's arms.

Chapter 20

Lightning flashed in the sky, momentarily illuminating the trail. Micah knew he should have taken Luther Cameron up on his offer to stay the night, but he'd promised Amy he'd be home tonight—and he knew the importance of keeping that promise. He hoped and prayed his delay wouldn't cause her undue worry. She hadn't wanted him to leave, but he had had no choice in the matter.

The unshed tears shimmering in her big brown eyes had made his heart ache. Was he doomed to always disappoint his wife? He'd only been married a few days and already he'd made Amy cry.

Micah shook his head, not willing to give in to those kinds of thoughts. He must fight the unseen enemy that would weigh him down and make him feel defeated. "Lord, please don't let this separation affect my new relationship with Amy. Take her fears away and heal her."

Huge drops of rain pelted his clothing, soaking him in seconds. Thunder boomed. The horses snorted and jerked in their harness, spooked by the storm. Micah cooed to them and hunkered down, wishing he had something to keep him dry. He'd not brought along a covering since it was summer and the nights warm.

Another bolt of lightning zigzagged above him. As miserable as he was, he couldn't help admiring the beauty of God's handiwork. He heard a *thud* in the back of the wagon, quickly followed by another. When a pea-sized piece of hail bounced off his arm, Micah knew he had to find cover fast. Lightning flashed again, and he noticed a grove of trees ahead. Trees and lightning were a bad mix, but if the hail got any bigger, he'd be in real trouble.

Wind whipped his face, and he urged the team forward. The hail increased to acorn size just as he pulled under the trees. "Thank You, Lord, for Your protection."

Micah reached for the brake and felt the hair on his arms rise. He looked up as the air around him sizzled. A horrendous boom exploded on his right, and suddenly he was flying through the air.

Amy stretched and kicked off the bedcovers. The rooster crowed, and she bolted upright. Once again she'd slept past daybreak. Sookie's place beside her was empty, but both Beth and Missy were still asleep.

Amy hurried out of the bedroom and found Sookie slicing a loaf of corn-meal mush. Already bacon fat sizzled in the cast-iron pan, awaiting the mush. When Sookie looked up and shook her head, Amy's heart dropped to her feet.

She opened the front door and stared out. Where was Micah? It had been three days since his team of horses had returned alone, towing the wagon. Ben had searched almost constantly since then, but he had seen no sign of his brother.

A deep sense of abandonment threatened to overpower her worry about her husband's condition. Regardless of what her own father had done, Micah loved his family. Even if she weren't there, he'd come home because he loved his children, his brother, and Jonah and Sookie. But she knew in her heart that he loved her, too. If he wasn't home, it was because he couldn't come home. Something had happened.

She closed the door and dragged herself back to the bedroom and dressed. All she wanted to do was crawl in bed and sleep until her husband returned. But she had a home and family to care for. She rubbed her gritty eyes and headed outside to visit the privy. Afterward, she walked down to the creek and splashed cool water on her face.

Would she face these struggles every time Micah left home? Somehow she thought she might. At least for a while.

Amy looked up at the clear blue sky. "Lord, it's me, Amy. I'm still not too good at praying yet, but I know You understand. Wherever Micah is, please watch over him. Keep him safe. If he's hurt, I pray that You show Ben where he is, so he can bring him home. And help me conquer these feelings of abandonment. Help me to believe in my husband's love."

"Amy! Micah's home!"

Startled at Ben's shout, Amy jumped and turned toward the house. She saw Ben running from the barn to the cabin. In front of the house stood a horse with a man slumped on its back. Another man, who looked like an old trapper, waved at Ben.

Amy's gaze pulled back to the man on the horse. *Micah!* She lifted her skirts and dashed forward. "Oh, thank You, God, for bringing him home."

"Micah!"

Slowly, he lifted his head and stared in her direction. Her heart nearly burst with joy. As she neared him, she saw a bandage wrapped around his head. Micah slid off the horse and steadied himself then turned toward her.

"Papa!" Beth charged out the door, jumped off the porch, and ran to her father, grabbing hold of his leg.

"Morning, Punkin." Micah laid his hand on the top of her head and gave her a tired smile.

Amy's heart beat a frantic pace, but her steps slowed as Micah was quickly surrounded.

Ben stopped right in front of his brother. "Where you been? What happened? We've been scared out of our wits." The men embraced and slapped shoulders; then Ben picked up Beth and handed her to Micah. Without waiting for Micah to answer him, Ben turned to the old man who'd brought his brother home and asked him where he'd found Micah.

Jonah shuffled up and patted Micah's arm. "Glad to have you back home. I been prayin' powerful hard."

Sookie stepped out the door and smiled. "Breakfast is ready." Just as quickly, she darted back inside.

Ben invited the old man for breakfast and introduced Jonah. Beth wiggled out of her father's arms and followed them inside.

Finally, Amy and Micah were alone.

She felt heat warm her cheeks as Micah gazed at her intently, seemingly taking in every square inch. He pulled his eyes from her and studied the ground. Amy's heart lurched when she noticed the spot of blood on his bandage. She moved toward him as he looked up.

"I'm so sorry, Amy. I planned on coming right home, but that storm messed things up. I know you were worried." His gaze begged her for understanding.

At that moment, all her concerns and fears were dashed aside. All she could think about was that Micah had been hurt and she hadn't been there to help him. Tears stung her eyes and made her throat ache. She could have lost him.

Stepping forward, she lifted her hand to his lips. "Shhh. God helped me, and I'm thankful He answered my prayers and helped you, too."

Hope sparked in his blue-green eyes, and he grabbed her hand, kissing each of her fingers. Shivers of delight raced up Amy's arm, and she felt as if her heart would burst with love for this man.

"Amy. . .I missed you so much."

Micah pulled her into his arms and pressed his warm lips against hers. Joy filled her being as she wrapped her arms around his waist and kissed him back.

Who would have thought a few months ago that she'd be married? Amy marveled at all that God had done in her life in such a short time.

Finally, Micah pulled back. He framed her face with his hands, and she noticed a bandage on one of them. "Amy Walsh, you have to know that I was an idiot to want to keep our marriage a business arrangement."

Feeling covered with a sudden blanket of shyness, Amy nodded and looked away.

"You think I'm an idiot?"

Her gaze darted back to his. "No—"

Micah's teasing smile sent butterflies dancing in her stomach. This time he covered her lips with his calloused finger. "I know you don't think that. As soon as I can finish Sookie's cabin, I'll move back downstairs."

It was Amy's turn to grin.

"What are you smiling at?"

Amy reached up and smoothed back a lock of Micah's dark brown hair that had flopped over the bandage, onto his forehead. "While you were gone, Sean came over with a friend, and they finished it. Tierney said you'd need to be in your own bed if something had happened, so I could nurse you."

Micah's eyes twinkled with delight. "I like the idea of you nursing me. I'm so grateful to God for bringing you here, Amy."

She managed to whisper, "Me, too," before his lips covered hers again.

The next day, Amy sat at the spinning wheel, pulling wool into thin strands and spinning it onto a spool. She'd used up Kathryn's bag of wool and had bartered a deal with a neighbor who owned sheep to trade their extra milk and eggs for wool.

Missy was asleep, and Sookie had taken Beth down to the barn to look for eggs and to see the horses. The men were down working in the cornfield. Amy took time to enjoy the rare moment of being alone.

So many times in her life, being alone had been a fearful thing, but now she cherished the few moments of quiet. As the big wheel spun around, Amy marveled at the changes that had happened in her life the past few months. She no longer feared men. She was even married to one.

She thought back to Jonah's word about how he knew God had plans for her the first time he saw her. She now believed that God had been directing her all along to come to the Walsh farm—only she never could have dreamed of the blessings God had in store for her.

"What are you smiling at?"

Amy jumped and turned toward Micah's voice. "What are you doing here? I thought you were working in the cornfield."

An ornery grin that resembled Ben's tilted his lips. "I was, but I missed my wife and needed a kiss to make it through the rest of the day."

Amy accepted Micah's outstretched hand and stood, then smacked him on his arm. "You goose."

"No goose, just a desperate man." He pulled her close, and his loving gaze roamed her face, sending shivers of excitement racing up her arms.

As Micah's face moved closer, Amy marveled at how she'd come to love her husband so much, so quickly. Once her life was spinning out of control, but God had taken the flailing strands and woven them into Micah's family, making a quilt of love, faith, and happiness.

VICKIE MCDONOUGH

Vickie is an award-winning inspirational romance author. She is the author of ten novels and novellas. Her second Heartsong book, *Spinning Out of Control*, placed in the Top Ten Favorite Historical Romance category in Heartsong's 2006 annual contest. Her stories have also placed first in several prestigious contests, such as the ACFW Noble Theme, the Inspirational Readers Choice Contest, and the Texas Gold contest. She has also written book reviews for over five years and enjoys mentoring new writers. Vickie is a wife of thirty-two years, mother to four sons, and a grandma. When she's not writing, Vickie enjoys reading, gardening, watching movies, and traveling. Vickie loves hearing from her readers at vickie@vickiemcdonough.com.

Weaving a Future

by Susan Page Davis

Dedication

To our second daughter, Megan, an author in her own right,
who is brave enough to critique her mom's work.
I can't wait to see our joint byline!

Chapter 1

May, 1848

Harry had never seen such fine country for horses. He had to admit, this Shenandoah Valley rivaled the rolling hills in Kentucky where he planned to set up his breeding farm. The meadows burst with a green opulence in the May sun. The grass grew so lush he was tempted to get down and roll in it and to take Pepper's saddle off and let him roll in it, too.

They trotted along a fencerow, and a half-dozen mares tore across the pasture toward them. They kept pace with Pepper as they strode along inside the rail fence, snorting and nickering, trying to capture Pepper's attention. The gelding snuffled and tossed his head but kept on steadily under Harry's firm hand. Every mare had a long-legged foal at her side, he noted. It would have been hard to choose among them for the best.

On Harry's left, a hardwood forest fringed the road. The oaks and hickories, in their full, glorious foliage, would offer some shade on that side of the lane in the morning; but now it was late afternoon, and the warmth of the golden rays striking him from the west, beyond the meadows and more rolling hills, was not unpleasant.

He heard muffled hoofbeats and turned toward the woods. Two horses charged neck and neck from a shady path and bolted into the lane in front of him. Pepper reared with an alarmed squeal as a bay mare rushed toward him. Harry's instantaneous impression of the rider was a young woman gone wild. Her features were lovely, lit with the joy of speed. As he jerked Pepper's reins she caught sight of him, and shock darkened her eyes as she realized the inevitability of the coming collision.

"Whoa!" She pulled back with all her strength, gritting her teeth in determination. Harry pivoted Pepper on his hind legs, attempting to lessen the impact.

He had no time to do more. In a split second her mare slammed against Pepper's hindquarters, sending the gelding in an awkward leap toward the pasture fence. Harry watched in dismay while trying to keep his balance. As she flew from the saddle, the girl's commodious burgundy skirts billowed with air, like the sails of the schooner Harry had called his home for the last three years. As she tumbled to earth, he had a glimpse of lace-trimmed linen and high black boots. Her bay mare veered to the left with an offended snort and skittered up the lane.

"Miss Sadie!" Beyond the fallen girl, a thin Negro boy was pulling up his own mount, a red roan, and staring with horror at the girl. At least he'd been riding on her other side and had avoided becoming part of the melee. Pepper lurched and snorted, but Harry held his head down, and the gelding halted, calming under the soft words Harry spoke in his ear.

He and the boy leaped to the ground at the same moment, and they knelt, one on either side of the girl. She lay on her back, staring up at them, breathing in quick, shallow gasps. Her blue eyes sought Harry's face in confusion. Her auburn hair was no doubt confined in a sedate knot at ordinary times, but now a long braid trailed in the dirt by her shoulder, and fine wisps fanned out around her face.

"Miss Sadie, you done what your papa said and broke your neck!" Tears streamed down the boy's face as he leaned within inches of her nose. "Tell me you ain't broke your neck, Miss Sadie!"

"Hush, Pax!" The girl hauled in a longer, slower breath and exhaled carefully. "I think I'll live, if you'll give me some air."

"Take it easy," Harry said. "Get your breath back."

"The horses." She struggled to sit up, swiveling to look. The bay mare had disappeared around a bend in the lane, and Pax's roan was snatching mouthfuls of grass at the edge of the road. The girl moaned and lay back gasping, putting one hand up to her head. "Get Lily."

"You sure you all right?" the boy asked uneasily.

"I'll be fine. Just get that horse!" She took several more shallow gulps and gasped, "If she gets back home without me, Papa will never let me ride again!"

The boy jumped up and ran to his mount. He scooped up the trailing reins and hopped into the saddle then tore off in the direction the bay had taken.

Harry watched the girl, waiting patiently for her to recover. She was older than he'd first thought—a young lady, of that he was certain from her clothing and her manner with the Negro boy. Probably the daughter of a planter. Her disinclination to swoon or cry assured him she had taken tumbles before and was not seriously injured. He was sure her corset was obstructing her breathing. Not much he could do about that.

She lay quiet for nearly a minute, her head turned away from him, gradually gaining control of her breath. At last she turned slowly toward him.

"May I help you up, ma'am?"

He read speculation, embarrassment, and something more in her blue eyes before the lids flickered down to conceal them.

"I don't believe I've ever laid eyes on you before in my life, sir."

Harry laughed. "I beg your pardon, miss. I should have introduced myself. My name is Harry Cooper."

"Cooper?" She sat up with a little moan, and Harry touched her shoulder gently.

"Are you certain you're not hurt?"

She rubbed her elbow then flexed her arm, frowning at the cuff of her dress where a button had been scraped off. "I'll be fine, thank you." She glanced up at him, wincing. "I've made rather a spectacle of myself, haven't I? I apologize, sir."

"No need, although spirited horses and daredevil riders can be a volatile combination."

She blinked once then smiled. "Indeed. It was a race."

"A very close one, I'd say."

"I'd have won if you hadn't been in the way."

Harry couldn't help smiling. "Are you sure? Those horses were pretty evenly matched."

Her cheeks colored slightly, and she looked away, but the smile didn't leave her lips. "Here comes Pax."

Harry bit back his disappointment at seeing the boy returning on his roan, leading the young woman's mare. She gathered herself to rise, and he slipped his hand under her uninjured elbow to give her a hint of leverage.

"I thank you for your concern," she said, facing him as she brushed a fine cloud of powdery dirt from her skirt. "Your horse wasn't injured, was he?"

"No, he's fine, ma'am. Allow me to see you home." His quick offer surprised him a little. He wasn't used to playing the gallant gentleman, but something about this untamed beauty drew him like north drew the needle on the captain's compass.

"No need, I assure you." Her breath came easier now but was still a bit choppy.

Harry looked the two mares over. Their conformation was nearly perfect, and both were walking sedately now, scarcely breathing hard.

The boy rode up close to where Harry and the young woman stood and halted, swinging down to the ground. "Lemme help you up, Miss Sadie."

Harry sensed the boy's mistrust directed at him, but he was no doubt the guardian for this lovely young woman and was privileged to ride his master's best mounts when the daughter of the house went out for exercise.

"The horses seem none the worse for the accident," Harry said.

"Yes. I thank you for your help." She stepped toward the bay, where Pax stood waiting to aid her. Harry knew he could easily pick her up in his arms and place her in the saddle.

Better belay that idea, he told himself. He was certain Miss Sadie and the fiercely scowling Pax would never allow it. She was about to leave him, a cheerless thought that set Harry to wondering how he could draw out the encounter without offending her. But she was astride now, settling her voluminous skirt around her with a couple of gentle strokes and gathering her reins.

She's left her hoops home, Harry thought with a wry smile. *She must be near twenty, but she has a child's unconscious freedom.* Her energy and boldness, coupled with a resolve to act the proper lady under the gaze of a stranger, made him envy Pax. *I wouldn't mind riding beside her day after day.*

"Good day then, sir." She turned and headed away, down the lane, and the boy scrambled aboard his mare.

"Wait!" Harry called. Pax looked back uncertainly, but the young woman kept her mare at a steady walk away from him.

"I'm looking for the Spinning Wheel Farm, owned by Mr. Oliver McEwan," Harry said to the boy.

Pax grinned. "This be your lucky day, suh. You done found it."

Harry was startled at how quickly the boy's animosity turned to welcome. "You mean this is McEwan land?"

The boy gestured to the fields on the other side of the lane. "Everythin' you see, suh."

"And the house?"

"Yonder." He nodded after the girl's retreating figure.

"Thank you." Harry stroked Pepper's neck and watched them ride out of sight before he mounted. He let Pepper amble along in the golden light of sunset. Beautiful country, absolutely gorgeous. There couldn't be two farms with such superb animals in the area. Did he dare hope he would once more meet the lovely young Sadie, who strove with marginal success to cloak her effervescence in propriety? He smiled to himself, remembering the quality of the horses Sadie and her faithful companion rode. Yes, he dared hope.

Chapter 2

Sadie donned a huge apron and tied the strings behind her. She loved the kitchen, with the savory smell of roasting poultry and the warmth of the cookstove. When she wasn't out feeding the chickens or in the barn coddling the horses, she spent many contented hours here with Tallie, the family's cook and housekeeper.

Tallie threw her an ominous frown. "You just get into the parlor and help your father entertain the gentleman."

"Don't fuss at me," Sadie said. "I always help you with supper. Papa's perfectly capable of keeping up a conversation with a customer."

"Hmm." Tallie plucked her green-handled masher from a nail on the wall over her worktable and plunged it into a pan of boiled potatoes. As she worked with strong, methodical strokes, she scowled at Sadie. "It's *dinner* tonight, served in the dinin' room, and I can fix it. Now that you're all cleaned up and lookin' respectable, you belong in there with the company."

"He'll see me soon enough." Sadie began arranging Tallie's golden biscuits on an ironstone platter.

"Pax said that gentleman was taken with you, though I don't know why, with you dashin' round the country like a hoyden." Tallie turned her brown eyes heavenward in despair. "I don't know how to keep you from shamin' this family, Miss Sadie."

"Now, you hush. Don't you dare tell Papa I fell off Lily this afternoon."

"It's a wonder you didn't meet your end." Tallie sighed, reaching for the butter. "And that dress you wore is near done for, I'll tell you!"

Sadie lifted the platter of biscuits and turned sideways, allowing her full hoopskirt to slide through the doorway to the dining room. She placed the platter on the table and tiptoed to the door on the far side of the room. When she held her breath, she could hear her father's warm voice coming from the parlor.

"You want six mares, Mr. Cooper? I'll have to think on that. Don't want to deplete my own herd too much. I can let you have four with no problem."

"Four will be a good start," Cooper said.

Her father went on. "If it's breeding stock you want, the sorrel is a good choice. She's dropped two good foals. And any of the others I showed you. Of course, I don't like to let my mares go until their foals are weaned."

Good! Sadie thought. *He's going to buy, and we'll have some money at last.* Her father had been short on cash this spring.

"Well, sir, I can come back in the fall if you'd like," Harry Cooper was saying. "I've picked out my property in Kentucky, but I haven't started building yet. I've got my summer's work cut out for me."

"It's a long ride," Oliver McEwan said.

"Not too far, sir, and I'd like to see this valley in the fall."

At that moment Tallie entered from the kitchen, holding a big porcelain tureen full of potatoes. "What you doin'?" she hissed, and Sadie straightened and pulled away from the doorway.

"Mr. Cooper's going to buy some horses from Papa," Sadie whispered.

Tallie smiled with satisfaction. "Isn't that fine? Now you get in there. Everythin's ready, and I don't want your papa waitin' on you until the biscuits get cold."

Sadie started to protest, but Tallie put her hands on her ample hips. "Git, git, git!"

Sadie could see she would have to do as she was told, and she reached behind her to untie her apron.

Tallie's eyes lit with admiration. "You gonna break that poor man's heart, sugar. That dress makes you look like a princess."

Sadie looked down at the rose silk gown. She didn't have many occasions to dress up anymore. Her father hadn't entertained much since her mother's death four years ago. Occasionally a neighbor would invite them to dinner. She hoped suddenly that her dress was still fashionable and that she would compare favorably to the other ladies Harry Cooper had seen in his travels. Her meeting with him had been so brief that she wasn't certain whether he was a courteous gentleman or a presumptuous bounder. She hoped her father liked him. That would tell her a lot.

She stepped toward Tallie and planted a kiss soundly on her plump, dark cheek. Then she took a deep breath and headed for the parlor.

Her father was standing near the fireplace with Harry, holding the small daguerreotype of Sadie's brother, Tenley. Sadie paused in the doorway. How well she knew that picture! Tenley stood stiff and proud in his dark forage cap and the white cotton uniform of the Second Dragoons. His eagerness and optimism glowed in his eyes.

"The boy's been gone a long time," her father was saying. "He wanted to go with General Taylor and whip those Mexicans. But it's been almost a year since we've heard from him."

"He's a fine lad," Harry said. "I'm sure you'll hear something soon."

"I hope so. We pray for him constantly. My solace is knowing he's in God's hands."

Harry nodded. "If your son is trusting the Lord, you know he'll be all right, sir, no matter what happens. But our troops took the capital last fall. I expect he's on his way home now."

"Maybe." Her father placed the frame back on the mantelpiece, and Sadie stepped forward. Her skirt rustled, and her father turned toward her. "Ah, here she is at last. Mr. Cooper, I'd like you to meet my daughter, Sadie."

She half expected the guest to laugh and accuse her of masquerading as a lady or at least to announce that they had met before, but Harry's expression turned serious as he took her hand and bowed over it.

"Miss McEwan," he murmured. "This is a pleasure."

A thrill of anticipation tickled Sadie's spine. Her dread had been for nothing. This dinner could turn out to be pleasant indeed, if Harry Cooper decided to make it so.

"Sadie, our guest is buying some mares from us. He'll come back for them in September."

"That's wonderful. I'm sure you'll be pleased with them." She didn't quite dare look at Harry again. She was grateful that he apparently hadn't spilled the tale of her breakneck ride to her father. For a fleeting instant she thought, *Maybe he doesn't recognize me! I must have looked like an ill-bred roughneck when I crashed into him.*

But a quick glance at him from beneath her eyelashes disabused her of that notion. A secret laugh danced in Harry's rich brown eyes.

"Come then," her father said, offering Sadie his arm. "I'm sure Tallie is beside herself, wondering how to keep the food warm."

During the meal Tallie and her husband, Zeke, served them with flawless precision. Harry Cooper was polite and carried on an animated conversation about horses, farmland, and politics, though he claimed to know nothing about the latter topic, having spent the last three years at sea.

"At sea?" his host asked. "Where did you sail to?"

Harry sat back with a little sigh and let Zeke take away his dishes from the main course. "The Caribbean mostly, sir. We made several runs to the islands—Tortola, Antigua, Trinidad. . . ."

"Trinidad," Sadie whispered, rolling the sound off her tongue.

Harry smiled at her. "We put in at Caracas twice. Went out to the Spice Islands one time. It's beautiful, but it's not home."

Her father nodded. "So you've had enough of the sea?"

"Yes, sir. The captain of the vessel I shipped on decided to do a transatlantic voyage, and I knew I didn't want to go along."

"Rum?"

"Yes, sir."

Tallie came from the kitchen at that moment, carrying a huge, white-frosted layer cake, and Zeke followed, bearing two golden fruit pies, still warm from the oven.

"Oh, my." Harry retrieved his napkin from the tablecloth and spread it in his lap again.

"We're blessed with a wonderful cook," her father said.

Tallie beamed at him. "Bless you, Mr. Oliver."

Sadie intercepted Harry's look of mild surprise and smiled at him. He smiled back, and she felt her face go crimson as Tallie handed her a small porcelain plate with a slice of layer cake.

"So, Mr. Cooper, you'll be returning to Kentucky soon to start construction?" her father asked.

"Yes. I'll put up the barn first, sir."

"And why did you come all this way to buy your foundation stock?"

Harry smiled. "There aren't many farms well established in Kentucky yet, but it's growing. I was raised near Williamsburg and thought perhaps I'd go there for horses, but when I set out, people kept telling me to go to the Shenandoah Valley."

"Can't beat this country for raising horses, and that's a fact." Sadie's father lifted his fork and surveyed his peach pie.

"Yes, sir. It's a beautiful place, all right. And the closer I got, the harder I prayed."

Sadie waited eagerly to hear what he would say next.

"What was your prayer?" her father asked.

"I asked the Lord to show me where to find the best horses. And the closer I got, the more I heard the name McEwan."

Her father's smile was the brightest Sadie had seen it since her mother's death. She eyed Harry, hoping he was sincere, not just trying to gain favor with his host.

"The last three places I stopped, folks pointed up the valley and said I couldn't do better than here, sir."

"Well, now." Her father gestured to Zeke to bring him more tea.

Their talk went on, and Sadie was glad to be a spectator. Occasionally one of the men would ask her a question, and she would answer quietly, but most of the time she sipped her tea and covertly watched Harry Cooper. She noticed many things: his strong, tanned hands; his direct, respectful gaze into her father's face when listening to him; a small, faint scar over the corner of his right eye; and a decidedly rebellious lock of dark hair that fell onto his forehead. He was the most personable and handsome horse buyer her father had ever entertained.

When Zeke and Tallie left the room, Oliver McEwan turned to the guest. "Zeke has been with our family a long time. My grandfather freed his father and six other slaves he'd maintained. Most of them scattered, but Zeke's father stayed on with us. Zeke and I are about the same age, and we were almost like brothers."

"And Tallie?"

He shook his head. "I had to buy her from a neighbor. It was the only way Zeke could marry her. I gave Tallie her papers nigh twenty years ago. Their children are free."

"I admire you, sir."

Her father ducked his head. "It's not such a big thing, but in my opinion it's the right thing. Of course, not everyone in these parts agrees with me."

"I understand."

He smiled. "It's getting dark, Mr. Cooper. You must stay the night."

"Oh, no, I couldn't, sir. It's only five miles back to the village."

"I insist." Her father rose, his decision made. "I've already spoken to Tallie about my son's room. I think you'll be comfortable there."

Harry hesitated a moment and glanced toward Sadie.

Her father said, "We'll be able to continue our pleasant conversation, and perhaps my daughter will show you her mother's watercolors. My wife was quite an artist."

Sadie stared at him. "Really, Father—"

"I'd love to see them, Miss McEwan."

How could she refuse his inviting smile? She walked with Harry into the parlor, behind her father. With every step, she was conscious of his nearness. He waited for her to compress her crinoline and pass through the doorway. Sadie felt her color rise again. She wished this ungainly style would go out of fashion.

As her father settled into his favorite chair, she led Harry to the far wall where her favorite painting hung between two windows. "That's my brother, Tenley, when he was about eight. It's a good likeness."

Harry studied the watercolor of the boy walking a rail fence, his arms outstretched to balance him. "It's unusual. So informal. I like it."

Sadie smiled at him then, not holding back what she felt. "Mother usually painted landscapes, like that one over the mantel." She nodded toward it, and Harry turned to look. It was the same view the McEwans had from their veranda, the sloping meadows in the pastel greens of spring rolling to meet the dark mountains in the distance. "But I like this one of Tenley."

Harry nodded. "It captures his temperament, does it?"

"Yes. He's idealistic and imaginative, but. . ." She hesitated, alarmed to find tears springing into her eyes. "His faith is strong," she whispered.

Harry leaned toward her and said softly, "You miss him."

"Terribly."

He looked at the painting again. "I'll pray for him, if you don't think it presumptuous."

"Of course not. Thank you."

Sadie found that she couldn't look into his eyes any longer. They were too intent. She glanced at her father, but he had taken out his pocket watch and was winding it.

"You don't mind me staying in Tenley's room?"

"Of course not," she said.

"I won't disturb his things." Harry was watching her again, with those expressive brown eyes. A vision of a possible future came unbidden to Sadie's active mind. Beautiful horses; children with dark, wavy hair; and Harry Cooper.

"Do you care for a game of dominoes?" Her father's voice drew her back to reality.

She would have declined, but Harry said quickly, "That would be a pleasure, if Miss Sadie would join us."

She gulped. "All right." It meant she would have to sit beside him for another hour and try to keep from staring at him. But she knew it wouldn't be torture.

Her father rose and went to the doorway. "Zeke! Zeke!"

Harry leaned close to Sadie's ear. "That gown suits you admirably, Miss McEwan. I've been thinking it all evening and wishing I'd have a chance to say so."

Sadie's heart raced, and she couldn't help giving him a slight smile, but she felt it only proper to take a small step backward before her father turned toward them again.

Chapter 3

Sadie couldn't help stroking the lush fabric as she spread out the end of the bolt to show her friend, Elizabeth Thurber.

Elizabeth sighed. "It's lovely."

"That green velvet is beautiful, Sadie," said Elizabeth's mother, Mary Thurber. "It would make Elizabeth look sallow, but you can wear it, my dear."

"I'm glad you didn't choose lavender," Elizabeth agreed. "You can wear bright colors with your complexion, and you should."

Tallie set the porcelain teapot down on the cherry table beside Sadie's chair. "That velvet gonna make her look like Queen Victoria's little sister." She smiled at Sadie and nodded toward the teapot. "You pour for the ladies now, Miss Sadie."

"Thank you, Tallie." Sadie reached for one of the thin china cups her mother had prized. Tallie had outdone herself with the tea tray today. She had artistically arranged wafer-thin sugar cookies and tiny butter tarts on the painted Italian charger Sadie's parents had received as a wedding gift more than twenty years ago. Small clusters of grapes were mounded in a cut-glass bowl. In spite of the warmth of the July afternoon, the tea was piping hot, served with honey, sugar, and cream.

Tallie smiled at Sadie and glided backward through the door, heading for her kitchen domain.

Mrs. Thurber accepted her cup of tea graciously but frowned slightly as Sadie began to pour a cup for Elizabeth.

"You're entirely too free with your help, Sadie, dear."

Sadie stared at her in momentary confusion. "But. . .Tallie is my friend, Mrs. Thurber. And she's a free woman."

"Yes, child." The older woman sipped delicately from her cup then blotted her lips with a linen napkin. "Still, I'm certain your mother wouldn't be quite so familiar with the servants."

Sadie thought about that as she passed the cup to Elizabeth. Tallie was no different in her manner from how she had been when Mother was alive, was she? She had always been loving toward Sadie and outspoken in her opinions.

"Thank you," Elizabeth murmured with a smile, taking the cup and saucer.

Sadie then passed the platter of sweets, and Mrs. Thurber selected a cookie and a tart. "Your Tallie certainly can cook, I'll give her that."

"Yes, she's a treasure." Sadie offered the charger to Elizabeth.

"I suppose you can put up with a lot in return for her skills," Mrs. Thurber went on, "but you must never let them get insolent, my dear." She bit into the flaky tart and closed her eyes for a moment in pure bliss. "Delicious."

A quick retort was on the tip of Sadie's tongue, but she swallowed it, along with a gulp of tea. Her mother had trained her to be courteous, and her father had warned her before to keep peace with the ladies in the neighborhood. *You'll need your neighbors one day, Sadie. Don't make yourself odious to them now, no matter how insipid you find them. Their good opinion will stand you in good stead when hard times come.*

Sadie wasn't sure about that, but her love for her father made her keep silent, even though Mrs. Thurber's comments about Tallie seemed unjust. Tallie had been mother and mentor to her for the past four years, since her own dear mother's death.

"The pattern for the walking dress will look lovely in that ice blue muslin," Elizabeth offered, and Sadie smiled on her with gratitude for gently turning the conversation.

"Thank you so much for letting me borrow all your patterns."

"Anytime," Elizabeth assured her.

"That velvet is perfect for the evening dress," Mrs. Thurber said with a pert nod. "Although you may need to adjust the bodice a little. The neckline is a bit low for our country dinners. Of course, for Elizabeth's Richmond gowns we've gone with the fashions."

Elizabeth's cheeks colored slightly. "I'm having three new day dresses and two evening gowns made," she told Sadie with an air of confession. "Father is all the time complaining about the cost, but Mother says I shall need them."

"Oh, yes, those and more, most likely." Mrs. Thurber waved her hand before her. "We plan to spend several months in Richmond, you know."

"So Elizabeth told me."

"It's a pity you have no one in the city now," Elizabeth said.

Sadie nodded. "My aunt Thompson would have invited me, I'm sure, but her health is so poor now that she keeps to her home by the sea."

"That lovely green velvet will be wasted here." Elizabeth giggled. "There are no eligible men in the neighborhood. Unless you count the Kauffman boys, of course."

Sadie returned her grimace, and they both laughed.

"You should come with us," Mrs. Thurber said, and Sadie stared at her in shock.

"Oh, I couldn't. Father needs me. I help him a lot with the business now, you know."

"Nonsense. You oughtn't to be tearing about the countryside on horseback the way you do, Sadie. It's time you were settled." Mrs. Thurber stirred her tea pensively. "And you don't even have a proper riding habit. Yes, I think I shall speak to your father. You ought to have some time in town. It will give you polish."

Sadie felt a sudden panic. "Oh, but I couldn't go in September."

"Why ever not?"

"We expect guests." She felt her cheeks going crimson. After all, Harry Cooper wasn't exactly a guest, but she wouldn't leave the Shenandoah Valley for the world now, not with Harry coming back in a matter of weeks. "And Father has several buyers coming. He'll need me here to entertain for him."

"My, my, entertaining your father's business clients," Elizabeth said.

"Yes, well, they often take luncheon or dinner with us after talking business with Father."

"Then you must have a suitable wardrobe." Mrs. Thurber held out her cup, and Sadie refilled it. "Is Tallie as handy with a needle as she is at the stove?"

"She's quite good," Sadie said. "Mostly she helps me cut out my dresses and stitch the seams and hems. I do the embellishments. My mother taught me, you know."

"Yes, she was a marvelous seamstress. No one can match her beadwork."

"Do you ever wear any of your mother's dresses?" Elizabeth asked.

Sadie lowered her gaze. "Well, no, I don't expect they would fit me right."

Mrs. Thurber eyed her figure without pretense. "Yes, you've grown a lot this last year. You might even be taller than your mother was. You're a might thin yet, but I suppose you could take in the seams." She nodded. "Those lovely fabrics she wore. You ought to consider it."

"It would save your father piles of money," Elizabeth said.

Sadie swallowed hard. She had tried several times to sort through her mother's things, but every time she opened the wardrobe, she found herself crying. Tallie had assured her she could take her time in deciding what to do with her mother's clothes.

"I recall the dress she wore to my husband's birthday dinner the year before she passed on." Mrs. Thurber's eyes were focused on something beyond the parlor walls. "It was exquisite. White tulle with Chantilly lace. A frothy confection, but she carried it off." She looked at Sadie with a bittersweet smile. "Your mother was stunning. I always envied her complexion. And now you have it."

Elizabeth scowled. "I pop out in freckles if I get the least bit of sun."

Mrs. Thurber remained in the nostalgic mode. "Do you still have the old spinning wheel?"

Sadie nodded. "Yes, Father was going to get rid of it, but I asked him if I could have it as a keepsake. It's in my bedroom upstairs."

"I recall your grandmother spinning in this very room." Mrs. Thurber's gray eyes went all dreamy again. "Her hands were never idle, even while she visited with company. She used to make the finest wool yarns in the county. She gave me enough for a pair of hose one year as a birthday gift. Softer, neater hosiery I never saw."

An hour later, when her guests had gone, Sadie changed into her plain gray housedress. Before going down to the kitchen, she paused before the mirror in her bedroom and put her hand up to her cheek. Did she look like her mother? She hoped so. She was glad she had listened to Tallie and worn her bonnet faithfully this summer whenever she went out to ride. Would Harry find her attractive? She thought he had last May. Of course, any number of things might have transpired in Harry Cooper's life this summer. He might even have found himself a wife in Kentucky.

She hurried downstairs. Tallie was sliding the roasting pan into the oven, laden with half a plump ham.

"Your papa's home from town," Tallie said as Sadie reached for her apron.

"Oh, good! I hope he found the notions I asked him to get."

Tallie wiped her hands on her calico apron. "You gave Mr. Oliver a list, and if MacPheters's store had it, he bought it. You can count on that."

Sadie smiled and reached for the everyday ironstone plates. She took a stack of five from the shelf and began arranging them on the broad kitchen table.

"What are you doin'?" Tallie asked sharply.

"Father and I can eat in the kitchen with your family."

"It ain't proper." Tallie frowned and shook her head. "You and Mr. Oliver need to eat in the dinin' room, like gentlefolks."

"That's so silly. We're all friends. You and Zeke happen to work for my father, that's all."

"No, that's not all, and you know it. What if those fine Thurber ladies showed up while you was eatin' in the kitchen? The news would be all over this county by the weekend."

Sadie laughed and started to renew her protest, but Tallie placed her hands firmly on her hips and scowled at her. "You mind me now, Miss Sadie."

"But I often eat out here with you and Pax and—"

"I been too lax with you, that's for sure. What would your mama say? Besides, what if Mr. Cooper came in the middle of dinner? Hmm? You just put two of them plates back and put the good china on for you and your papa, in there." She pointed toward the dining room door with a stern look that left no room for argument. "Your papa wants you to turn out a lady, just like your mama was, and that's a fact."

Sadie sighed and picked up two of the plain white plates. She replaced them on the shelf and headed for the doorway. Her mother's best china was kept in a cabinet in the dining room.

"You do think he'll come back, don't you?" Immediately she wished she hadn't asked. She'd tried so hard not to show how eagerly she awaited Harry's return, but what use was it? Tallie knew her so well that it was probably no secret.

Tallie smiled as she opened the flour bin. "He'll be back for certain. That man prayed to God, just like Abraham's servant, and God brought him here for a reason."

Sadie couldn't hold in the shy smile that pulled at her lips. "Do you think I'm that reason, Tallie?"

"Well, you just don't know, do you? Not only that, but he gave your papa half the money for them horses he's buyin'. He won't forget his unfinished business."

"I suppose you're right." Sadie pushed the door open with her hip. She set the table carefully for two, waiting for the heat to leave her cheeks before she rejoined Tallie in the kitchen. When she returned, Pax was coming in through the back door.

"Mr. Oliver say he'll be up to talk with Miss Sadie, soon as he and Pa take care of the horses."

"All right." Sadie wondered what lay behind this odd bit of news. It sounded as though her father had something special to discuss with her. Perhaps he hadn't been able to fill her list of sewing notions, after all. "Do you know if he got the things I asked for?"

Pax shrugged. "First we took the colt to Mr. Glassbrenner. Then he and Mr. Oliver went to the bank together."

"Good! That means he paid Papa in cash, and we're solvent again." Sadie grinned, but Pax's smooth face still held a worried look. "What is it?"

"Well. . .we went over to the store, and Mr. Oliver gave Mr. MacPheters his list. Then Mr. MacPheters gave him the mail, and Mr. Oliver started reading it while they got his goods for him."

Sadie watched him closely, wondering where this rambling tale was headed.

"Spit it out," Tallie chided, and Pax glanced at her then down at the floor.

"Then Mr. Oliver told me to bring everythin' out to the wagon, and he went outside."

Sadie stepped over close to Pax. The boy had been like a little brother to her—a pesky, troublesome little brother at times, and they didn't stand on ceremony with one another.

"Pax, you just tell me what's going on right now, or I'll box your ears."

"Me, too," Tallie said ominously.

Pax looked from Sadie to his mother then stepped back toward the door. "Ain't nothin' goin' on that I know of, except Mr. Oliver didn't speak to me after that, except to ask if I was sure I got everythin'."

Pax sidled toward the door, not looking at her, and Sadie reached out and grabbed the collar of his shirt. "You're not going anywhere."

"That's all I know, Miss Sadie. Honest."

She looked deep into his dark eyes then released her hold on him. "Fine. I'll find out soon enough anyway. Just you be ready to ride tomorrow before breakfast, you hear me?"

Pax grinned. "I be ready right after I milk the cow, Miss Sadie, unless your papa tells me to do somethin' else for him."

She nodded curtly and turned away. She hadn't ridden for a week, and she missed the long rambles with Pax. The heat had been overpowering throughout July, and her father and Tallie had both advised her to stay out of the sun. But enough was enough, so she had made a date with Pax to ride early before the worst heat overtook them again.

Tallie selected a sturdy wooden spoon and returned to her worktable. "I keep telling your papa he needs to put you in a sidesaddle, but he won't listen to me. Lets you ride all over the valley like a farmhand."

"Only sissies ride sidesaddle. I have to ride spirited horses and keep them in condition. You know I have to keep Mr. Cooper's mares fit."

Tallie shook her head. "They're already fit."

"Ha! That's what you know. I haven't ridden them all week. Every one of them needs a good workout."

"Pa and me took Maude and Buttercup out yesterday," Pax said sheepishly, and Sadie stared at him.

"What? You and Zeke? You didn't tell me!"

"Mr. Oliver say they need exercise. He knows you want to ride them, but it was too hot yesterday."

Just then the dining room door opened, and her father looked in.

"Sadie, I need to see you for a moment." He turned and let the door swing to.

Sadie stared at Tallie as she fumbled with her apron strings.

"Probably nothin'." Tallie picked up her tin measuring cup and stooped over the flour bin.

"I should have gone with Papa myself." Sadie walked slowly through the dining room, across the entry, and into the parlor. A queer feeling of dread was settling in her stomach.

"Papa?"

He was sitting in his armchair, and he looked up from the paper in his hand. His solemn expression did nothing to dispel her anxiety. "Sit down, daughter."

Sadie took one of the side chairs. She wanted to ask him what was wrong, but she waited, clutching a handful of the gray fabric of her housedress. They sat in silence for a long moment, and her father stared down at the sheet of paper. She saw that it was a letter, and her fear multiplied.

"Papa?"

He looked at her then, and she could see tears standing in his eyes. "It's Tenley."

"No!" She left her chair and knelt beside him, grasping his arm and peering at the letter. "Tell me, Papa."

Her father swallowed hard and reached out to her. His hand shook, but he placed it on her head and stroked her hair.

"I'm afraid he's gone. It was in the battle—"

"No, that can't be!"

"Hush, child. Listen to me. He was wounded in the battle for Mexico City. He didn't survive his wounds."

"But that was. . ." Sadie stared up at him, unable to accept his words. *Not Tenley!* First her mother, now her precious brother. It was too much to bear. Her chest tightened, and she had to struggle to breathe. "They captured the city almost a year ago, Papa!"

"Yes, in September." He sighed and held the letter out to her. "This is dated January first. It seems he lingered for several weeks in the field hospital; then it took his commanding officer awhile to write the letter. And who knows where this letter's been in the past six months? But it's here now, and so now we know."

She refused to look at the creased letter or read the fateful words. "No, Papa. We would have known. *I* would have known."

He shook his head helplessly. "We've all prayed so hard."

"I've prayed every day," Sadie agreed, tears choking her and making her voice crack. She leaned her forehead against her father's knee and sobbed.

"We'll get through this," he whispered, patting her shoulder. "Sadie, child, it's a cruel thing, but we've still got each other."

Chapter 4

Harry tested the latch on the door of the tiny, one-room cabin. It was good enough to keep the door shut while he rode to Virginia and collected his brood mares from Oliver McEwan.

It was late August, and he'd planned to be on the road by now, but everything had taken longer than he'd anticipated. Thanks to several kind neighbors, his barn was now complete. That was the critical structure. All summer Harry had prepared timber, cut and stacked hay, and split firewood, then built a paddock. Last of all, he had thrown up the little cabin that would shelter him this winter. He'd planned a bigger building—a real house—but setbacks in building and haying had cut short the time he could spend on it, and he'd settled for this barely adequate cabin. No matter. He would add on to it next spring.

The important thing now was to bring the mares home. McEwan had agreed to have them bred to drop spring foals and ready to go when he arrived. In his mind's eye, Harry could see the mares trotting across his pasture with their colts at their sides. Of course, he had yet to fence the pasture, but he ought to be able to do that before cold weather set in.

He sighed and looked out over his property. There was still so much to do! He'd better not linger too long at McEwans', tempting as the thought was.

The image of Sadie in her rose-colored gown came unbidden to his thoughts as it had many times since his trip to Virginia. She was a budding rose, a girl maturing into womanhood, and he could hardly wait to see the full-blown flower.

Another picture of her flashed across his consciousness then—the wild Sadie dashing out of the woods on that exquisite mare then hauling back on the reins in a desperate effort to avoid disaster. Then the subdued Sadie, lying in the dust and looking up at him cautiously, gasping for breath while he tried not to stare.

Harry stooped to pick up his tools. He would leave at first light. He didn't want to put the trip off any longer or delay seeing her.

"Papa, are you all right?"

Her father had dismounted and stood beside the stallion, pressing his fist against his lower back. He gave out a sigh and smiled at her. "Just growing old."

"It's Clipper's rough trot that's getting to you."

"You may be right." He eyed the horse critically. "He looks so good, but his gaits are downright painful."

"Not to mention that little bucking trick he does if you touch his flanks."

He gave her a rueful smile. He'd been trying to break Clipper of that habit, with no success.

Zeke came from the barn and reached for the horse's reins. "Let me walk him, Mr. Oliver. Pax, you get Miss Sadie's horse."

"Nonsense. I can cool down my own mount." Sadie clucked to Lily and led her along behind Zeke across the barnyard. She knew her father was wondering if he'd made a mistake in keeping Clipper as a stallion, but he wouldn't discuss such matters with her. Clipper was young, only four years old, and had been earmarked to replace their aging stallion, Star. In Sadie's opinion, there would never be another horse like Star, but she knew he was getting on in years, and the farm's income depended on the McEwans finding another exceptional stallion soon.

She glanced back at her father. He seemed to move a little slower since the letter had come from Tenley's commander, and Sadie was startled to note that his hair was graying quickly. Throughout the month of August, he had thrown himself into the work of the farm, and Sadie began to worry. He was working too hard. His grief drove him, she knew. Tenley's death had devastated him, but instead of languishing in his sorrow, he spent long hours in the fields and at the barn, working with the horses, haying, and most recently harvesting wheat and oats.

She had begged him to hire more help, but he had insisted he could do the work with Zeke and his two sons, Pax and Ephraim, the older son who lived a few miles away. Ephraim eked out a living for his young family as a blacksmith, but every summer he devoted a few weeks to work on the McEwan farm.

Zeke turned ahead of her and walked toward the barn with Clipper straining at the lead rope. Her father had given the stallion a good run, but he was still dancing and tossing his head. He reached over to nip Zeke's sleeve, and Zeke slapped him on the nose.

"Quit that, hoss!" Zeke glanced at Sadie. "Your papa ought to sell this one for a racehorse. That all he's good for."

"Pa!" Pax shouted.

Sadie jerked her head to stare at him. Pax was standing just inside the barn door, and he appeared to be wrestling with her father.

No, she realized in horror, Pax was holding her father up, keeping him from falling to the ground.

"Pa, help!"

"Zeke!" Sadie shrieked. Lily snorted and shied, and ahead of them Clipper neighed and reared. Zeke kept his hold on the lead rope and yanked down on it firmly.

"Ho, you hoss! Easy now."

Sadie realized she had broken one of her father's ironclad barn rules. Instead of helping in an emergency, she had screamed and caused the volatile stallion to panic.

She ran in agonizing slowness toward Pax and her father, pulling Lily along with her. "Come on, Lily! Come!" She would not break another rule and drop the lead rope. Loose horses would only cause more mayhem.

As she ran, she saw her father slide from Pax's grasp and crumple to the straw-strewn floor.

Dear God, no!

A fractured prayer left her heart as she thrust Lily's reins into Pax's hands and knelt beside her father.

———

"Mr. Cooper's here, sugar." Tallie smiled in apology from the doorway to Sadie's bedroom.

Sadie wiped a tear away. "He's really here?"

"He just rode up to the barn. My Zeke is taking his horse. He'll show him the mares so Mr. Cooper can see how nice and fat they are; then he'll show him to the house."

Sadie nodded and pushed herself up out of the rocking chair. "What am I going to do, Tallie?"

"Why, the same as your papa would do."

"But everything's changed now that Papa's dead."

"I know, child." Tallie opened her arms wide, and Sadie flew into them with a sob.

"What if he doesn't want to buy the mares anymore?"

"Of course he does! If he didn't, he'd have sent your papa a letter."

Sadie nodded and sniffed, and Tallie turned to open a small inlaid box on top of Sadie's dresser. She took out a clean muslin handkerchief and handed it to her.

"Here now, mop your face. You need to look your best when you greet him."

Sadie pulled in a shaky breath. "What if he wants his money back? Because—"

"Whoa now! You just borrowin' trouble. That man came for his horses, and you're gonna give them to him. He gives you the money, and that's that."

Sadie nodded and exhaled slowly. *That's that,* she thought. It wasn't at all how she had pictured her second meeting with Harry Cooper. She had imagined her father would invite him to spend the night again so they could enjoy another long evening of conversation. She'd thought she would at least have a chance to sit at dinner with him again. She'd planned it for months, down to the menu Tallie would prepare and the imported lace on her gown.

"You freshen up," Tallie said. "Put on your new blue dress. I'll go down and start the fried chicken for supper."

"No, Tallie, not the fried chicken."

Tallie stared at her. "Why not? Just like you said, Miss Sadie. Fried chicken, biscuits, butter beans, and carrots, then the pies. He liked my pie, remember?"

"I remember, but, Tallie, I can't invite him to stay to dinner tonight."

Tallie pressed her lips together. "Well, maybe not." Her shoulders drooped as she left the room.

Sadie stared into the mirror over her vanity. How could she face Harry with these red eyes and this haggard face? And yet she didn't have the energy to try to do anything about it.

At last Harry got Zeke to stop extolling the virtues of the McEwan horses and take him to the house. He was a bit surprised and disappointed that Oliver hadn't come out to the barn on his arrival, but Zeke had explained that his boss had been "poorly."

"Will I be able to see Mr. McEwan?" Harry asked as they entered the house and Zeke steered him toward the parlor.

"Oh, I don't think Mr. Oliver can see you today." Zeke shook his head with doleful regret.

Sadie jumped up from a chair and stood facing Harry as he entered the room.

"Miss Sadie. How wonderful to see you again." He stepped forward eagerly and tried to hide his dismay. She wore a fetching ice blue crinoline dress, but her face was pale and drawn, and her hair was poorly dressed, put up in a loose knot from which tendrils were escaping. She must have been at her father's bedside.

"Mr. Cooper," she murmured, and Harry bent over her hand.

"I'm sorry to hear that your father is ill."

Sadie stared past him at Zeke with a look of shock. Had she expected the servant to hide the fact that his master was gravely ill?

"I—"

Her face flooded with color, and Harry smiled as a trace of the old, excitable Sadie appeared. Zeke had embarrassed her, no question, and Harry determined to do whatever he could to put her at ease.

"Do you have a few minutes?" he asked.

She hesitated then nodded. "Won't you sit down?" When she led him to a seat near the fireplace, he looked up at the painting on the front wall and smiled.

"I've thought many times of that picture this summer. I confess there were many evenings when I longed to be back here again."

Sadie swallowed. She seemed to be struggling with every word today.

"I—I hope you found the mares in good condition."

"Excellent, thank you. Miss McEwan, if your father is too ill for guests today, perhaps I can stay in town tonight and come back in the morning."

"Mr. Cooper," she said, eyeing him carefully, "I must tell you that our family has suffered a great tragedy."

He nodded, his heart filled with sympathy. "I'm so sorry about your brother. Zeke told me you received the news a few weeks ago, and it distressed me. I know how much you loved him."

Sadie bit her lip, and he thought she was holding back tears. He stood hastily. He longed to stay there and try to be a small comfort to her, but a gentleman would not presume to do that. A gentleman would express his condolences and leave.

"Miss McEwan, forgive me for intruding at this time. I'll come back tomorrow, and perhaps your father will be able to see me then."

"Oh no, really, Mr. Cooper, he won't be able to. You see—"

Zeke stepped forward. "Mr. Oliver is restin'."

Sadie stared at him. "Zeke!"

He shrank back toward the doorway, his hands folded and his eyes downcast.

Sadie cleared her throat and looked up at him, and Harry's heart pounded. She was the Sadie he remembered, even though she was grieving for her brother and worried sick about her father's health.

"You see, Mr. Cooper, Papa's heart hasn't been strong lately, and. . .and. . ."

She sobbed, and Harry couldn't help stepping closer and touching her shoulder ever so lightly.

"Don't distress yourself. I'll come back tomorrow."

She sobbed once more. "Perhaps it's best."

He nodded and backed away, not wanting to leave her, yet determined to abide by the social code. He would do nothing to upset or offend her family. At all costs, he wanted to stay in the good graces of the McEwans. Seeing Sadie again, even in her sorrow, had taught him that. If he had his way, this would not be his last visit to the Spinning Wheel Farm.

Zeke walked slightly behind him on the way to the barn. Harry wondered if Sadie would chastise the servant later for being too forthcoming. Dark clouds were forming over the ridge of mountains in the west, and Pax was leading two horses in from the pasture. When they reached the barn he brought out Harry's horse, Pepper, and Zeke silently brought the saddle.

"I take it Mr. McEwan's condition is very grave," Harry said. He took the bridle from Zeke's hand. "Here, I can do that."

"Well, suh," Zeke said, "it ain't good. A few days back, Mr. Oliver just collapsed. Right over there." He pointed toward the barn door.

"Has he seen a doctor?"

"Ain't no doctor close, suh."

Harry frowned, wishing there was a way to help. He liked Oliver McEwan and had felt they might be friends if they lived closer. And his daughter. . .that was another story.

"Is there anything I can do, Zeke?"

"I don't think so. But if you's coming back tomorrow, I'll keep your mares in so they'll be ready for you in the mornin'."

"Thank you, Zeke. It looks like we're in for a storm tonight. I expect there's an inn in Winchester?"

"Yes, suh."

Harry nodded. "All right. I'll come back midmorning. If Mr. McEwan can't see me then. . ."

Zeke said quickly, "Miss Sadie, she can do business just like her papa. That gal can ride like the best, and she's not afraid of work. She's had it hard these last few weeks, with the bad news and all, but she's strong, Miss Sadie. She'll get through this trouble."

Harry smiled at his enthusiasm. "Yes, she's got character. I expect she'll weather the storm."

Chapter 5

W
hat are we going to do?" Sadie asked, watching from the parlor window as Harry rode down the lane. Was she also bereft of Harry now? Her sadness weighed on her, a heavy burden pressing on her heart.

"I dunno, Miss Sadie." Tallie stood next to her, holding the lace curtain back.

"I just wish I knew what Papa would do."

"Why, he'd sell that gen'leman some hosses, of course," Zeke said from the doorway.

They both turned toward him.

"You think so?" Sadie faltered. Never in her life had she been called upon to make important decisions. Could she go forward, as her father would have, do business, and bring in money to keep the farm going?

"I know so. This gen'leman said he prayed and asked God to show him where to buy. Seems like you're the answer to his prayer, and he might be the answer to yours, too."

"What do you mean, Zeke?" Sadie felt a blush coming on. Was Zeke implying that she should pursue Harry? Was a husband the solution to her problems?

"I just mean you need cash right now, Miss Sadie. You know your papa already spent most of what he got for that colt last month. You'll need some money to get you through the winter."

She gulped. "Do you think I can stay here alone?"

"Child, you won't be alone." Tallie slipped her arm around Sadie's shoulders. "You've said before we's your family. Well, now is the time you need us. It'd be different if you had kin close by, but you don't."

Sadie nodded. "Oh, Tallie, what would I do without you and Zeke?"

"Likely you'd be just fine, Miss Sadie. But you's better with us here."

"That's so."

Zeke smiled down at her. "Don't forget your heavenly Father, Miss Sadie."

"Of course not."

"That's right," said Tallie. "You talk to Him every day, and He'll tell you what to do."

Sadie sighed. "Right now everything seems so jumbled that I don't know where to begin. And you shouldn't have lied to Mr. Cooper. You know that, Zeke."

"It wasn't a lie," Zeke said, his eyes wide in surprise.

"Listen to you!" Tallie scowled at him with evident disapproval.

"I said Mr. Oliver is restin'. Well, he is. Permanently."

Sadie felt she was helpless to change Zeke's way of looking at things. She looked to Tallie for support.

"You just should have told him straight out," Tallie said, shaking her head.

"I think it's better this way. We don't know Mr. Cooper very well."

Tallie arched her back and glared at him. "That man is a gen'leman, and you know it!"

"Well, I do like Mr. Harry." Zeke scratched his chin. "I don't expect Miss Sadie needs protectin' from him."

"I should say not!" Tallie was not mollified, Sadie could tell. The woman had appointed herself Harry's champion, and besides that, she was obviously disappointed he hadn't stayed to dinner.

"When he comes back tomorrow, I'll tell him the truth," Sadie said. "If he doesn't want to do business with me, I can't help it, but I won't continue this lie, Zeke."

Zeke had the grace to look down at the floor. "I'm sorry, Miss Sadie. I didn't mean to deceive. I did tell Mr. Harry you'll be speakin' to your Father tonight about his business deal, though."

"You *what*? Zeke, how could you do that?"

"Easy now, missy." Zeke held out his hands beseechingly. "I just thought you'd be talkin' to your heavenly Father. You know you're on good speakin' terms with Him."

"Well, of course. But—"

"So I put Mr. Harry at ease. He was askin' for particulars on Mr. Oliver, and I cogitated he'd feel better about the whole thing if I told him that." He looked up at Sadie and said quickly, "And it weren't no lie. You will be asking the Almighty what to do, won't you, Miss Sadie?"

"Well, of course." She looked uncomfortably at Tallie.

"The truth, Zeke," Tallie said. "The truth is always the best. You know that."

Zeke shrugged, and his wife sighed in exasperation.

"Fine," Zeke said. "I just thought that poor Miss Sadie didn't need to be tellin' menfolk who aren't much more than strangers that she's got nobody here to protect her now. And we don't know what will happen to Mr. Oliver's property, with Mr. Tenley gone and all. It just seemed to me that until she finds out what will become of the estate—"

Tallie's dark eyes threw defiant sparks at him. "We can take care of Miss Sadie! Whatever happens to her, she has us and the good Lawd!"

After a mediocre dinner at the inn, Harry settled into a tiny attic room under the eaves. He'd chosen this accommodation over sharing a larger, more comfortable room on the second floor with a team of surveyors.

A deafening bolt of thunder cracked as Harry reached his room. He blew out the candle the landlady had given him and stared out the window. He was glad he'd found the livery stable and seen to Pepper's care early. His horse shouldn't be too uneasy, although the high winds worried Harry a bit. A few scattered papers blew about the street below, and as he watched, a limb was torn from a large elm tree across the way. It was early for the trees to shed their foliage, but the wind whipped the leaves so hard that many loosed their hold and flew with the maelstrom.

A scattered pattering of rain on the roof above him became a roar as the clouds dumped their load and millions of drops pounded down on the shingles. His room had no ceiling, just the underside of the boards of the roof, and Harry eyed them speculatively, wondering if the shingles on top would hold their places. The rain pummeled the street, turning the powdery dust to muddy soup in minutes, and a change in the wind sent a torrent of water against his window, sheeting down the glass before him.

Harry sighed and stretched out on the rickety cot. He wondered how the folks at McEwans' were doing. He ought to have stayed there. With Oliver so ill, Zeke and Pax would need help with the chores and making certain everything at the farm was battened down before the storm.

Sadie would be right out there with them, helping secure the livestock, he was sure, and Tallie would be in the kitchen. No matter what the weather, Tallie would conjure up a huge, tasty meal, one much better than the poor fare he'd found at the inn. Miserable excuses for biscuits they had here, and the stew was composed of overcooked vegetables and some unidentifiable meat. It was worse than what had come out of the galley of the *Swallow*. The more he thought about it, the more certain he was that Pax, the half-grown servant boy at McEwans', had eaten much better than he had this night. Yes, and he probably had a cozier berth, too.

Harry was too restless to sleep, and the intermittent thunder and surges of rain would have kept him awake anyway. He got up and stood at the window again. Great. Pepper would probably have to slog through five miles of mud in the morning. But he knew it was more than Tallie's cooking and more even than the four superior mares he was buying that drew him to the Spinning Wheel Farm.

Sadie, his heart cried out. *Lord, I don't know what it is about that gal, but I truly believe You engineered our first meeting. Something inside me is mourning with her. I want to see her carefree and eager for life again.*

His anticipation had grown all summer and had peaked as he approached the farm that afternoon. But his eagerness had dissipated when he saw her again, and his brief meeting with Sadie had been a disappointment. Something was wrong there, very wrong.

Of course her father was sick, perhaps fatally so, and it was only a few weeks since she'd learned of her brother's death. Still, he couldn't forget the wariness and melancholy in Sadie's eyes today. She was not the cheerful, outgoing girl he'd remembered and dreamed of all summer. In fact she'd seemed almost frightened of him today. She hadn't been that way in May. Had he imagined the spark in her eyes back then and the secret smiles they had shared over a simple game of dominoes? No, it was real. She had regretted the parting as much as he had.

He lay down again, determined to catch some sleep. As soon as it was daylight he would go for Pepper and head back to the farm. If she still held him off, he would pay for the mares and leave. But he hoped. . . .

Harry sighed. What did he hope exactly? That Oliver would be well enough to see him, of course, and that their business would be concluded satisfactorily. But that was secondary, he knew, to his longing to see Sadie's eyes light up. He had hoped to deepen his acquaintance with her—there was no denying it. If he were honest, he would admit he had hoped he would find her receptive to his interest. A courtship even? It would have to be either a short one or a protracted one conducted long-distance.

But he knew he had at least hoped for encouragement, and he hadn't gotten that today. He closed his eyes. There was only one place to turn when things weren't going the way he planned. After all, God was in charge of these events, from the long-decided battle in Mexico to the storm that tore at the inn and made the timbers shudder.

Sadie sat up in bed, shivering. She fumbled in the darkness to light her bedside candle. The thunder didn't frighten her exactly, but she didn't like being alone in the big house during the violent storm. She felt isolated and vulnerable.

Tallie and Zeke were battened down in their little house beyond the big barn. The house had been two slave cabins in the old days. Zeke and her father had torn them apart and made one snug little dwelling from the lumber years ago, before Sadie was born. Zeke and Tallie had raised their five children there, and Sadie had played with them all. The girls had kept watch of her while her mother was busy. Pax, the youngest, was the only one left in their home now, and Sadie knew he was warm and dry in his loft above his parents' small bedroom.

A sharp crack made her jump, and she heard lightning strike nearby. She threw back the covers and hurried to the window, gazing out over the yard. She couldn't see anything amiss, but she wished Tallie had stayed in the big house with her tonight.

As she stared out into the darkness, she made out rivulets of water coursing across the barnyard and down the lane. The trees near the pasture fence tossed fitfully. The booming of closer lightning strikes now and then drowned out the rumbling background of thunder.

She reached for the woolen coverlet her grandmother had woven and pulled it around her. It was chilly, but she knew that if she stayed in bed she would only toss and turn.

She thought back to the event that had consumed her mind today. Harry Cooper was in town. He would be back in the morning. Tears filled her eyes as she realized how the long-awaited day had turned to ashes. She would have only one brief chance to set things straight with him. She wanted to, but she wasn't sure how he would receive her news.

And when he had gone, what would become of her then? She had to think beyond Harry's visit, to tomorrow and the next day and the rest of her life. Would she be forced to leave here soon? Did she even have a right to be here now? Would she have to seek a new place to live and a way to support herself that did not include the farm?

Dear Lord, she prayed silently, *there's so much I need Your help with. Please give me wisdom and show me what to do.*

She felt calmer and a bit more optimistic. She sat watching the flickering lightning and began to pray for those she loved, although that circle had grown quite small.

Thank You, Lord, for Tallie and Zeke. Thank You for—

Crack! Her eyes flew open, and she jumped from her chair. The sharp lightning strike was followed by a ripping, tearing crash that rocked the house.

Chapter 6

Harry reined in Pepper and stared at the McEwans' house. A huge limb had apparently been torn from the towering oak tree on the south side of the house and was now wedged in the upper story. The roof had been torn open, exposing the interior of one of the bedchambers. Unless he was mistaken, it was Tenley's room where he had spent a comfortable night last spring.

Harry spurred his gelding into a gallop and tore up the lane, searching all the while for movement amidst the rubble. There was Zeke, climbing over the debris. Relief swept over Harry, and he halted Pepper once more.

"Zeke! Hey, Zeke!"

The black man straightened and peered down at him from between the branches of the oak. His face opened in a wide grin, and he waved with enthusiasm.

"Mr. Cooper! Hello, suh!"

"Anyone hurt?" Harry called.

"No, suh. The good Lawd was choosy about where He dropped this limb."

Harry smiled and dismounted. "I'll put Pepper in the barn and come help you."

"No need, suh. I'll send my boy to tend him." Harry saw then that Pax was also in the shambles with his father, pulling at the wreckage.

"No, I'll do it myself; then I'm coming up there to help you."

Zeke grinned down at him. "As you say, Mr. Harry. Just make yourself to home, suh. We'll tell Miss Sadie you're here, and she can see you in the dinin' room when you come in. The parlor window's broke, but that's all right. Won't take much to fix that."

Harry relaxed then, knowing Zeke had accepted his presence. He led Pepper toward the large barn, stepping around the biggest puddles.

"All right, fella," he said, opening the half door to the first empty stall he came to. "I know you're muddy and tired, but you'll be all right in here for a while." He noted with satisfaction that the manger was filled with hay. "I'll bring you some water in a while and clean you up."

Pepper whinnied and poked his head out over the Dutch door, snorting when another horse stuck his head out of a stall farther down the aisle.

Sadie met him at the door to the house.

"Mr. Cooper, it's good of you to offer to help us, but Zeke can—"

Harry brushed her protest aside and stepped into the entry. "Nonsense, Miss McEwan. Your roof is severely damaged. It will take days to clear out the mess and make it weather-tight again."

Sadie hesitated, and he smiled down at her.

"Please let me help. I'm here, and I'm strong. There's no way I'm leaving without lending a hand. Let me do what I can today."

She bit her bottom lip and nodded. "All right. Thank you. I admit, it's too big a job for us."

He saw she was wearing a patched apron over a worn gray dress. The hemline and sleeves were a bit shorter than was customary, and he guessed she had put on an old, outgrown dress so she could join in the work. A suggestion of plaster dust tinged her rich hair where it peeped out from beneath a cotton scarf. Harry looked into her blue eyes and felt the same spark of joy he'd known in May when he'd first seen her. She was the same Sadie, after all, even with all the trials she had encountered.

Her long lashes swept down over her eyes, and she stepped aside with a sudden air of shyness. "Let me show you upstairs. Zeke can tell you best what needs to be done. There's a lot of water damage. Tallie and I have been getting out the bedclothes and rugs to try to salvage them."

He followed her up the stairway, questions flooding his mind. "Was your father's bedroom damaged?"

"No." She stepped up into the second floor hallway and turned partway toward him. "Mr. Cooper, Father is—" She looked at him then away.

"He's not injured then?"

"No, but—"

She turned away, bringing one hand quickly to her lips, and Harry wished he hadn't spoken. Apparently Oliver was no better today.

"I'm sorry, Sadie," he said softly.

She gave him a watery smile and seemed about to speak again when Zeke clumped out of the wrecked room in his rough boots.

"Mr. Harry, I have to say I'm glad to see you, suh!"

He smiled and extended his hand. "I'll be glad to help any way I can."

Zeke hesitated, looking at him with a question, and then clasped his hand. "I thank you, suh."

"Since Mr. Cooper insists, I suppose we'd be foolish to turn down his offer of help." Sadie pushed aside an oak branch and wriggled into the room. "Zeke, I think we can dismantle the bedstead and take the pieces out of here."

"We'll do that, Miss Sadie, soon's we cut a few more limbs away. Whyn't you and Tallie see if you can find a sheet of canvas to hang over that parlor window. I misdoubt we'll be able to go for glass today. Too much to clear away up here." He nodded sagely at Harry. "Good thing you spent the night in town, suh."

"Truly spoken." Harry looked at the bed in grateful awe. The heavy oak branch must be a third part of the ancient tree. It had smashed through the roof and front wall of the room diagonally, crushing the armoire that had stood near the window and cracking at least one of the bed rails. The heaviest part lay across Tenley's bed, and a gnarled limb gouged deep into the mattress where Harry's chest would have been if he had slept there.

Zeke placed a saw in his hand, and he set about cutting the smaller branches off the huge fallen limb. He put Sadie out of his thoughts and concentrated on the job. Zeke sent Pax down to the lawn in front of the porch to gather up the wood they threw down and stack it around behind the house near the kitchen door.

The tear in the roof extended over the bedroom and a storage room, but the ridgepole seemed solid, and Harry agreed with Zeke that only the east half of the roof's front side would need replacing. The outer walls of the bedroom would need new framing timbers, and the plaster would have to be redone, as well. The sashes and glass in two upstairs windows were destroyed, in addition to the parlor window below, and the whitewash would need to be freshened when the repairs were completed.

"I can work on the inside this winter if need be," Zeke said after an hour's work. "If we can get the roof fixed before another storm, we'll be in good shape."

Harry stooped to examine the frame of the bed. "I think we can get this out of here now. You'll have to mend this side rail, but the damage isn't too bad, considering."

Zeke went to the doorway and called, "Miss Sadie! Miss Sadie, where you say you want this here bedstead?"

Harry wrestled the plump featherbed off onto the floor. By the time he had the footboard separated from the side rails, she was in the room.

She directed Zeke on where to take the featherbed then turned to Harry. "Just follow me, Mr. Cooper."

Harry picked up the heavy footboard and carried it carefully through the doorway and to the opposite end of the hallway. She opened a pristine white door and stepped into another bedchamber.

He knew at once that it was her room. Even without her sidelong glance and the becoming pink of her cheeks, he'd have known. The embroidered bed hangings were embellished with decidedly feminine lilac blossoms, and a green gown was hanging on the door of the armoire. He made himself quit looking around as his curiosity seemed to raise her anxiety.

"Just lean it against the wall there." She nodded toward the longest stretch of bare wall.

Harry set the footboard down and straightened. He couldn't help noticing an old spinning wheel in one corner. "That's a very old piece, isn't it?" he asked, more to relieve her uneasiness than anything else. "Do you spin?"

"No. It belonged to my great-grandmother Walsh. My grandmother used to spin wool on it, and my mother did some when she was a girl. I never learned, but I asked Papa if I could keep it."

He nodded and stepped over to give the wheel a spin. "It's in good condition. My mother used to spin, too."

They smiled at each other, a small, tentative smile on Sadie's part, but it sent his pulse racing. Given enough time, he was sure he could regain the ground he'd lost with her since May. But time was the one thing he wouldn't have with Sadie.

She ran her hand over the scarf that covered her hair. "I'd best go help Tallie."

"I'll bring the rest of the bed in here."

He met Zeke in the hallway, awkwardly carrying the headboard. Harry grabbed one end and walked backward along to Sadie's room. When they had set it down with the footboard, they made their way back to the scene of destruction.

"I can get the rails and slats," Zeke said.

Harry nodded, surveying the room. They had sawn up the lesser limbs and thrown the wood down into the yard below. Just the main part of the big oak limb was left, and it would take a lot of energy to cut it in pieces small enough to toss out.

The cherry armoire had been smashed by the falling tree, and a small side table and lamp were broken. The washstand seemed to be unscathed except for some scratches on the wood. The porcelain bowl and pitcher stood miraculously unharmed in the corner of the room farthest from the breach.

"This was a beautiful room," Harry said, shaking his head.

"Yes, suh." Zeke wiped the sweat from his forehead with his sleeve then glanced up through the gaping roof toward the sun. "I'd best get down to the barn. Those animals had ought to be put out to pasture now that the weather's cleared."

"Would you like me to help you, or should I stay here and keep on with this?" Harry asked.

Zeke looked around. "It's gonna be a big job, ain't it, Mr. Harry? I don't think we can fix this roof today."

"No, we can't. But I can measure what we'll need for timbers while you're at the barn. Do you have a measuring line, Zeke?"

"Mr. Oliver has one. I'll ask Tallie to see if she can find it. We'll have to get some lumber and shingles." Zeke headed for the stairs.

"I'd better go and see to my own horse," Harry said.

"My boy and I can tend him, if you want."

Harry hesitated. "If you don't mind."

"Not a bit, Mr. Harry."

"All right, thank you. Could you see that he gets a drink of water then?"

"Yes, suh, I'll do that. If you want, I'll have Pax put him out to grass after."

When Zeke returned, Harry had made a careful inspection of the damage and prepared a list of the lumber he estimated they would need to complete the restoration. Zeke sent Pax to the sawmill two miles downriver with a wagon and Harry's list. The two men tackled the heavy log that was the last of the tree limb. When it had been sawn into manageable pieces and ousted, they began clearing away the ragged, broken boards and plaster in preparation for the repairs. By noon Harry was certain he and Zeke had become lifelong friends. They worked well together, with few words needed between them.

Sadie appeared in the doorway. "I've got a basin of water at the back door so you gentlemen can wash up for dinner."

"I don't know," Harry said with a grin. "It might take the whole Shenandoah River to get us clean."

Zeke laughed and brushed at the plaster on his sleeve, but it was damp and mushy from his exposure to the rain-soaked room.

"Yep, we are two filthy field hands. I expect we'd both best eat in the kitchen, Miss Sadie."

"We're all eating in the kitchen, although Tallie's a mite scandalized." Sadie shot a sideways glance at Harry. "No offense, sir, but the time it would take us all to clean up and change—"

"I agree," Harry said. "Especially when we'll be coming back to this job as soon as we're finished eating."

He bowed solemnly and gestured toward the hallway. "After you, sir."

Zeke grinned. "No, suh, you first."

Sadie was not in evidence when they passed through the kitchen. Tallie looked at Zeke, her eyebrows arched high. "You done gone and turned Mr. Harry into a no-account."

Zeke laughed. "He's a hardworking no-account."

When they reached the lean-to at the back door, Harry peeled off his shirt and shook it outside, but it was a sorry mess. If he was still there for the evening meal, he'd have to retrieve his extra clothing from his pack in the barn. He splashed water from the tin basin over his face and hands.

"I hope Mr. McEwan wasn't disturbed by all the racket we've been making this morning." He reached for one of the towels Sadie had left on the bench beside the basin.

Zeke tossed the water onto the row of zinnias outside the lean-to and refilled the basin for himself from a bucket. "Oh, no, suh, I can assure you, Mr.

Oliver wasn't disturbed by us."

"Glad to hear it. I asked Miss Sadie about her father, but she seems quite distressed about his condition. I don't like to press her."

"Well, I can tell you, Mr. Oliver is no different today than he was the last few days, and the storm and all didn't bother him a bit."

Harry nodded, thinking about that. It seemed to him that a man would have to be comatose not to have been disturbed by the jolt the house had taken in the night.

His muscles ached from the morning's labor, but sinking into the sturdy oak chair across from Sadie for lunch was worth every minute of work. She had washed her face, brushed her hair to a luster, and removed the faded apron. It was hard to decide which reward was better—Tallie's cooking or Sadie's shy smile.

———

They were all exhausted by suppertime. Sadie had scrubbed and swept and mopped most of the day. When Pax returned with the lumber and nails in the middle of the afternoon, the men unloaded it all. The boy ate a late luncheon then set about splitting and stacking the rest of the wood from the oak tree. Harry and Zeke made a temporary covering over the yawning hole in the roof in case more rain came in the night. Tallie did her usual kitchen chores and helped Sadie wash the curtains, blankets, and sheets from Tenley's bedroom.

"We ought to ask Mr. Cooper to stay." As they folded the dry linens in the bright sunshine, Sadie looked to Tallie for guidance, uncertain as to what course she should take.

"Yes, you should. That man's worked like an ox all day, for nothin'."

"Can we feed him again tonight?" Sadie felt the least bit timid to ask the favor, and Tallie looked over at her as if she were crazy.

"Why, child, I've got fresh johnnycake in the oven, and I kept over the chicken and sweets I was planning to serve Mr. Harry last night. You know I forbade Zeke and Pax to touch those pies. Why you think I didn't serve them this noon?"

"I was wondering," Sadie admitted. *Those are for Mr. Cooper,* Tallie had told them last night, even though at the time Sadie was sure Harry would return briefly for his horses and be gone before another meal was served at the McEwan house. Yet Tallie had served gingerbread after luncheon this noon.

"They're for his dinner."

Sadie frowned as she pulled a linen towel from the clothesline. "Well, I can't have him stay here in the house tonight. I mean, not if I'm alone here. And he thinks—oh, Tallie, what am I going to do? Zeke has muddled everything!"

"Should have told him straight out," Tallie agreed with a shake of her head.

"I know it, but it's too late now! How would it look? Mr. Cooper would be shocked, and who knows what he'd do? He might tell someone who could do us harm, Tallie!"

"Mr. Harry wouldn't do that."

"No, I suppose not." Sadie stood in indecision. "But Tenley's room is ruined, and Papa's room is full of the extra furniture. Where would we put him, even if you slept up here for appearances?" Suddenly the tears that had hounded her for days gushed from her eyes, and Sadie sat down with a plunk on the grass and buried her face in her apron. "Tallie, I had to have Harry put the bedstead in my own room, because if he went into Papa's room. . ." She sobbed, unable to continue.

"There, child." Tallie came close and hugged her. "You've had a lot to deal with lately. There now."

"Tallie, tell me what to do!" Sadie sobbed and put her arms around Tallie. "Please tell me. I'm so tired and confused."

"Well, we's all tired, that's for sure. We can't send Mr. Harry back to town."

"No, no, we can't. Oh, Tallie, you don't think he'll ask for his money back?"

"Of course not."

"I do hope you're right, because what with having to buy lumber and all, we're going to need cash really soon."

"Your papa had nothin' at all in the bank?"

"I don't think so, and even if there's a little bit, it's not rightfully mine."

The door to the lean-to opened, and Zeke strolled out with a bucket in each hand.

"You frying that chicken tonight, sugarplum?" he asked Tallie as he headed for the well.

"Iffen I don't, it'll spoil," she replied. "I kept it in the spring house all day, but it's going in the pan shortly."

"Sounds good to me. Mr. Harry and me'll be ready to tuck into it whenever you say."

Tallie frowned at him. "Mr. Harry is eatin' in the dinin' room tonight with Miss Sadie."

"Yes, ma'am, I hear you." Zeke ambled on toward the well, but Tallie's next statement brought him to a halt.

"You quit feedin' Mr. Harry full of lies. You tryin' to wreck Miss Sadie's prospects with that gen'leman?"

Zeke turned to face her. "I ain't told no lies."

"Oh, listen to you! Surely, surely, my ears ain't workin' right!" Tallie looked pointedly at Sadie. "You hear him say he don't lie?"

"Well, Tallie, I'm not sure Zeke intended to be deceptive, but Mr. Cooper made certain assumptions, and—"

"That's right," Zeke said. "He assumpted. Now what was I supposed to tell him, with Miss Sadie here worried sick over what's to become of her? Mr. Harry, he's a good sort, but we didn't know that for sure yesterday. Now we know it."

Tallie nodded. "A man works that hard all day for you—he's a true friend."

"That's right. He's upstairs right now workin' on that mess. And tomorrow me and Mr. Harry is going to get that roof closed in."

"Tomorrow?" Sadie blinked at Zeke. "He's coming back tomorrow?"

"Comin' back?" Zeke set his buckets down and slapped his thigh. "Miss Sadie, you not going to make that fine young man ride all the way to Winchester tonight when he's bone tired!"

"Well. . ." Sadie looked once more at Tallie and saw that Tallie was coming to a decision.

"We was just talkin' about that," Tallie said. "We got no place for Mr. Harry here in the big house."

"Well, then, he'll just have to bunk with me and Pax in our cabin, and you can join Miss Sadie for tonight," Zeke said.

"Would you?" Sadie asked, searching Tallie's face for an indication of her feelings.

Tallie's teeth gleamed as she smiled. "Why, surely! That's the answer. That is, if Mr. Harry don't care about sleepin' with the poor folks."

"Mr. Harry don't stand on ceremony," Zeke said.

"But still. . ." Sadie looked doubtfully from one to the other. She was certain it wasn't socially correct to ask a guest to sleep in the hired help's home especially when they were a black family. Mrs. Thurber would be shocked. "I—I'm just not sure. . . ." She stood up. "Oh, Tallie, I'm so tired. I don't know what's right and what's not! I suppose Zeke can ask Mr. Cooper if he's willing, and if he's insulted he can take his mares and leave."

"No worry about that," Zeke said, smiling and reaching into the pocket of his trousers. "Mr. Harry done told me he's stayin' 'til the roof is tight, and he asked me to give you this."

"What is it?"

"It's the rest of the money for the horses. He said he'd like to give it to your pa direct, but since we had these unexpected expenses and all, he thought maybe he'd best give it to you, and you can give it to your papa."

Sadie gulped and reached for the money. "I feel like I'm taking this under false pretenses."

"Nonsense, child," said Tallie. She glared at Zeke. "Mr. Harry is a fine man. He would have understood. Why did you have to muddle things up so? You ought to be sleepin' in the barn for three nights—you're so bad! If I wasn't sleepin' with Miss Sadie tonight, I surely wouldn't sleep with you! I'd make you—"

Sadie burst into tears, and Tallie caught her breath and drew her close in her embrace. "See what you done, Zeke? Now git your water, and git on out of here. Miss Sadie's gone all weepy 'cause of you, and I've got chicken to fry!"

Chapter 7

Four days later Harry and Zeke worked side by side, nailing shingles into place on the roof. Pax went up and down the ladder, bringing them supplies. Harry's knees ached from kneeling on the staging, but he didn't dare stop hammering.

"I'm thinkin' we're in for rain before nightfall," Zeke said, casting a worried glance toward the sky.

Harry had several nails protruding from his mouth, but he grunted in reply.

"Think we can finish before it hits, Mr. Harry?"

He took the nails out and shook his head. "I doubt it. But we should be able to cover what's left with that canvas so it won't leak in."

Zeke nodded. "That's my thinkin', too."

They worked on steadily, course after course of cedar shingles.

"Got to move the staging," Zeke said at last.

Harry looked out over the valley. Dark clouds were brewing. "Maybe we'd best cover it up and get off this ridgepole before the lightning commences to look for a target."

"You think so, suh?"

In answer to Zeke's question, thunder rumbled ominously.

"Come on!" Harry stood up, flexing his back wearily. The canvas was folded back each morning and weighted down on the upper part of the roof. He and Zeke scrambled up the slant.

"Yes, suh, we'd best start makin' things shipshape," Zeke said.

Quitting early was a blessing, Harry thought. For once he'd have time to bathe at leisure then spend a pleasant evening with Sadie. All week they'd worked until the sun set, and every night when they quit at last for supper, they were so tired they all retired as soon as the meal was finished. There was never time for a detailed conversation.

As the first raindrops pattered on the canvas, they were scooting down the ladder with their tools. They dashed inside just as Pax came sprinting up from the barn.

"Hosses all under cover," Pax told his father, and Zeke clapped him on the shoulder.

"Good boy! We'd best go wash up, or your mama won't give us any supper."

Harry was pleased to find that Tallie had carried warm water to Tenley's room for him. The chamber was still bare of furniture, and the walls needed plastering and painting, but it would do fine as a bathroom.

"I washed all your extra clothes this morning, Mr. Harry," she told him with a satisfied grin. "They dried out just in time. I brung your things in before the rain started."

"Thank you, Tallie." He hated to cause her extra work, but his two changes of clothing had become offensive from grime and sweat.

As he mounted the stairs, Sadie approached.

"Harry, since you've been so kind and stayed on to help us, I wanted to offer you these."

She held out a bundle of clothes, and he took it with mixed emotions. He badly needed the extra clothing, and he didn't want to embarrass her with his meager wardrobe. On the other hand, it must be stressful to her to offer him things that had perhaps belonged to her deceased brother.

"Sadie, I. . .this is very thoughtful of you."

She shook her head and raised one hand. "Father. . ."

"Your father suggested you give me some of Tenley's clothes?"

"No, actually. . ." She winced then took a deep breath. "These were my father's things. You're larger than Tenley. I'm afraid the cuffs of his trousers would be above your boot tops, and I don't like to contemplate your trying to fit one of his shirts."

Harry chuckled. "Well, please express my warmest thanks to your father. How is he?"

"He's. . .the same."

Harry nodded. He'd tried not to ask too often. Sadie, Zeke, and Tallie all seemed on edge when he inquired about the master of the house.

"Well," he said, and she looked up at him. Her blue eyes were trusting now, and Harry felt a sweet longing. A longing for a permanent home, not the little hut he had erected in Kentucky. A longing for many evenings with Sadie, a lifetime of cozy, companionable evenings.

"How is the roof coming?" she asked.

"Good. I think we can finish it tomorrow if it dries out enough."

"Yes. I wouldn't want you and Zeke up there if it's still wet. We don't need any accidents now."

He nodded. "If it rains, we can work inside, on the walls that need redoing. And if it's dry, we'll finish off the roof and get at those windows next."

"Harry. . ."

"Yes?"

"You don't have to stay, you know." She flushed, and he could almost read her mind. She didn't want to sound ungrateful, and she didn't truly want him to leave, but she didn't want to hold him either, if he wished to go.

"I want to stay a little longer, Sadie, and make sure you're comfortable again before I leave you."

The corners of her lips curved in a delicious smile. "Thank you," she whispered and headed down the stairs.

"Sadie!" When she turned back, he couldn't resist asking, "Are you ever going to wear that green velvet gown?"

Her face went scarlet, and he wondered if he'd been too bold in mentioning the dress he'd seen hanging in her room. He'd thought of it several times, wishing she would wear it to dinner some evening, but she hadn't. It was probably a ball gown, made for fancy parties she would attend this fall if her father's health improved. She wouldn't put the lovely creation on for a simple family dinner, but he still wanted to see her in it.

"Perhaps I shall, if you wish it, Harry."

Their gazes met, and he felt a flutter in his heart. Sadie wasn't a flirt by any means, but she was daring to respond to his suggestion.

—

After helping Tallie set the table, Sadie went back up to her bedroom. Maybe she was taking a risk, offering Harry some of her father's clothing. Tallie had insisted he let her wash and mend his extra things that day since his clothes were filthy and his shirts were torn. She didn't want to further embarrass him by giving him the clothes, but it was silly for him to go around threadbare because he had extended his stay, when there were plenty of clothes in the house.

Be careful, Sadie, she warned herself. She liked Harry. She liked him a lot. But she mustn't lose her wariness. Harry meant her no harm, she was sure; but if he learned her secret, he might feel it was his duty to take action.

She sighed and studied her face once again in the mirror. Why did they have to deceive him? Why? But she couldn't correct things now. It had been too long. They had to go on as they were. In a sense, it would be a relief when he was gone. She wouldn't have to go on pretending anymore.

No! her heart cried. *Life will be unbearable when he's gone.*

She turned and opened her armoire. The deep green velvet was softer than lamb's wool. Why shouldn't she wear the dress for Harry? She had planned it this way. She had sewn every stitch dreaming of the night he would see her in it. Hour after hour she had labored over the detail on the bodice, the layers of whisper-soft fabric, stitching and nurturing her dreams of Harry.

She undid the buttons of her blue dress and pulled it off. A quiet dinner tonight with Harry. Joy shot through her, and she stood still for a second then tiptoed across to the mirror again. How could she feel such anticipation and eagerness again? Was it right to feel this way? Perhaps the green velvet should wait. Tears welled up in her eyes.

Papa, I don't know how to behave anymore. I'm sorry. I want you to be proud of me.

She sat down on the edge of her bed, inhaling long, deliberate breaths. *Heavenly Father,* she prayed, *please help me to do what is right.*

A quiet tap came at the door, and she jumped up with a gasp. Here she was, lolling about in her underclothes.

"Miss Sadie," Tallie called.

"Yes?"

"Mr. Kauffman is in the parlor, inquirin' after you and Mr. Oliver."

Sadie swallowed hard. "I'm dressing, Tallie."

"I'll tell him you be right down. He don't expect to stay long. He's just on his way home from town and stopped in."

Sadie quickly put the blue dress on again. She would feel foolish going down to meet her stolid neighbor wearing the lavish gown. And besides, later on, after things had calmed down a bit, he might recall seeing her in a fancy evening dress this night. *No,* she decided, *it's not proper. Thank You, Lord, for sending Mr. Kauffman.*

As she entered the parlor a few minutes later, Zeke was placing a cup of tea in her neighbor's hands. Mr. Kauffman's clothes and hair were damp, and she realized he'd turned in at the lane as much for shelter from the rain as for a neighborly visit. Perhaps she ought to invite him to stay to dinner. Her heart sank at the thought of losing that intimate hour at the table with Harry.

"No, suh," Zeke said, "Mr. Oliver's no better today, but he's no worse."

The farmer caught sight of Sadie and rose. "My dear, I'm sorry we've neglected you so. I had no idea you received such severe damage in the storm last week. Zeke was just telling me about all you've been going through, and your father so ill."

"It's all right," she faltered. "We've been managing."

"But you could have used some help!"

"That's all right, suh," Zeke said. "We've had a guest helping us."

"A guest?" Mr. Kauffman looked at Zeke then at Sadie.

"Well, yes." Sadie could feel the heat flooding her face at the mention of Harry, but she supposed Zeke was right; there was no point in concealing Harry's visit. It would only look bad later if people found out he had been here for nearly a week, and she hadn't mentioned it to anyone. "Mr. Cooper was here to see Papa on business when we had the storm damage, and he's been helping Zeke with the carpentry work."

Zeke nodded, smiling at her. "That's right. And Miss Sadie's Father says—"

"Zeke!" Sadie glared at him. She would not stand by and listen to him add to the lie they were living.

"But, Miss Sadie," he said in an injured tone, "you know you been speakin' to your Father about all this business, and He been tellin' you things will be all right. Isn't that what you told me this mornin'?" His meaningful stare pierced her heart.

Sadie swallowed hard. She had mentioned to Tallie and Zeke that her prayers had been a great comfort to her and that God had assured her of His care for her and her people.

"Well, I—" She heard a light step behind her and turned. Harry was entering the parlor with an inquisitive air.

Suddenly Sadie knew she couldn't bear it any longer. She could not, *would not*, stand there and imply things that were not true. And yet she couldn't blurt out the truth in front of Mr. Kauffman. She felt as though she couldn't breathe.

"Excuse me!" She pushed past Harry and dashed through the doorway, across the hall, and out the front door. She ran through the yard, aware that the rain had slackened to a light mist.

She pushed open the barn door and ducked inside. It was dark and warm inside, with the homey sounds of horses chewing their evening rations and the smells of manure, leather, and sweet hay. How many times had she found solace in the company of horses?

Harry's gelding, Pepper, was in the stall nearest the door on the right, and she stepped toward him. His large head was a dark bulk in the dimness, and he nickered softly. Sadie reached up and stroked his long, soft nose. Little sobs began low in her chest and made their way up her throat, escaping in gasps. She leaned her arms on the half door of the stall and wept, not caring that Pepper was snuffling at her hair.

Everything was wrong, and she couldn't fix any of it.

"Sadie."

She caught her breath and raised her head.

"Sadie?"

Harry was standing very close to her, and she sniffed. The one moment in the last four months when she didn't want Harry within a mile of her, and he'd found her.

Chapter 8

"Come here." Harry's warm fingers closed on Sadie's wrist, and she did not resist his gentle pull but went into his strong arms and let him hold her while she sobbed. He stroked her hair and her shoulders, saying nothing. Sadie found her anguish subsiding as she absorbed the warm, solid security of Harry's embrace.

At last she straightened and pulled back a few inches, but he kept his firm hold on her. She fumbled in her pocket for a handkerchief and chased her tears with it.

"I'm sorry, Harry. I've soaked your clean shirt."

"It's all right." He pulled her back in against his chest, and she went willingly.

"Is Mr. Kauffman all in a dither?"

"No, but he's heading home. The rain's let up, and he expressed his condolences."

"What did you tell him? About me, I mean? I shouldn't have left you to make my excuses." Perhaps she should have asked what Zeke said to Mr. Kauffman, she thought bitterly. Wasn't this all Zeke's fault?

"I just told him things have been difficult for you. I think he understood."

"Thank you."

"He offered to send his two sons over to help with the roofing—"

"Oh, dear! They're not coming, are they?"

He smiled. "No, I assured him we were doing fine, and he admitted he needs his boys on the harvest right now."

Sadie sighed in relief. Wilfred Kauffman ogled her every time he had a chance, and it was very disconcerting. She realized suddenly that she was clinging to Harry, her arms encircling his waist, and she jerked away from him, appalled at her behavior. "Harry, I—"

He bent toward her, and Sadie caught her breath. He was going to kiss her. It caught her off guard, but in a flash she knew she had longed for this second. For one instant, all thoughts of propriety fled. There was only Harry for that moment, that one long, delightful moment when anything seemed possible, even a carefree future.

Her wickedness struck her suddenly, and she tore away from him with a gasp. It was terribly wrong for her to let him assume things could be good and sweet between them when she had been lying to him for more than a week now.

Harry let her leave his arms with a pang of regret. It was too soon—that much was clear.

"I'm sorry, Sadie. Please forgive me."

She stood before him in silence. He could barely see her face in the dimness of the barn, but he could feel the confusion in her hesitation, and he could hear her breath coming in shallow gulps.

"I'm. . .not angry with you," she said.

He reached out and brushed her cheek with the backs of his fingers. "I should have spoken to your father first, but you know that's been impossible. It just. . .it seemed like the right moment, but I know how distressed you've been. This isn't the right time, after all, is it?"

She sobbed once more and raised the handkerchief quickly to her lips, as though to smother the sound. "Please, Harry. I don't think I can go on like this. Maybe it's time for you to leave."

He stood still, trying to take it in. She didn't mean for him to leave the barn. No, with a sinking heart he realized she was asking him to leave the farm.

He took a deep, slow breath. "If I've offended you—"

"No, it's not that."

"The neighbors then?" he hazarded. Was she mortified that Mr. Kauffman knew she was entertaining a guest while her father was bedridden? He could set that straight and squelch any rumors. "Sadie, we can explain to people how things were. You don't need to worry about gossip. You've been the model of propriety."

"It's—it's not that."

"What then?"

He waited, but she said nothing. His stomach began to churn with anxiety. Something was terribly wrong, at least from Sadie's perspective. At last he felt he needed to break the silence.

He stepped toward her. "If it's my trying to kiss you that's upset you, please know I didn't mean anything dishonorable by it."

"No, no." She stepped away, toward the barn door. "You've been a true gentleman, Harry. But I can't go on saying one thing and living another. I shan't be eating dinner tonight, so don't wait for me."

His concern changed to alarm, and he followed her out into the barnyard. "What are you talking about? Sadie, tell me what's bothering you so."

She was closing the door without comment.

"Here, let me do that."

She stepped aside, and he drew the heavy door into place. When he turned around, she was walking quickly toward the house. He hurried to catch up with her.

"Sadie, stop, please."

She paused and looked at him in the twilight, and he took that as a good sign. At least she would hear him out.

"Look—I can't leave until I know you're secure again." He shoved his hands into his pockets so that she wouldn't wonder if he was going to reach for her again, although he longed to do just that. "If it's fair tomorrow, Zeke and I can finish patching the roof, but we need to get the broken windows fixed, too. After that, Zeke can probably go it alone, or he can fetch his older son to help him, the one he told me sometimes helps around here."

"Ephraim." She nodded.

"Well, we ought to get that far within a week. Then I can go and feel peaceful about it."

Her troubled eyes regarded him, and he knew that peace was the last thing he would feel. She wanted him to go. He couldn't help believing the moment in the barn had something to do with that, regardless of what she had said.

The days went too quickly. When Harry awoke each morning, the first thing he did was go outside the little cabin and glare at the rising sun. Rain would serve him far better.

Sadie had kept a cool distance between them since their conversation in the barn, and he was beginning to doubt he had enough time to unravel her reasons. She was polite, and sometimes at dinner he even caught her watching him with what he could only feel was a mournful longing, but she gave him no encouragement. Any suggestion of playful banter was gone, and the spark he had felt jump between them on other occasions was conspicuously absent.

They didn't speak of his leaving again, but they both knew it was imminent. The roof was done, and when the outside walls were patched and the windows replaced, his sojourn at the Spinning Wheel Farm would end.

"One of us had best go to town for the windowpanes," Zeke said one morning, "or else we can't finish the job."

"You go," Harry said. "I'll keep at the sashes while you're gone. I ought to be able to finish the one for the parlor this morning. Then the two for the upstairs windows, and I guess you won't need me anymore."

Zeke eyed him with open curiosity. "You welcome to stay as long as you like, Mr. Harry."

"Thank you. I should get back to my place."

Zeke nodded. "We'll be sorry to see the back of you."

Harry sighed and leaned on the rail fence that edged the pasture beside Zeke's house. "Zeke, I hate to go. I truly do, but I can't stay much longer."

"Why not, Mr. Harry? You like it here."

"I do, but. . .Zeke, you know I've got obligations in Kentucky, and besides,

Sadie wants me to go."

"No, suh."

"Yes."

Zeke pulled a dry grass stem and stuck it between his teeth. He glanced at Harry then looked thoughtfully out over the pasture. "Miss Sadie sets a lot of store by you, suh."

Harry shook his head. "Maybe a few days ago, but not now. She's asked me to leave, Zeke."

"I. . .just can't believe it, Mr. Harry."

Harry turned around and leaned back against the rails with a sigh. "I was all primed to speak to her father, you know. I wanted to ask for her hand." He gave Zeke a rueful smile. "Wasn't sure if Mr. McEwan would go along with it, but I had hopes. We got along pretty well last spring. But now. . . well, Sadie pretty much let me know she wouldn't consider it, even if her father would."

"No." Zeke was very quiet, and his frown stretched from his wrinkled forehead to his drooping mouth.

"She's the kind of woman I was hoping for," Harry said with a shrug. "She's prettier than a sunset in Jamaica, and she works hard and doesn't complain. Treats you and Tallie well, too. But besides all that about Sadie, as long as I'm here, I'm keeping your family apart. While Tallie stays up yonder with Sadie, you have to bach it down here with Pax. No, Zeke, it's time for me to meander."

"Well, I know one thing," Zeke said. "It's time for breakfast now. Grab your hat, suh, and let's get movin'." He stuck his head inside the cabin and shouted, "Pax! Come on, boy! You know your momma won't keep breakfast all day for you."

On their way up to the big house, Pax wrangled with Zeke over the question of the trip to Winchester for the glass.

"I can handle it, Papa. I been to town a thousand times with you or Mr. Oliver. I know what to do. And I can make sure Mr. MacPheters packs the windowpanes so's they won't break on the way back."

"I don't know," Zeke said.

"The boy can do it," Harry said, even though he knew that would leave Zeke here to help him, and the job would be done faster. By supporting Pax, he was shortening his stay.

Sadie didn't appear at breakfast while he was in the kitchen with Zeke and Pax, and Harry assumed she was with Oliver. Tallie went upstairs and came back a few minutes later with money for the glass.

"You'd best go with the boy," she told Zeke. "Miss Sadie say Mr. MacPheters might want cash, and Pax ain't never carried this much before. Besides, if the boy break the windows, she be out her money."

"I suppose," Zeke said.

Harry said nothing, but when Zeke told Pax to go to the barn and prepare the wagon, Harry pulled the boy aside just behind the lean-to.

"Pax, while you and your pa are at the store, can you do a little errand for me?"

"Oh, yes, suh." Pax's dark eyes shone as Harry drew a handful of coins from his pocket.

"You get yourself some candy, and I want something pretty for Miss Sadie and your momma. I want to thank them for letting me stay so long, you see."

Pax nodded, staring at Harry all the while. "What kind of pretties, suh?"

"Oh, maybe some new gloves?"

Pax's brow furrowed.

"Ask your papa," Harry said. "If he thinks that's too personal, he'll know what to get."

Zeke came out the back door and scowled at Pax. "You ain't got the wagon ready?"

"My fault," said Harry.

"I'm doin' Mr. Harry's business, Pa." Pax drew himself up with importance.

"Well, git on to the barn now and do your own business." Zeke drew his arm back as if he would swat the boy, and Pax ran for the barn, but Harry knew it was all a show.

"Zeke, I really, really need to talk to Mr. Oliver," Harry said.

Zeke shook his head sorrowfully. "I wish you'd quit askin' me, suh. I just can't let you. If anything bad should happen, Miss Sadie wouldn't forgive us."

Harry sighed. "Just how bad is he, Zeke? Tell me the truth now."

Zeke's mouth worked for a few seconds, and he glanced at Harry then looked down toward the barn. "Well, suh, he's bad. Real bad."

"But Sadie spends a good part of the day with him every day, and you told me she talks to him."

"Yes, suh. Miss Sadie talks to her Father every single day. That's a fact."

"Does Oliver talk back?" Zeke wouldn't meet his gaze, and Harry pressed further. "Well, Zeke, what I don't understand is how your boss can be so very ill that he can't even see me in his bedroom once in a week's time, and yet you claim he's talking to his daughter about business and such all the time."

Zeke drew himself up and looked him in the eye with the air of a martyr. "I can assure you, suh, that Miss Sadie receives guidance from her Father every day on how to run the farm."

Harry shook his head, at a loss to comprehend the situation. All he knew was that he wanted some sort of permission from Oliver McEwan to pay his addresses to his daughter. Surely if she knew she had her father's approval, Sadie would agree. Harry couldn't forget the sweetness of her embrace before she had torn away from him that night in the barn. For a few seconds it had been the culmination of his dream. He realized that since May it had been in the back of his mind. If Sadie lived up to his memories of her, he had intended to speak to her father about marrying her. He tried to keep his exasperation in check as he told Zeke, "I would really like to see Oliver before I go, if only for a few minutes. You know that, don't you?"

"That's impossible. I'm sorry, but it can't be done."

Harry pulled his felt hat off and dashed it to the ground. "Zeke, I'm losing my patience. I can't understand how Oliver can be giving Sadie so much help if he's too sick to see a client, even in his bedroom. You know what I want to talk to him about, don't you? And I don't mean horses."

Zeke stared down at Harry's dirty hat. "Yes, suh, I reckon I do."

"That's right, you do. I want to speak to him about Sadie, to see if he'd be averse to me courting her. You don't have a reason to keep that from happening, do you, Zeke? Do you have something against me?"

Zeke looked up at him with wide eyes. "Oh, no, suh. I like you fine, Mr. Harry, and I think you'd be a wonderful husband for Miss Sadie. But you told me yourself, she give you the broom."

Harry heaved a sigh and tried once more to reason it out. "But it's her father's illness that's holding her back, don't you see? It's got to be that. I know she cares for me." He stared at Zeke. "Has anyone actually told Oliver I want to see him? Does he even know I'm here, Zeke?"

Zeke stooped and picked up the hat. He dusted it off and handed it to Harry. "I'm truly sorry, suh. It ain't going to happen."

Harry stared at him for a long moment. Maybe he should just march upstairs and go to Oliver's room and ask him. But, no, he couldn't override Sadie's wishes so blatantly. She would surely be angry then. Or would she? Maybe she would be relieved if he took the initiative and forced the issue.

Harry pulled in a deep breath, realizing his feelings for Sadie were keeping him from looking at the situation rationally. His hostess had asked him to leave as soon as possible. He couldn't disrespect that. It wasn't in his nature, and it wouldn't win him favor with Sadie if he acted that way. He put on his hat and headed for the lean-to where he had laid out the wood needed to repair the window sashes.

Chapter 9

Sadie stuck out her tongue and squinted in fierce concentration. Harry and Zeke were fitting the new window into Tenley's bedroom, and Harry had entrusted her with putting the glass panes in the second frame, for the room next to her brother's. She bent over a makeshift worktable the men had set up in the front yard—two sawhorses supporting a couple of planks that held the window.

The work was exacting, as Sadie had to fit the panes to the wooden sash Harry had built to replace the one that was crushed. She inserted tiny glazier's points on the outside of the glass to hold each pane in place then applied the putty carefully to seal each pane to the wooden frame. Then she had to wipe away the excess before it dried, leaving the windows clear and sparkling.

Harry had done a good job, and the spaces were precisely the right size. Her task was tedious, rather than creative, but she was determined to do it well.

Of course, when these two windows were in place, Harry would be leaving. He had saved her a lot of money by making it unnecessary to hire a skilled carpenter. The parlor window was finished. If she hadn't known better she'd have thought it was the old one, but Harry had totally rebuilt it. It had taken him three days to do it right.

The smaller bedroom sashes hadn't demanded as much time, but still Harry had been here two weeks now.

Sadie thought her heart would break when he finally left, but even so she looked forward to the relief his departure would bring. The strain between them was almost unbearable.

Zeke and Pax had come home from Winchester with the windowpanes a few days ago, bearing candy, a colorful new head scarf for Tallie, and several spools of fine lace and ribbon for Sadie. She had begun to scold Zeke for spending her scarce resources on trifles, but Pax had cried, "It was Mr. Harry's money, Miss Sadie. He paid for your pretties."

She nearly lost control then and had to flee to her room so no one would see her weep. Harry was too dear. In the middle of her agony and sorrow, he bought treats for her poor friends and showered her with fancy trimmings.

"There will be better days," he told her that evening at dinner when she thanked him. "You'll feel like sewing again. I know you love to design pretty clothes, and Zeke thought you'd enjoy those gifts sometime when things are looking better."

At that moment, she'd almost wished she had worn the green gown. She knew Harry wanted to see her in it, and she wanted to see his reaction when she wore the dress with its intricate stitching.

I can't encourage him, she reminded herself. It seemed so unfair. They could have had such lovely times together.

She bent over the window sash where it rested on the sawhorses. Now and then she glanced toward the house where the men were working. Zeke had stood the tall ladder against the side of the house and mounted it. She couldn't help looking up to where Harry was leaning out Tenley's window, steadying the sash as Zeke fitted it into the frame. They had torn out and replaced the broken lumber around the window, and now the new one was almost in position. Pax stood below, bracing the ladder.

A sudden shout from Zeke made her look up, just in time to see the heavy window frame falling.

"Pax!" Sadie screamed.

The boy jumped back away from the ladder, but the corner of the window caught him on the head, and he crumpled to the ground as the glass shattered around him.

"Pax!" Zeke scrambled down the shaking ladder. Sadie ran toward them. Harry had the presence of mind to lean out the window hole and grasp the top of the ladder to keep it from sliding to the side. As soon as Zeke reached the ground, Harry let go and disappeared from the window.

Zeke huddled over his son, moaning, "My boy, my boy."

Sadie reached his side. "How bad is it, Zeke?"

"He bleedin' bad, Miss Sadie. He got a big gash on the side of his head, and his arm's bleedin'."

"The glass got him," she said.

Harry came tearing out the front door and hopped over the side railing of the porch, landing a few feet from the ladder.

"Be careful." Sadie straightened and held up her hands. "There's glass everywhere, Harry. Stay back."

Zeke picked up the boy and carried him out away from the side of the house, laying him tenderly on the grass. "He's breathin', Mr. Harry. What do we do?"

"We need to stop the bleeding. But be careful. If there's glass in his cuts, we don't want to push it in deeper." Harry looked at Sadie. "Can you get us something to bandage him with?"

As Sadie turned, Tallie charged around the corner of the house. "What happened? What's all the ruckus?"

She stopped as she saw Pax's prone form then turned her eyes heavenward. "Oh, dear Jesus! Help us now!"

"Where's the nearest doctor?" Harry asked.

"I done told you—they ain't a doctor," Zeke said grimly. "If they was, we'd have had him here for Mr. Oliver when he needed him."

"Oh, Lawd, oh, Lawd!" Tallie wailed, clasping her hands together. "My baby! Save my baby boy!"

Sadie ran to her and put her arms around her. "Come, Tallie. We can pray while we fetch what's needed. I'll get some hot water and clean linen. You fix my bed so they can bring him there."

"Not in your bed, Miss Sadie. It ain't right."

"Well, that's what we're doing."

"Where will you sleep tonight?" Tallie asked.

"We'll worry about that later. Now do as I say!"

Tallie blinked at her then lifted her skirt and ran for the front door. Sadie followed, shouting to Harry, "As soon as you can move him, take him up to my bedchamber!"

———

At midnight Tallie sat by her son's bedside, humming a dolorous hymn. Harry stepped softly into the room, and Tallie said, "You sleep, Miss Sadie. I want to stay with him."

"Tallie, it's me."

She jumped and turned to look at him.

"I thought I'd sit awhile with the boy."

"Bless you, Mr. Harry. You don't have to do that. I won't be able to sleep anyhow."

Harry felt tears threaten him as he looked down at the boy's angelic, dark face, still against the snowy pillow, but he smiled at her. "I guess this is a mother's post."

"That it is."

"I just wanted to help, Tallie."

"I know. I know."

He saw a straight chair before Sadie's secretary and pulled it over beside the rocker Tallie occupied. "If I'd only kept a better hold on that window. I'm so sorry, Tallie."

"It ain't your fault, Mr. Harry. Don't you be a-thinkin' that way."

"I can't help it."

"It was my Zeke dropped the window."

"No, you mustn't blame him. It was me, too. Both of us lost our hold."

Tallie was silent for a minute. "I don't blame neither of you."

Harry bit his upper lip. Better she feel that way than to have her blaming her husband. He would say no more on the subject.

"Where did you put Miss Sadie?" he asked, and Tallie glanced at him.

"She in her brother's old room. She put the bed back together in there herself."

Harry nodded. "I didn't know but she might have a cot in her father's room."

"No, no, she'll sleep better where she is."

"I think Pax will be better tomorrow, Tallie. I truly do."

"I hope so, Mr. Harry."

Harry stretched out his long legs and leaned back with a sigh. "I'm sure he's concussed, but the skull wasn't broken."

"That good or bad?"

"I think it's good. We'll know more when he regains consciousness."

"Them big words." Tallie shook her head.

"If he comes to, we'll know," Harry said.

"Will you pray for him?"

"Of course. I have been already since the minute it happened." Harry reached for her hand, and Tallie squeezed his fingers.

"I'm glad you're a prayin' man. We need a lot of prayer just now."

Harry bowed his head and earnestly sought the Lord's mercy for Pax. He'd spent two weeks living with this boy and his father, and the family was precious to him now. He'd had enough conversations with young Pax to know the condition of his heart.

"Dear Lord," he prayed aloud, "you know this brother in Christ is in need. We ask for Your will, Father. We know that if You should take him home now, he'd be in a wonderful place with You. But his momma and his pa would be devastated, Lord, and we beg You to spare Pax's life. Give him health and strength again so Tallie and Zeke won't have to worry about him. And we pray for Mr. Oliver, too, Lord. Please help him to regain his health."

Tallie began to sob, and Harry said quickly, "Amen."

"Amen." Tallie blew her nose on a square of calico.

"Are you all right?" he asked, leaning toward her.

"Yes, suh. I be as good as I can be."

"Can I do anything for you? Maybe I could check Mr. Oliver—"

"No!"

Harry was startled, but Tallie patted his arm. "It's best to leave him be."

"If you're sure he's resting. Isn't there anything else I can do, Tallie?"

She shook her head. "You'd best sleep, suh. In the mornin' you can fetch my older son to come and see his brother. And, like you say, maybe things be better in the mornin'."

Sadie lay awake, staring at the canvas that covered the hole where the window should have been. She could have spent the night in her father's room, but somehow she'd known that sleep would elude her in that chamber. Why she'd imagined she would find it here in Tenley's room, she had no idea.

They had to end this charade. Harry had done nothing to deserve the shabby treatment they had given him. The irony was that Harry himself would say they had been kind to him. The knowledge of their deception and of the lies she herself had tacitly told made her physically ill. Even Tallie was ignoring the little things Zeke let fall that implied Sadie's father would be up and about again one day. The dear servant's loyalty to her mistress was causing Tallie to go against her honest nature, and that grieved Sadie.

Harry's compassion for Pax when the boy was injured had touched her deeply. Sadie knew Harry blamed himself for the accident. He was becoming like family to Zeke and Tallie, and now he felt he had let them down. He had injured their son, perhaps fatally. That was the way Harry saw it. Sadie wished she could take that sickening guilt away for him.

"Dear Lord, I care too much about him," she whispered in the dark. "You've got to take him away from here. I fear I'm past beginning to love him. Lord, please, if You have a way for us to straighten this out, show us now. Otherwise, what can I do but send him away believing a lie?"

If only she had told him everything from the start. But that would have meant betraying Zeke's deception. They had all thought it was only for a day and it wouldn't matter, but now it had gone so far that Sadie didn't see a way to make it right without hurting several people.

The last two weeks had opened up a new world for her as she got to know Harry. Tallie said they had seen the stuff he was made of. Sadie didn't want to think about how bleak her life would be when Harry left. If only she had the courage to tell him, even now, and face whatever came. Rejection? Anger? Condemnation? Could she take that from Harry? It was too dire to contemplate. Tears left the corners of her eyes and streaked down her face to her ears.

I'm so tired of crying, dear Father. I've lost Tenley and Papa, and now I'm losing Harry. Please, don't take Pax away from us, too.

Chapter 10

Sadie lingered in her room before dinner, wondering again if she was making a huge mistake. In the three days since Pax's injury, the boy had made a marvelous recovery. He was back in the little cabin with Zeke and Harry now and today had even gone back to helping feed the horses and performing his barn chores.

Sadie had her own bedroom back, and her daily routine seemed more normal. The windows were finished—Harry had gone to town himself for more glass the day after the accident while Tallie and Zeke hovered over Pax.

This would be their last dinner together. Harry had no reason to stay on now; the outside repairs were done, and Pax was on the mend.

She knew he didn't want to leave, and she didn't want that either. The things she had learned about Harry in the last few days only confirmed what she already knew. He was witty, intelligent, diligent, and compassionate. Her love for him had blossomed, and yet she'd kept it in check out of necessity.

But now, on this final evening together, she had made a momentous decision. She would wear the velvet gown.

Was that foolish?

Dinnertime arrived, but still she hesitated, wondering if she should go down in the dress she loved. If only her mother were there to advise her! She stared into the mirror. Her auburn hair gleamed in the lamplight, and her eyes were huge. They picked up the color of the dress and seemed more green than blue this evening. She had added an extra row of lace at the cuffs and neckline from the trimmings Harry had paid for. She wasn't sure he would notice it, but that was all right. She wanted to be wearing something that he had given her tonight. The dress suited her. For once she did not think she looked gawky and immature. Would Harry see her as. . . beautiful?

Her conscience told her she was a fool. This was no way to send a man packing. The conflict in her heart was clouding her reasoning. She should put on her dowdiest housedress and treat him with cool courtesy tonight and not go downstairs in the morning until he had gone.

But she knew she couldn't do that. And here she was, wearing the gown he had requested that she wear a week ago.

Before she could change her mind, she strode from the room and down the stairs.

Harry rose when she entered the parlor, and his eager smile sent a thrill through her. His eyes glowed as he took her hands.

"Sadie, you look wonderful."

Her lips trembled as she gazed up at him. All she could get out was a whispered "Thank you."

Dinner was a bit strained at first, but Zeke and Tallie livened things up. They insisted on serving the two in the dining room as they did every evening. They were on familiar terms with Harry now, and Zeke soon had them both laughing with his comments. Tallie's motherly instincts were at the forefront.

"You eat up, Mr. Harry. You got a long trip ahead of you tomorrow." She brought the platter of meat to him, her meaning unmistakable. If Harry didn't take seconds, she would be insulted.

"Yes, Tallie. I'll miss your scrumptious cooking." He speared a slab of roast beef with the serving fork.

Tallie looked at her husband. "Zeke, get some hot gravy for Mr. Harry."

"This is fine," Harry said, reaching for the china gravy boat, but Zeke snatched it up before he could lift it.

"Oh, no, Mr. Harry. That gravy's cold. You need hot gravy for my Tallie's biscuits and roast beef."

He hurried toward the kitchen. Harry looked at Sadie and shrugged, his eyes twinkling. "I'll miss the service, too."

"Spoiled you, have we?" Sadie asked.

"I'll say. Things were never like this on board ship."

"You got people to look after you in Kentucky?" Tallie asked.

Harry's eyebrows shot up. "You mean. . .family?"

"Slave folks."

"No, Tallie, I don't. No kinfolk there, either."

"Well, what you want to live in Kentucky for?" Tallie shook her head.

When they were alone in the parlor half an hour later, Sadie's nerves assailed her. She sat in a chair, and Harry paced the room slowly, examining all the paintings once more and touching the knickknacks on the mantel.

"I am glad we have this evening together," Harry said, staring down into the empty fireplace, not looking at her.

"So am I."

He turned and smiled at her. "That gown is magnificent on you. Thank you for wearing it."

"You're welcome." Sadie swallowed hard. There were many things she wished to say, but she wasn't sure she could voice any of them. When she inhaled, her chest hurt, so she kept quiet.

Harry went to the settee and sat down facing her. "Sadie, I want to tell you how much I've enjoyed my stay here."

"Oh, that's. . .there's no need."

He shook his head. "You've been wonderful, all of you."

"Harry, we should be thanking you for staying. You've helped us in so many ways!"

He sighed. "I hate to leave, but I know the time has come. Sadie, I can't go without telling you how much I admire you."

She shifted uneasily in her chair. This was what she wanted to hear, but it only brought more turmoil to her heart. He admired her! And yet she was a lying hypocrite.

Harry went on quickly. "I know you're a modest woman, but your faithfulness and tenacity are undeniable. I've seen how much this farm means to you. You've run it admirably, even during this time of stress and illness. Your family—and I'm including Zeke and Tallie and Pax in that—comes first with you. I believe you've broken my heart because of that, and I'm not sure why."

Sadie caught her breath and stared down at the figured carpet. "Harry, I never meant to hurt you."

"I know that. I just wish you could be open with me and tell me all your troubles. I can only think I could help you change things."

Sadie felt a crushing weight on her chest. If only she could do that! He might be right—so far he'd been right about most things. Maybe if she told him now, he could help her with the legal and social morass she knew would envelop her soon.

A montage of images flashed through her mind. It was possible she could be evicted from her family home. She might be forced to flee, penniless and without hope, and be separated from her beloved family servants. The thing that frightened her most, the one she didn't dare mention even to Tallie, was that she might be arrested. Yes, she and Zeke and Tallie might all be charged with. . .something, she wasn't sure what, but a vague certainty that they had broken multiple laws of the Commonwealth lurked in the back of her mind.

Harry left his seat and knelt beside her chair.

"You must know that I love you."

She drew in a shaky breath and avoided looking at him. If she gazed into those earnest brown eyes, she would be lost.

She felt his warm, strong hand cover hers.

"Sadie, tell me you love me, too."

As she struggled for her answer, tears welled in her eyes. He slid his arm around her.

"Sadie, dearest, look at me."

Slowly she turned her head. "Harry." It was all she could get out, and even that was a little squeak. Her heart raced, and his melting brown eyes had the effect she'd known they would have.

"I'm going to do one of three things," Harry said.

"What?" she managed.

"Either I'm going to run up those stairs and speak to your father—"

"No! You mustn't."

Harry frowned. "All right then." He took a deep breath. "All right, I'm going to do one of two things. Either I'm going to kiss you, or you're going to tell me to leave now, and I won't see you again."

She stared at him.

"Sadie?"

"I. . ."

"It's up to you."

"I don't want you to leave, but—"

Harry didn't wait for her to finish. He drew her up out of her chair, and his lips found hers. Sadie tensed for an instant. Had she given the wrong answer? *No,* her heart told her. *You love him. This is the right thing.*

She let him draw her closer, reveling in the joy his touch brought her. It was far beyond her expectations or imaginations, and she wanted the moment to last forever. He held her in his arms and showered soft kisses along her temple, to the corner of her eye.

"Sadie, I love you so much."

She gulped for air, knowing that all she needed to say was two words: *Don't leave.*

And then what? Would he be embroiled in their troubles, too? Or would he betray them when he found out the truth? The joy that had flooded her a moment ago was overcome by guilt, and she pushed him away reluctantly.

"Harry, we mustn't. You know my father is. . ." She sobbed. "His condition is very serious."

"Yes. Yes, I know."

"I do love you, Harry, but—" As triumph leaped into his eyes, she pressed her hands against the front of his shirt to keep him from sweeping her into his embrace again. "But that doesn't change anything."

"I don't understand. It should change everything."

She sighed. "Please respect my wishes. You need to leave in the morning. That's the way it is right now. There are things I have to face on my own."

He studied her face, and Sadie made herself return his gaze. Her heart hammered, and she longed to nestle against his chest again and feel safe, but that would be a false security.

At last he stood back, his head bowed. "All right. I've done everything I know how to do. But tell me, Sadie. If I were to come back, say in the spring, would things be different?"

Her heart lurched. She hadn't considered this possibility. Would she even be here next spring?

"Sadie?"

"It's. . .possible." She looked up at him. He was smiling. He grasped her hands and lifted them to his lips.

"In the spring, then, when the mountains are passable."

———

Harry went to the barn with Zeke and Pax at dawn to tend the livestock. While the father and son fed the horses, Harry tied his pack to the cantle of his saddle and gave Pepper a grooming.

His heart was heavy. He didn't want to ride back to Kentucky and leave Sadie behind. He would spend all winter pining for her. She had admitted she loved him. He smiled at that. It was a start, but her father needed her here. Harry was certain now that it was Oliver's health that was weighing her down. She didn't feel she could make a commitment to him while her father was so ill, and she felt bound to the farm and her family.

Harry sighed and fastened a lead rope to Pepper's halter. Maybe he was too aggressive last night, but at least it had brought a declaration from her. He could live all winter on that if he had to. She loved him. She wasn't as ready to start a new life as he was. He could wait. He didn't know what would come of it in the future, but one thing he knew for sure: He couldn't ride off and forget her. He would hold the memory of Sadie in his heart all winter and come back in the spring to see if she was ready for his suit.

"You sure you'll be all right alone with those mares, Mr. Harry?" Pax asked him, leaning against a post between the stalls.

Harry smiled. Pax would love it if he offered to take him with him to Kentucky. He wouldn't mind the company himself, but he was sure the boy would get homesick before they left the Shenandoah Valley, and Tallie wouldn't abide the idea of her youngest leaving home so early. Harry had learned that all four of her daughters lived at least a day's ride away, and only Pax and his married brother, Ephraim, were close enough now for Tallie to spoil them. No, she wouldn't let the youngest go easily.

"I'll be fine, Pax. They're well-behaved horses. You folks have taught them good manners."

"You gonna lead them all, suh?"

"Most likely your pa will help me tie the lead ropes into a string. I don't expect much trouble."

"What if a Injun tries to steal them while you're sleepin' at night?"

"Not too many Indians left where I'm headed, son. You'd have to go a little farther west for that."

Pax was disappointed, he could tell.

"How's your head feel?" Harry asked.

"Fine, suh. Pa said I could ride today."

Harry nodded. "Glad to hear it. You be good now and help your pa get things ready for winter."

Pax scuffed his toe in the straw on the barn floor. "Yes, suh. We gonna miss you."

"I'll miss you, too." He ruffled the boy's woolly hair. "You want to take Pepper to the water trough for me?"

Pax grinned and hurried to take Pepper out into the barnyard. Harry followed him. He took a deep breath and looked toward the house. Would Sadie show herself this morning? He'd promised Tallie he'd eat breakfast in the kitchen before leaving.

A flash of color caught his eye, and he saw a figure disappearing among the trees at the side of the house toward the river, beyond the vegetable garden. It was a slender woman in a full mulberry-colored skirt. It had to be Sadie!

He stepped forward eagerly then thought to call to Pax, "Just put him away when he's finished drinking. I'll see you at breakfast."

Pax waved his acknowledgment, and Harry hurried toward where he had seen her. He found a narrow path, leading between the apple trees and beyond. He followed it and mounted a gentle knoll. At its crest he stopped in surprise. A burial plot lay on the south slope, overlooking the river. Perhaps twenty stone grave markers were in it, and a rough rail fence bounded the area. In the middle, kneeling before a wooden cross, was Sadie.

Chapter 11

Harry squinted at the headstone nearest her. Her mother's grave. Then what was the cross beside it for? They had only learned of Tenley's death a few weeks ago. Zeke and Sadie had both spoken of the letter Oliver received from Tenley's commander. Neither had said a word about his remains being received. Surely Sadie's brother couldn't be buried here in Virginia.

But the earth where she knelt was just growing up in tender grass, and he could see that the grave was much newer than Mrs. McEwan's.

The obvious truth broke on him, but Harry refused to believe it. Against his will, the many comments Zeke had dropped flooded his memory.

Mr. Oliver is resting. Mr. Oliver wasn't disturbed by the storm. Mr. Oliver is no better today, but no worse.

It couldn't be. Sadie wouldn't lie to him so blatantly. He tried to recall the things she had said about her father, and suddenly he was sure. Her statements that she couldn't go on living as she was, and her cryptic remark about saying one thing and living another. . .it all made sense now.

He wanted to go to her, but the incredulity he felt brought on a heavy dread. Did he really want to know the truth? That would mean confronting the woman he loved. Harry didn't want to accuse people he had believed to be his closest friends of lying to him. But then, wasn't that why she hadn't told him? She didn't want to face that kind of chaos, either. Perhaps they would all be better off if he left without saying a word.

He needed time to think. He started to turn away, wondering if he could escape without Sadie knowing he had seen her, but at that moment she rose and turned around.

She gasped and clutched her hands together at her breast, staring at him. Her lips were parted, and the anguish he saw in her eyes stabbed through the dull pain that had encased him.

She knew he had figured it out; his expression must have revealed it. There was no way to make her believe otherwise. Harry wished he weren't so transparent.

He took a few steps forward, and she met him at the low gate.

"Why didn't you tell me?" he whispered.

She swallowed hard then caught a ragged breath. She looked at him then away. "Tell you what?"

Anger spouted up inside him so suddenly that it shocked him. "Oh, stop it, Sadie. Your father's dead. He's been dead for weeks, hasn't he? If anyone had told me you would do this, I'd have called him out. You are the last person on earth I would expect to lie to me, the very last." He ignored the tears in her eyes. "I begged you to tell me what was wrong. Why, Sadie? Why couldn't you trust me?"

She dashed tears from her eyes with one hand. "I wanted to, but I was so afraid."

"Afraid of me?"

"We didn't know you well, not at first. How could I tell if you were trustworthy? I'd only met you once."

"Why should that matter? Sadie, I heard Zeke tell your neighbors your father was alive. What is going on? Why on earth would you try to hide his death? It makes no sense at all."

She sobbed into her hand, turning partly away from him. "When he died, we had to bury him. Ordinarily we'd have sent for the preacher, but the reverend had left shortly before on his circuit. It would have taken Zeke a week or more to catch him. We couldn't wait. It was so hot. We couldn't wait."

She was shaking, and Harry's love for her struggled against the outrage he felt.

"Even so. . ."

"And then we got to worrying about the property. You see, my father had left his estate to Tenley, but with Tenley dead we weren't sure what would happen to us."

Harry frowned. "What do you mean?"

"I. . .Zeke and Tallie and I aren't sure whether I'll be allowed to inherit the farm. Zeke recalled the Widow Scott. When her husband died, their farm went to his cousin's son, and she was turned out. We didn't know what would become of us if I lost the farm, and. . .well, when you came, Zeke said something about Papa, and you thought he meant. . ."

"You should have seen a lawyer."

She shook her head hopelessly. "I don't know any lawyers, Harry. I wouldn't even know where to find one." She looked off downriver. "Washington, maybe? There was no one within several days' journey who could issue a death certificate."

"What do your neighbors do when somebody dies? What did your father do when your mother died?"

"I don't know! I don't know!" She slumped against the low fence, holding on to the top rail and weeping.

"I can't believe you lied about it. Just because you couldn't get a doctor or a preacher—" Harry shook his head as if to clear the cobwebs. "I can't believe you all conspired against me. Even Pax? I love that kid. How could he not spill it to me?"

Sadie winced. "Pax is very loyal to this family."

"But Tallie. There's not a dishonest bone in her body."

"We were afraid, Harry. We wanted to tell you. Tallie has been distraught over this, but we were afraid."

"I would never do anything to hurt you."

"We didn't know that then. Don't you see? When you arrived, we thought it was just for a day, and Zeke thought it would be best to say nothing and let you assume Papa was ill. We didn't know but what you'd tell someone, and the law would come and evict us all. But when you stayed and we got to know you, it was too late. We couldn't tell anyone then that he was dead. How would that look? It just got worse and worse the longer you stayed, even though we were thankful you came, and we. . .grew to love you." She hid her face then, sobbing uncontrollably.

"What you did was foolish, Sadie." It came out more harshly than he'd intended, and she jerked her chin up.

"Don't speak to me in that tone, sir, or I shall have to ask you to leave at once."

He took a deep breath. "No need. I was just leaving anyway."

He walked quickly over the knoll and through the orchard. The confusion in his mind was nearly as painful as the sorrow in his heart. He ought to be holding her in his arms this moment, but he couldn't make himself turn back. She had lied to him, not once, but many times. He'd thought he knew her, but apparently not.

Pax was still holding Pepper near the water trough, and Zeke stood with him, anxiously watching Harry approach.

"Mr. Harry, everythin' all right?" Zeke asked. Harry thought his grin was a little strained.

"Bring my saddle, please." Harry clipped out the words, and he could tell by the way Zeke's face fell that he knew the ruse was over.

"Yes, suh. Right away." Zeke hurried into the barn, and Pax stood staring at Harry with wide eyes.

"You leavin' us now, Mr. Harry?"

"Yes, Pax."

They stood in uneasy silence until Zeke came from the barn carrying Pepper's tack.

Zeke kept his eyes lowered. "Please don't go off in a tear, Mr. Harry. It started out all innocent. We didn't mean to—"

"Zeke, I've lived with you for more than a fortnight. We're as close as brothers, or so I thought. But you still don't trust me." Harry seized the saddle blanket and tossed it onto Pepper's back. Pepper snorted and sidestepped, and Harry placed his hand on the gelding's shoulder. "Easy now." If he didn't calm himself, Pepper would fidget all morning. He smoothed the blanket then gently settled the saddle over the withers.

"Just tell me, who buried Oliver?"

Zeke sniffed and kicked at a pebble. "I did, suh. I dug the grave. Then we all. . . It was hard for Miss Sadie, suh, but I made a box in the barn here, and we. . .we said some words and sung the doxology."

"You couldn't have got a few neighbors together to give him a respectful funeral?" Harry made himself stand still and breathe deeply. His anger was resurfacing.

Zeke glanced at Pax then said quietly, "We was afraid what would happen to Miss Sadie if people found out he was gone, suh."

"So Sadie told me. Did you expect to hide it forever?"

Zeke had no answer. He and Pax watched in silence as Harry tightened the cinch strap. He took the halter off Pepper and handed it to Pax then slipped the bridle over Pepper's ears. The bit slid into the horse's mouth, and Harry worked at the buckle. Pax stood twisting the lead rope in his hands.

"Mr. Harry, don't leave like this," Zeke pleaded.

"Oh, sure. I ought to go into the kitchen and have breakfast first with you all." Harry's laugh was bitter.

Zeke shook his head, and his shoulders drooped. "It's just a pity you came when you did."

Harry refused to consider that remark. He needed to get away from this oppressive place. Without another word, he mounted and pushed Pepper into an extended trot.

———

Sadie stumbled up the path to the dooryard. Zeke stood with his back to her, watching as Harry's horse trotted down the lane.

"Zeke," she called, and he turned toward her.

"Miss Sadie!"

"He knows, Zeke. Harry knows everything."

"I'm sorry—truly I am." His shoulders slumped. "I wanted to help you, Miss Sadie. When your pa died, I only wanted to protect you."

"I know." She put her hand to her forehead. "I'm so tired. I'm sure things will look better when we've had breakfast."

Zeke leaped to her side. "Let me take you inside. You need to sit."

She took his arm, and they turned toward the house. She could almost read her faithful servant's thoughts. Once again he had failed her. All his efforts to shield her from the consequences of her father's death had come to nothing. Perhaps he'd even hoped that he and Tallie had found a husband for her, a man who would love her and protect her from the legal entanglements brought on by this tragedy, a man they could serve with contentment and pride.

Suddenly Pax raced up from behind them. "Pa! Mr. Harry done forgot his mares! Let me go after him." He would have run for the barn, but Zeke grabbed the back of his shirt and held him in place.

"Pa, we gotta catch him. Let me ride after him." Pax squirmed out of Zeke's hold and turned to face him.

Zeke shook his head. "Let him go, boy. This ain't over."

"But them mares! He paid for 'em."

Zeke nodded with a grim smile. " 'Zactly. Mr. Harry needs to put some distance between us and him for a while, but he'll be back."

"I'm not so sure," Sadie said.

"Oh, he'll be back," Zeke insisted. "Meanwhile, we'll be prayin' that things will turn out right."

"Was he right about us lying, Pa? You said it wasn't lying."

Zeke sighed. "I been wrong about things before, son. Now you go and put Mr. Harry's mares out to grass for today then come for breakfast. I'll see Miss Sadie inside."

Sadie knew Zeke would catch it from Tallie as soon as she found out what had happened. She was certain he would rather stay down at the barn with Pax and let her break the news to his wife. But he held on to her firmly and squared his shoulders as they approached the lean-to.

"It's gonna be all right, Miss Sadie," he said just before opening the kitchen door for her.

"God will help us through this." She brushed away a tear, wondering if she could face Tallie without weeping.

Zeke nodded. "I'm powerful sorry I caused all this."

"It wasn't you. It was all of us. I should have known better. That first day, I should have told him everything and let whatever happened happen." She gulped for air and wiped her eyes again.

"I expect my wife will be hoppin' mad when Mr. Harry don't come to eat her special breakfast."

"I'm not sure I can eat, Zeke. Perhaps I'll go in the front door and up to my room."

Zeke sniffed. "I be very, very sorry, Miss Sadie."

She knew she couldn't leave him alone to broach the subject with Tallie.

Chapter 12

B y the time the farm was a mile behind him, Harry's blood had cooled to a simmer. It was early, and the day spread before him, empty and bleak. He rode automatically, letting Pepper choose his footing. Then, as the gelding clopped over a wooden bridge that spanned a placid stream, it struck him: He'd left his brood mares behind.

He pulled up for a moment and looked back. It was downright idiotic of him to forget them, but it had completely slipped his mind. Maybe he should turn around and ride back for them. He could be forty miles on the road by nightfall.

No, best go on to the little town ahead. He wasn't ready to face Sadie again, and he had a feeling he wasn't up to seeing Tallie just now either. Zeke might cringe and humble himself before Harry, but Tallie would do no such thing. She would do anything to protect her mistress; she'd proven that. She'd rake him over the coals but good, and somehow the whole calamity would wind up being Harry's fault. And maybe, in some way, it was.

He decided to take a room for the night in Winchester and see how things looked in the morning. After all, he did pay a large sum of money for those mares. He'd better go back and collect them or have his money back. He knew Sadie needed the money, and he did want the mares, so he'd have to go back. He couldn't see any other solution.

He rode on, ruminating on the events of the morning. Why had they lied to him? While Zeke's explanation made some sense, he still couldn't believe Sadie would go along with the deception. Had she truly been afraid of him?

Harry shook his head. The anger still glowed inside him. He'd have done anything for her. Anything! He'd been starting to dream of relocating his horse breeding operation to the Shenandoah Valley. There was no chance of that now. His heart cried, *I love you, Sadie! How could you not trust me?*

He took Pepper to the livery stable and ambled about the town. His wrath still stewed inside him, but it was less urgent now. By noon he didn't feel angry at all, unless he was angry with himself. He had handled the entire situation badly. His wrath dissipated and was replaced by a painful wound that throbbed every time his thoughts came near it.

As he wandered aimlessly down the dusty streets, he remembered that he'd missed breakfast and set about to find a place to eat. He didn't care if it was a late breakfast or an early dinner; he just wanted something filling. He found a boardinghouse that served meals to travelers, but they wouldn't serve luncheon for two hours yet. His stomach was growling by then, and he gave up and walked back to the inn on the main street. The hurt Sadie had inflicted on him had eased to a mournful sadness so long as he didn't think about her. When he did, it flared up and stabbed his heart once more.

Two men in tattered uniforms were leaving the inn. Their faces were hard, and the taller one glanced warily at him. Harry stepped aside to let them come down the steps and watched them as they started down the road on foot, the way he had come.

A wagon rumbled past, and Harry recognized the driver as the McEwans' neighbor, Mr. Kauffman. He raised his hand in greeting, but Mr. Kauffman didn't see him. Just as well, Harry thought. He didn't feel like having a neighborly visit and explaining why he was in town today.

The uniformed men hailed Mr. Kauffman as his wagon came abreast of them, and he pulled his team up. They talked for a few moments. Kauffman was nodding and gesturing toward the road up the valley. To Harry's surprise the two vagrants climbed into the back of the wagon and rode off with Mr. Kauffman.

Guess they prefer bouncing around in a wagon box to wearing out their shoe leather, Harry thought. He hoped Mr. Kauffman arrived home with his pocketbook intact.

He didn't relish the thought of eating the landlady's nondescript stew again, but by this time he was ravenous, so he turned resolutely toward the door of the inn.

———

"Sadie, baby, you got to eat somethin'." Tallie sighed when she got no response. She set the tray down on the small table beside her mistress's bed. "I brung you a good chicken soup now and fresh bread and apple tart. You need to nourish yourself, child. You gonna make yourself ill."

All morning Sadie had lain in bed. Occasionally Tallie had heard her weeping, but mostly there was a heavy silence throughout the house.

Tallie left the room in defeat and shuffled across the hall to open the door of Mr. Oliver's bedchamber. Time to get the room aired out and go through the master's things. She would begin cleaning in there this afternoon, and perhaps she could interest Sadie in sorting her father's papers and clothing.

She threw the windows open then went downstairs. When she entered the kitchen, Zeke and Pax peered at her silently.

Tallie shook her head. "She still won't eat."

Zeke sighed. "Maybe she'll perk up tomorrow."

"Mr. Harry will come back tomorrow, won't he, Pa?" Pax's earnest question demanded an answer, but Zeke only shrugged so the boy turned to Tallie. "Ma? Won't he?"

"I don't know, son. I didn't see Mr. Harry when he left, so I don't know how overset he was." She sent her husband an icy glare. "I wasn't there when the arsenal exploded, so to speak, unlike some people. I wasn't the one who let Mr. Harry gallop off in a fine pucker."

"He wasn't gallopin'," Zeke protested, "and he wasn't red-hot mad."

"Oh, you tellin' me he's not upset? Sure. That's why he wouldn't come in and eat my flapjacks." She picked up a big wooden spoon and began to stir the chicken broth.

"Well, he wasn't rantin'." Zeke avoided her scathing gaze.

"So Mr. Harry wasn't put out with you?"

Zeke shrugged. "I didn't say that. He just. . .well, he let me know I went down a notch or three in his respect."

Tallie frowned and shook the wooden spoon at him. "One more hour. One more hour, husband, and he would have rode out of here happy."

Zeke put his fists to his forehead. "I know. I know."

"If you ever tell a lie again, I'll. . .I'll. . ."

Zeke shot a sideways look at Pax and hissed, "Hush now, Tallie. The boy!"

"Is Miss Sadie gonna be all right?" Pax blinked at his mother, and she thought he was holding back tears.

"I don't know. Right now she's feelin' so guilty, she's just crushed. If she don't come out of this soon, she gonna get sick." Tallie set a bowl of hot soup before her husband and dipped up another for Pax.

"He'll come back, and when he does, we'll straighten everythin' out," Zeke said, but Tallie thought he lacked confidence.

When they had eaten and she had cleaned up the kitchen, she left Pax drying the dishes and went back upstairs. Sadie was sitting up in bed, sipping a spoonful of broth.

Relief flooded Tallie's heart, and she hurried to the bedside.

"There now! That's a good girl!"

"I knew you'd keep fussing at me if I didn't touch it." The listlessness in her voice still troubled Tallie, but they had made a beginning, and she felt sure Sadie would recover from her crisis.

Tallie pulled the rocking chair over and sat down. "Miss Sadie, you know the Lawd will forgive us if we ask Him to."

Sadie's face screwed up into a grimace. "I've asked Him and asked Him, Tallie, but I still feel guilty."

"There, there." Tallie patted the smooth skin of her forearm. "You got to stop blamin' yourself, child. It was me and Zeke more than you, especially Zeke. And we're all sorry. The Lawd knows it, and when we truly repent He stops rememberin' our foolishness, and we got to, too."

Sadie sniffed. "Thank you, Tallie. I know you're right, but I feel positively filthy. I never did anything like that before. Harry said I lied, and he was right. It was a black, putrid lie."

"Hush, hush. It's all forgiven now."

"But what are we going to do, Tallie? Nothing is solved."

"The Lawd knows, and that's what matters. When Mr. Harry comes back for his horses—"

"I don't want to see him if he does come back!"

Sadie's vehemence sent a wave of apprehension through Tallie. "Why not, child?"

"I can't. I can't look into his big, brown eyes ever again. He trusted us, Tallie, and we deceived him. I let him—" She bit her lip, and the tears started again. "I let him kiss me last night, Tallie, and he said he'd come back in the spring, and I let him go on thinking my father would see him then! It was wicked of me."

There was a timid tap on the door, and Tallie turned toward it. "What you want?"

Pax peeked in at them, his eyes wide in the dim light. "They a man at the door, Ma."

Tallie jumped up. "Is it Mr. Harry?"

Pax shook his head. "No, he all ragged, and he limps. I never saw him before."

Tallie took the bowl from Sadie's hands. "You stay put, and I'll send him away. Don't you worry none. I'll just get rid of this tramp. You rest now."

Sadie lay back on the pillow, and Tallie was satisfied. She went down the stairs with Pax close behind her.

"Where's your pa?" Tallie whispered to the boy.

"Yonder at the barn. He's cleanin' out."

Tallie saw that her son had left the door ajar, but no one was on the porch. "Where he go?" Pax whispered.

Tallie heard a step behind her and whirled toward the parlor door. A man stood in the doorway to the front room, peering at her. He had a thin, wolfish face, and Tallie's heart began to pound. She noted that his ragged jacket had a military cut, and the tarnished buttons looked official.

She felt like scolding him and tossing him right out, but a sudden thought stopped her. If he was from the army, he might have some word of Mr. Tenley.

She looked him up and down. He was sizing her up with the same shrewdness.

"What you want?" she asked, not bothering to pull out the courteous phrases Sadie's mother had taught her to use with guests.

"I'm here to see Mr. Oliver McEwan," the man replied.

Tallie looked into his eyes. She didn't like what she saw, but she didn't draw back. Her job of protecting Sadie was not done yet, and her caution took over. She straightened her shoulders. Before she had time to think, she opened her mouth.

"Mr. Oliver can't see you today, suh. He's been ill, and he's restin'."

Chapter 13

I appreciate you seeing me."

Sadie could smell the filthy man from six feet away. She tried not to let her nose wrinkle. She sat down in one of the parlor chairs and studied him. "I'm only seeing you because my maid said you'd been to Mexico City."

"That's right, miss. I was in the battle there a year ago." He shook his head. "Seems like another life."

"You. . .fought under General Scott?"

"Yes, miss, and a rough time we had of it."

Sadie nodded. "I didn't get your name."

"Mitchell." He paused. "Sergeant Dan Mitchell."

Sadie noted he wore the cotton summer uniform of the Dragoons, which had no doubt been white once but was now a grubby gray.

"And what brings you here, Sergeant Mitchell?"

"Why, young McEwan, of course."

Sadie swallowed hard. "You are speaking of my brother?"

"If Tenley McEwan was your brother, miss. If you don't mind my saying so, I see a resemblance. You must be Sadie."

It took her a moment to regain her composure. "You were acquainted with him?"

"Yes, ma'am."

She gestured toward a chair, and he seated himself. "What can you tell me about him?"

Mitchell leaned forward and frowned. "I know this is a difficult time for you, miss, but I wanted to meet your father. You see, Tenley told me all about him and this place before he. . .passed on."

Sadie caught her breath. "You were with him when he died?"

"Yes, I was. As a matter of fact, without me he might have been left lying on the battlefield and. . .well, he wasn't. I got him to the field hospital afterward. I made sure the doctor saw him, but. . .well, it wasn't enough in the end. I'm sorry. He was a fine young fellow."

Sadie came to a decision. She didn't like this man. He was dirty, he smelled of sweat and beer, and he had a shifty manner, but he had been with her dear brother during the chaotic last weeks of his life. She had lost so much so quickly that her grief left her feeling drained and empty. This man was offering her a glimpse of the void she had felt since Tenley went away to war almost two years ago. She wanted to learn everything she could about her brother's last days, and Dan Mitchell might be the only one who could enlighten her.

"Would you care to stay to dinner, Sergeant?"

A look of awe came over his face. "Why, miss, that's mighty gracious of you. I'd be honored if I weren't so scruffy. I'm afraid I don't have any proper clothes now."

Sadie stood. "My maid will bring you some things. You can bathe in the barn. We have a servant who will fix a bath for you there. I believe my late brother's things might fit you."

He was too smelly to continue the conversation as he was. She would give him dinner, but there she drew the line. She wouldn't have him upstairs in the house. She had no reason to trust him, but she would take a small risk to gain an insight into Tenley's death.

"Why, thank you, miss. And I'm sorry your father's not well."

She went to the hall, and he followed her. She called Pax and told him to take the guest to Zeke in the barn and then return for the clothes and linens Tallie would have ready. Tallie wouldn't like it, and Sadie couldn't blame her. She was a little afraid of Mitchell herself. But she knew that if she turned him away without hearing his story she would always regret it and wonder what he could have told her.

———

When Dan Mitchell appeared for dinner, Sadie was pleasantly surprised at the improvement in his appearance. A pang of loss struck her as she noted how well Tenley's clothes fit him. He was shorter than Harry and not so broad through the shoulders. His sandy hair was clean now, and he'd shaved.

Sadie had put on one of her nicer day dresses, knowing her guest would not be sporting evening wear. Tallie and Zeke served them in silence, watching the stranger's every move. Sadie knew Tallie had planted a rolling pin in the sideboard, and Zeke had concealed her father's pistol in a cupboard just inside the kitchen door. They had both scolded her for her hasty invitation.

The longer she conversed with Mitchell, the less she felt their caution was needed. It was true he was roughened by his years of harsh living in the army, but he seemed to have a rudimentary command of the manners acceptable in polite circles, and he was eager to please Sadie.

"I believe you said you helped my brother off the field of battle." As she handed him the plate of biscuits, Sadie was careful not to let any emotion creep into her voice.

"Yes, ma'am. I started to carry him. The carnage was awful that day when we attacked the *presidio*, as I'm sure you've heard. I saw Tenley go down, and I knew if I left him there, he'd either be hit again or he'd bleed to death. As soon as there was a lull in the shooting, I went to move him farther back where we had men to tend the wounded. But just as I hoisted him on my shoulder, I took a musket ball in my leg." Mitchell rubbed his thigh and frowned. "It was a terrible day, miss."

"How did you manage to escape?"

"Well, I went down, but I knew we both had to get out of there. Our troops were pulling back, and if we got left there, we'd be right in the line the Mexes were going to take to try and rout our forces. I decided it was do or die for me and Tenley. I picked him up and hobbled along after our detachment."

Sadie was silent for a moment, considering his tale. Was this man truly a compassionate war hero? "That's quite remarkable. My family owes you its deepest gratitude, Sergeant Mitchell."

He looked at her from hooded eyes. "That's partly why I'm here, Miss McEwan. I don't like to put it to you, but if your father is too ill to give me an audience, I suppose I'll have to put myself on your mercy."

"To what are you referring?" She stared at him with apprehension.

He smiled and tilted his head to one side, reaching for his water glass. "Your brother and I were very close, even before we got to the capital. We slept in the same tent for a while, and we swapped a lot of stories."

Zeke was standing in back of Mitchell near the kitchen door. He was scowling and shaking his head behind the soldier. Sadie ignored him.

"Before we went into that last big battle, he asked me to do him a favor," Mitchell went on. "It's not unusual. Lots of men write letters home before they go into battle or give last messages to their friends."

Sadie caught her breath. "Did Tenley write a letter to us? We received nothing."

"No, ma'am, I'm sorry. I didn't mean to raise your hopes like that. What he did was to ask me, if anything happened to him so's he didn't make it home, to visit his family here in Virginia and tell his father how it was at the end."

Sadie felt tears prick her eyes, but when she looked toward the sideboard and caught Tallie's eye, Tallie was frowning.

"I appreciate your making the journey here, sir," Sadie said. "Where are you from? It must have been an inconvenience for you to seek us out."

"Well, miss, I'm not really from anywhere. I was born in Connecticut, they tell me, but then my folks moved to Pennsylvania. After they died, I drifted around here and there, seeing the country and taking jobs where I could. I've been to Georgia, Ohio, and New Jersey, and everywhere in between. Then one day I joined the army, and, well, I got to see a lot more country." He shook his head ruefully. "This here is heaven compared to Mexico, I'll tell you. You don't want to plan a pleasure trip down there."

"The officer who wrote us said Tenley survived several weeks at the hospital in Mexico City."

"Yes, that's correct. At first I thought he'd get better, but he kept going downhill."

"You were close by and saw him while he was being nursed?"

"Yes, ma'am. I spent a few weeks in the hospital myself. It was a big building near the palace, and they'd commandeered it for medical purposes. You see, my wound got infected. The heat and bugs down there are awful, and I think more men died of sickness and infections than from their wounds."

Sadie felt slightly nauseous, and she raised her napkin to her lips. "I'm pleased you recovered," she murmured.

"Yes, well, while I was there I was able to see Tenley every day. He talked to me a lot before he got feverish."

She nodded expectantly, and he went on.

"Your brother told me a lot of things about his family, miss, and one thing he told me was how generous his father was."

Mitchell swabbed the gravy from his plate with half a biscuit and took a large bite. Sadie sipped her tea, grateful he was waiting until he finished chewing before continuing his story.

"The last time I saw him alive, he was in dire straits. He knew he wasn't going to make it."

Sadie winced but could not tell him to stop. She wanted to know everything, every scrap, no matter how painful the knowledge was.

"He told me. . ." Mitchell smiled at her suddenly. "He talked a lot about his daddy. He told me if I ever needed help, to find Oliver McEwan. He said his father would help out a friend of his son's."

He paused, apparently assigning great significance to these words. Sadie waited, certain there was more to come.

"If I ever needed a job or a loan or maybe a letter of reference, his father would help me out, he said."

"I see." She looked at Tallie and Zeke. Both were staring in disapproval at the back of Mitchell's head. "Zeke, perhaps you could serve us coffee in the parlor." Sadie rose, and Mitchell jumped up.

"That sounds lovely, Miss McEwan. Might I be so bold as to ask if you can offer anything stronger?"

She stared at him in embarrassed shock. His manners were less polished than she'd thought.

He added hastily, "My wound, you know. It bothers me some."

"We do not keep spirits in the house, sir. Now, if you would excuse me for a moment, Zeke will show you to the parlor."

Sadie pushed through the door to the kitchen and waited for Tallie to join her.

"You got to get that fellow out of here," were Tallie's first words as she entered carrying two serving dishes. "It's plain he wants more than a fine dinner and some of your brother's cast-off clothes."

"That's unkind, Tallie," Sadie said. She looked toward the window and saw that it was nearly full dark outside. "It's getting late."

"Yes, but—" Tallie set the dishes down and placed her hands on her hips. "You not thinkin' of lettin' him stay here tonight?"

Sadie shrugged. "I don't like him, but he was kind to Tenley when he needed help."

"Maybe he was and maybe he wasn't."

"What do you mean?"

"You want my opinion? Anybody could say someone told them such and such, just to make folks feel sympathy."

"But he obviously knew Tenley. He knew my name."

"Oh, and he couldn't pry that out of the person who told him where the house was?"

Sadie frowned. She felt a strong discomfort in Mitchell's presence, but she didn't like Tallie implying she was naive. "You're too skeptical, Tallie. He's a veteran who needs a boost."

"Humph! He's a bad egg what needs a kick in the pants. He wants your papa to give him a job, that or some money."

"You may be right, but what can I do? I wasn't the one who told him Papa was ill now, was I?"

"No, but it's a good thing I was the one to see him first. If you'd blurted out the truth with this one, he'd have seen a golden opportunity, and I mean golden. He'd be calculatin' how to get this property away from a simple little orphan girl. Right now he's just expectin' a little silver."

"That's enough, Tallie."

Zeke entered the kitchen just then, and Tallie pounced on him.

"What you want to leave that grifter alone in the parlor for? He'll be pocketin' Miss Sadie's valuables."

"He asked me to get his coffee right away."

"I just bet he did," Tallie said. "He wants a chance to look things over again."

"All right, I'll go tell him you're gettin' it." Zeke pushed the door open.

"Wait, Zeke!" Sadie held herself tall. "I would like Sergeant Mitchell to stay at your house tonight."

"What? No! That bum? He's not sleepin' in my cabin."

"But I thought—well, I can't have him here under the circumstances," Sadie faltered. "I thought perhaps he could stay with you one night. You know, like Harry Cooper did."

Zeke shook his head. "Don't go comparin' that man and Mr. Harry, Miss

Sadie. The answer is no, no, and no."

Zeke left the kitchen, and Sadie stared after him. "Well then, I guess he'll have to have Tenley's room."

"No, Miss Sadie!" Tallie cried. "Listen to me. That man is no good. Zeke brought his dirty uniform up for me to wash, and he said, 'that's not any officer's uniform.' He's right. There's no sergeant stripes on it, and I can't see where there ever has been. Don't you let him stay here."

"Perhaps he lost his original uniform while he was in the hospital," Sadie said.

"Oh, and perhaps General Scott slept in the tent with his men, too, and played cards with them."

"Just one night," Sadie said, setting two china cups on a tray.

"Rubbish." Tallie wagged her finger under Sadie's nose. "You just pinin' for Mr. Harry, and you all wrathy because he left so sudden. That's no reason to bring a shiftless stranger into the house."

"I'll take the coffee in. You see that his room is ready." Sadie picked up the tray.

"No. You can't do that." Tallie scurried around the worktable and tried to beat her to the door, but Sadie was too quick.

"I'm doing it," Sadie said.

"Then I have to sleep up here with you. Can't let no vagrant stay here with you unchaperoned."

"Fine." Already Sadie regretted her impulsiveness, but she was too stubborn to admit when she was wrong. Tallie's remark about Harry hit close to home. Her heart was aching, and this diversion had taken her mind off it. Well, she would send Mitchell away right after breakfast.

Sadie woke and lay still for a moment. Moonlight shone in through her window, but it wasn't near dawn yet. She sat up and listened. Was that a step she'd heard? Too early for Tallie to be starting breakfast.

Another stealthy sound drew her attention. It sounded like the front door closing softly. She rose and tiptoed to the window, standing to the side and peering down into the yard.

It's nothing, she told herself. *Lord, calm my heart and let me rest.* She couldn't help but add, *And please let Harry forgive us, Lord! Give him peace, too.*

She still found it hard to believe Tallie's admission that she had continued the lie. She had told Mitchell that Papa was sick. How many tongue-lashings had she given Zeke for that very thing?

Sadie went back to bed and tossed fitfully, thinking about Harry and all the things they'd told him that couldn't be unsaid. At last her thoughts grew fuzzy with sleep.

Chapter 14

Harry left his garret room at the inn and went down the two flights of stairs to the dining room. Breakfast here was better than the dinner fare. He was served a high stack of flapjacks with sorghum, fried sausage, applesauce, and plenty of hot, strong coffee.

"You heading out today, Cooper?" the landlord asked when he pushed back his chair.

"I believe I will, sir."

The landlord nodded. "Good. I could rent your room three times over tonight."

"Something happening in town?" Harry asked.

"The traveling preacher pulled in yesterday. He's holding services today, and lots of folks will come in from the countryside."

Harry wondered if Sadie knew about this. If she did, she would probably come to Winchester to worship.

"Guess I lost track of the days," he said, trying to count them off mentally.

"It's Sunday all right," the landlord told him. "We take the parson whenever we can get him, though. Sometimes we have church on Friday or Tuesday. Folks stop their work and come."

Harry nodded. It was almost three months since he'd had the opportunity to attend a church service, and he felt a sudden longing to drink in God's Word. And this preacher knew the McEwan family. Harry might get a chance to talk to him. It wouldn't hurt him to stop over a day and let the dust settle between him and the McEwan farm.

"Where is the church service to be held?" he asked.

The landlord smiled. "At the schoolhouse."

"I think I'll stay until tomorrow, take a day of rest, and attend the service," Harry said.

The landlord's smile drooped. "As you wish. You're welcome."

"You won't lose money if I keep my room, will you?"

"Well, I suppose not. Not too much."

"What, you'd squeeze five or six people in that little closet?"

The landlord shrugged. "I might put a family with kids up there."

Harry thought that over for about a half second. "Well, I tell you what. If you can serve me breakfast again for supper tonight, I'll pay you extra."

"Oh, I don't know, sir. Mrs. Ferguson doesn't like to make special orders at dinnertime. It's too busy in the kitchen."

"Isn't it busy in the kitchen now?"

"Well, yes, sir, but the hired girls, Bessie and Emma, fix breakfast. My wife does lunch and dinner."

Harry reached into his pocket and produced a silver dollar. "Well, I'm paying for my room and tomorrow's breakfast in advance, and when I come back tonight there'd better not be any drunks or kids in my bed."

Mr. Ferguson nodded. "Yes, sir, and I'll tell Bessie you're partial to her flapjacks."

When Sadie descended to the kitchen on Sunday morning, Tallie was preparing a breakfast tray.

"Is that for me?" Sadie asked. "I'm up."

"No." Tallie did not look up from her work but arranged the plate of bacon, eggs, and fried potatoes with painstaking care. "This is for your friend, Sergeant Mitchell. He can't come down for breakfast this mornin'. It's his leg, you know. It bothers him sometimes."

Sadie watched her with growing dismay. "Well, he was wounded in battle."

"Is that so? I never would have guessed it, but then I didn't have to. He's told me a hundred times in the last twelve hours." Tallie poured out a mug of tea for the tray.

Sadie wished she hadn't come downstairs. Tallie had lavished love on her since she was born, and Sadie knew she only wanted the best for her. Realizing she had been foolish in allowing Mitchell to stay overnight made it worse.

"He's making extra work for you, isn't he? Here, I'll take the tray up."

Tallie's back straightened, and she slapped at Sadie's hand. "Don't you touch that. You aren't going near that man's bedroom."

Sadie pulled away and twisted her hands together. "I'm sorry. You shouldn't have to wait on him."

"Not goin' to. I'll get Zeke to take the tray up as soon as he's in from the barn. Of course, the sergeant may object to his breakfast being served by a man who smells like the stable, but it'll be good for him to know that's part of life on a farm."

"He can't think we're rich, Tallie. This place is comfortable, but it's not like the grand places over near Richmond."

"I can't say what Sergeant Mitchell thinks, but I don't suppose it's anything good."

Harry enjoyed the church service. He joined in with the others, singing hymns he had learned as a boy. Pastor Richards was of middle age, but robust and passionate. His sermon focused on God's holiness, and his message touched Harry's heart.

At the end of the service, the pastor announced that worship would reconvene at two o'clock. Folks brought lunches from their wagons and spread blankets on the grass in the schoolyard for a picnic.

Harry walked over to the boardinghouse for lunch then returned to the schoolyard. He spotted the pastor eating dessert with a family under the trees. When Pastor Richards rose and drifted toward another group, Harry walked over to him.

The pastor smiled and paused to talk to him, and Harry gave him a brief description of his background and the business that had brought him to the area.

"I've known Oliver McEwan for many years," Richards told Harry. "He's a fine man, and you can't do better than his horses. I was hoping to see him here today."

"Well, sir. . ." Harry stopped, wondering how much he should reveal. Since several families were within earshot, he decided it was not his place to break the news.

The pastor said with a frown, "Mr. McEwan wasn't well the last time I passed through. I hope he's not worse."

"Perhaps you could visit the family if you have time," Harry suggested.

"Yes, I think I can do that. He lost his son recently and was taking it quite hard when I saw him a month ago."

Harry nodded. "It would be a good thing for Miss Sadie if you could stop by and encourage her, I think. She's having some trouble handling her grief."

"I'll do it. Thank you, Mr. Cooper. It may be a day or two before I get out there, but I plan to stay with the Clarks until at least Wednesday. I'll be visiting folks in the area, and we'll hold another service Tuesday evening. I understand I've a wedding to perform, as well."

"They keep you busy when you come this way, sir?"

"Oh, indeed they do. My parish is large and scattered, Mr. Cooper, but I love serving the people."

The afternoon service gripped Harry's heart even more than the morning sermon had. When the pastor spoke of repentance and forgiveness, Harry at first thought about Sadie, Zeke, and Tallie, and the lies they had told him. He prayed silently that they would seek God's forgiveness. But soon his thoughts turned inward, and he recognized his own anger and self-righteousness. He was not only in need of forgiveness; he had been unforgiving.

When the pastor closed the service, Harry slipped away and walked toward the river. He found a secluded spot beneath a large willow and dropped to his knees. *Lord, please take away all my selfishness and pride. Show me how to help Sadie.*

After a long time, he rose and headed back toward the inn. The sun was low over the mountains to the west, casting long shadows on the road. When he entered the dining room, Mr. Ferguson approached him with a smile.

"Glad to see you, Mr. Cooper. Bessie's husband let her come back after church to fix your supper. Or should I say breakfast?"

Harry grinned. "I'm obliged. If you don't mind, I'd like to meet Bessie."

"I guess she can spare half a minute. You want to wash up before you eat?" Harry nodded.

"You wait here," Ferguson said.

A minute later a thin young woman came from the kitchen carrying a steaming pitcher.

"You Mr. Cooper?" she asked, approaching Harry.

He smiled at her. Her huge apron enveloped her like a shroud. She must have borrowed one from Mrs. Ferguson. "Thank you for coming back to work just for me. I didn't mean to take you away from your family on the Lord's Day."

Bessie smiled as she held out the pitcher of water. "My Joe says I make the best flapjacks in Virginia. To hear him tell it, that's why he married me."

Harry chuckled and reached into his pocket. "Is Mr. Ferguson paying you extra?"

"My regular wage, sir, but don't you worry none."

Harry slipped a coin into her hand. "That's for you, not the boss."

Her eyes widened. "You don't need to pay for your supper twice, sir."

"Consider it a tax on my selfishness. Reverend Richards and the Lord have been working on me this afternoon." Harry took the pitcher from her.

Bessie's warm smile rewarded him. "Thank you, sir. Wasn't the service wonderful? Your plate will be ready in five minutes."

Harry went up the stairs as quickly as he could without spilling the water. Again he wished he was dining at the McEwan table tonight, and Tallie's cooking was only a small part of his longing.

Lord, take care of Sadie tonight. Ease her sorrow, and please, if You don't mind, I'm asking You to prepare her to let me take care of her.

Tallie trudged up the stairs with an early supper tray. Might as well feed the voracious visitor before the others came in for their supper. All this stair climbing was wearing her out. She missed Sadie's help in the kitchen this evening, but Zeke had gotten behind in the barn chores. Even though it was Sunday, Sadie had put on her old gray dress and gone down to help him and Pax tend the horses.

Tallie didn't like it one bit when her mistress worked like a field hand. Maybe they should send Pax to his brother's house in the morning. If Ephraim could give them a few days' work now, it would be a big help. Of course, they needed to straighten out this business of Mr. Oliver's death before too many people came around. If only Sergeant Mitchell would leave!

She reached the landing and paused for breath before heading for Tenley's old bedroom. They had put just the barest of furnishings back in there as the wall repairs were not completed. *Besides,* she thought, *no sense making the stranger too comfortable.*

The door was open, and she stopped just outside it. "Mr. Mitchell? Got your supper here."

There was no response, and she cautiously peeked around the doorjamb. The bed was empty.

Tallie's heart skipped a beat. She walked into the bedroom and took a good look around to be sure. She set the tray on the stand next to the bed. He must have decided to make a trip out back to the necessary, but if so, she ought to have heard him go down the stairs.

She hurried back into the hallway. As she reached the top of the stairs a muffled sound reached her, and she froze. Someone was in Mr. Oliver's bedroom.

Chapter 15

W hat are you doin' in here?"

Mitchell quickly shut the top dresser drawer and faced her. He was fully clothed, and he looked fit to her.

"Well now, it's Tallie, the efficient cook-housemaid. I was just looking for some company. Got lonesome down at the other end of the house and thought maybe Mr. McEwan was as bored as I was. Thought we could have a game of checkers maybe. But it seems Mr. McEwan stepped out." His feral smile made Tallie shiver.

"You nothin' but trouble. You git out of here!" She stepped aside, indicating that he should avail himself of the open door.

"Here now, is that any way to talk to your master's guest?"

"What do you know about it?"

"I know plenty. I know no one's living in this room. Somebody's been sorting through Mr. McEwan's things." Mitchell nodded toward the bed where Tallie had spread out piles of clothing she removed from the wardrobe, hoping Sadie would go through them tomorrow. He ran a finger along the edge of the dresser and looked at it critically. "Dust, too. For shame, Tallie. You haven't been doing your job. Letting the patient's room get all dusty. I've been listening, too. No one took Mr. McEwan a tray all day. I thought the poor man was starving, but now I see it's worse than that."

Tallie shifted her weight, making herself stare back at him. "You don't know what you're talkin' about. Now go on out of here."

He smiled and walked past her into the hallway. Tallie leaned against the door and took a deep breath. She looked about the room, wondering if he had stolen any of Mr. Oliver's things. She couldn't tell without making a careful examination. *I'll come up after dinner,* she decided. She closed the door.

Mitchell had stopped in the hallway near the top of the stairs. Tallie heard Sadie's surprised voice.

"Why, Sergeant Mitchell, you're up and about. That's good news. Your leg must be better."

"Yes, ma'am, it is," he said smoothly. "I was just casting about for some company."

Tallie strode up to stand near Mitchell. "He been snoopin' in your father's room, Miss Sadie."

A look of fear crossed Sadie's face. "What—" She stared at Mitchell.

Tallie said, "I was gonna tell him Mr. Oliver is gone, but he got no manners."

Mitchell smiled. "Oh, he's gone, all right."

Sadie swallowed hard. "If your leg is so much better, Sergeant Mitchell, I expect you are able to leave us."

"Well, miss, it's a trifle better, but I wouldn't want to try to walk five miles into town on it tonight."

Sadie hesitated, and Tallie tried to think of a solution. *Don't give in,* she thought, and she tried to send semaphore to that effect in Sadie's direction with her eyes.

"Fine," Sadie said. "Our man, Zeke, can drive you to Winchester in the morning."

"I'd be grateful, miss. And I do regret not being able to see your father. My condolences. I'll see you at dinner." He turned toward his room.

"I done put your supper tray by your bed," Tallie called.

He smiled at her then looked at Sadie. "That's very kind, but I feel well enough to get to the dining room this evening."

Tallie scowled at Sadie, but Sadie merely said, "Then I shall see you in thirty minutes, sir."

———

Tallie followed Sadie to the door of her room.

"Please, Tallie, I need a few minutes alone."

"I was just goin' to help you get changed, Miss Sadie."

"Send Pax up with some hot water. I can do for myself. When I'm dressed, I'll come down to the kitchen, and we can discuss this."

"Yes'm." Tallie faded back behind her, and Sadie entered the sanctuary of her bedroom. Had Mitchell sneaked in here, as well? Had he looked at her personal things, handled her clothing, books, and stationery? She looked around carefully and decided he had not. Not a thing was out of place, so far as she could tell. She had left a silver dollar and two nickels in plain view on her secretary, along with a silver pen and some stamps. If Mitchell had been in here and his purposes were as nefarious as Tallie and Zeke indicated, he surely would have pilfered the coins.

Pax knocked at the door and delivered her hot water. Sadie hastily washed and changed into her blue dress. She brushed her hair smooth and took a moment before the mirror to check her appearance. How she wished Harry were here, preparing to meet her for dinner! How could she have been so foolish as to deceive him and drive him away? If he'd been present when Mitchell arrived, no doubt he'd have run him off immediately.

She wished she didn't have to face the sergeant over the dinner table. He made her nervous, and apparently he saw through Tallie's attempt to continue the fiction that her father was alive. Mitchell wasn't a large man, but he seemed fit and agile. She doubted he would attempt to harm any of them physically, but his implications put her on edge. He had made himself charming last night. She hoped he would again be on his best behavior tonight. At any rate, she'd be glad when he was out of the house.

When she entered the kitchen, Zeke and Pax were seated at the table eating their supper. Sadie knew Pax would start washing the dishes afterward while Zeke and Tallie waited on her and Mitchell. It was the dinnertime routine of the household.

"I wish he was gone," she blurted. "I wish I was eating in here with you all tonight!"

"There now," Tallie said. "He be leavin' in the mornin'. Then we'll get back to rights."

Pax stared at her. "You look fine, Miss Sadie, but your face is as white as Mama's apron."

"Thank you, Pax. It gave me a start to see Sergeant Mitchell looking so. . . healthy."

"Healthy and active," Tallie said as she lifted the fried chicken pieces onto a platter. "He was making free of the house, and that ain't right. I don't believe his leg was botherin' him. In fact—" She shook her long-handled fork at Sadie. "In fact, I don't believe he ever was wounded. He made that up for sympathy and for an excuse to stay longer."

Sadie grimaced, ruing her gullibility. "He does look spry this evening."

"That's right," said Tallie. "This mornin' he claimed he couldn't get down the stairs 'cause he hurt so bad, but now he's right as a trivet."

"It must have been all the exercise he put in last night that made him sore," Zeke said, sipping his tea.

Sadie frowned at him. "What do you mean?"

"Nothin' except the little stroll your guest took last night—or should I say this mornin'? It was past midnight, after all."

Sadie remembered her restlessness in the night and wondered if Mitchell's movements had wakened her. She stared at Zeke, but he wouldn't look back, so she walked over to the table and stood directly across from him. Pax looked up at her in surprise.

"If you know something I should know, Zeke, you'd best tell me now." Sadie tapped her foot impatiently.

Zeke wiped his mouth with his sleeve and finally met her gaze. "I don't know nothin', Miss Sadie. I just saw your friend leave the house last night, and it didn't look to me like his leg was botherin' him then, not one little bit. He wasn't favorin' it in the least."

"Where did he go?"

Zeke shrugged. "He started down the lane then took off into the woods. Your guess is as good as mine."

Sadie took three deep, controlled breaths.

"I've asked him to leave in the morning. As a matter of fact, Zeke, I told him you'd drive him to town."

"I'll do what you say, Miss Sadie, but I don't think that tramp is helpless. He takes on about his leg painin' him so, and that makes folks cater to him." Zeke lifted his teacup.

"Should I march upstairs and demand that he vacate the premises immediately?"

"Do it!" Tallie cried.

Zeke shook his head. "Let's not give him any reason to be huffy with us. You've been nothin' but gracious, Miss Sadie. If I take him to town in the mornin', we'll be sure he gets there, and he can't say we weren't polite to him."

Sadie nodded slowly. "All right then. First thing after breakfast."

———

Mitchell poured on the charm at dinner, but Sadie wasn't receptive this time. When he hinted that she might hire him to help with the farmwork, since she seemed a little short on manpower these days, she bristled.

"Excuse me, Sergeant. I'm very fatigued. Zeke will bring you coffee."

Mitchell jumped up as she rose. "Wait! Aren't we going to sit in the parlor? I thought I'd tell you more about Tenley. Maybe you'd like to hear about how we marched across the desert for weeks, chasing Santa Anna."

Sadie shook her head. "I believe I've heard enough. I hope you'll have a good journey in the morning. Zeke is having an early breakfast and leaving for town immediately afterward. Good-bye, Sergeant Mitchell."

She swept around, hoops and all, and glided through the door and up the stairs. When she reached her room she closed the door behind her and exhaled. She hoped Tallie would come up soon to unlace her corset. She ought to go and help with the kitchen work, but it seemed beyond her strength tonight. She wanted to be alone and safe in her room. She didn't have her father, and she didn't have Harry, but she had God with her always, and she would enjoy His company tonight.

She untied the waist of her crinoline and dropped the awkward skirt hoops, stepped out over them and sat down in her rocker. She sat deep in thought for several minutes then reached for her Bible. Only one person could show her what best to do now, and she would listen to Him.

A half hour later she heard Mitchell's heavy, uneven steps on the stairs. It was nearly as long again before Tallie came to help her undress, and Sadie noted how slow her steps were.

"You're working too hard, Tallie."

"Just doin' my job."

"No, you're doing the work of three people. I should have stayed downstairs to help you with the kitchen work."

"I'll be fine as soon as we get that baggage out of your brother's room. But you can help me make jelly tomorrow. Pax tells me the grapes are just right."

Sadie smiled. "I'll do that."

Tallie untied the corset laces, and Sadie shrugged out of it and into her warm flannel nightgown. "You could sleep in Papa's room now," Sadie said.

"You afraid to be up here alone with him?"

"No, it's not that. I just thought you might be more comfortable than in that little cot you have in the pantry."

Tallie sighed. "If the truth be told, I'd be more comfortable in my own bed, but I couldn't never sleep in the master's room. But I don't like you bein' up here with him."

"We could put a cot here in my room for you," Sadie suggested.

Tallie frowned. "Not tonight, we can't. Zeke's gone down to the cabin. You just lock your door tight, you hear me?"

"I will."

Tallie sighed. "What we gonna do, Miss Sadie? After he's gone, I mean. We can't have you rattlin' around in this house alone every night, but Zeke won't put up with this arrangement forever."

"I don't know. I did think perhaps Ephraim and Dulcy might come stay here and help us."

"Eph won't want to give up his blacksmithin' business."

"I know. Maybe we could let him build a cabin here. They're renting where they live now. If they'd live on McEwan land, I'd give him free rent just for the security, and his smithing customers could come here. It's only a few miles from where he is now, and folks will travel a long ways for a good blacksmith."

"Maybe," Tallie said with a yawn. "But Dulcy wouldn't be sleepin' here in the big house, and you know you can't afford to pay much extra help right now."

Sadie frowned and sat down on the edge of her bed. "We need to clear things up about the title to the land. If I can own the farm outright, we can make a go of it, Tallie. I know we can, even if we have to hire more help. Zeke is smart when it comes to horses. I know Papa wasn't too happy with Clipper's prospects, but there's that yearling colt, the one Papa called Smidge. Harry was impressed with his conformation. If Smidge turns out as well as we think he might, I'd have the stallion we need, and we could expand our breeding operation in a couple of years."

"Hush now," said Tallie. "It's not proper for you to talk about those things. You ought not to say *stallion*."

Sadie giggled. "All right then, *gentleman horse.*"

There was a moment's silence as Tallie began to brush her mistress's hair. Her touch was gentle, and Sadie felt the tension drain out of her.

"Mr. Harry knows about things like that," Tallie said. "Maybe if he comes back, you can have Zeke ask him for some advice."

Sadie felt a lump in her throat. "I don't think he's coming back, Tallie. He's had all day yesterday and today. He's probably halfway to Kentucky by now."

"He left those mares."

Sadie turned and looked up at Tallie. "What if he never comes back? Even worse, what if he writes and asks for his money? You know I can't pay it back."

Tallie was silent for a moment. "You been prayin', child?"

Sadie was humbled by her simple question. "Yes. When I pray I get to thinking everything will turn out all right, but afterward I forget, and I get to worrying again. Tallie, I can't count on Harry's goodness. Men fail you. Even the Bible says so. And I failed him so badly, I don't blame him."

"Yes, men do fail you on occasion, but the Bible also tells you not to fret."

Sadie inhaled slowly. "Tallie, will you pray with me now?" She grasped her cook's hand and pulled her down on the quilt beside her. They murmured their petitions quietly. Tears rolled freely down Sadie's face as she prayed.

"And help me to trust You more and to quit worrying so about Harry and the property and everything, Father. In Jesus' name—" She heard a thud, seemingly from below them. "Amen," she said quickly. "Did you hear that, Tallie?"

"I heard it. My menfolk left the house a half an hour ago."

They both stood up. Sadie fumbled for her dressing gown.

"You can't go downstairs like that," Tallie chided.

Sadie hesitated then grabbed her gray housedress. "We could be robbed blind in the time it takes to do all these buttons," she muttered.

"Let me take a quick look. It's probably just Zeke checkin' on things." Tallie lit a candle from the flame of the oil lamp and headed for the door.

"I'm coming, too." Sadie grabbed the poker that hung beside the hearth. She rarely had a fire in her bedroom fireplace, but the small poker Tallie's son Ephraim had made for her seemed the perfect size for a defensive weapon.

"Watch out," Tallie hissed. "You gonna get soot all over your clothes."

"Well, Zeke took Papa's pistol down to the kitchen yesterday. We don't have anything else."

Tallie said no more but tiptoed into the hall carrying the candle.

When they reached the top of the stairs she stopped, and Sadie pushed in beside her, staring downward. Light came from the parlor doorway, and they could hear low voices. Tallie blew out her candle, and they stood listening.

"No, don't bother with that," Mitchell said distinctly. Another male voice answered, but Sadie couldn't make out what he said.

Sadie started down the stairs.

"Come back here!" Tallie whispered. "Where you goin'?"

Sadie stopped with one hand on the balustrade, looking up at her. "I'm not going to stand by and let my home be ransacked under my nose."

"You ain't even fully dressed, child."

Sadie gave a soundless laugh. "I have to wear a corset to confront a thief?"

She hurried down the steps and to the door of the parlor. The small oil lamp was burning on her father's desk, illuminating Dan Mitchell and another man. Mitchell was wearing the clothes she had given him, and the other man was dressed much as the sergeant had been on his arrival. He was larger, and the side of his face was scarred. In one hand he held a bulging cotton pillowcase, one Sadie recognized as having been on Mitchell's bed. Many years ago her mother had embroidered it with magnolias. The idea of the filthy robber carrying off her mother's delicate work enraged Sadie.

"You want these doodads?" the man nodded toward the porcelain figurines on the mantelpiece.

"Yes, but be careful not to break them," Mitchell said. "Those knickknacks can be valuable. There's a lot of stuff upstairs. I got what cash I could find before I was interrupted, but I saw a rifle and a store of lead balls in the old man's room and a couple of knives, besides a pocket watch and a fine painting. I expect the girl has jewelry, too."

"We'll get those after," the second man said.

"You'll do no such thing." Sadie stepped into the room.

Chapter 16

Mitchell whirled, and both men stared at her.

"Well, now, if it isn't the lady of the house," Mitchell said, smiling as he stepped toward her.

"Stay back." Sadie brandished the poker and held her ground. Her heart raced as she met the sergeant's malevolent glare.

Mitchell laughed. "My, oh, my, we are fierce."

"You didn't tell me she was a firebrand," the big man said. One step and he was so close that, before Sadie could swing the poker, he had it in his hands and twisted it, wrenching it away from her. He tossed it to Mitchell and jerked Sadie around so that her back was to him, and she felt something sharp at her throat.

"All right, Miss McEwan." Mitchell smiled and paced before her as the larger man held her. "Moe doesn't want to hurt you. Just tell us where the family fortune lies, and we'll be gone."

Sadie stared at him, too terrified to squeak. *Family fortune,* she thought. *Either Tenley painted a very rosy picture of our life to this fellow, or he's gotten the impression somewhere else.* It was true her father had a large piece of land with prime river frontage. The house was adequate, but not opulent. The horses were the finest, but that was because her father had spent many years working hard to build up his breeding stock.

The man holding her squeezed her until she could barely breathe. "Where's the money?" he croaked in her ear.

Sadie struggled to turn her head away. The stench of his breath was sickening, and his body odor made her feel ill. She hated the way he held her so tightly.

"Let me go," she whispered. "I don't have any money."

Mitchell laughed. "I heard the slave boy say you sold several horses a week or so ago. Where's the cash? There's got to be more than we've found lying around."

Sadie held perfectly still, trying not to visualize the carved pine jewel box on her dresser. In it lay the money she had left after buying the lumber and new windows. She had hoped to purchase winter supplies with it. Of course, they would find it sooner or later.

"Where is it?" Moe snarled in her ear.

Sadie gulped for air and managed to gasp, "He's not a slave."

"Oh, that's right. Your brother told me his grandpa was a soft touch and freed them all." Mitchell came close and leaned toward her. "He also told me your old man was well-fixed. The sooner you tell us, the sooner we'll be gone."

"Tenley wouldn't—" Sadie broke off as Mitchell raised his hand.

He's going to strike me! She tried to pull back, but that meant leaning closer to Moe. She sobbed at her own helplessness and fear.

"Hold it, mister!"

Both men turned in surprise to the doorway. Tallie stood there in suppressed fury, and in her hands was Oliver's old pistol.

There was an instant of silence; then Mitchell laughed.

"Tallie, Tallie, Tallie. Don't expect me to believe that thing is loaded." He started to step toward her, and the pistol fired with a deafening roar that made Sadie's ears ring. One of the new windowpanes shattered. They all stood staring at Tallie; then Mitchell smiled.

"Well done, Tallie. Now we know how serious you are about protecting your mistress. We also know the chamber is empty now. Give me that thing." He stepped forward and took the gun from Tallie's nerveless hand. "These old pistols." He shook his head as he examined it. "Single shot. Not much good once you've fired it."

Sadie caught Tallie's eye, hoping to see some reassurance there. Had she awakened Zeke and Pax, or had she only had time to go to the kitchen for the pistol? Tallie's eyes were dull with despair. Sadie refused to let herself give up hope. Maybe Zeke had heard the gun's report.

"What are you going to do with us?" she asked.

Mitchell looked up. "You got more ammo for this?"

Sadie and Tallie kept quiet, and he laughed. "Right. You know, Moe and I aren't murderers, which is more than I can say for you, Tallie. You'd have blown my head off with glee if you could've held your hands steady."

Moe let out a guffaw, and Sadie renewed her struggle. His grip tightened, and she hated having his hands on her.

"Easy now," Mitchell said. He gestured toward the door. "Ladies, upstairs, please."

"You want them in the heiress's bedroom?" Moe asked, allowing Sadie to precede him into the hallway.

"No, put them in the room where I've been staying." Mitchell came behind them, carrying the lamp. "We know there's nothing worthwhile in there. It will keep them out of our way while we finish our work."

Sadie thought of making a break for the front door, but Moe placed his hulk of a body between her and freedom. He cut the air before him with his knife and said, "Go on now. Get up those stairs."

Sadie and Tallie went up in silence. Mitchell herded them into his bedchamber and took a quick look around. "I think they'll be secure here, Moe, but let's be quick."

He took the key from the inside of the keyhole, and the two men went out.

It was dark when they closed the door. Sadie heard the click of the key in the lock. Her knees went weak all of a sudden, and she felt for the edge of the bed and sank down on it.

"Tallie, we'd best pray."

"That's right," Tallie said, walking to the window. "But we'd best be thinkin' while we pray."

"Do you think Zeke will help us?"

"Can't count on it. If he was still up, he'd hear that pistol shot for certain. If not...well, when that man is out, he's out."

Sadie nodded in misery. "He said he didn't sleep well last night so he was tired tonight. He's probably down there in the cabin, snoring away."

"Sawin' logs," Tallie agreed. "So it's up to us."

Sadie joined her at the window. "Too bad they finished the outside work and took the ladder down."

Tallie grunted. "I be too wide to get through this window anyway. I'd bust the nice frame Mr. Harry made. But you now..." She turned to Sadie. "You can get out the window. I'll help you."

Alarm shot through Sadie as she eyed the window casement. "But there's no ladder."

"Bedsheets. Good, sturdy, linen bedsheets. Come on. We'll tie them together. Hurry up. Those men won't stick around long, and we want to put Zeke onto them before they get away with everythin' you own."

"Do you think Zeke can stop them any more than we did? I don't want anyone to get hurt."

"I don't know if he can or not, but my man has a strange habit of thinkin' when he needs to. Sometimes you'd guess he didn't have a brain in his head, but when he wants, he can be smart as a steel trap."

Sadie sobbed as she yanked the comforter off the bed. "Tallie, I left all the money Harry gave me in my jewel box. They've probably found it by now."

"Well, we can't help that." Tallie knotted two corners of the sheets together. "You think this will be long enough, or should we tear them in two?"

"Don't do that! Linen sheets don't grow on trees, you know. I can jump the last bit, if I need to."

"All right, but you be careful! Remember all the glass that was under the ladder? I think Zeke got most of it, but they might be a few pieces left."

Sadie stared at the window. "I can't go out that one, Tallie. It's right above the front parlor window. Those hooligans might see me." She went to the second window, on the sidewall of the house.

"That one's above a parlor window, too," Tallie said.

"Not directly, and besides it's not where the broken glass was." Sadie raised the sash.

Tallie brought the one chair over and planted it beneath the window. Sadie climbed onto it and stuck her feet out, clinging to the sheets.

"You hang on tight," Sadie said.

"I will," Tallie assured her. "It's too short to tie around the bedstead. Maybe we ought to rip them, after all."

"No! Besides we don't have anything to cut them with, and they're too stout to tear with our bare hands."

Before Tallie could say any more, Sadie lowered herself from the window frame. She dangled above the earth for a second, wondering if she could survive this escapade. She knew she didn't have the strength to pull herself back up to the windowsill, so there was only one way to go. She inched downward as slowly as she could, hoping to touch the ground soon with her toes.

She heard Tallie moan, and Sadie called softly, "You all right?"

"Hurry up, gal. I'm no great shakes as a hitchin' post."

Sadie almost lost her grip when she reached the knot at the bottom of the first sheet. The bulk of the second sheet seemed too thick for her hands to grip firmly. She realized her legs were close to the side parlor window. What if the men were in there and saw her or heard her feet bump the wall? The sheets billowed out in a sudden breeze, and she slipped unceremoniously the last four feet, landing in a heap between the side of the house and a rosebush.

She held her breath. No sound came from within the house, and the parlor window was dark. They must not have returned to the room.

Probably tearing my bedroom to pieces, she thought bitterly.

"You alive?" Tallie called in a stage whisper.

"Yes. Now hush. I'll get us some help."

Sadie stood up and edged past the prickly rosebush, shaking out her dress. She lifted her skirt and prepared to dash around the corner and across the yard toward Zeke's cabin. She rounded the corner at a full run and slammed into something firm but yielding.

"Oof!"

Sadie and the man she had collided with tumbled to the ground.

Chapter 17

H old it!" Zeke yelled.

Sadie wanted to laugh, but she couldn't catch her breath. "It's me, Zeke," she gasped.

"Miss Sadie?" He clutched her arm then fumbled in the dimness, roughly patting her head. "Well, sure enough. Where'd you come from?"

"I dropped from the sky."

Zeke shook his head and pulled himself to his feet then offered her his strong hand. "I thought I heard a gunshot."

"You did. Tallie fired my father's pistol at Mitchell and his thieving pal, but unfortunately she missed them both."

"Do tell!" Zeke peered at her in the little light offered by the thin crescent moon. "Where are they now?"

"Probably stealing the cash Harry gave us out of my jewel box. They're taking everything they can lay their hands on, Zeke! And the big fellow, Moe, has a knife." She brushed at her skirt.

"Are you all right? Where's Tallie?"

"I'm fine. She's up in Tenley's room. They locked us in there a few minutes ago, and Tallie let me out the window. I climbed down the bedsheets."

Zeke laughed. "Well, well. Ain't you some punkins?"

"It's not funny, Zeke. What can we do? They're robbing us blind, and the big man doesn't care if he knocks a few heads together."

Suddenly she heard hoofbeats, and she stared toward the barnyard. "What's that?"

"Don't worry, Miss Sadie. I woke Pax when I heard the shot and told him to get over to the barn and saddle Clipper and ride for town. There's no horse faster than Clipper in these parts."

"That was good thinking, if Pax can handle him."

Zeke smiled. "He'll do, and he's got the moonlight to guide him, praise the Lawd. I figured whatever was up, we'd need some help. Maybe I should have sent him to Kauffmans'. It's closer, but the road is poor goin' that way, and I figure there's a chance Pax will find Mr. Harry at the inn."

Sadie caught her breath. "Do you really think so? I expect he's long gone."

"Well, then, I allow Pax can raise the alarm in town."

Relief swept over Sadie. "I'm so glad I found you! I was frightened for a while, I don't mind telling you."

Zeke pulled her up against the side of the house. Sadie followed his gaze and saw that a light had appeared in the parlor window. She held her breath.

Zeke edged toward the glass and peered into the room then ducked down beside her. "They's goin' through Mr. Oliver's desk."

"Oh, Zeke, there's no time!" she whispered. "They'll be out of here long before Pax gets back with help."

"Listen now. They're collectin' a lot of booty."

"Yes, I saw them with a pillowcase full earlier, and that was just from the parlor."

Zeke stroked his chin. "They've got your papa's rifle now and a pile of other stuff. So I asks you, Miss Sadie, how's they going to carry all that stuff away from here?"

She drew in a quick breath. "The horses! They're going to steal some horses and maybe the buggy or the farm wagon."

"That's right. For a quick getaway, I'm bankin' on two horses."

"What can we do?"

"Come on!"

He grabbed her hand and pulled her toward the barn. When they reached the door he opened it quietly. Several horses whinnied and shifted in their stalls.

"Here now. Can you lead that first mare out in the dark without gettin' stepped on? I don't think we'd ought to light the lantern."

"I can do it," Sadie said.

"Good. We'll put them all out to pasture. That will at least slow them crooks down some."

Sadie reached up and gave him a swift hug. "Thank you, Zeke. It's a good thing they didn't hear Pax leave."

"Godspeed that boy. Now you get the mares one at a time. We'll get Mr. Harry's mares out first. Don't want them stolen. Then your mares and the colts. I'll see to Star last, and if there's time we'll hide all the bridles in the hayloft."

They ran back and forth, releasing the horses into the pasture. Sadie led one mare on each trip, but Zeke was able to control two horses at a time, and the barn emptied swiftly. Sadie puffed at the exertion and was grateful she wasn't wearing the despised corset.

We're going to make it, she thought as she released Lily's five-month-old filly into the fenced field. She wished Tallie could know what they were doing, but there was no time to get word to her now. Sadie hoped her dear servant would take her own advice and not fret.

She bounded along the path toward the barn door. Zeke had gone in to get Star, the last horse. While he took the aging stallion to the pasture, she would conceal the bridles.

A glow of light caught her eye, and she stopped in dismay twenty yards from the barn. Dan Mitchell and his friend had come down from the house and had nearly reached the barn door. They each lugged a sack of plunder, and Moe was carrying her father's rifle.

Sadie sank into the shadows at the edge of the barn and sent up a quick prayer for guidance. The two men lowered their pillowcases full of loot to the ground outside the door then went inside. She listened intently but didn't hear anything. Her heart raced as she crept forward. Feeling her way gingerly, she took hold of the first pillowcase and dragged it toward the watering trough then got the second bundle. She didn't take the time to remove them farther, but the dark shadows concealed them.

She tiptoed to the doorway and leaned her head past the edge to look inside. Mitchell and Moe had their backs to her. Mitchell was holding the lantern high while Moe aimed the rifle at Zeke.

Zeke stared at the men in the glare of the lantern. His eyes flickered from one to the other, and for an instant Sadie thought he focused on her then looked back at Moe. He held the lead rope with his left hand, and his right was grasping Star's halter with a firm grip. The horse fidgeted and snorted then pawed the earthen floor impatiently.

"Well now, Sergeant Mitchell," Zeke said. "Were you aimin' to take a ride this evening? It's a mite late."

"What are you doing out here in the dark, Zeke?" Mitchell asked.

"Just tendin' this here horse, suh. He was makin' a ruckus, and I thought I'd put him out in the paddock, or he'd never let me get any sleep."

Mitchell looked around at the empty stalls. "Where are the other horses?"

"They all out to pasture for the night, suh. We let them stay out to graze sometimes when the weather's good."

"Step away from the horse," Moe said.

"Oh, no, suh, I couldn't do that. If I let go of his halter, they's no tellin' what this horse will do."

Sadie gulped down the fear that rose in her chest. She had the feeling that if Zeke did as told, Moe would shoot him as soon as he was clear of the horse.

Lord, show me how I can help Zeke! She wondered where the pitchfork was, but it was probably down at the other end of the barn, beyond Zeke, where they usually stored it, along with the other tools and all the harnesses. She crept through the doorway and flattened herself against the wall.

"Oh, that horse is a brute, is he?" Mitchell asked.

"I'll take him," Moe said with a laugh.

Mitchell nodded at Zeke. "Tie him up and throw a saddle on him."

"Oh, suh, don't make me do that. This here's Mr. Oliver's special horse, and he never lets anyone else ride him."

"Shut up! You fool, you think I don't know the truth? Your master's dead, and you've been helping the girl keep it quiet so you can go on living here. Got yourself a pretty soft place so long as no one knows about it, don't you?"

Zeke's eyes were wide with fright. "That's not so, suh."

Mitchell smiled. "The way I see it, her brother was the heir, and now he's dead. Sadie McEwan is paying you and your wife to help her out, and you're giving her a facade of respectability. If no one finds out she's alone, she can go on living as she's accustomed, until she snares a husband."

Moe shook his head dolefully. "Too bad she didn't like you, Dan. Think she'd like me? Maybe we should stay."

Mitchell scowled. "No. If we did, Miss McEwan would have the law on us before sunset tomorrow. Time to move along, Moe."

Zeke's eyes narrowed. "If we're gonna talk plain, mistuh, you'd best think twice before you rob the McEwan family blind."

"Oh, you're going to stop me?"

"I might."

"You'll do what I tell you," Mitchell snarled. "Now saddle that horse and fetch me one from the pasture. A fast one, you hear?"

"I told you, suh—this horse ain't the one you want to take for a pleasure ride."

Sadie knew Zeke was trying to buy time, but she couldn't think what to do that would help him. In an alcove near the door was a barrel of oats, and on a ledge in the barn wall were several brushes, a tin of salve, and a used horseshoe with several bent nails still dangling from its holes.

She eased cautiously toward the wall and grasped the horseshoe. She remembered playing a game with Tenley once where they'd tried to throw the horseshoes Ephraim pulled off the carriage horses' feet into a bucket. She hadn't been very good at it.

———

"Mr. Harry! Mr. Harry! Wake up!"

Harry sat bolt upright in bed. Someone was pounding on the door. In an instant he remembered he was in the attic of the inn in Winchester, Virginia. His next conscious thought was that Pax was screaming for him to open the door.

"Mr. Harry!"

"I'm coming!" He grabbed his pants and pulled them on hastily then dashed to unlock the door.

Pax fell into the room, and Harry caught him.

"Easy now. No sense busting your noggin. What's the matter?"

"The soldier." Pax panted.

"Soldier? What soldier?"

"The one called Mitchell. He's doing somethin' bad. My pa heard a gunshot from the house where this soldier is. He sent me to get you. You gotta come, Mr. Harry. We don't know what he's doing to my mama and Miss Sadie."

Harry stared at him.

"You telling it straight? Who is this fellow?"

"We don't know, suh. He showed up yestiddy, out of nowhere, saying he was a friend of Mr. Tenley."

Harry threw his shirt on as he talked and sat down to poke his feet in his boots.

"I'll have to get Pepper from the stable, out back of the inn."

"No, suh, I done brought Clipper. You take him, and I'll come along on Pepper. Iffen you don't mind, suh."

"Good plan!" Harry grabbed his hat and wallet and tore down the stairs. He heard Pax behind him, and at the bottom of the second flight of steps, he turned for a moment.

"Get Mr. Ferguson. Tell him to raise some other men and come out to the farm."

"Yes, suh."

"Good lad." Harry ran outside and found the four-year-old stallion fighting the rope that held him fast to the hitching rail in front of the inn. He untied the rope and gathered the reins. Clipper snuffled and stepped away from him. Harry remembered Zeke cautioning him once that Clipper didn't like to stand still to be mounted. He didn't like to be switched back of the saddle either, if Harry recalled it right. He took a few precious seconds to calm the stallion and push him up against the edge of the porch then jumped quickly onto his back. Clipper leaped toward the street, and Harry let him tear for home.

———

"Here, take this." Mitchell thrust the lantern toward his partner. Moe took it and reluctantly surrendered the rifle to him. Mitchell stepped closer to Zeke. "All right now, saddle that horse, or I'll blow your head off."

"Yes, suh." Zeke meekly turned Star toward the back wall of the barn. Sadie knew an iron ring was in a post there. One was closer to the barn door, right beside where she was standing. Zeke was taking Star as far away from the door and her as possible, to delay the thieves' discovering her presence. As the two ruffians watched Zeke and Star move away from them, Sadie figured it was now or never.

She swung her arm back and put all her strength into the toss, aiming for the back of Mitchell's head.

To her horror she saw the horseshoe fly over Mitchell's shoulder and beyond him. He and Moe both jumped and stared as the shoe hit Star squarely on the hindquarters.

The stallion screamed in terror and reared, jerking his head away from Zeke.

Zeke lost his grip on the halter, and Star pivoted on his hind feet then lunged toward the barn door with Zeke doing his best to hang on to the lead rope. The horse ran between Mitchell and his friend. Mitchell was jostled so that he stepped backward, flinging the gun upward, but Star's shoulder slammed into Moe. The big man lost his balance and fell backward to the floor.

"Run!" Zeke yelled to Sadie, struggling to hold Star back by the rope, but as Moe's lantern struck the floor the bedding straw of the nearest stall burst into flames, and Sadie shrank into the corner by the oat barrel. Star squealed and turned again, kicking as he wrenched the rope away from Zeke. The horse bolted to the back of the barn once more and stood trembling and pawing the ground.

"Miss Sadie!" Zeke grabbed her wrist. "Quick now! Get out of here!"

"No, Zeke! The barn!"

"We can't stop it," he cried. The flames were already engulfing the dry wood of the stall dividers. She knew it might only be seconds before the hayloft above them erupted into a crackling inferno.

"We can't leave Star!" She clung to Zeke's hand.

Mitchell dashed through the burning straw on the barn floor and past them toward the open door. Sadie choked as the roiling smoke reached her. The stallion's shriek came to her from beyond the spreading fire.

Chapter 18

Harry galloped up the lane to the McEwans' house, praying he would be in time to help. The house was dark, but he saw movement at an upper window, the one he and Zeke had dropped the frame from. A stout figure leaned from the window. The face was dark above a snowy white garment.

"The barn!"

"Tallie?" he called.

"The barn, Mr. Harry! Hurry!"

Clipper was already fighting him to return to the barn, and Harry let him have his head. As they sped closer to the large structure, he saw the flicker of flames through the doorway, and a wave of smoke hit him.

Clipper whinnied and reared. As Harry tried to control the stallion, a man came running out the barn door. Harry didn't stop to think, beyond the certainty that the pale-faced man was not Zeke, and leaped from the saddle onto the fleeing figure.

He carried the man to the ground with him, and they rolled in the dust of the barnyard, wrestling for control. Harry concentrated on subduing his adversary, but he was also conscious of Clipper snorting and dancing about them and a second man yelling.

It was only seconds, but it seemed forever before he pinioned the man on the ground. In a glance he saw a huge man pulling Clipper's head around toward his shoulder and struggling to mount.

"Harry!"

He glanced up briefly to see Sadie and Zeke emerging from the barn, through a dense cloud of black smoke. Sadie was coughing as she led out a horse, and Zeke was on the other side, holding a cloth over the stallion's head.

"Hey!" Zeke shouted toward the man mounting Clipper. "Don't do that! Come back here!"

The man Harry was holding down stirred, and Harry was forced to give all his attention to keeping him prone, but he was aware of Zeke rushing past him and the clatter of hoofbeats growing fainter as Clipper galloped away down the lane.

Within moments, Zeke was at his side with a short piece of rope.

"Here, Mr. Harry, let me tie him with this."

The prisoner was soon trussed and left lying near the well and water trough.

"Where's Sadie?" Harry asked.

"She puttin' Star in the paddock. Come on, Mr. Harry. You think we can do anything about that fire?" Zeke's eyes were bloodshot and streaming tears, and beads of sweat rolled down his face.

Harry looked toward the barn and shook his head. "We might be able to keep it from spreading to the haystacks and your house."

Sadie ran toward them out of the darkness. "The horses are safe. Where are Mitchell and Moe?"

Zeke grimaced. "Mr. Harry got the sergeant. He's tied up over there. That big fella jumped on Clipper and streaked it."

"We need sacks," Harry said. Somehow he felt he ought to greet Sadie and apologize for the way he had left, but there was no time for any of that now.

Sadie cried, "There are two right here. Just dump out the silver. Oh, be careful. I expect my mother's porcelain figurines are in there, too."

Harry and Zeke emptied and soaked the two pillowcases and began to beat out cinders that flew away from the barn. Sadie filled the two buckets that were handy by the water trough.

"Run to the cabin for more buckets and some blankets," Zeke told her.

———

Harry and Zeke battled the flames with all their energy. Harry was exhausted, but he kept going, moving things they could salvage away from the burning building and beating back the small blazes that flared up wherever flaming debris landed.

He didn't have time to worry about Sadie but was aware of her running back and forth to the water trough, soaking the wool blankets from Zeke's cabin for them to use in smothering the small fires and hauling more buckets of water from the well.

As they struggled to hold their own against the raging blaze, several horses thundered into the yard. At a shout, Harry looked up to see Pastor Richards jumping down from Pepper's back and Pax clambering down from his perch behind the saddle.

Nearly a dozen men joined him and Zeke as they renewed their efforts to keep the damage to a minimum. The loft full of hay went up in an inferno that drove them back with its stifling heat. Harry watched in awe as the roof turned crimson and collapsed. The men rushed to stamp out the brands that flew throughout the yard and into the paddock. A few small fires even began in the pasture, and men rushed out there with blankets to smother the flames.

At last the blaze was confined to devour what remained of the ruined barn. Harry joined the others at the well. Mr. Ferguson, the innkeeper, poured a bucket of cold, clear water over his blackened head and shoulders. Zeke came toward Harry with another bucketful.

"Here, Mr. Harry. Let me douse you."

Harry let him pour the water over him. It felt good. He shook his head and looked toward the blazing embers of the barn. What a waste! But at least the horses were safe.

———

Sadie stood back and watched with tears in her eyes as the barn roof caved in, throwing sparks and burning splinters many yards into the air. At least there was no wind to carry the fire farther afield. Her father's old friend, Heinrich Glass-brenner, had arrived with Pax, the pastor, and the other men from town. He had quickly recruited several men to go with him down the nearby path to the river and fill barrels, but it was too late to save anything from the barn.

Sadie's throat hurt as she swallowed back the tears.

Thank You, Lord, she prayed. *Thank You for sending all these friends to help!*

And what about Harry? She couldn't think yet about what his presence meant to her. That was up to him and God.

"Sadie!"

She turned in shock and looked toward the upstairs window.

"Tallie!" Sadie clapped her hand to her mouth. How could she have forgotten about Tallie?

She ran into the house and up the stairs to the door of Tenley's room.

"Tallie, I don't have the key! Are you all right?"

"I'm fine, child. Is everyone out there, too?"

"Yes, I think so, and we got all the horses out. What should I do? The key isn't on this side."

"Send my man in. He'll know how to get me out of here."

Sadie ran down to the yard and found Zeke hauling more buckets of water up out of the well in the barnyard. She reminded him of Tallie's plight, and he quickly located Harry.

"Think we ought to bust the door down, Mr. Harry?"

"Where's the ruffian who locked it?" Harry asked.

Zeke pointed toward a hulk near the paddock fence. They had dragged Mitchell out of the way earlier so the men wouldn't stumble over him when they wet their cloths and filled buckets.

"He be the one," Zeke said, "that fella you rassled with."

Harry strode over to where Mitchell lay and kicked him, but not nearly as hard as Sadie felt like doing.

"Hey!" Harry said. "Where's the key to the room you locked Tallie in?"

Mitchell blinked up at him. "Leave me alone."

Harry grabbed his shirtfront and lifted him a few inches off the grass. "This isn't a good time to make me angry, mister. Where's the key?"

Mitchell was trembling. He looked from Harry over to Sadie. "Don't let him hit me, Miss McEwan!" His brow furrowed, and he stared at her. "How did you get out?"

Zeke leaned down close to Mitchell's face. "God gave her wings, you scoundrel. Now give it up!"

"This isn't my fault," Mitchell screamed as Zeke began rifling his pockets. "I didn't set that fire! Let me go! I can explain everything."

"You'll have plenty of time to do that later," Harry said.

"Here we go!" Zeke straightened and held up the key. He handed it to Sadie. "Tell Tallie I's proud of her and you, and there's about a dozen men here that'll need breakfast once we cool that heap of coals down."

Sadie grabbed the key and ran for the house.

———

"Tell me ever'thing!" Tallie rushed into Sadie's arms as soon as the door swung open. "Are you hurt? How's my Pax? I thought I seen him once, runnin' to the water trough."

"Pax is fine. No one was hurt, unless you count a few scrapes and bruises."

"Did you get them two no-accounts? What happened to them?"

Sadie frowned and led her toward the stairs. "Harry caught Dan Mitchell, but his friend got away on Clipper. We've probably lost that horse for good. And the barn! Oh, Tallie, it's my fault the barn burned. We're out half our winter's hay, and the buggy, and all the tools and harnesses that were in there!"

"No sense cryin' over it now," Tallie said. "Tell you what. You come wash up and get dressed proper, and we'll give this crew a breakfast like they've only imagined before. Mm-mm! Bacon and flapjacks, eggs, coffee, hash, doughnuts. . .what else?"

Sadie laughed, but she was on the edge of breaking down in tears.

"What do I say to Harry?"

Tallie paused and looked deep into her eyes. "I expect you'll know when the time comes. All right now, put on your corset. Can't let them gentlemen see you like that in the light of day. I'll lace you up; then we'll set to work. The chicken coop didn't get burned, did it?"

"The men let the chickens loose and hauled the coop over near your cabin. We'll have to see how many hens come home to roost when things calm down, but I doubt we'll get many eggs today."

"Well, I've got a couple of dozen in the springhouse. Good thing. I just wish I could have been out there helpin' you! Maybe we could have put that fire out."

"It spread so fast. . . ."

Sadie stopped in the doorway, staring in shock at the shambles of her pretty bedroom. The bedclothes had been torn from the bed, and the mattress was askew. The drawers were open, and her clothing strewn about the room. The jewelry box was gone, as was her toiletry set. Her secretary was tipped over, and her stationery scattered over the rug.

Tallie pushed past her and stood looking at the chaos. "Well, they made a mess, but they left your clothes." She stepped toward the old spinning wheel in the corner. "Good thing you brought your grandma's old wheel in from the barn last winter."

"Yes," Sadie agreed. "We'd have lost it for sure."

Tallie found Sadie's foundation garment in the corner behind the old spinning wheel and held it out.

"They. . .they touched it."

Tallie grimaced. "Let's not fuss now. This is the time to show what kind of woman you are, missy."

Sadie swallowed and began to unbutton her dress.

Chapter 19

Dawn was breaking when the men decided it was safe to leave the smoldering ruins and eat breakfast. They washed at the riverbank and came toward the house in a herd. Looking out the window, Sadie realized that more men had joined them from the town, and Mr. Kauffman and his two sons, her nearest neighbors, were among the crowd.

She and Tallie had set up a trestle table outside the lean-to, and they had most of the food laid out already.

"Grab that coffeepot!" Tallie edged past her with a platter of brown sausage and fried potatoes.

They used every plate Sadie could lay her hands on, from her mother's fine china to the battered tin ones Zeke and his sons took on hunting trips. The men stood under the singed trees or sat on the grass that was still green near the house and wolfed down the provisions. Harry mingled with the others, and once Sadie saw him deep in conversation with Pastor Richards.

Wilfred Kauffman came back for seconds and held out his plate, grinning at Sadie. He was the older of Mr. Kauffman's two sons, and it was obvious he was enamored of her. He was a nice enough fellow and would be a good farmer, Sadie supposed. Tenley used to play with him, but she had never liked him much. He was clumsy and a bit dense, she thought. The whole family had the same blond hair and blue eyes, but Wilfred's dull eyes were always watching her, and she didn't like that.

"I'm so glad you're all right, Sadie. We came as soon as we heard."

"Thank you, Wilfred." She placed two more flapjacks on his plate.

Mr. Glassbrenner came back to the table to refill his coffee cup. "Where's your father?" he asked Sadie with a smile. "Not still sick, I hope?"

Sadie gulped. "He..."

"He'll be wanting to rebuild that barn," said Mr. Thurber, her friend Elizabeth's father. "You tell him when he's up to it, we'll all come help him clean up the mess and raise a new one."

Mr. Glassbrenner nodded. "He'll be needing supplies. You tell him to come by the mill and see me. We'll work something out."

"Thank you." It was all Sadie could say. She snatched up the empty biscuit platter and dashed into the lean-to.

Harry was just coming out of the house with a pitcher of milk. "Sadie! Are you all right?"

She gasped and stepped aside, out of his path. "Yes, I'm. . ." Suddenly she couldn't stand it a minute longer. "Harry, I'm so sorry! I meant to wait until the others were gone to try to have a word with you, but I can't. The neighbors are all asking about Father, and I don't know what to tell them. I can't go on with this lie. I can't! Not another minute!" She burst into tears, and in her embarrassment she turned away from him, clutching the platter to her breast.

Harry set the pitcher down on the back step and came toward her. She felt his hands on hers, gently prying her fingers loose from the platter. He took it from her and laid it next to the pitcher then drew her toward him.

"Let me handle this for you, Sadie," he whispered, folding his arms around her.

Her breath came in a little gasp. "How can you be so. . .kind? Don't you hate me?"

He sighed and laid his cheek against the top of her head. "No. I never hated you. Can you forgive me for leaving the way I did?"

"Oh, Harry!" She clung to him for a moment then stepped back, brushing the tears from her cheeks. "I'm sorry. I shouldn't be so forward."

He smiled. "Would you mind if I told the folks about your father? I think it would make things a lot easier for you."

"Would you?"

"Yes. And as to the rest of it, well, perhaps we can talk again later."

She made herself meet his steady gaze. His brown eyes were clear and bright, and their tender expression made her heart leap. She nodded. "I'd like that."

He picked up the milk pitcher and stepped outside the lean-to. Sadie abandoned the platter and went to stand near Tallie behind the table.

"Folks!" Harry shouted, raising his hand, and the chattering stopped. "A few of you know me," he said, "but for those who don't, I'm Harry Cooper, a friend of the McEwan family."

Sadie's breath went out of her in a puff. He wasn't angry. He was representing himself to her neighbors as a friend. *Thank You, Lord!* She breathed. Even if he left now and never came back, she was content. But she realized she hoped fiercely that he wouldn't go. Not now, not until things were settled between them. *We can talk again later,* he'd said. Sadie seized the joy that prospect brought her.

"Several of you have inquired about Oliver McEwan today," Harry said, and all the men gathered closer, eager to listen.

Sadie glanced at Tallie. Pax came and stood between them, and Tallie placed her hand on the boy's shoulder. "Mr. Harry's goin' to straighten things out," Tallie whispered, and Sadie nodded.

"It grieves me to have to give you the news," Harry said, "but in order to spare Miss McEwan the pain of doing so, let me tell you that Oliver McEwan has passed away." A murmur ran through the crowd, and Harry went on. "There's been a lot of confusion here, with the house being robbed and the fire, but I'm certain Oliver would be glad to know how many of his friends are here to help his family in this time of need. Miss McEwan hasn't had a chance to make arrangements yet, but I'm sure the word will get around to all of you soon, and perhaps a small memorial service will be held."

He glanced around and found her, a question in his dark eyes. Sadie nodded and pressed her lips together.

As the men stood staring at Harry, hoofbeats sounded along the road, growing louder, and a lone horse trotted up the driveway.

They all stared in silence at the empty saddle as Clipper entered the yard and stopped, shaking his head and eyeing the smoking rubble of the barn in confusion.

"Isn't that your father's stallion?" Mr. Kauffman called to Sadie.

"Yes, it is. One of the robbers rode off on him before you got here."

"That must be the man who raced past us when we came to the lane," Pastor Richards said. "We called out to him, but he didn't stop."

Sadie looked to Harry. He'd left his spot and was walking toward Clipper.

"That hoss is an ornery one," Zeke said. "Let me get him, Mr. Harry." He walked toward the stallion, passing Harry, and held out half a biscuit. "Here now, fella. You're home now."

Clipper stretched his neck out and delicately took the biscuit with his lips. Zeke snatched the trailing reins, and the horse immediately threw his head back and tried to pull away.

"Here now." Zeke spoke softly to him until Clipper let him stroke his neck. He led the horse to the hitching rail near the house and unsaddled him. Harry followed and ran his hand down Clipper's sweaty shoulder.

"I don't know as we want to turn him into the pasture, Mr. Harry," Zeke said. "He's been known to jump a fence or two. The small paddock will hold him, but I've got Star in there. Wouldn't want two stallions in such a small pen."

Harry nodded. "I guess we'll have to tie him up someplace until we sort things out, Zeke." He turned and looked toward the barn. "We've got a lot of work to do."

Zeke smiled. "Yes, suh!"

The men had gone back to eating and talking to each other. Harry shot a sidelong glance at Sadie, and her pulse accelerated. He smiled, and she tried to smile back, wanting him to know how much she appreciated all he had done. But her lips trembled. Her love for him surged up, taking her breath away.

She didn't deserve Harry Cooper! He was too fine for her. She'd deceived him all that time, and then she'd brought this new calamity on them all by letting Dan Mitchell in the house. And she had burned the barn down to save a little money and a few trinkets! Something in the far reaches of her mind told her that wasn't accurate. She'd been trying to save Zeke, too, when she'd thrown that horseshoe and caused the fire, but she couldn't quite piece it together and make sense of it. She was so tired!

She hurried in through the front door and up the stairs.

———

"You're needed down below, Miss Sadie."

Sadie wiped her eyes, rolled to the edge of the bed, and sat up. "I'm sorry, Tallie. I shouldn't have left you alone with all that work."

Tallie shrugged. "I was hopin' you'd rest, but I see you been feelin' sorry for yourself instead."

"I'll come now and help you clean up."

"We got all day to clean up. Most of them men are gone. They took that thief Mitchell with them. But they's two gen'lemen waitin' in the parlor to see you."

Sadie swallowed. Her throat still hurt, and the smell of smoke was still in her nostrils. "Two?"

"Uh-huh. Pastor Richards and Mr. Harry."

Sadie stood up. Her legs didn't feel strong enough to hold her, and she grabbed the corner post of the bed.

"Please tell them I'll be there shortly."

Tallie's expression softened. "Let me help you freshen up a little, child."

Sadie looked in the mirror. Although Tallie had helped her scrub away the soot earlier, her face was still dirty with smudges where her tears had smeared. Her eyes were red from the smoke and weeping, and the skin beneath them was puffy.

She washed her face, patting the cool, wet cloth against her swollen eyelids. Then Tallie insisted she sit down and let her comb out her matted hair.

"Mr. Kauffman and Mr. Thurber both say they'll come over tomorrow to help Zeke and Mr. Harry, and their wives will send some food."

"That's kind of them," Sadie said.

At last Tallie stood back and said, "There. You still smell like smoke, but I expect they'll understand."

———

Harry stood at the side parlor window, carefully removing the shards of glass from the frame with his handkerchief. At least Tallie hadn't splintered the sash. Harry had spotted the broken window when Tallie asked him and Pastor Richards to wait in there for Sadie, apologizing for the state of the room. Harry thought there might be an extra pane left in the lean-to. He'd check on it later. Meanwhile Pastor Richards gathered scattered papers and accessories from the floor, returning them to the oak rolltop desk.

Sadie came to the doorway, and Harry turned toward her. She had been weeping, and he didn't blame her. He wished he could take her into his arms again, but with Pastor Richards present, he couldn't do that. He smiled at her.

"Sadie, I'm so sorry you had to go through all this."

The pastor stepped forward and took Sadie's hand in his. "Yes, my dear. Mr. Cooper has explained some things to me, and I must tell you how my heart aches for you. You've been a very brave girl."

"No," she said, blinking back her tears. "I wasn't brave at all, Pastor. I was a coward, and so I did the cowardly thing. I let Harry think. . ." She pulled in a deep breath then looked directly at Harry. "I let him think Papa was alive, and that was a lie."

"Sit down, Sadie, dear," said the pastor. "From what I hear, most of this deception was Zeke's doing, not yours."

She shook her head. "It may have started with Zeke, but I let it go on. I could have stopped it at the very beginning, but I didn't. And after awhile I joined in it. Harry begged me to tell him what was wrong, but I wouldn't." She looked down at her hands and sighed. "I'm so sorry, Harry."

"I told you, Sadie—that's forgiven."

Sadie pulled her handkerchief out of her sleeve and wiped her eyes.

Pastor Richards cleared his throat. "Perhaps when you feel better, you could show me your father's grave."

"Yes, of course." She sniffed. "We could go out there now, if you wish."

Harry hung back, letting Richards walk with Sadie, and followed them into the front hall.

"I think Mr. Cooper's suggestion is a good one," the pastor said. "If you'd like, we can have a brief graveside service. Perhaps on Wednesday. There would be no need to tell folks how long your father's been gone."

Sadie sobbed and put her handkerchief to her lips for a moment then whispered, "Thank you, sir. I'd like that."

They stepped outside and were heading for the path that led to the burial plot when once more a horse came up the drive. Zeke came from the lean-to, looking toward the approaching horse.

Harry recognized the rider as Mr. Ferguson.

"We found that fellow!" the innkeeper shouted.

Sadie, Harry, Zeke, and Mr. Richards walked toward him, and Ferguson dismounted.

"You found the second robber?" Harry asked.

"Yes, a great big man with a scar." He touched his left cheek.

Sadie said, "That's Moe, the one who rode off on Clipper. I'm sure of it."

"What happened?" Harry asked.

"He was lying in the road beside the bridge between here and town. I beg your pardon for being indelicate, Miss McEwan, but. . .well, his neck's broken. Looks like the horse threw him."

"Don't surprise me none," Zeke said. "That hoss would buck if the least little thing hit him back of the saddle."

"They're taking him into town in Glassbrenner's wagon," Mr. Ferguson said. "Oh, and these were in his pockets, Miss McEwan. We thought perhaps. . ."

He held out a wad of folded bills and a gold pocket watch. Sadie stared down at them. "The watch is my father's. There was some money taken, too."

Ferguson pressed the items into her hand. "I'll be going now. See you later, Mr. Cooper. Breakfast for your dinner tonight?"

Harry said, "Oh, well, I may be dining here this evening." He looked at Sadie with a question in his eyes.

"Please do," she said.

"You'd best stay right here, Mr. Harry," said Zeke. "Iffen you want, I can go get your things from in town."

Ferguson laughed as he mounted his horse. "You want your stuff, Mr. Cooper? Because I can still rent your room out. Big wedding tomorrow, right, Parson?"

Pastor Richards nodded. "Yes, Sarah Murray and John Hofstead."

Harry hesitated. "Well. . ." He glanced at Sadie again, and to his consternation, felt his face flushing.

"Please stay, Harry," she said, not looking at him, in a voice so low only he could hear her.

It was all he needed. "All right then, Zeke. I'd appreciate it if you'd do that for me."

Zeke's grin made everything seem right again. "Yes, suh, Mr. Harry! I'd be pleasured to do that thing! I'll get me a horse to ride and be back in an hour with your things from the inn." He turned and trotted toward the pasture gate.

Harry walked with Sadie and Pastor Richards as far as the fence surrounding the burial ground. He left them there together and walked on to the river, taking his time, and went along the bank to the place where the McEwans had a boat landing. He circled back by another path to the barnyard and stood looking at the remains of the barn. Here and there a wisp of smoke escaped the charred ruins. Harry tried to figure when they could begin the cleanup and how long it would take to get the materials and raise the new barn. If all the neighbors pitched in, they ought to be able to do it before winter set in.

The circuit rider and Sadie came back from the graveyard, and Sadie slipped into the big house through the lean-to. Mr. Richards joined Harry in the barnyard.

"Is she all right?" Harry asked.

"She's been through a great deal," the parson replied. "She's a strong woman, though. With loved ones to support her, I'm sure she'll get through this."

Harry nodded. "Did she mention how frightened she was of losing her home?"

"Yes. I think that can be straightened out. She told me her father left the estate to Tenley, but of course he predeceased Oliver. That might complicate things, but I offered to look into it for her."

"That's good of you, sir."

Richards shrugged. "I do many things to help my flock. I often meet Judge Ryerton in my travels. Our circuits intersect every couple of months, you see. The next time I see him, which I calculate will be soon, I'll make a discreet inquiry on Miss McEwan's behalf."

"Thank you," Harry said. "If she needs to go into town and sign papers or anything like that, I'll take her."

"It might help if she could find her father's will," the pastor said. "Lawyers like to see a document. They'd rather not take your word for something like that."

Harry frowned. "There must be a will. She was certain the property was left in her brother's name."

"She says there is, but she's not sure exactly where it is. It may be in her father's room or in his desk, but things are in quite a jumble now. It may have been misplaced. I advised her to ask Tallie if she knows about it, since Tallie usually does the cleaning."

It was nearly noon, and Harry turned toward the house. They walked to the back door, and Harry showed Pastor Richards where he could wash in the lean-to. As they were finishing, Tallie looked out the kitchen door.

"Mr. Harry, you ought to know better than to have comp'ny wash out here," she said, her eyebrows almost meeting in a frown.

"I'm sorry," Harry told her. "I've gotten used to it, and I don't stand on ceremony here."

"Well," Tallie said, nodding, "that's right. You's family now. But the preacher is another story."

Mr. Richards laughed. "I'm all right, Tallie. You don't have to give me a fancy china basin to wash in."

"Well, at least I can get you a fresh towel." Tallie disappeared for a moment, and the pastor waited with his hands dripping over the tin washbasin. When she reappeared with a clean towel, he took it with a smile.

"Thank you. You make a man feel right at home."

"Well, now, you just get around to the front door, both of you," she replied. "I sent Miss Sadie into the dinin' room, and she'll sit down with you now."

Harry glanced at the pastor. Richards was holding his smile in check. They walked around to the front of the house, and Harry led the minister through the hall and into the dining room.

Sadie whirled from the window as they entered. Her cheeks flushed as she met Harry's gaze.

"I'm so glad you could both join me for luncheon," she murmured. "Mr. Cooper, will you sit here, please?" She touched the back of the chair at the head of the table.

Harry looked at her in surprise. That was her father's place, he knew, and in all the time since he had returned to the Spinning Wheel Farm in September, no one had sat in that chair.

She was waiting for his response, he realized. He nodded and stepped forward.

"Thank you," she whispered. "And you here, Pastor, across from me, if you don't mind."

Harry pulled out the chair in which Sadie customarily sat. Her flush was pronounced as she took her seat. Harry sat down in Oliver's chair. Sadie wasn't looking at him. Instead, she held the circuit rider's gaze.

"And, Pastor, if you would be so kind as to offer grace?"

They bowed their heads, and as the pastor spoke, Harry breathed carefully. Things would work out. They had to.

Please, Lord, he prayed silently, *show me what to do next.* Even with his eyes closed, he could feel Sadie's energy. The pastor's voice went on at length, seeking God's blessing on Sadie and her dependents. Harry exhaled and sent up another prayer. *Let her love me, Lord, even a tenth as much as I love her. And let her allow me to take care of her.*

At Richards's amen, Harry opened his eyes. Sadie glanced at him, and he smiled. She smiled back with a hopeful gladness that spoke to Harry's heart.

Chapter 20

areful now." Sadie took her mother's china figurines from Tallie's hands and turned to place them with care on the mantelpiece.

"At least we got back all your things." Tallie ran her dust rag over the windowsill and the frames of the paintings.

"Yes," said Sadie. "The barn is the biggest loss. I'm afraid the buggy and harness will be costly. We may have to wait awhile to replace them."

"Well, Mr. Harry says we can get the lumber in and have a new barn raised before long." Tallie began to hum as she plumped the cushions on the settee.

Sadie bit her lip. She wasn't sure how to take Harry's actions. Apparently he and Zeke were already deep into their plans for a community barn raising. Did that mean he would stay here for several more weeks? They definitely needed to discuss some things.

Zeke had insisted on carrying Harry's luggage to Tenley's bedroom. Sadie had consented to this arrangement on condition that Tallie sleep in the little room off the kitchen. To her surprise, neither Tallie nor Zeke had objected this time.

After the pastor left, Harry and Zeke had gone out to poke around the ruins of the barn, and Sadie didn't expect to see Harry again until suppertime. She and Tallie had begun to clean up the parlor in earnest. Nothing seemed to be missing or broken. Harry had already cleaned up the broken glass from the window and replaced the pane. How many things had he done for her today? From the moment he'd galloped into the yard and leaped on Dan Mitchell, he had gone about making things right at the McEwan farm. Sadie would never be able to express her gratitude to its full extent.

As if her thoughts had drawn him, Harry appeared in the parlor doorway. His endearing smile warmed her, and she marveled that she felt so contented when only a few hours ago she'd been in turmoil.

"I wanted to tell you, Zeke and I think we can salvage a lot of hardware from the barn."

"Praise the Lawd," Tallie said.

Sadie smiled. "Yes, that will be a savings for us."

Harry nodded. "The only saddle that survived is the one Pax had on Clipper, but at least we have that one saddle and bridle. Oh, and we have some boards Zeke had stored behind the chicken coop. We thought we'd knock together a few benches for seating at the memorial service on Wednesday."

"Do you think many people will come?" Sadie asked.

"Judging by the turnout last night, I wouldn't be surprised if quite a few came, and the pastor said he'll spread the word in town. If the weather is fine, you can hold it outside near the graveyard."

Sadie nodded, looking around at the parlor. "If it rains, I suppose we'll have it in here."

"Oh, we'd best do some baking tomorrow!" Tallie closed her eyes and smiled.

"Folks will bring food, won't they?" Sadie asked.

"Yes, they surely will, but the dainties they'll talk about most will come right out of our kitchen."

Sadie laughed. "Careful, Tallie. You're getting mighty proud of your cooking."

"With good reason," Harry said with a grin. "Now don't you ladies wear yourselves out with cooking and cleaning."

"Two of the neighbor ladies are comin' tomorrow to help us, and my Ephraim's wife, Dulcy," Tallie assured him. "I sent Pax over to tell Ephraim what happened, and Dulcy said she'll come right after breakfast and bring her big girl, too."

"Good," said Harry. "I'm glad you'll have some help."

"They's soot and ashes everywhere," Tallie said. "It'll take us a week to get everything clean, but we'll make sure this parlor and the dining room sparkle on Wednesday for Mr. Oliver's service." She stooped and picked up an envelope that had slid along the floor and was almost hidden under the settee.

Harry looked toward Tallie then took a step nearer Sadie. "May I count on having some time alone with you this evening?"

Sadie drew in a slow breath, savoring the moment. "Yes, Harry."

He smiled and reached to give her hand a squeeze, and she thought her heart would burst.

"Oh, glory, glory!" Tallie shrieked. "Praise the Lawd! Praise the Lawd!"

"What is it?" Sadie asked.

Tallie held out the envelope she had retrieved. "This be what you said to look for, Mr. Harry. It's that paper Mr. Oliver signed when Mr. Tenley went away with the army. He had me and Zeke put our marks to it."

Sadie's hand trembled as she reached for it and took the document from the envelope. She had never seen it, but she knew at once what it was. "She's right, Harry. It's Papa's will." She sat down in one of the cherry side chairs, feeling a bit unsteady. "Would you mind reading it?"

She held it out to him, and Harry took it, his face full of compassion.

"If you're sure you want me to."

"Yes! Waiting any longer won't do us any good."

Tallie clasped her hands at her breast and watched as he glanced over the sheet then separated it from a second one and stood staring at it, frowning.

"What is it?" Sadie asked.

Harry looked up. "It's. . .Sadie, did you know your brother made a will?"

"I. . .no." She caught her breath and turned to Tallie. "Did you know of such a thing, Tallie?"

Tallie shook her head. "I never."

Harry nodded slowly, looking at the papers again. "Well, this first sheet is Mr. McEwan's will all right, and it's as you said, Sadie. He's left his entire estate to his son, with the provision that Tenley would give you tenancy here at the farm as long as you want it." He slid that paper behind the other. "This second sheet appears to be a will that Tenley made when he joined the army. It's witnessed by a private and a corporal. Apparently he entrusted it to your father, and Mr. McEwan placed it in the envelope with his own document."

Sadie felt tears flooding her eyes once more. "Papa never told me."

Tallie was also weeping openly, and she mopped her eyes with her apron.

Harry stepped closer to Sadie and placed his warm hand on her shoulder. "Sadie, dearest, your brother left his worldly goods to you."

"Bless that boy," Tallie cried. "Oh, Mr. Harry, does that mean Miss Sadie gets to keep her home?"

"I think it does."

"Glory, glory! Thank You, Lawd!"

Sadie couldn't help but smile. "Tallie, if you'd like to go and tell Zeke. . ."

"Yes'm, I'll do just that!" Tallie rushed out the doorway.

Sadie sniffed and blinked a couple of times then wiped her cheeks with her handkerchief. "What do I do now, Harry?"

"Pastor Richards mentioned a judge who comes around on a circuit."

She nodded. "Judge Ryerton. He's dined here before."

"Well, Pastor Richards will be here Wednesday for the memorial service. Perhaps he'll advise you on the best way to contact the justice and take care of this. I confess, I'm not up on legal matters, but probably these will go through probate court."

Sadie sighed. "Papa never said a word, even after we heard Tenley was dead. But perhaps he was waiting for Judge Ryerton to come around again."

"I'm not an expert," Harry said, "but God has allowed us to find these papers, and I think what it says here should comfort you."

"It does." She stood and looked at him, managing a trembling smile. "So does your presence, Harry."

He leaned toward her and brushed her lips with a soft kiss then stepped back as they heard Tallie's footsteps in the hallway.

On Wednesday Sadie sat beside Harry on a wooden bench just outside the graveyard fence. Forty neighbors and friends filled the benches behind them, and more than a dozen men stood at the back. Zeke, Tallie, Pax, Ephraim, Dulcy, and their children stood to one side. Pastor Richards led them in hymns of praise to God then spoke with affection and respect for Oliver McEwan's life.

The late October breeze was cool but not bone chilling. Zeke and his sons had gathered late blooms from the flower beds and heaped them over Oliver McEwan's grave. No one asked how long he had been buried.

At Sadie's request the pastor included Tenley in the memorial. Her brother's body was buried outside Mexico City and would remain there, but Sadie had decided to have a small stone prepared in Tenley's memory when she had her father's done and have it placed between the graves of their parents.

Her sorrow made a fresh assault on her as she listened, and she soaked both the handkerchiefs she'd stowed in her pockets. Harry's eyes were moist, too, as he reached over to squeeze her hand. She clung to him, and he held her hand through the closing prayer.

The neighbors lingered to commiserate with Sadie over strong tea and luncheon. The women of the neighborhood had contributed enough food to provision a small army. Tallie's roasted haunch of beef and berry pies took pride of place on the dining room table. Guests filed through and filled the plates loaned for the occasion by the women of the neighborhood then found places to sit in the parlor, on the porch, or on benches the men had brought up from the cemetery to the dooryard. Harry never left Sadie's side.

The sun was falling over the mountains to the west before the guests left. Elizabeth Thurber and her mother lingered to help with the cleanup while Mr. Thurber engaged Harry and Pastor Richards in conversation.

"You didn't tell me about your beau," Elizabeth whispered to Sadie as they cleared the table.

"My...you mean Harry?"

"He's splendid!" Elizabeth picked up two pie tins. "Poor Wilfred was despondent. Did you notice?"

"No," Sadie admitted.

"Of course not. You weren't thinking about things like that today." Elizabeth gave her a squeeze. "I love you, Sadie. I'm sorry about your father."

"Thank you." Sadie hugged her back. "You and your family are good friends."

"Well, if you need anything or you just want to have a good talk, ride over and see me."

"I will."

At last Elizabeth's family drove away in their wagon, with Mr. Thurber assuring Harry he would be back with his farm wagon on Saturday to help cut some logs to make beams for the new barn. Pastor Richards declined supper and left on horseback, promising Sadie a speedy resolution to her legal situation.

Ephraim and his family were the only ones remaining, and they were staying for a supper of leftovers in the kitchen with Zeke, Tallie, and Pax.

Sadie tried to enter the kitchen to help with the meal preparation, but Dulcy shooed her away, so she hastened upstairs. She'd been in her room only minutes when Tallie knocked on her door.

"I brung you some warm water," Tallie said, carrying in a steaming pitcher.

"Thank you. I just want to wash up and fix my hair before dinner. I'm rather windblown, I'm afraid."

"Let me help you, child."

Tallie reached to unbutton Sadie's black dress, but Sadie shook her head. "I'm going to wear this tonight."

Tallie frowned. "Seems to me you ought to spruce up a bit for Mr. Harry after all he's done for us."

Sadie felt the blood rush to her cheeks. "Harry doesn't expect me to try to dazzle him."

"All the better," Tallie said. "Surprise him. If you put on that green velvet dress, he'll know you did it just for him."

Sadie bit her lip. "Today was my father's funeral," she whispered.

Tallie nodded. "I know it, and Mr. Harry knows it. Your papa wouldn't want you to mope around in black, and you know it. Why, if he was here he'd say, Pretty up for your guest tonight, Sadie, and be a good hostess like your mama used to be. Then git up at dawn and go ride one of them hosses with Mr. Harry."

Sadie smiled. "He wouldn't really say that."

"Oh, wouldn't he just? He liked Mr. Harry. You know he did." Tallie opened the wardrobe and lifted the heavy green gown out. "This is what we been prayin' for. The man you love is downstairs waiting."

Sadie closed her eyes for an instant, seeking guidance. She went to Tallie and took the hanger from her hands, returning the gown to the wardrobe. "I'll save it for another evening, Tallie. Tonight I just need to be. . .plain Sadie."

Harry talked quietly during dinner, explaining to her his plan to help Zeke and the neighbors build a new barn.

"It will be smaller than the old one, but it will get you through the winter," he said. "If we can put it up and get the roof on within two weeks, I think I can get to Kentucky while the mountains are still passable."

She nodded, fighting the lump that was forming in her throat. Harry was leaving again. She had expected it, but it hurt.

"Do you think you'll be all right for a while if I do that?" he asked.

"I. . .yes. We'll be fine, Harry. You'll want to get the mares home as quickly as possible."

His eyes widened. "Well, no, I. . .thought I'd leave them here. If it's all right with you."

Tallie removed their plates, frowning but silent.

Sadie looked up at Harry. "I don't understand."

He took a breath then glanced toward Tallie's retreating figure. "Sadie, could we. . .perhaps we could go into the parlor now."

"You don't want dessert?"

"No, I'm fine, and I need to speak to you alone."

She swallowed hard. Tallie returned from the kitchen carrying two dessert plates.

"Please bring Mr. Harry's coffee into the parlor," Sadie said, rising.

Tallie blinked at her in astonishment then turned to Harry. "I've got pecan pie, Mr. Harry."

"Oh, Tallie, that sounds wonderful, but I ate so much after the funeral that I think I'd better pass on the pie tonight. Will you save me a piece for tomorrow?"

" 'Course I will. Go on now."

Harry held his hand out to Sadie, and she took it. She went with him into the parlor and sat down on the settee, unable to meet Harry's burning gaze.

"Sadie, dearest," he said, sitting down beside her, "I hope you understand. I need to go back to Kentucky, just for a short time. I don't want to leave you in a mess, so I'll wait until we have the new barn up, but. . ."

Sadie sat speechless, staring at him, and Harry winced.

"I'm coming at this backward, aren't I?" he asked.

"Well. . ." She wasn't sure how to respond so she waited, her heart hammering.

Harry slid off the settee to one knee and reached for her hands. "I love you, Sadie."

She could breathe then. She squeezed his hands and tried to speak, but nothing came out, and tears were threatening her again.

He looked at her with his tender, purposeful brown eyes. "Will you marry me?"

She gasped. "Oh, Harry, do you mean it? I've been so wicked!"

"No. Don't think that."

"But I do! And you have your farm in Kentucky."

"Yes, but that's what I was going to tell you. If you'll be my wife, we can go there if you want and build a new farm, or we can stay here. Sadie, I know you love this place, and it's your home. I'd be willing to sell my land in Kentucky and move here. A neighbor out there would love to have it. But I don't want you to think I'm only doing this because of the land. If the judge told us tomorrow you couldn't keep this place, it wouldn't make any difference to me. I love you so much that it doesn't matter to me where we live, just so you'll be happy." He stopped and bit his lower lip. "Does that make sense to you?"

She smiled, wishing she could banish the tears in her eyes. "Yes, Harry. It makes perfect sense. I'd like to stay here and get the farm back to how it was when Papa ran it. That may take awhile, though, with this setback."

He shook his head. "Darling, I'd be happy to invest in this place. In the spring we can be married, and we'll build a bigger barn then. And if that stud colt of yours doesn't turn out the way we want, we can ride over to Richmond together and look for another one, and. . ."

Sadie felt her cheeks go scarlet, but she couldn't make herself look away from his eager face.

"Sorry," Harry said. "I was getting a bit carried away there, but you understand."

"Yes. Yes, I do."

"Does that mean. . .you'll marry me?"

"Yes, Harry. Nothing would make me happier."

He smiled and whispered, "Thank you! Whatever it takes, Sadie, I'm sure we can make a go of it together."

"Are you certain you want to give up your dream in Kentucky?"

"Yes. I have a new dream now, and you're in the center of it."

He sat beside her on the settee once more and pulled her into his arms. Sadie thrilled at his touch. She closed her eyes as his lips met hers, losing herself in the dream of their future.

Harry held her for a long moment, with her head nestled over his heart.

"Praise the Lawd!"

Sadie's eyes flew open, and she sat straighter, pulling away from him as Tallie entered the room with Harry's coffee cup on a tray.

He laughed. "Thank you, Tallie. You can tell Zeke to be up bright and early, and we'll get to work on the barn. I need to finish it quickly so I can get to Kentucky before the snow flies."

"I'll do that, Mr. Harry, but. . .you are coming back, aren't you? 'Cause iffen you're not. . ." Tallie threw a meaningful glance at Sadie.

"You don't have to worry about your mistress," Harry assured her. "Miss Sadie is going to become Mrs. Cooper as soon as I return from my trip to sell my farm in Kentucky."

"Glory, glory!" Tallie shouted. She set the tray down and bustled toward the kitchen.

Sadie smiled at Harry. "You'd better relax and enjoy your coffee while you can. When Zeke hears the news, he'll want to talk everything over with you and make plans."

"Zeke can wait." Harry drew her into his arms again, ignoring his coffee.

Epilogue

May 1849

Sadie held her hoops in and stepped carefully through her bedroom doorway into the hall. Dulcy followed, holding up the hem of her white satin skirt in the back. Elizabeth Thurber came toward them from the stairs.

"Oh, Sadie, you look marvelous!"

"So do you." Sadie hugged Elizabeth then stood back to admire her friend's frothy apricot gown. Tallie and Dulcy fussed about her.

"Careful now, girl. You mussin' up your bride's dress." Tallie arranged the folds of Sadie's skirt while Dulcy smoothed the lacy veil.

"Is everyone ready?" Sadie asked, a little breathless.

"I'm ready, and the minister's ready." Elizabeth laughed. "But if you mean Harry, yes, he's more than ready. Papa said he's been pacing like a panther in a cage this last half hour."

Sadie smiled. Harry had returned from Kentucky three weeks ago and had made no secret of his anticipation of the wedding day.

She and Elizabeth slowly descended the stairs. Mr. Thurber met them in the lower hall, outside the parlor door.

"You look lovely, my dear," he said. "Are you ready?"

"Yes, sir. Thank you for standing in for Papa."

Mr. Thurber stooped and kissed Sadie's cheek. "I'm honored. Oliver was a good man and a good friend."

Tallie lowered the veil over Sadie's face then slipped away with Dulcy to squeeze into the far corner of the parlor with the rest of their family.

Elizabeth kissed Sadie and went through the door. Sadie found herself gripping Mr. Thurber's arm and stepping forward. The Thurbers, the Kauffmans, the Glassbrenners, and several other neighbors were packed into the room, and Zeke's family beamed at her from the corners. Harry stood before the fireplace where large vases of apple blossoms graced the mantelpiece. Clara Glassbrenner played softly on her dulcimer. Everyone was smiling, but Sadie had eyes only for Harry. As she walked with Mr. Thurber between the rows of guests and drew closer to Harry, she could see love radiating from his eyes. She stood trembling as Pastor Richards welcomed the people, and Harry's warm smile calmed her. At last she was able to place her hand in his and begin their new life together.

SUSAN PAGE DAVIS

Susan and her husband, Jim, have been married thirty-two years and have six children, ages thirteen to thirty. They live in Maine, where they are active in an independent Baptist church. Susan is a homeschooling mother and writes historical romance, mystery, and suspense novels. Visit her Web site at www.susanpagedavis.com.

A Letter to Our Readers

Dear Readers:

In order that we might better contribute to your reading enjoyment, we would appreciate your taking a few minutes to respond to the following questions. When completed, please return to the following: Fiction Editor, Barbour Publishing, Inc., P.O. Box 719, Uhrichsville, OH 44683.

1. Did you enjoy reading *Virginia Brides*?
   ❑ Very much—I would like to see more books like this.
   ❑ Moderately—I would have enjoyed it more if _____
   _____
   _____

2. What influenced your decision to purchase this book? (Check those that apply.)
   ❑ Cover   ❑ Back cover copy   ❑ Title   ❑ Price
   ❑ Friends   ❑ Publicity   ❑ Other

3. Which story was your favorite?
   ❑ *Spoke of Love*   ❑ *Weaving a Future*
   ❑ *Spinning Out of Control*

4. Please check your age range:
   ❑ Under 18   ❑ 18–24   ❑ 25–34
   ❑ 35–45   ❑ 46–55   ❑ Over 55

5. How many hours per week do you read? _____

Name _____

Occupation _____

Address _____

City _____ State _____ Zip _____

E-mail _____